THE SAVIORS

THE SAVIORS

CREATED BY
JAMES ROBINSON
& J. BONE

WRITTEN BY
JAMES ROBINSON

ART BY
J. BONE

EDITED BY
JOEL ENOS

IMAGE COMICS, INC.
Robert Kirkman – Chief Operating Officer
Erik Larsen – Chief Financial Officer
Todd McFarlane – President
Marc Silvestri – Chief Executive Officer
Jim Valentino – Vice-President
Eric Stephenson – Publisher
Corey Murphy – Director of Sales
Jeff Boison – Director of Publishing Planning & Book Trade Sales
Jeremy Sullivan – Director of Digital Sales
Kat Salazar – Director of PR & Marketing
Branwyn Bigglestone – Controller
Drew Gill – Art Director
Jonathan Chan – Production Manager
Meredith Wallace – Print Manager
Briah Skelly – Publicist
Sasha Head – Sales & Marketing Production Designer
Randy Okamura – Digital Production Designer
David Brothers – Branding Manager
Olivia Ngai – Content Manager
Addison Duke – Production Artist
Vincent Kukua – Production Artist
Tricia Ramos – Production Artist
Jeff Stang – Direct Market Sales Representative
Emilio Bautista – Digital Sales Associate
Leanna Caunter – Accounting Assistant
Chloe Ramos-Peterson – Library Market Sales Representative
IMAGECOMICS.COM

A LETTER FROM
JAMES ROBINSON

I'm equal parts proud, happy and also a bit sad as I write about my collaboration with J. Bone and our series THE SAVIORS. It was my first creator-owned series in over a decade (God, maybe even longer -- two decades?) and so it's a work I hold very close to my heart. This was J. and my attempt at "alien invasion with a twist" with some cool intentions for where we were taking it in the future. As it stands now, some of those intentions may still come to pass one day, maybe not. For now at least, what you hold in your hands is the beginning of something, at least.

As I sit writing this, I muse over my accomplishments and failures, both in work and life. I realize creatively I've made more mistakes and missteps than ten creators combined could have if they've actually contrived to do so. But hey, there have been some successes and noble efforts along the way too. I think THE SAVIORS falls somewhere in between.

THE SAVIORS, the comic (as opposed to the collection in your hands), was I feel, an example of a bare-bones Image book. That was a mistake, in hindsight. I see that. The thing about Image is they give you everything in terms of the property. Full ownership, full freedom. And if you know what you're doing going in, it can be truly liberating. I don't need to tell you some of the creators who have ascended to the Heavens of the art form due to their Image output. Indeed, those wonderful books are on the shelves now for us all to enjoy. There is a flipside to this too however, one that I wish I'd known when J. and I began THE SAVIORS. Namely, that in return for creative freedom and ownership, there's also a degree of overseeing: You're responsible for yourself. With that understanding, many creators go nuts with extras, conceptual art and playlists, letters pages and all the other fun things that get the readers invested in the book and follow it on a monthly basis, instead of "trade waiting" (two words that will kill a comic series out of the gate, if enough people decide your book isn't worth the monthly purchase and they'll pick it up later.) THE SAVIORS, the comic, on the other hand was an example of what an Image book could be in the worst way. It merely had our story, and then trade ads for other books. Bare-bones. It wasn't enough. I see that now. At the time, having worked at DC and later Marvel, where editors and publicists and designers help you (or just outright take care of it) with every step of the process, I was completely out of my depth.

J. and I should have made THE SAVIORS more ours, filled the back with art and text and made it something readers could really get involved in. We didn't know. Hindsight is 20/20, but I so wish I'd had more clarity regarding this aspect of things when we did our series as a monthly.

What remains instead is the five issues you have before you. Five issues I remain very proud of. It was a joy to work with J. seeing his art change for this project just subtly but definitely, from his looser cartoon style and into something akin to animation. There was an edge and bite to the art of THE SAVIORS that was so exciting to see as the pages came in. The shadows and mood. J's art in THE SAVIORS is, I feel, among his best and I'm incredibly thrilled to have been a part of this. I also loved the coloring style he/we chose, using minimal color to convey shifts in mood and location. It's something I loved then and I'd definitely like to do more of.

I also love that we basically did a pro-marijuana series, neatly wrapped in an alien invasion comic. "Want to stop the aliens? Get high!" Truthfully, the more I look at what Jay and I did, the prouder

I feel of it. The pacing, the mood, the cinematic "editing" of the cuts from panel to panel that J. brought to the series, elevating it even more than I'd hoped.

It's been a long time since J. and I did THE SAVIORS, with the promise of more stories to come after Issue 5. I'd intended single issues to intersperse the ongoing present-day narrative that would jump about in time, showing the history of the alien presence on Earth and showing the story from their side too. In their eyes, and those of the readers too if the series had progressed, they were perceived as mankind's saviors. Anyway, the first of these, set in 1870s New York would have been Issue 6. (As the teaser pages at the end of Issue 5 show.)

And then on to the next arc, set in Paris and featuring a completely different cast. That was the plan, different arcs and casts, some living, some dying -- until slowly the narrative strands were drawn together and we'd see Tomas again (around Issue 12), now a hardened (but still-stoned) alien fighter. Oh, it would have been a wild series -- if J. and I had been in a creative place where we felt we wanted to continue it. And if it had sold more.

Now, like I say, I see it as part success and part not. Looking at it now, perhaps our biggest failure was simply not continuing onward with it. And perhaps we will. I admit that reviewing the issues, prior to my writing this, has brought about a degree of creative excitement to do more with this premise.

We shall see.

For now, enjoy THE SAVIORS for what it is -- a good story with fantastic art by my alien-bashing partner-in-crime, J. Bone. I'm certainly happy to finally see the whole collected, with color fixes and corrections, along with the short story we did for a CBLDF book that many people aren't even aware of.

Apart from that, let me end with a small piece of advice...

You don't need to get high to fight aliens and you don't need to fight aliens to get high.

Enjoy.

-JAMES ROBINSON

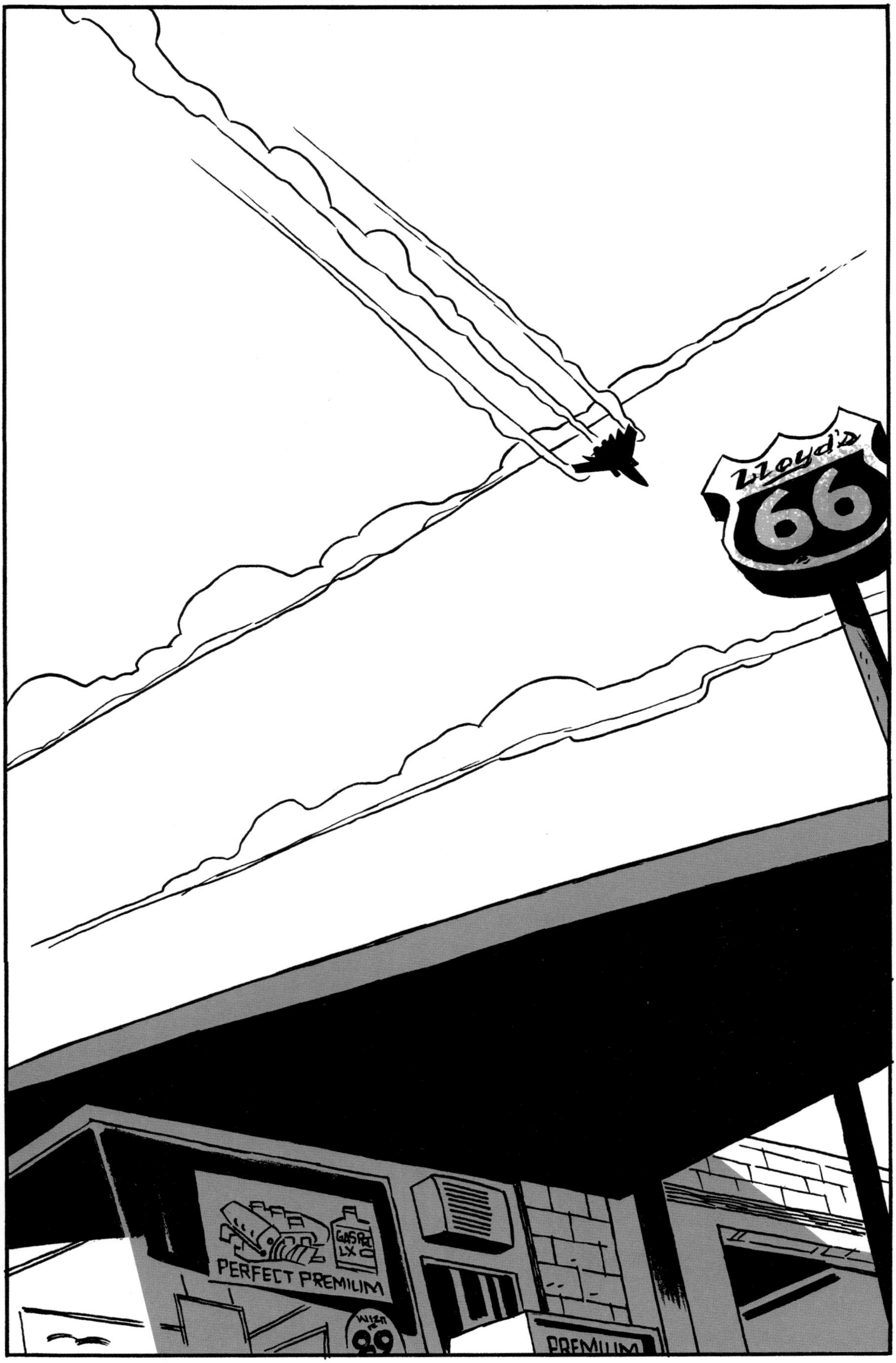
Lloyd's
66
PERFECT PREMILIM

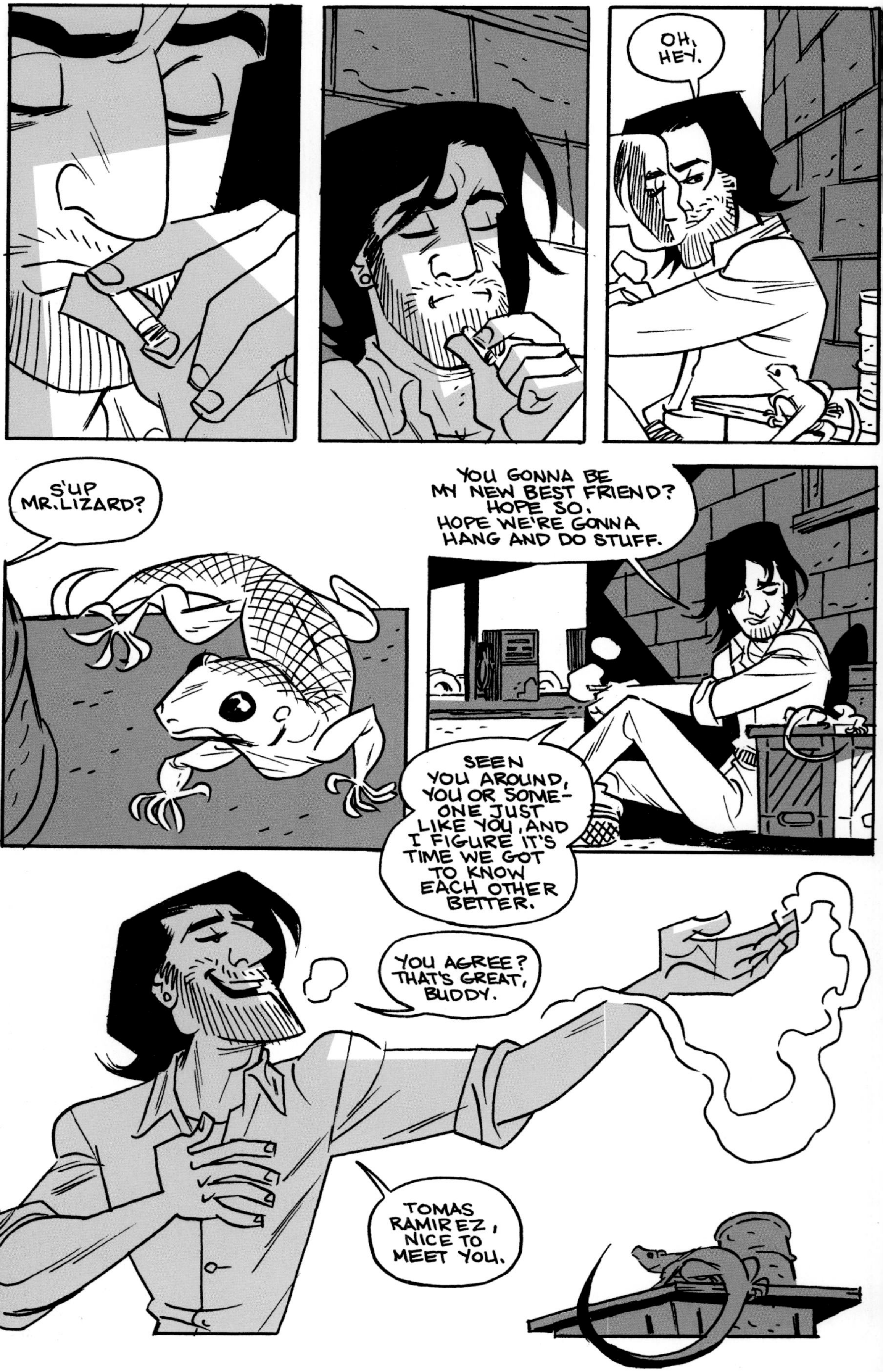
OH, HEY.
S'UP MR. LIZARD?
YOU GONNA BE MY NEW BEST FRIEND? HOPE SO. HOPE WE'RE GONNA HANG AND DO STUFF.
SEEN YOU AROUND, YOU OR SOME-ONE JUST LIKE YOU, AND I FIGURE IT'S TIME WE GOT TO KNOW EACH OTHER BETTER.
YOU AGREE? THAT'S GREAT, BUDDY.
TOMAS RAMIREZ, NICE TO MEET YOU.

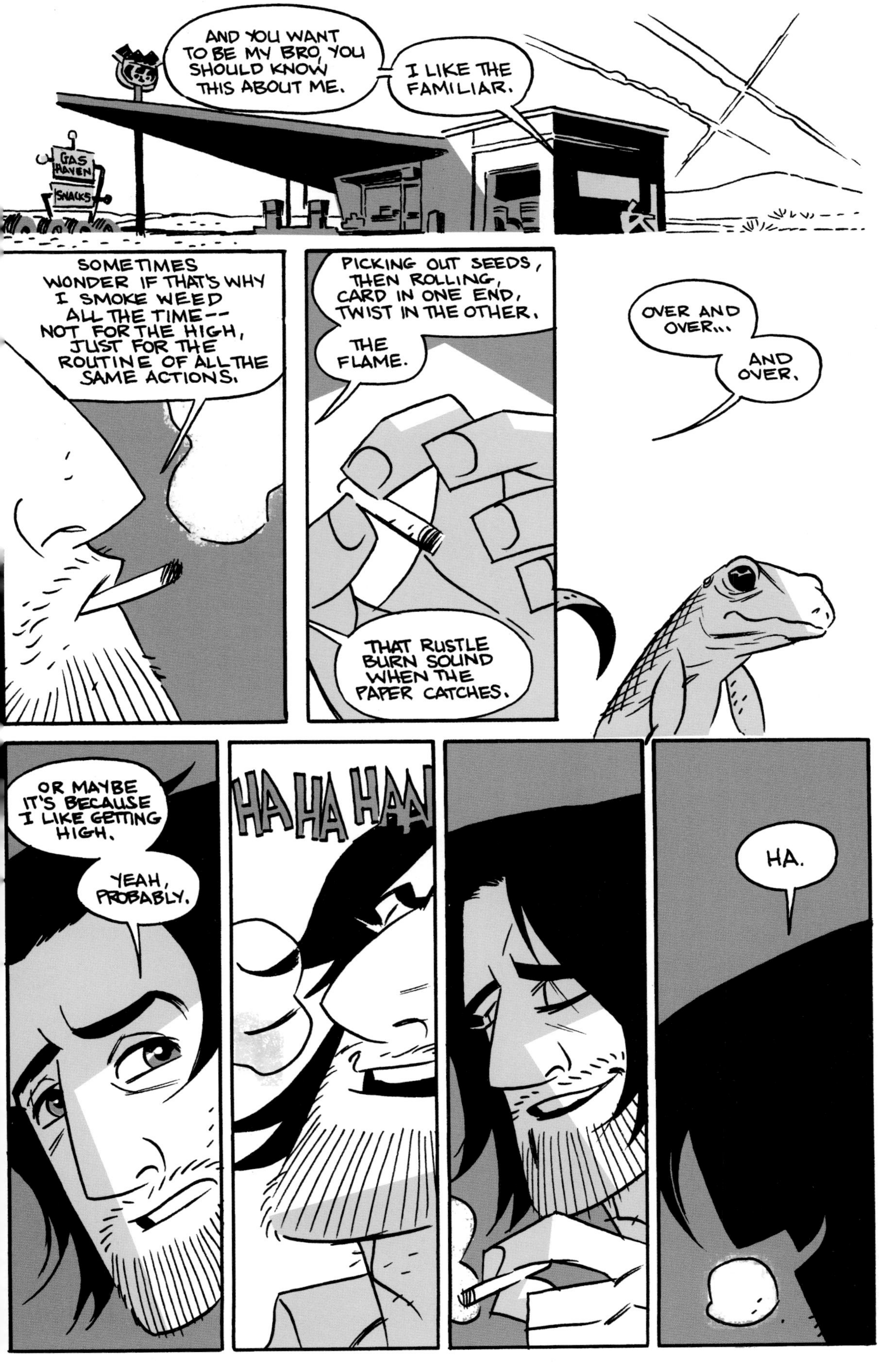

AND YOU WANT TO BE MY BRO, YOU SHOULD KNOW THIS ABOUT ME.
I LIKE THE FAMILIAR.
GAS HAVEN
SNACKS
SOMETIMES WONDER IF THAT'S WHY I SMOKE WEED ALL THE TIME-- NOT FOR THE HIGH, JUST FOR THE ROUTINE OF ALL THE SAME ACTIONS.
PICKING OUT SEEDS, THEN ROLLING, CARD IN ONE END, TWIST IN THE OTHER.
THE FLAME.
THAT RUSTLE BURN SOUND WHEN THE PAPER CATCHES.
OVER AND OVER...
AND OVER.
OR MAYBE IT'S BECAUSE I LIKE GETTING HIGH.
YEAH, PROBABLY.
HA HA HAA
HA.

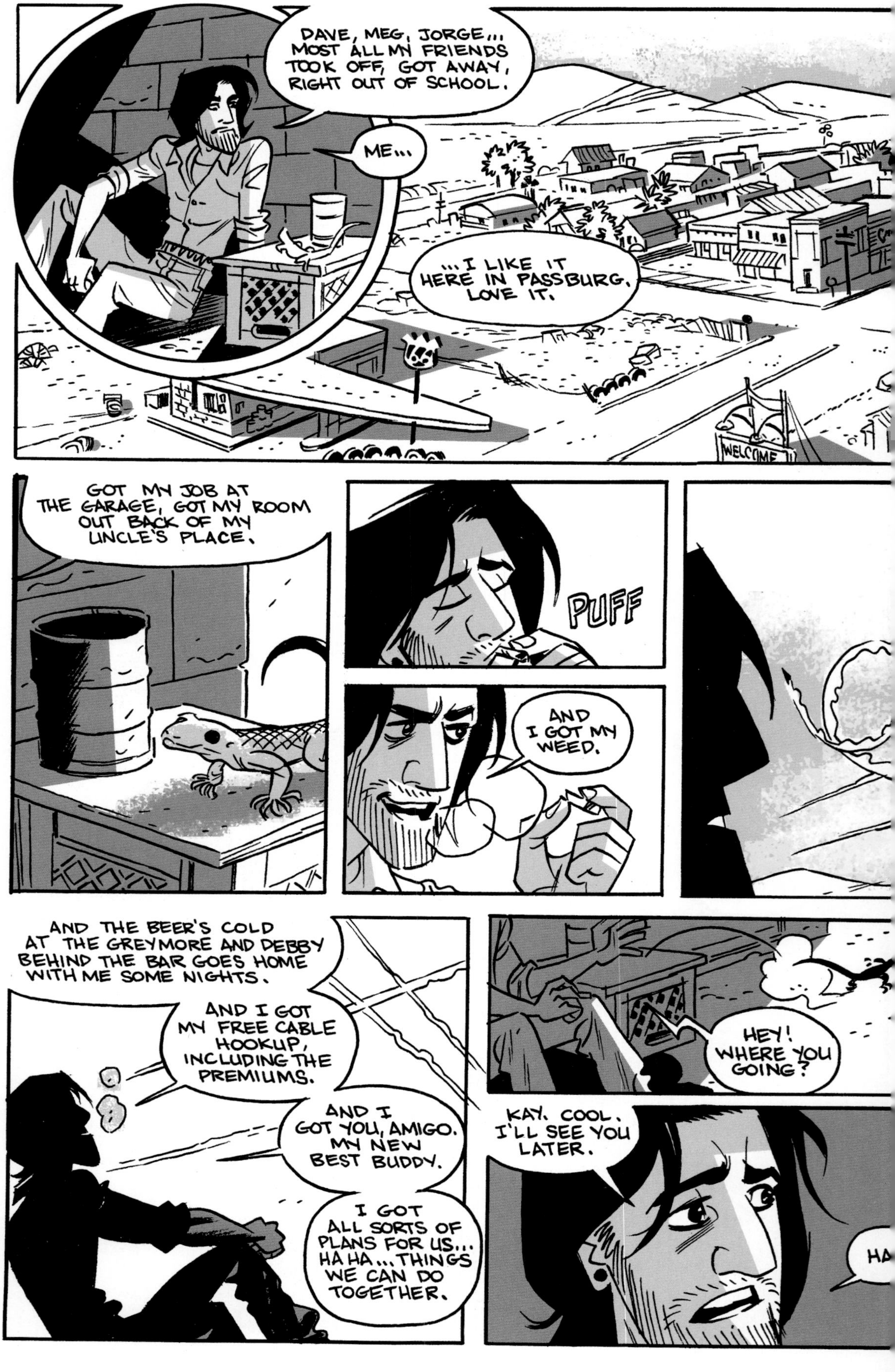
DAVE, MEG, JORGE... MOST ALL MY FRIENDS TOOK OFF, GOT AWAY, RIGHT OUT OF SCHOOL.
ME...
...I LIKE IT HERE IN PASSBURG. LOVE IT.
WELCOME
GOT MY JOB AT THE GARAGE, GOT MY ROOM OUT BACK OF MY UNCLE'S PLACE.
PUFF
AND I GOT MY WEED.
AND THE BEER'S COLD AT THE GREYMORE AND DEBBY BEHIND THE BAR GOES HOME WITH ME SOME NIGHTS.
AND I GOT MY FREE CABLE HOOKUP, INCLUDING THE PREMIUMS.
AND I GOT YOU, AMIGO. MY NEW BEST BUDDY.
I GOT ALL SORTS OF PLANS FOR US... HA HA... THINGS WE CAN DO TOGETHER.
HEY! WHERE YOU GOING?
KAY. COOL. I'LL SEE YOU LATER.
HA

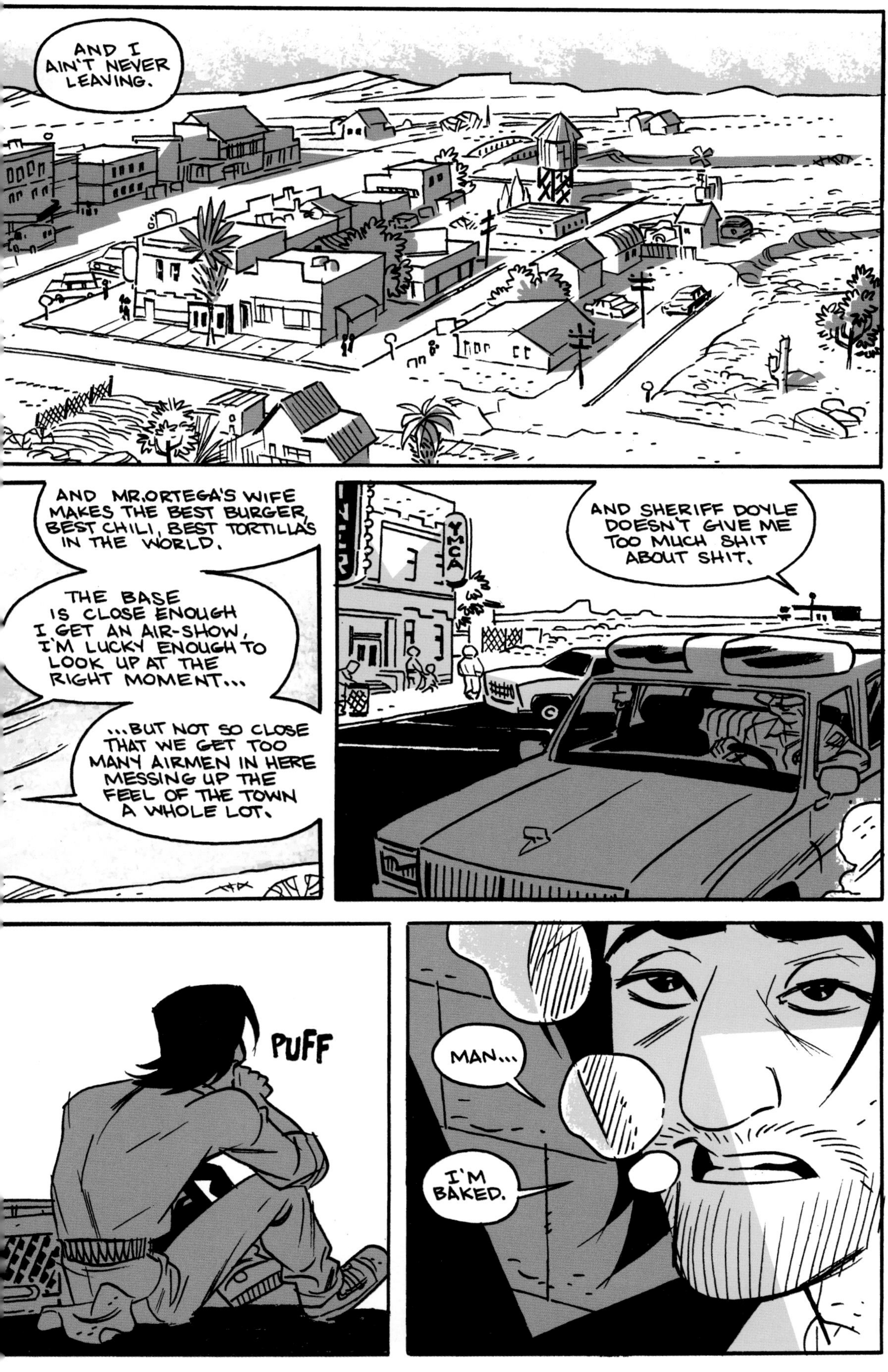
AND I AIN'T NEVER LEAVING.
AND MR. ORTEGA'S WIFE MAKES THE BEST BURGER, BEST CHILI, BEST TORTILLAS IN THE WORLD.
THE BASE IS CLOSE ENOUGH I GET AN AIR-SHOW, I'M LUCKY ENOUGH TO LOOK UP AT THE RIGHT MOMENT...
...BUT NOT SO CLOSE THAT WE GET TOO MANY AIRMEN IN HERE MESSING UP THE FEEL OF THE TOWN A WHOLE LOT.
YMCA
AND SHERIFF DOYLE DOESN'T GIVE ME TOO MUCH SHIT ABOUT SHIT.
PUFF
MAN...
I'M BAKED.

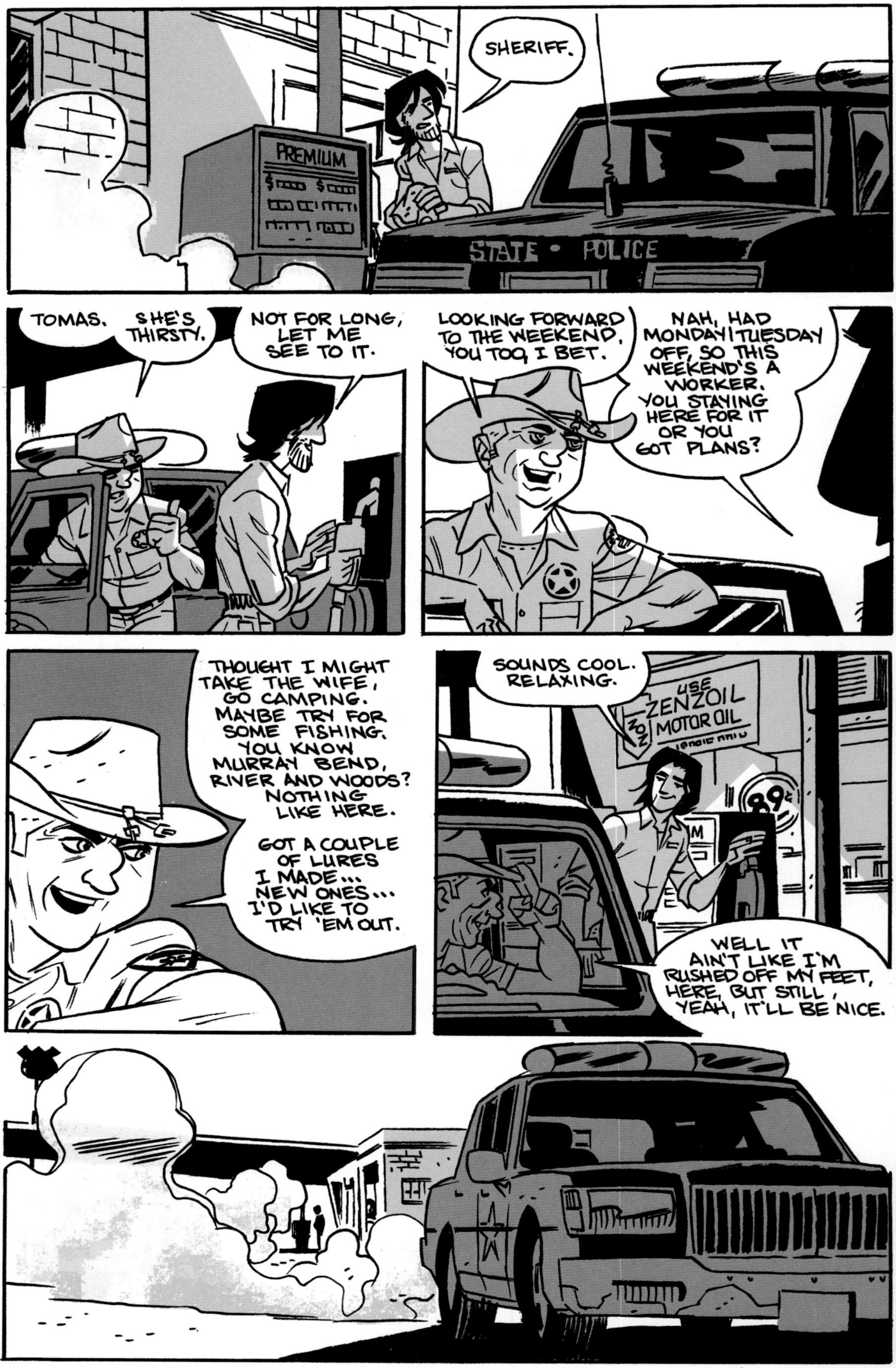
SHERIFF.
PREMIUM
STATE • POLICE
TOMAS.
SHE'S THIRSTY.
NOT FOR LONG, LET ME SEE TO IT.
LOOKING FORWARD TO THE WEEKEND, YOU TOO, I BET.
NAH, HAD MONDAY/TUESDAY OFF, SO THIS WEEKEND'S A WORKER. YOU STAYING HERE FOR IT OR YOU GOT PLANS?
THOUGHT I MIGHT TAKE THE WIFE, GO CAMPING. MAYBE TRY FOR SOME FISHING. YOU KNOW MURRAY BEND, RIVER AND WOODS? NOTHING LIKE HERE.
GOT A COUPLE OF LURES I MADE... NEW ONES... I'D LIKE TO TRY 'EM OUT.
SOUNDS COOL. RELAXING.
USE ZENZOIL MOTOR OIL
89¢
WELL IT AIN'T LIKE I'M RUSHED OFF MY FEET, HERE, BUT STILL, YEAH, IT'LL BE NICE.

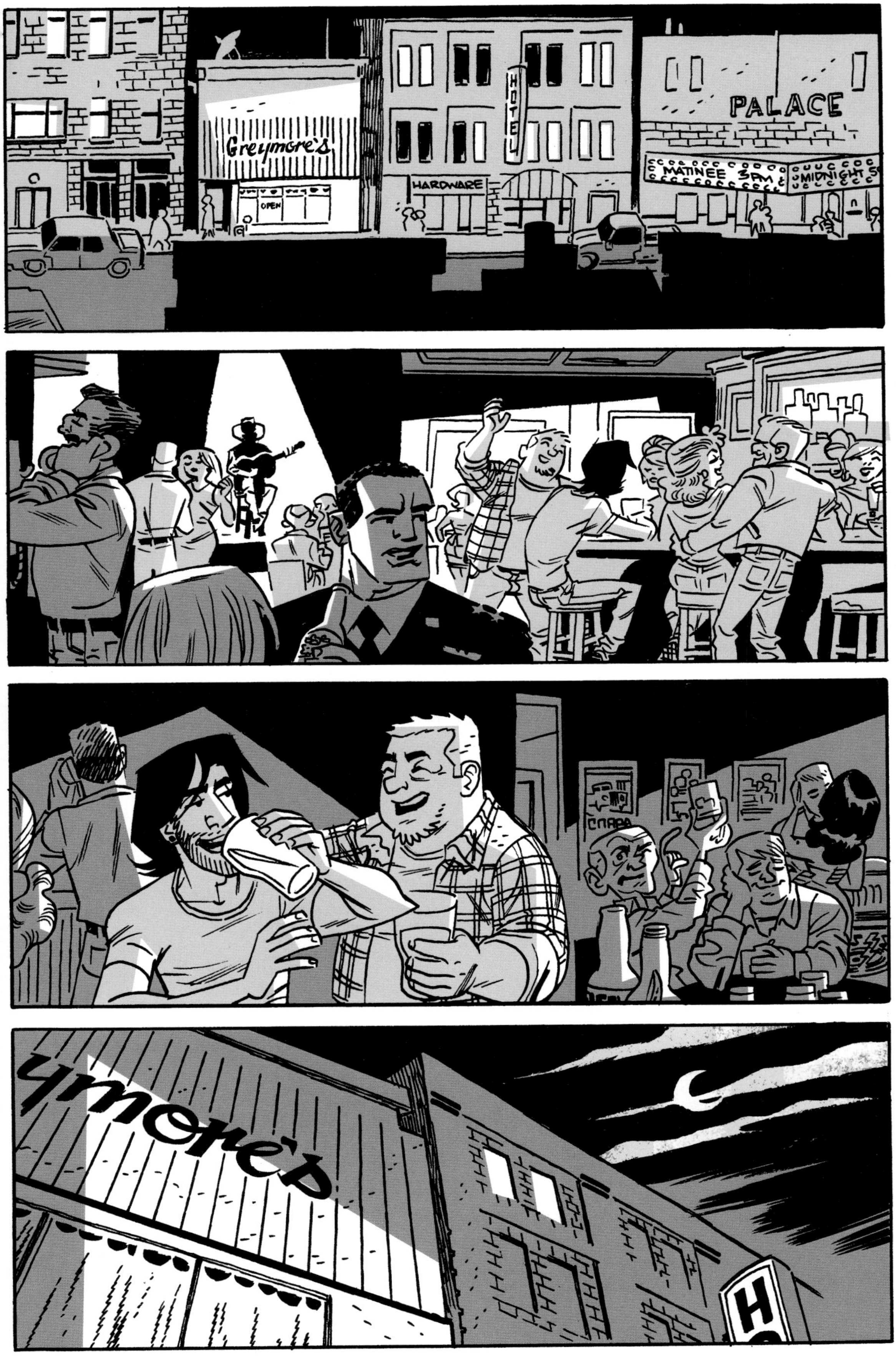
Greymore's
OPEN
HOTEL
HARDWARE
PALACE
MATINEE 3PM &

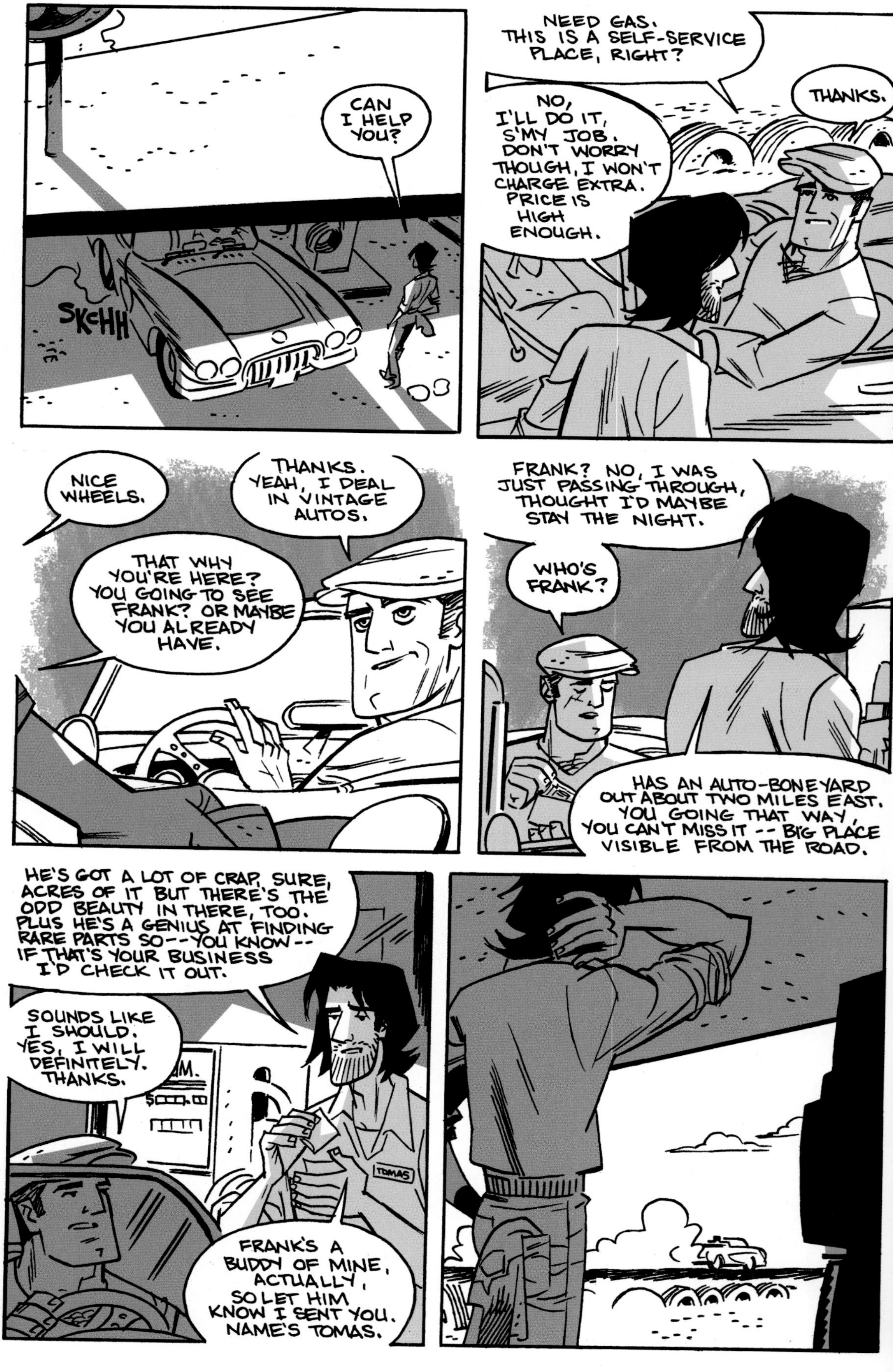
CAN I HELP YOU?
SKCHH
NEED GAS. THIS IS A SELF-SERVICE PLACE, RIGHT?
NO, I'LL DO IT, S'MY JOB. DON'T WORRY THOUGH, I WON'T CHARGE EXTRA. PRICE IS HIGH ENOUGH.
THANKS.
NICE WHEELS.
THANKS. YEAH, I DEAL IN VINTAGE AUTOS.
THAT WHY YOU'RE HERE? YOU GOING TO SEE FRANK? OR MAYBE YOU ALREADY HAVE.
FRANK? NO, I WAS JUST PASSING THROUGH, THOUGHT I'D MAYBE STAY THE NIGHT.
WHO'S FRANK?
HAS AN AUTO-BONEYARD OUT ABOUT TWO MILES EAST. YOU GOING THAT WAY, YOU CAN'T MISS IT -- BIG PLACE VISIBLE FROM THE ROAD.
HE'S GOT A LOT OF CRAP, SURE, ACRES OF IT BUT THERE'S THE ODD BEAUTY IN THERE, TOO. PLUS HE'S A GENIUS AT FINDING RARE PARTS SO--YOU KNOW--IF THAT'S YOUR BUSINESS I'D CHECK IT OUT.
SOUNDS LIKE I SHOULD. YES, I WILL DEFINITELY. THANKS.
TOMAS
FRANK'S A BUDDY OF MINE, ACTUALLY, SO LET HIM KNOW I SENT YOU. NAME'S TOMAS.

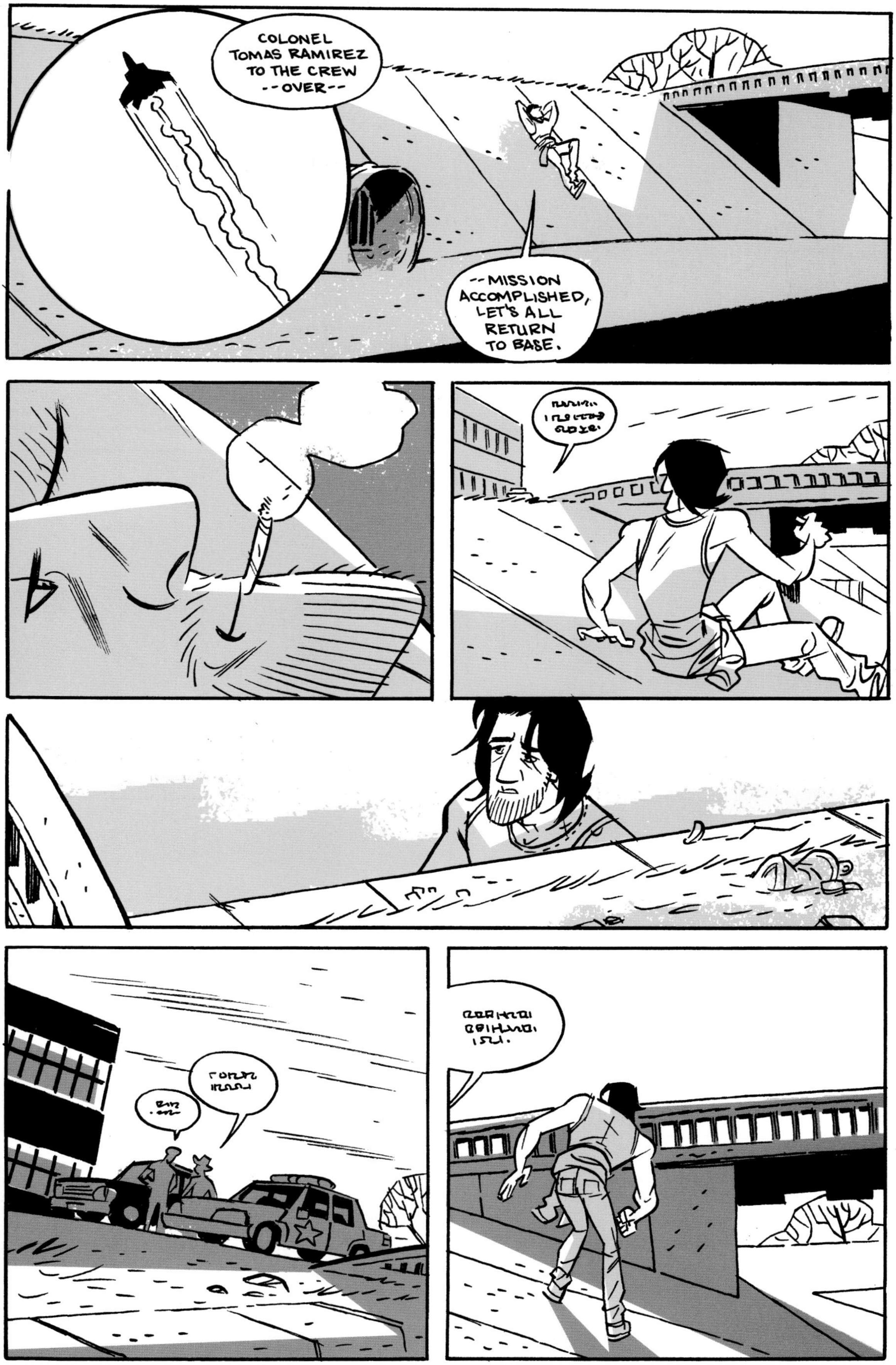
COLONEL TOMAS RAMIREZ TO THE CREW --OVER--
--MISSION ACCOMPLISHED, LET'S ALL RETURN TO BASE.

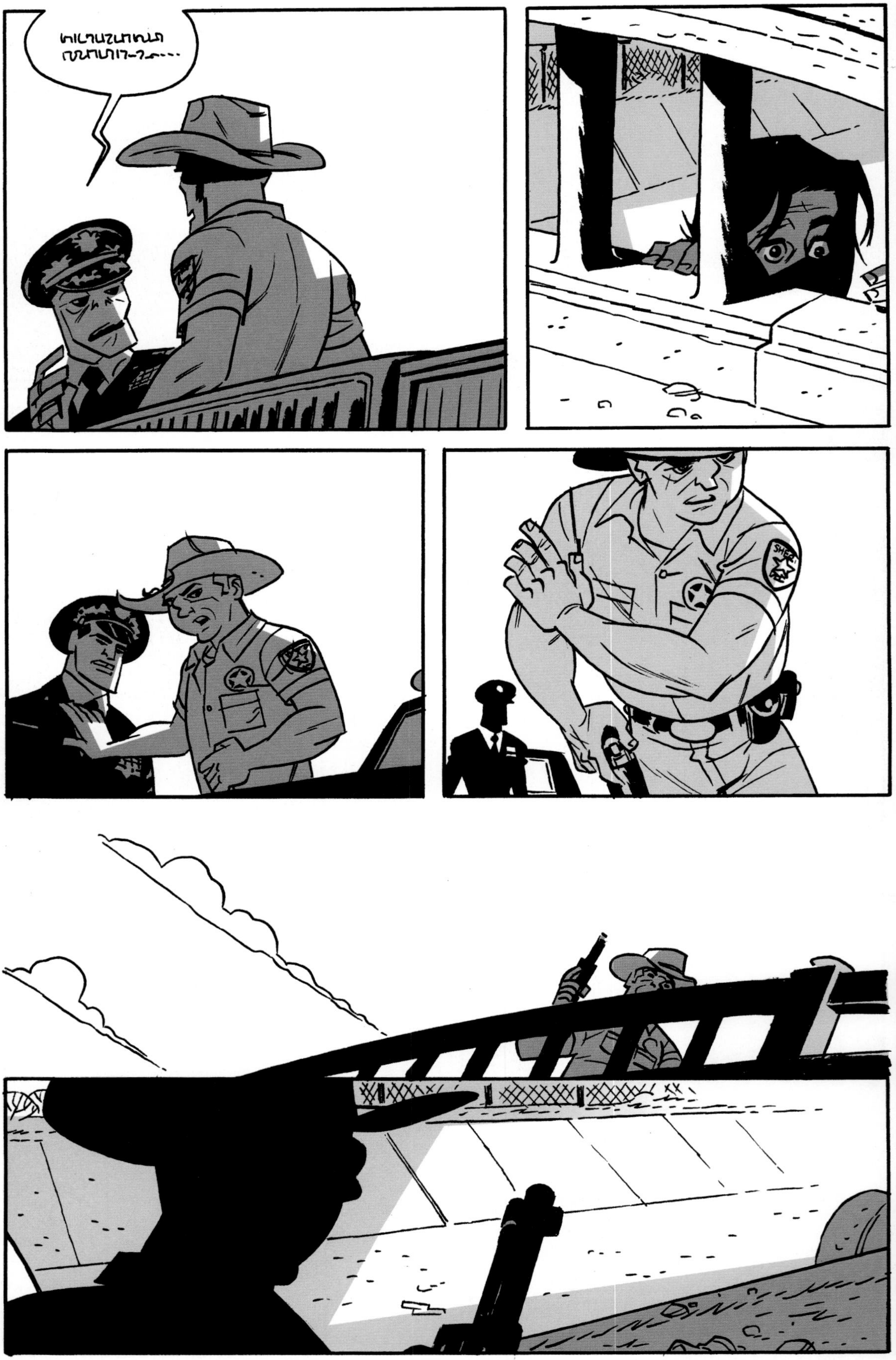

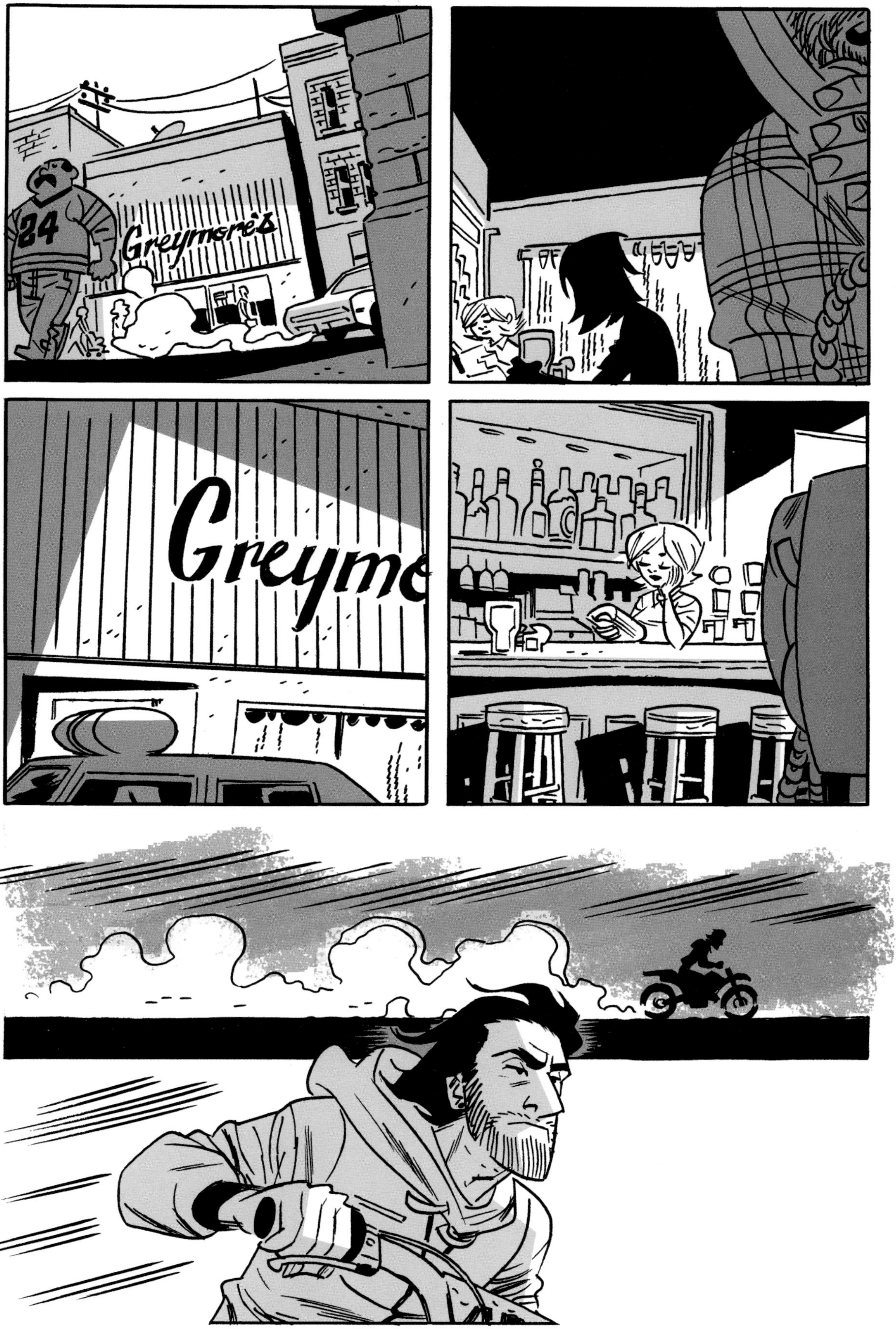
24
Greymore's
Greym

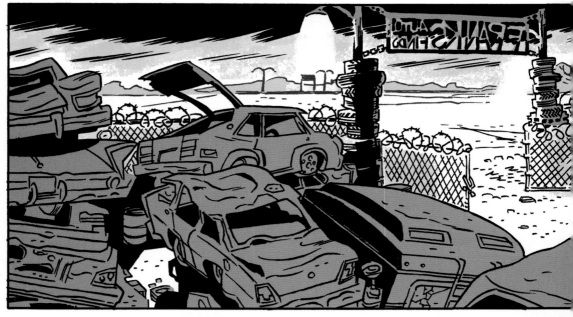

...WELL YOU'RE CERTAINLY NOT THE FIRST TO CLAIM THEY EXIST.

PHEW! SUCH A RELIEF, FRANK, YOU BELIEVING ME.

OH, I BELIEVE YOU THINK YOU SAW LIZARD MEN, TOMMY. DO I THINK YOU ACTUALLY DID THOUGH? NO.

PLAIN AS DAY, FRANK, I SWEAR.

WOW.

I DIDN'T EXPECT THIS FROM YOU.

'CAUSE I'M YOUR FRIEND? SURE, I LOVE YOU. BUT SOMETIMES PEOPLE HAVE TO HEAR WHAT THEY HAVE TO HEAR.

GO HOME, TOMMY. NO BOOZE, NO WEED. TAKE A BREAK. GIVE IT A WEEK, YOU'LL SEE I'M RIGHT. I SWEAR.

K. YOU KNOW-- MAYBE YOU'RE RIGHT AT THAT. MAYBE THIS IS A SIGN I SHOULD CHANGE.

LIZARD MEN, HUH?...

LISTEN. LISTEN TO ME. FRIEND TO FRIEND. YOU ARE ALWAYS HIGH -- LIKE --ALWAYS.

YOU COME OUT HERE AND WE SMOKE IT UP ONCE IN A WHILE, BUT THEN YOU LEAVE AND I GET BACK TO THE REAL WORLD. MY BUSINESS.

THE AMOUNT OF WEED YOU SMOKE, TOMMY, I DON'T THINK YOU'VE SEEN THE REAL WORLD IN A LONG TIME.

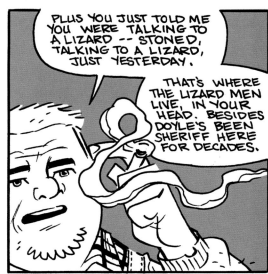

PLUS YOU JUST TOLD ME YOU WERE TALKING TO A LIZARD -- STONED, TALKING TO A LIZARD, JUST YESTERDAY.

THAT'S WHERE THE LIZARD MEN LIVE, IN YOUR HEAD. BESIDES DOYLE'S BEEN SHERIFF HERE FOR DECADES.

I DON'T KNOW YOU NEED TO GO THAT FAR. JUST MODERATION, YOU KNOW.

FRANK, BUDDY, THANK YOU SO MUCH.

FOR WHAT? YOU JUST SAID IT-- "BUDDIES" --I'M HERE FOR YOU.

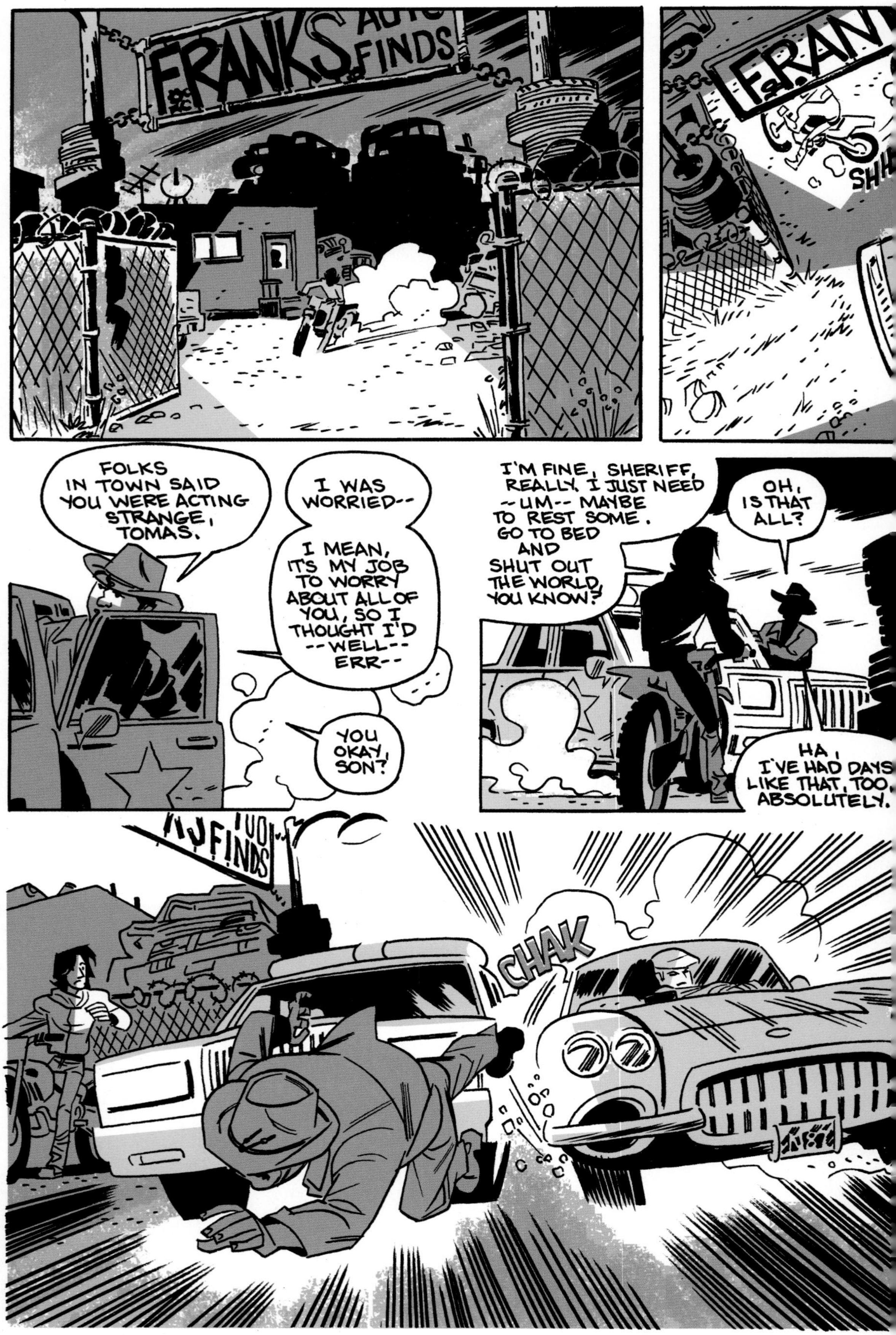
FRANKS AUTO FINDS
SHH
FOLKS IN TOWN SAID YOU WERE ACTING STRANGE, TOMAS.
I WAS WORRIED--
I MEAN, IT'S MY JOB TO WORRY ABOUT ALL OF YOU, SO I THOUGHT I'D --WELL-- ERR--
YOU OKAY, SON?
I'M FINE, SHERIFF, REALLY. I JUST NEED --UM-- MAYBE TO REST SOME. GO TO BED AND SHUT OUT THE WORLD, YOU KNOW?
OH, IS THAT ALL?
HA, I'VE HAD DAYS LIKE THAT, TOO, ABSOLUTELY.
FINDS
CHAK

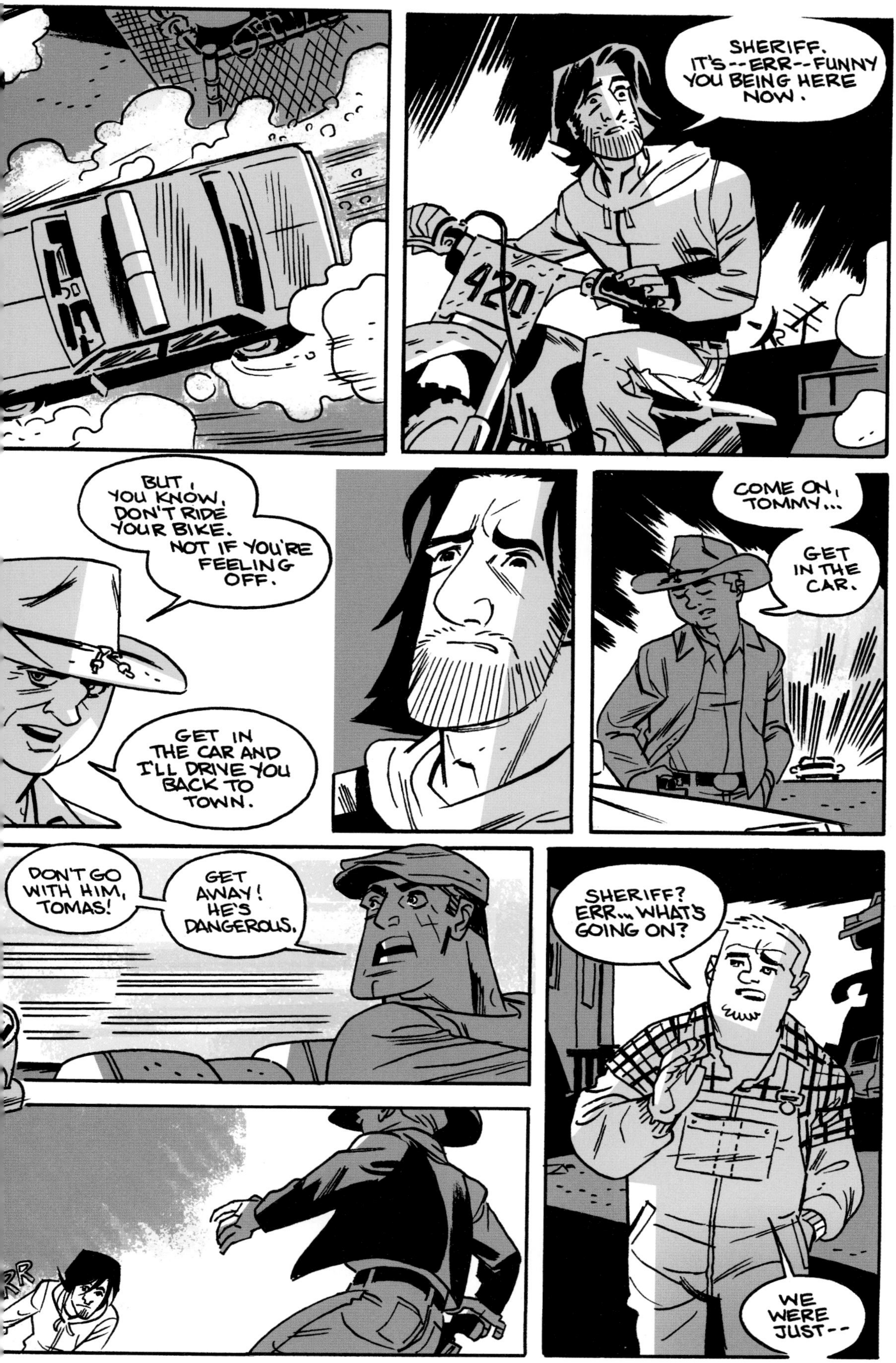
SHERIFF. IT'S--ERR--FUNNY YOU BEING HERE NOW.
BUT, YOU KNOW, DON'T RIDE YOUR BIKE.
NOT IF YOU'RE FEELING OFF.
GET IN THE CAR AND I'LL DRIVE YOU BACK TO TOWN.
COME ON, TOMMY...
GET IN THE CAR.
DON'T GO WITH HIM, TOMAS!
GET AWAY! HE'S DANGEROUS.
SHERIFF? ERR... WHAT'S GOING ON?
WE WERE JUST--

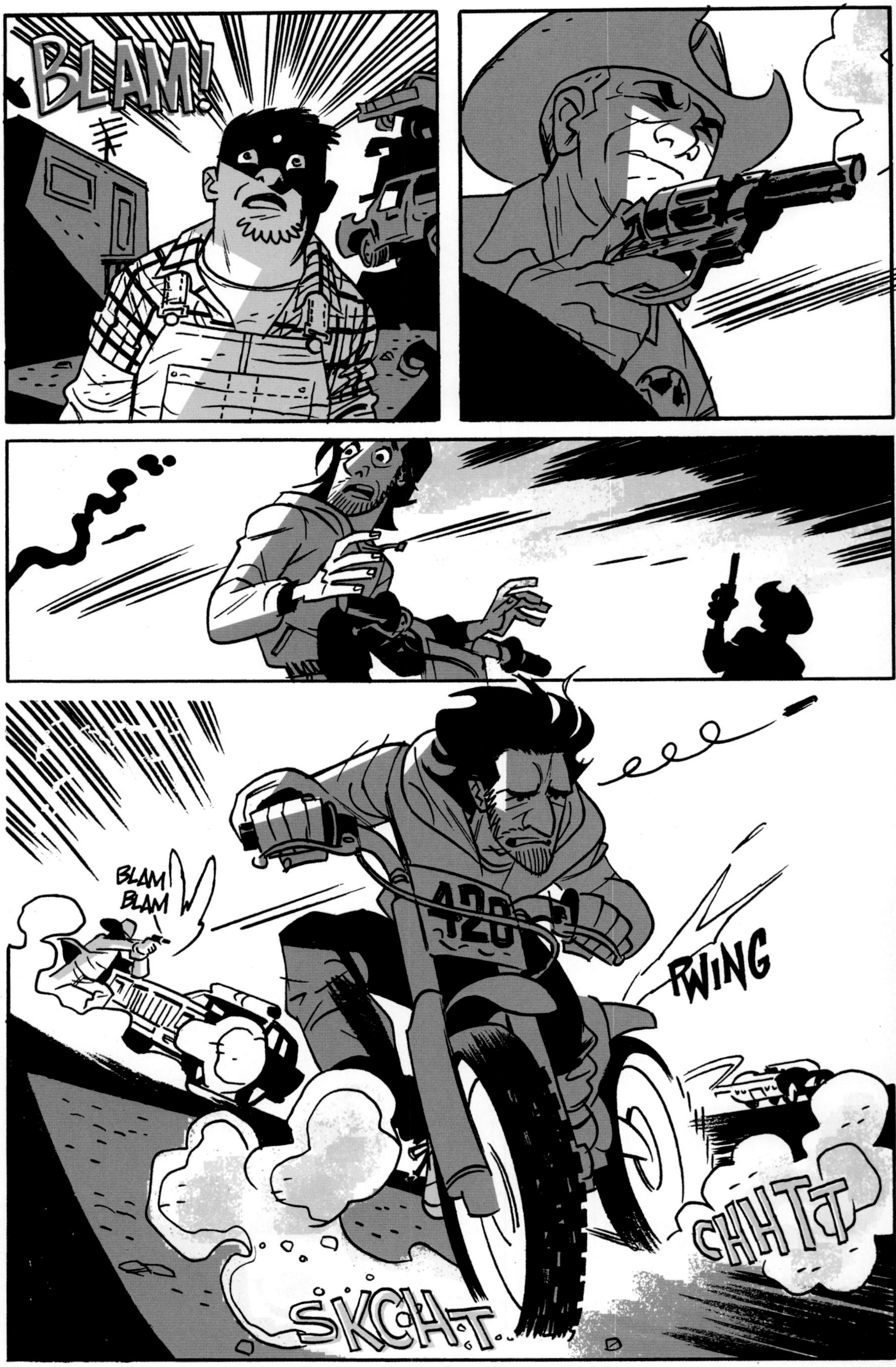
BLAM!
BLAM
BLAM
PWING
CHHTT
SKCHT
420

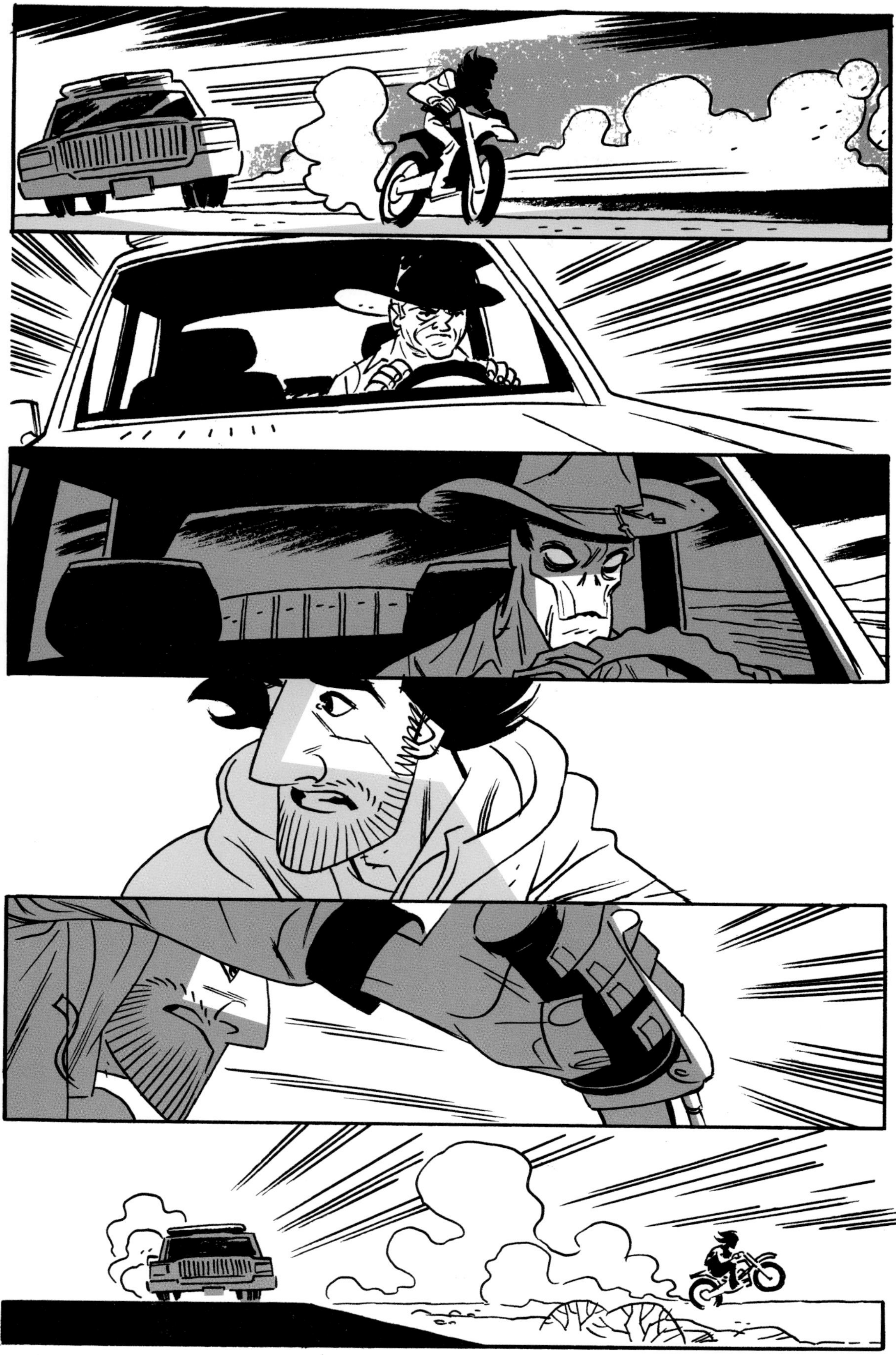

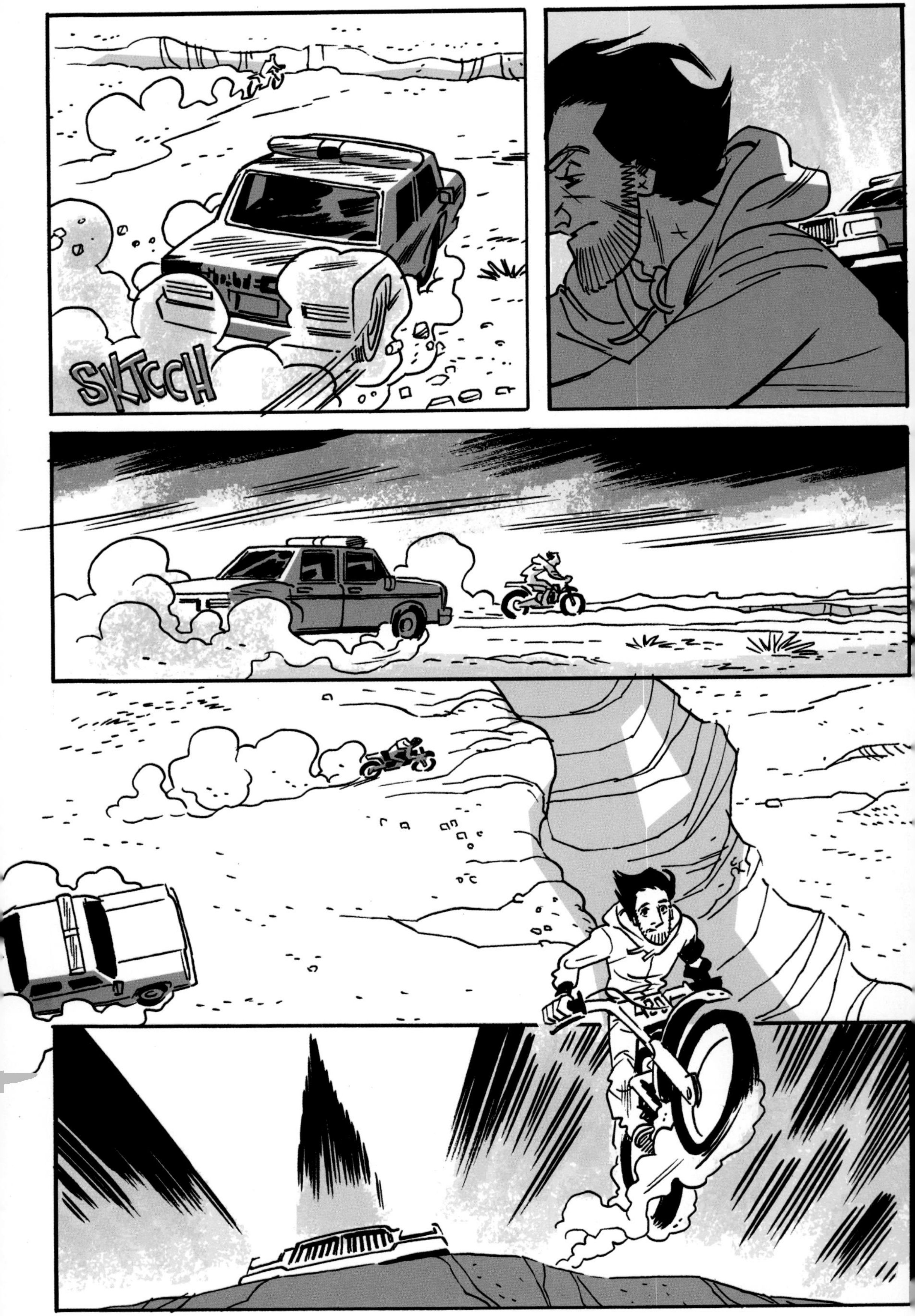
SKTCCH

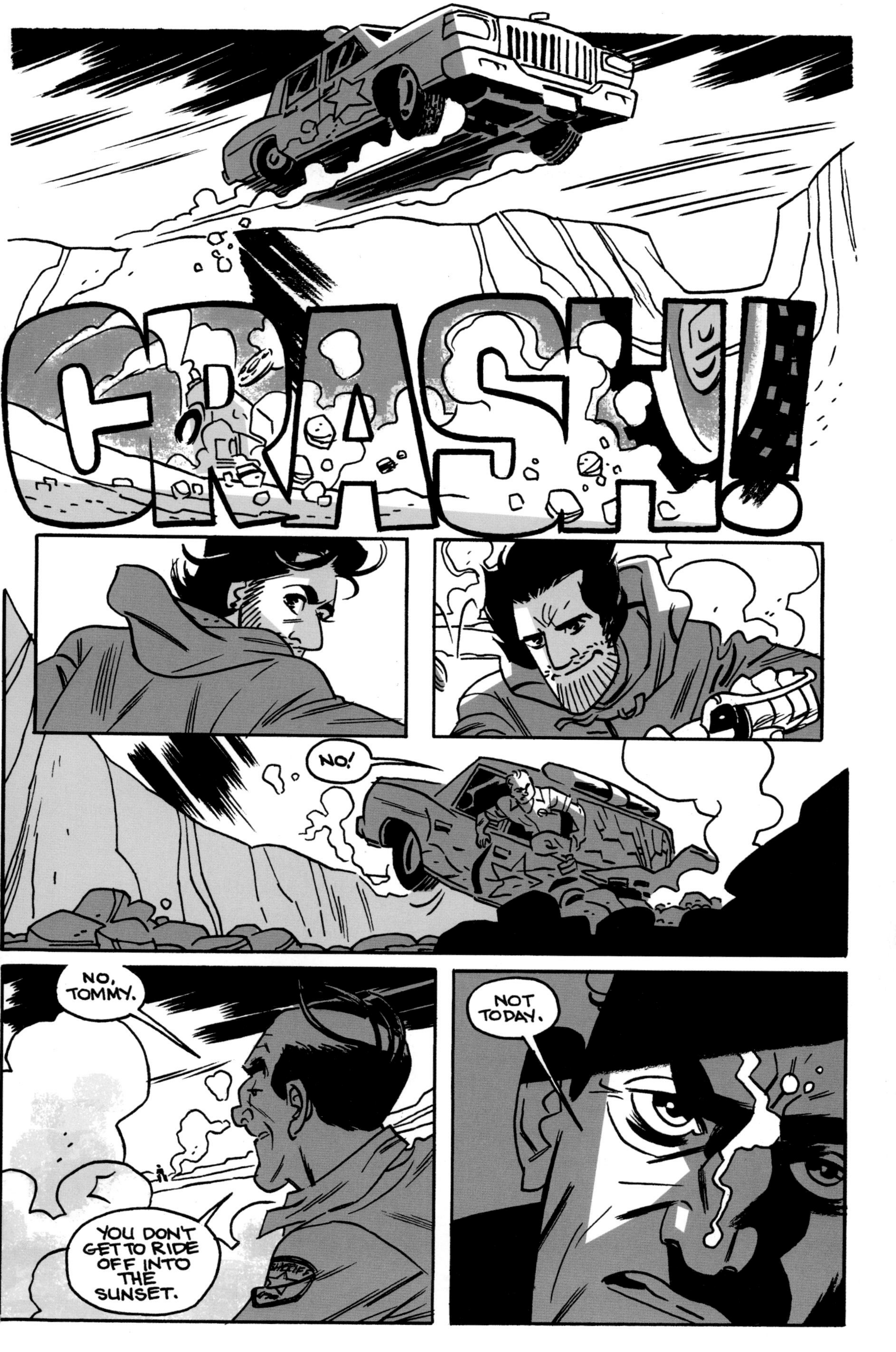
CRASH!
NO!
NO, TOMMY.
YOU DON'T GET TO RIDE OFF INTO THE SUNSET.
NOT TODAY.

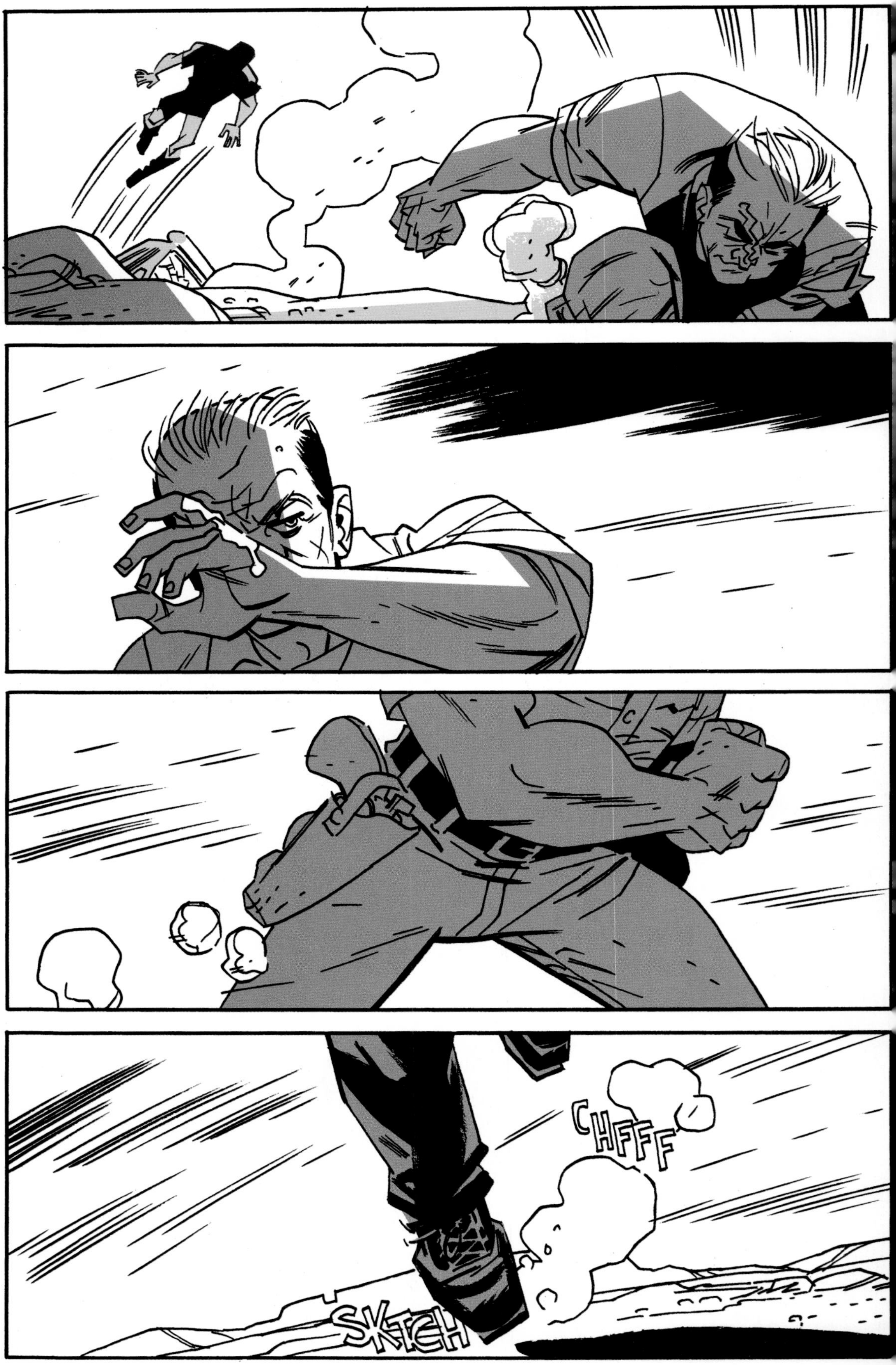
CHFFF
SKTCH

KRKKT

RIP!

SNAP

BAF!

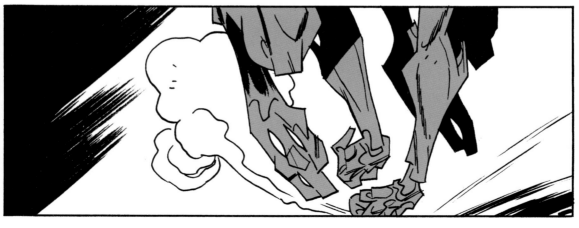

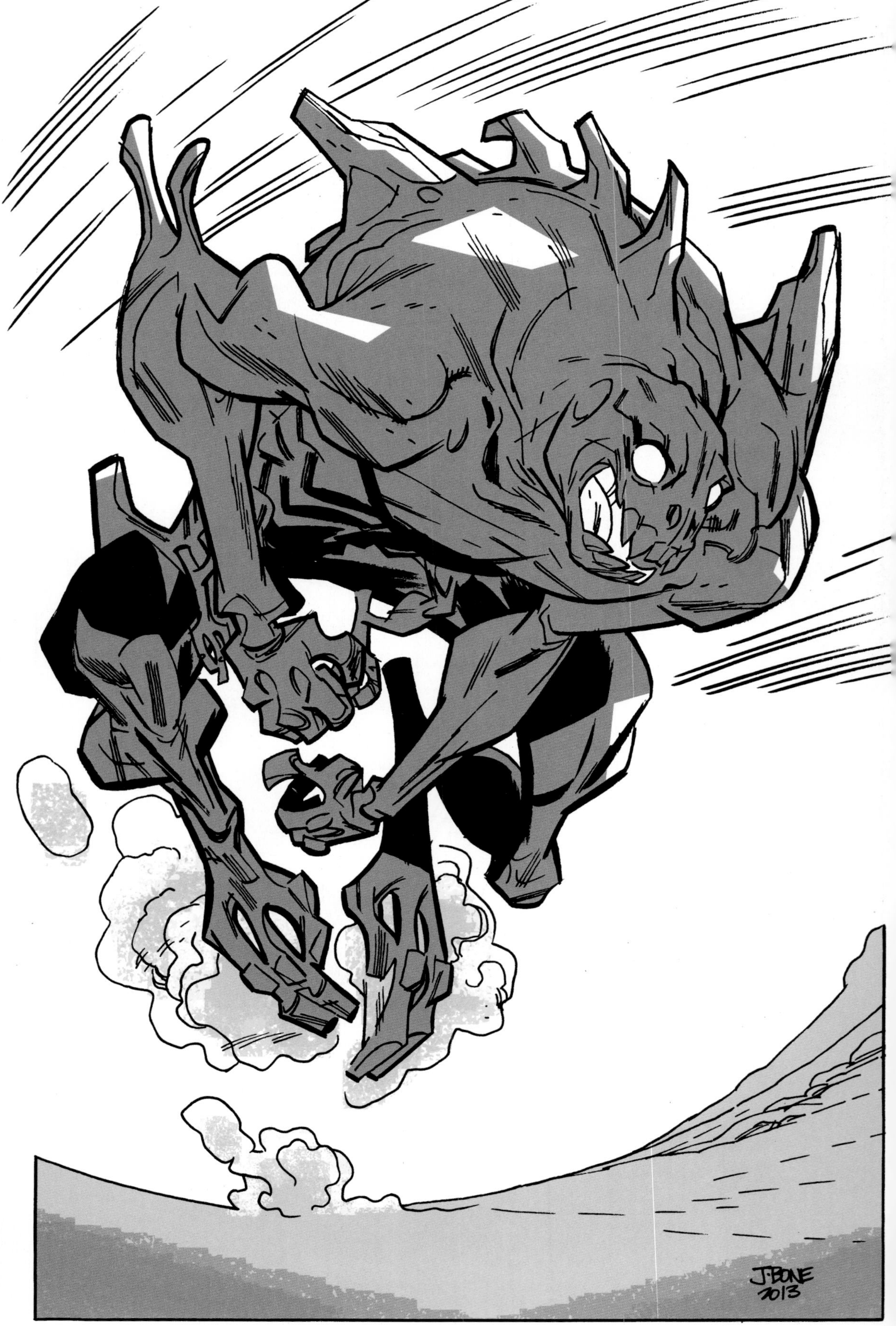
J·BONE
2013

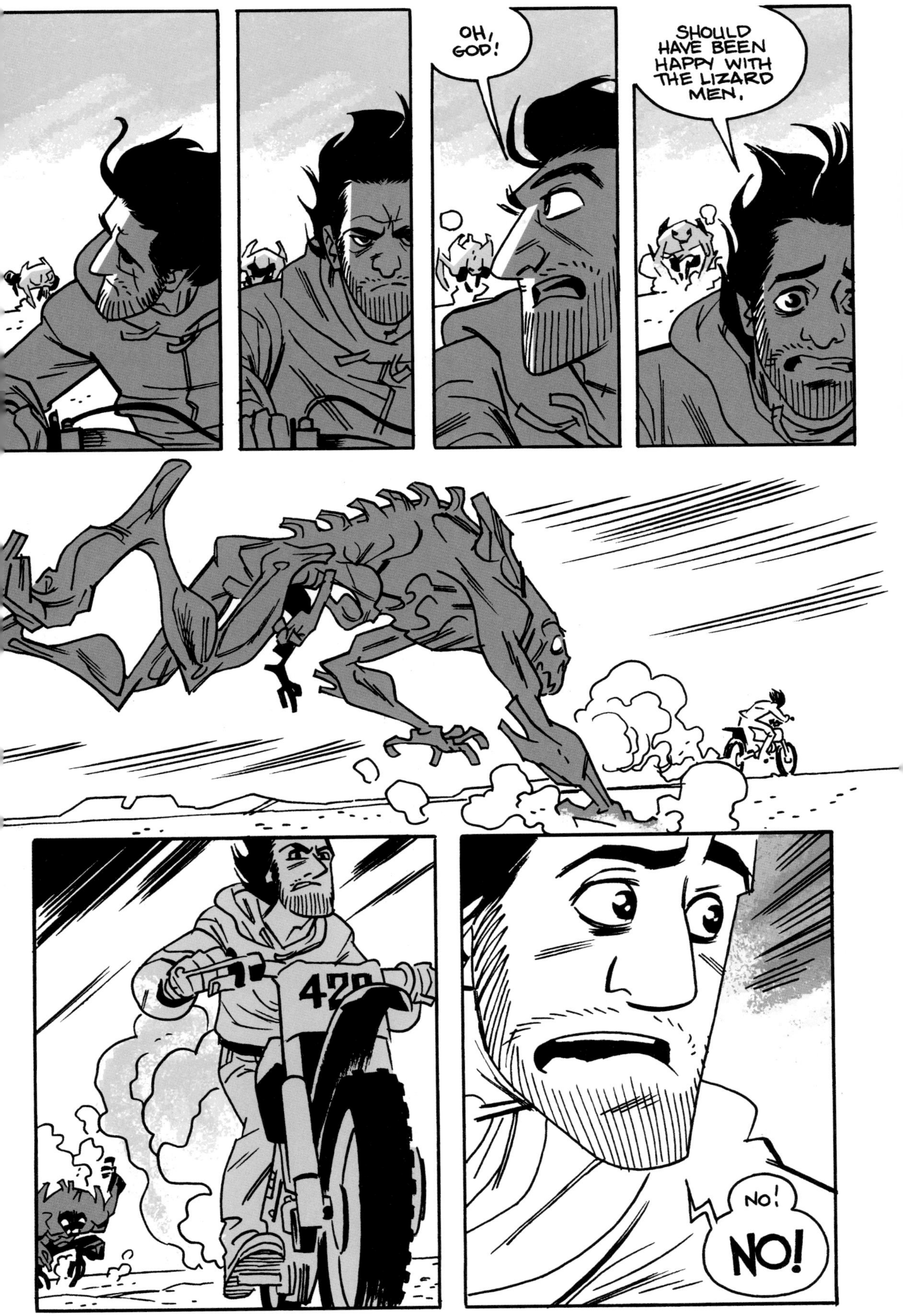
OH, GOD!
SHOULD HAVE BEEN HAPPY WITH THE LIZARD MEN.
429
NO!
NO!

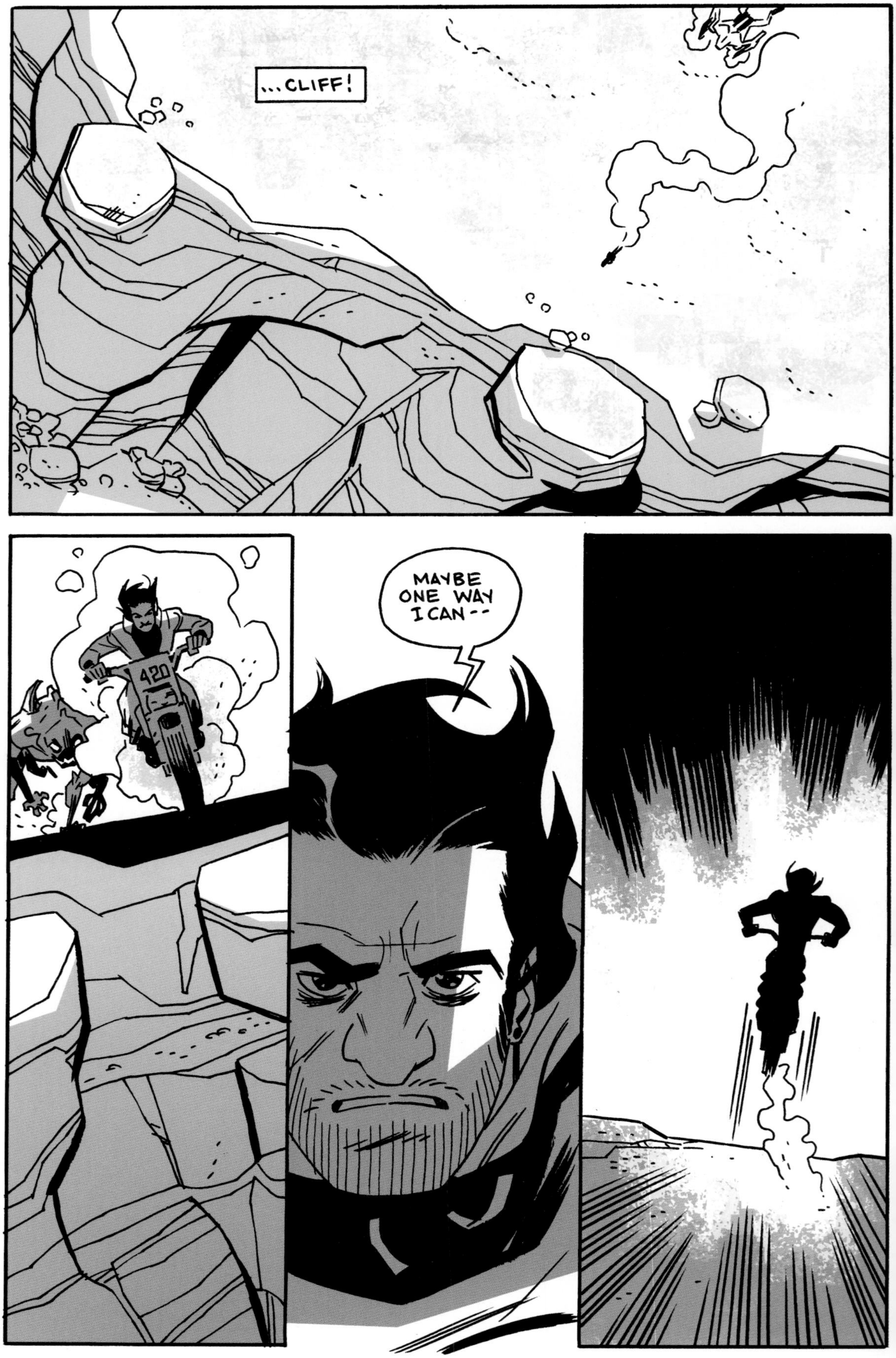
...CLIFF!
MAYBE ONE WAY I CAN--

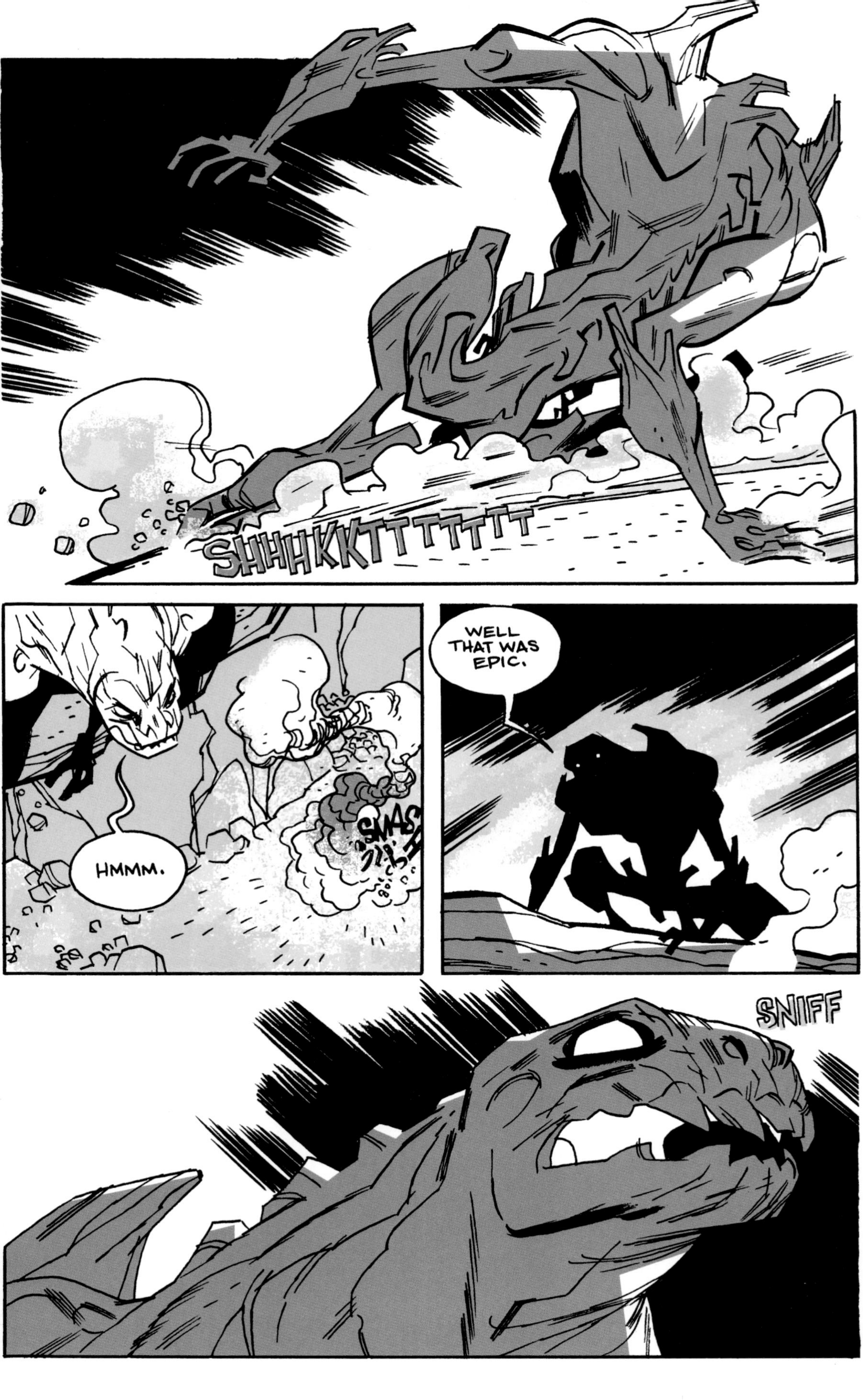
SHHHKKTTTTTTT
HMMM.
SMASH
WELL THAT WAS EPIC.
SNIFF

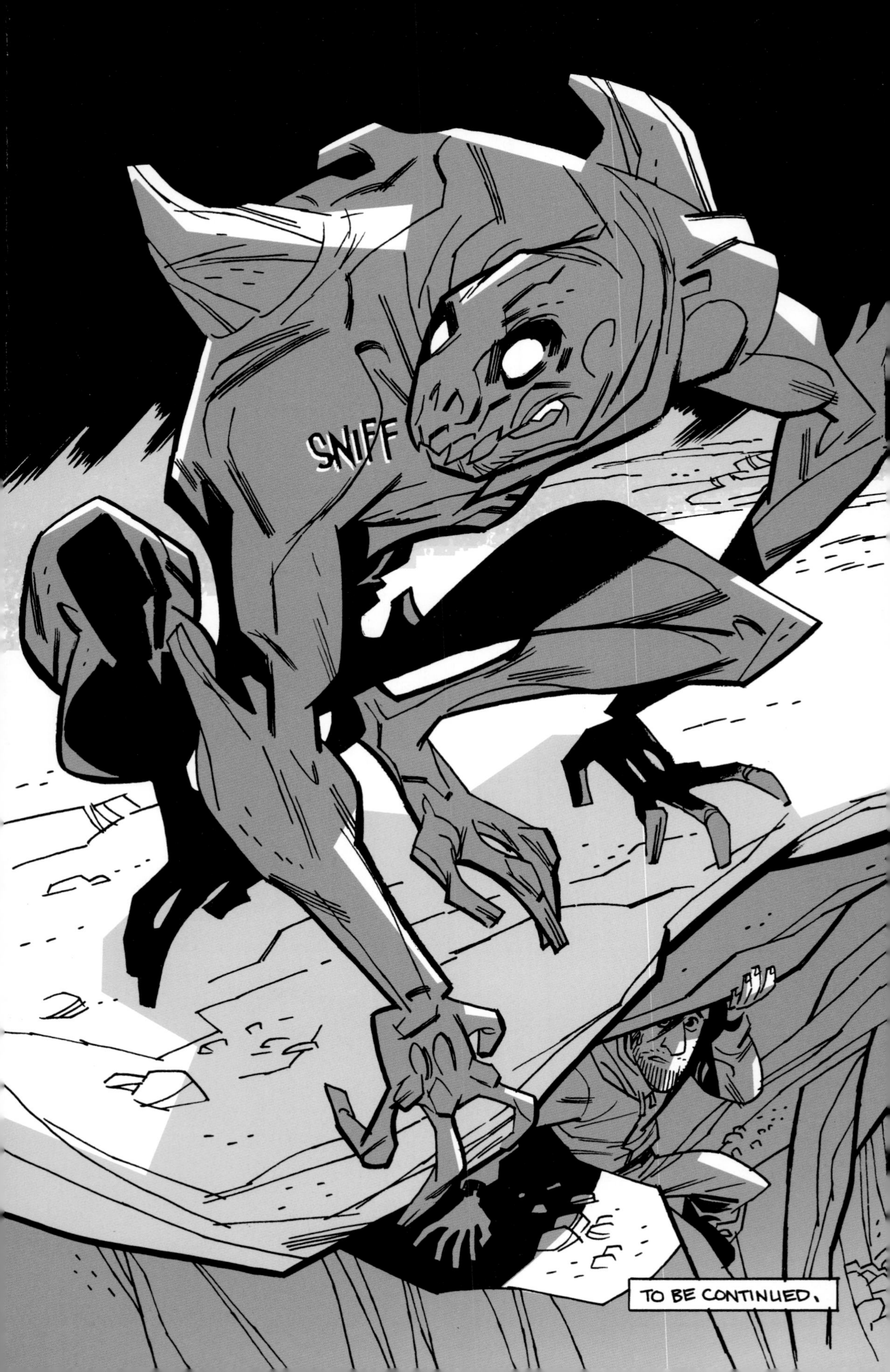
SNIFF
TO BE CONTINUED.

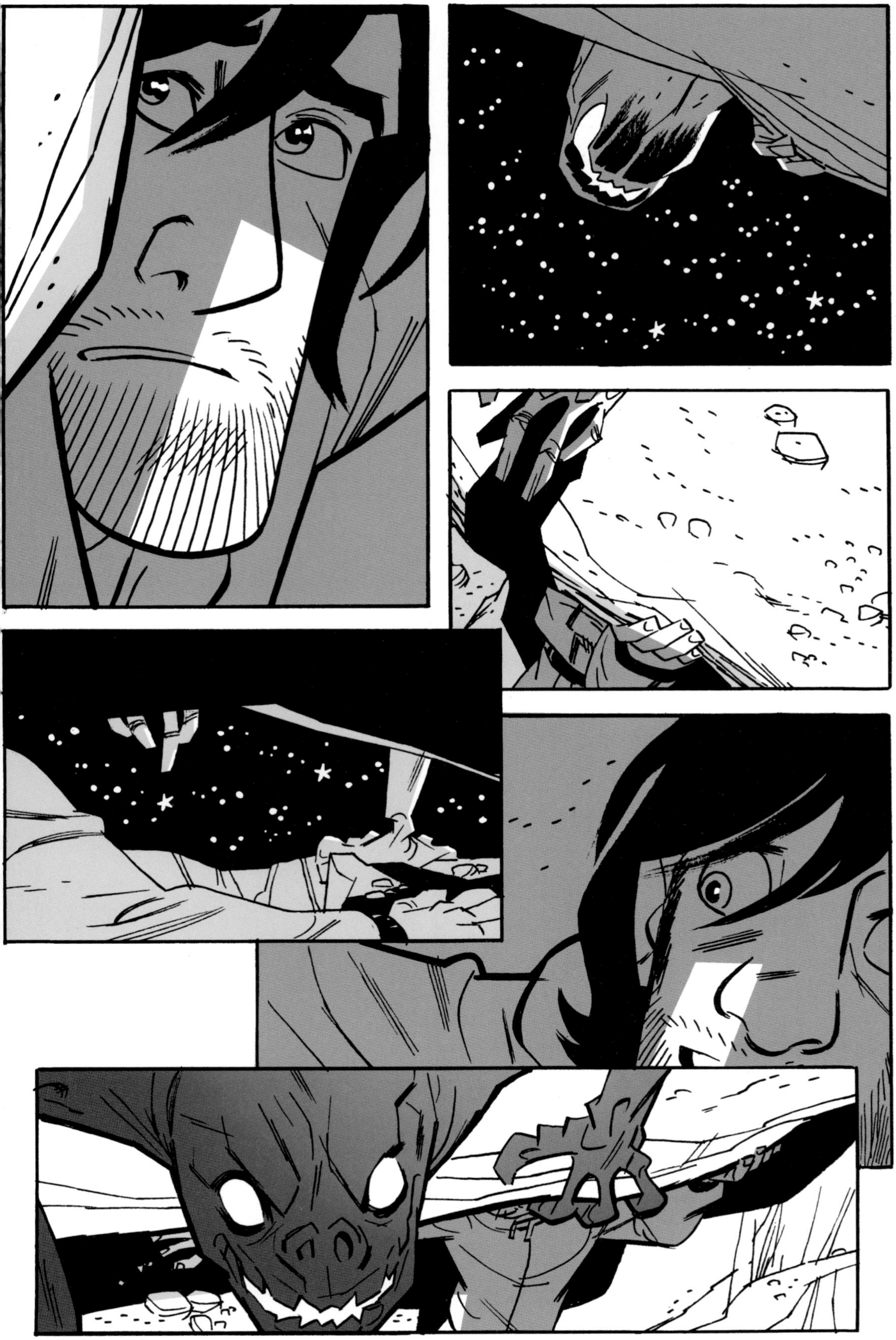

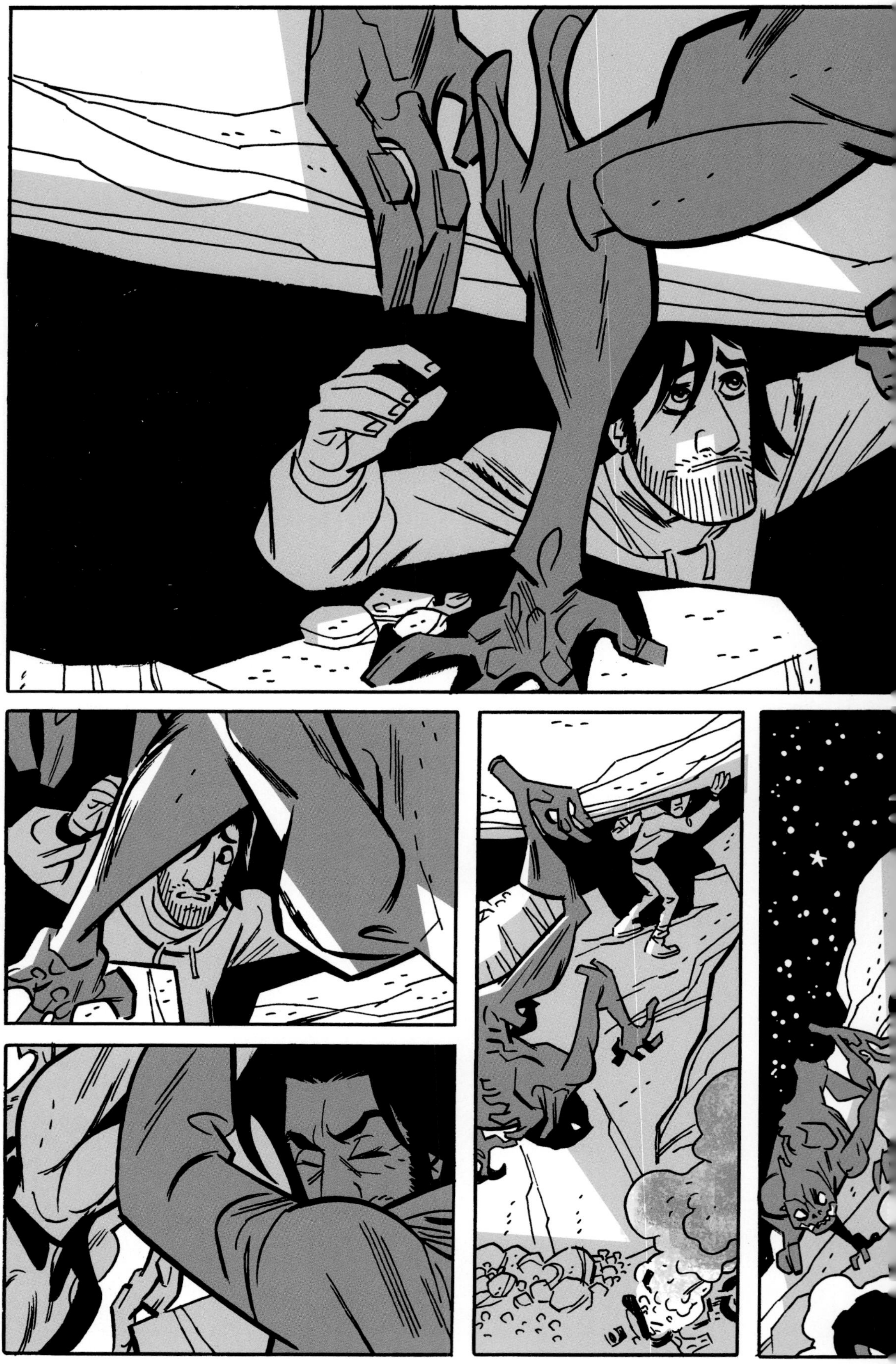

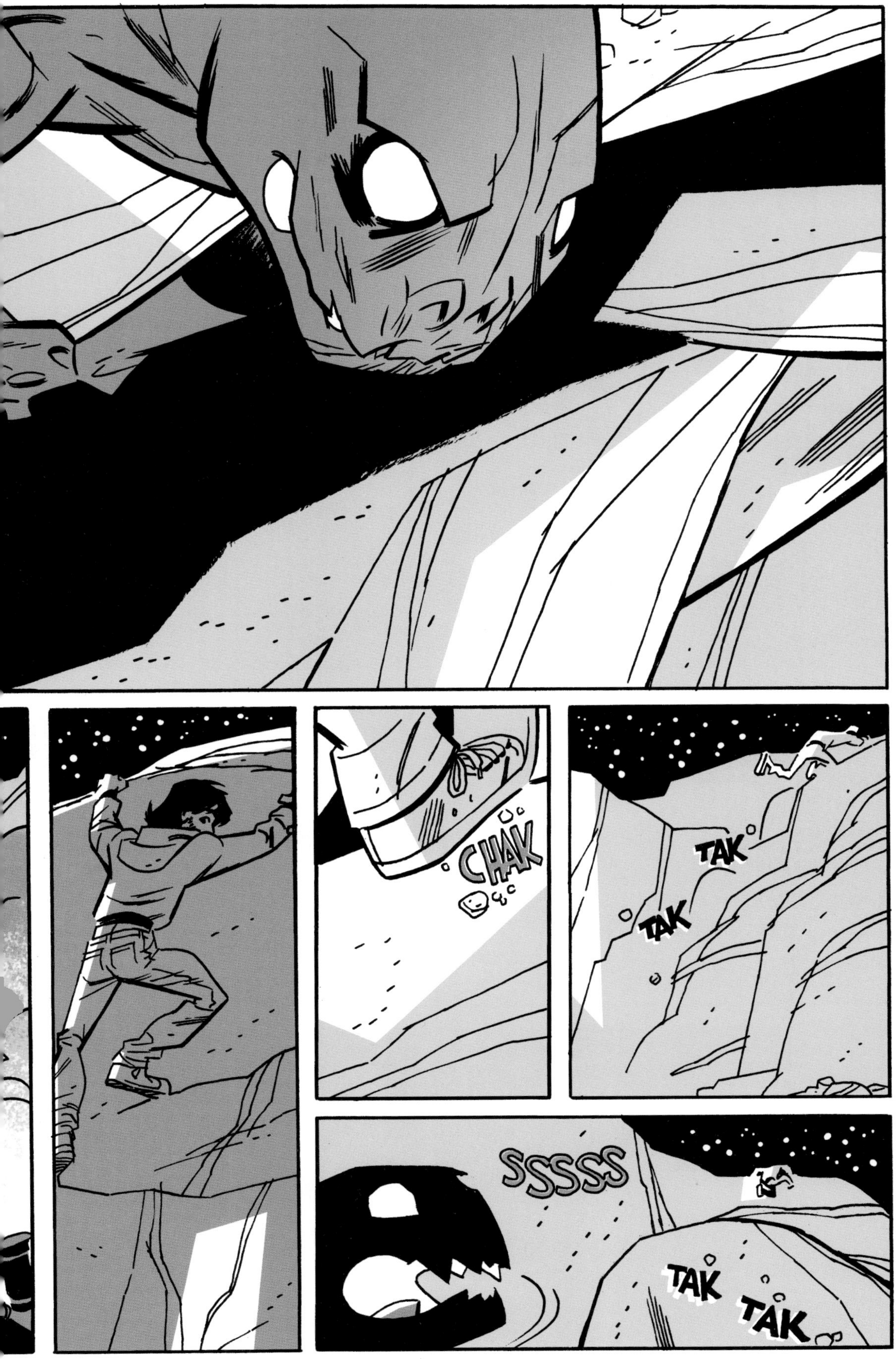
CHAK
TAK
TAK
SSSSS
TAK
TAK

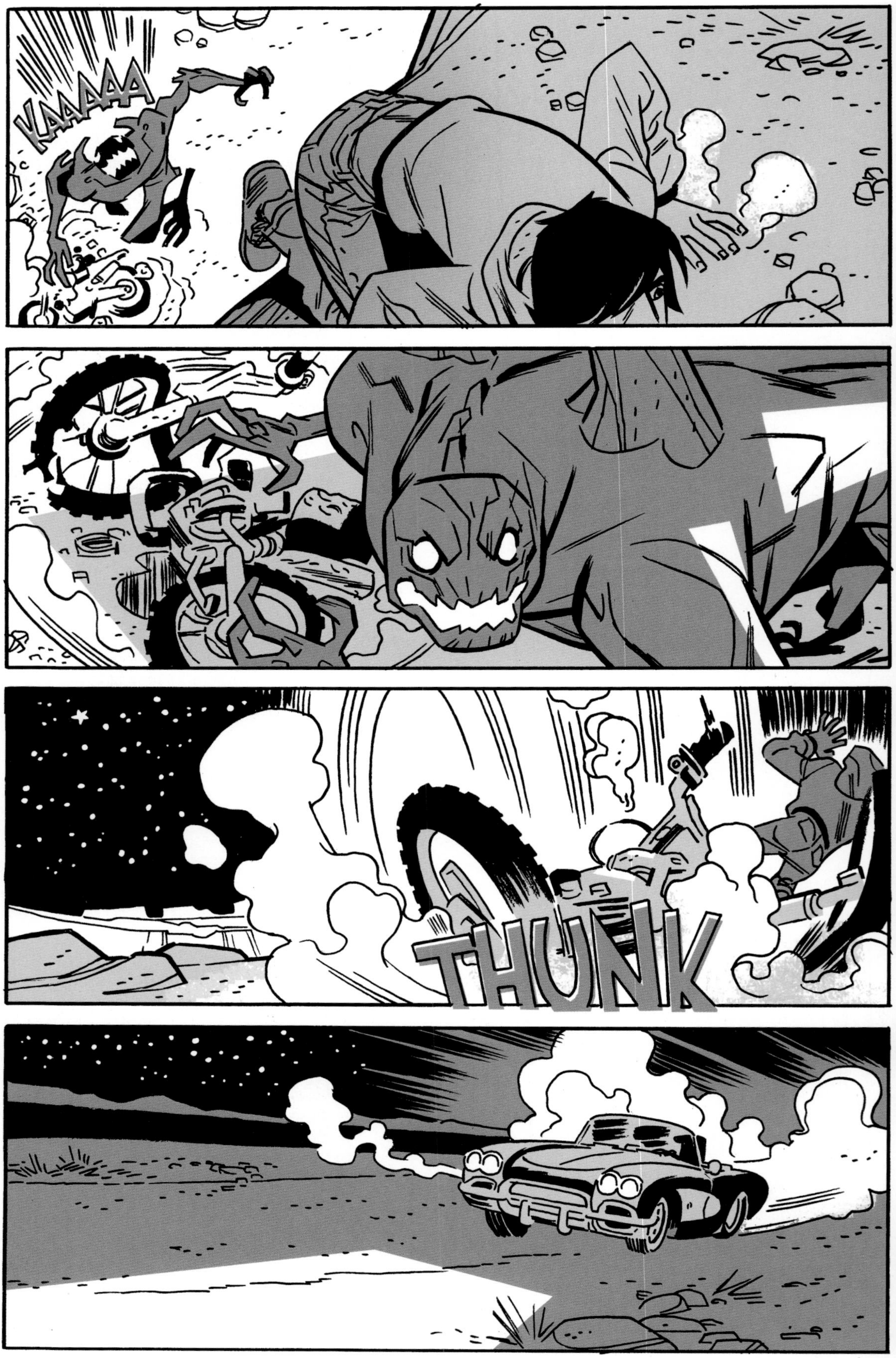
KAAAAA
THUNK

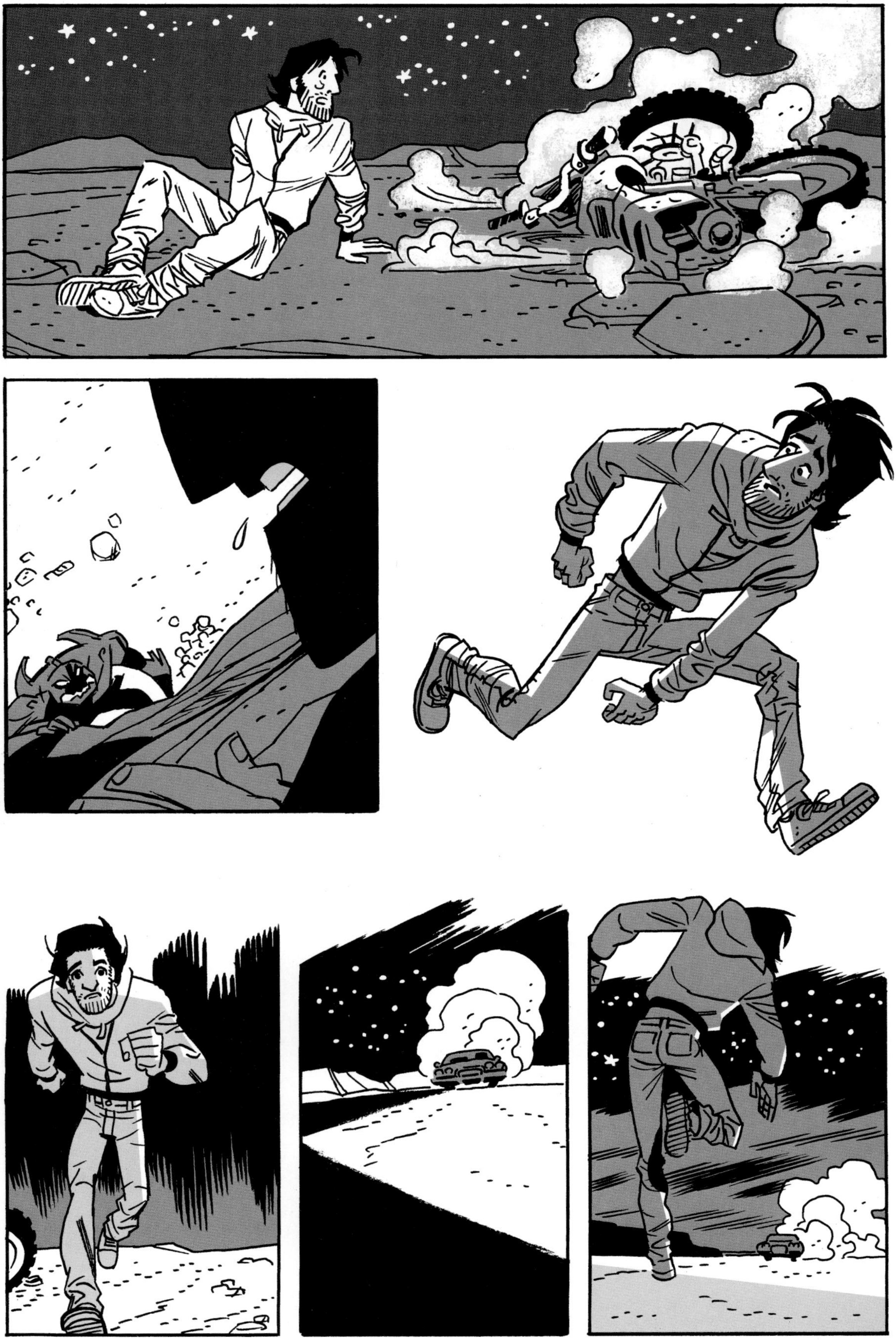

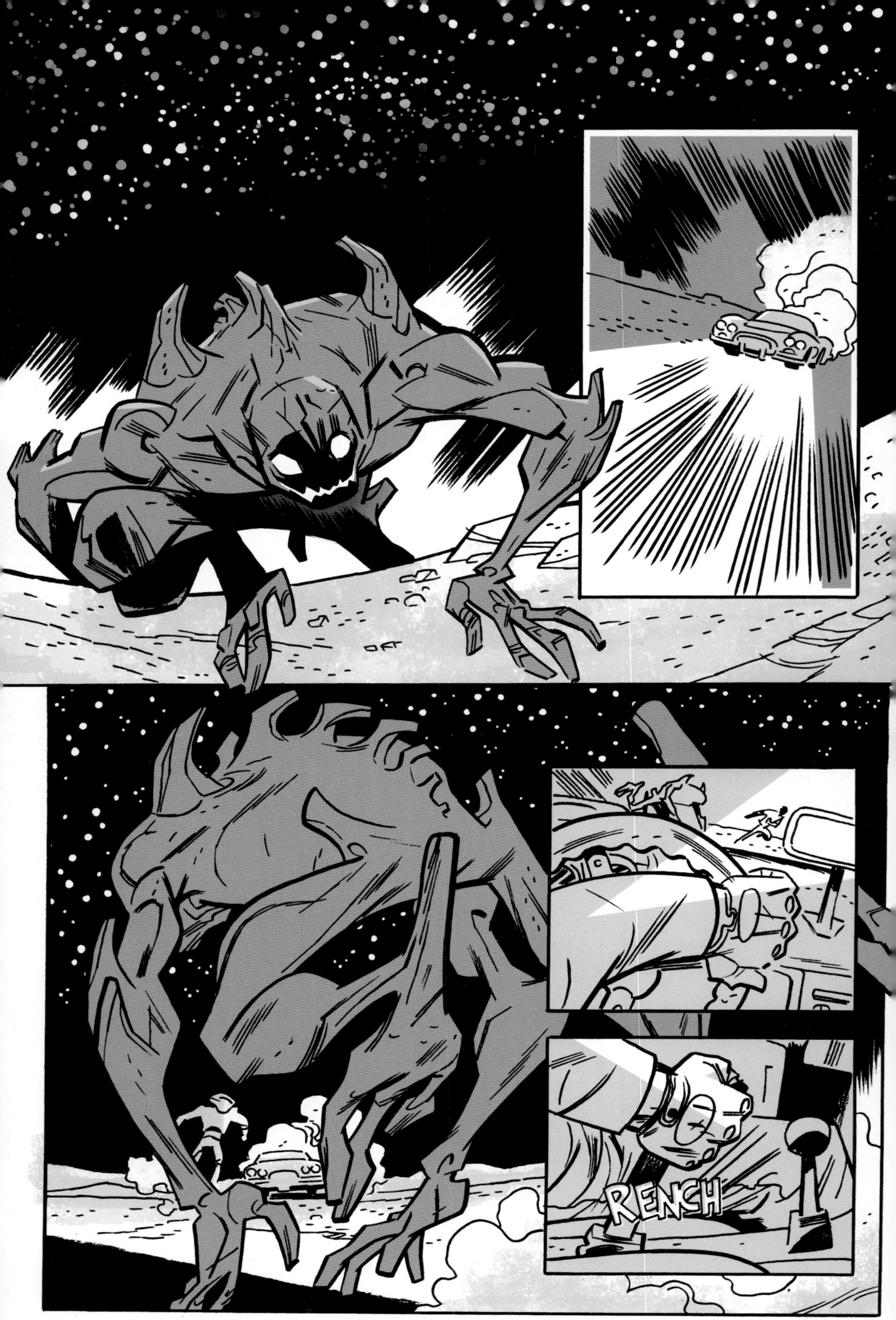
RENCH

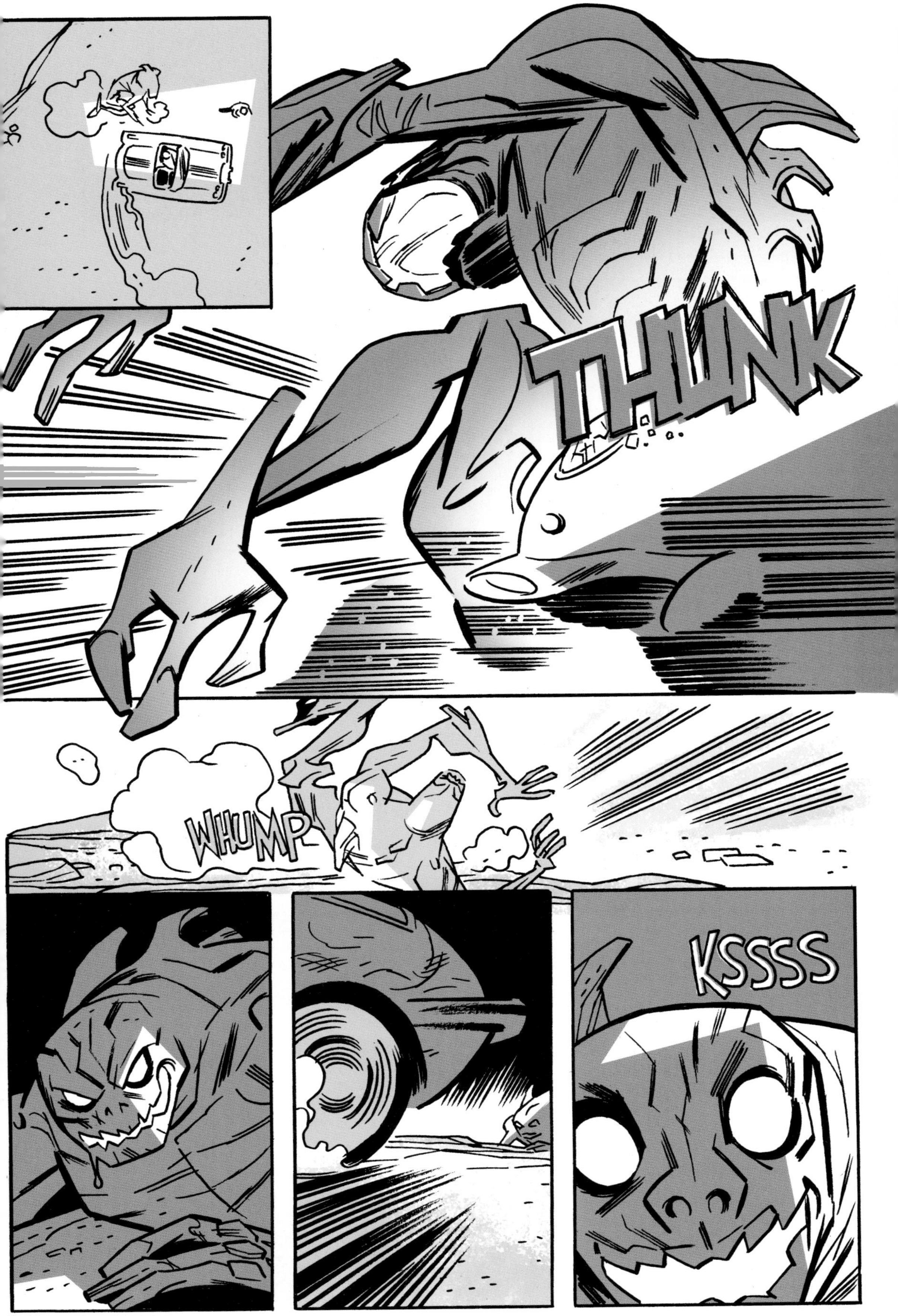
THUNK
WHUMP
KSSSS

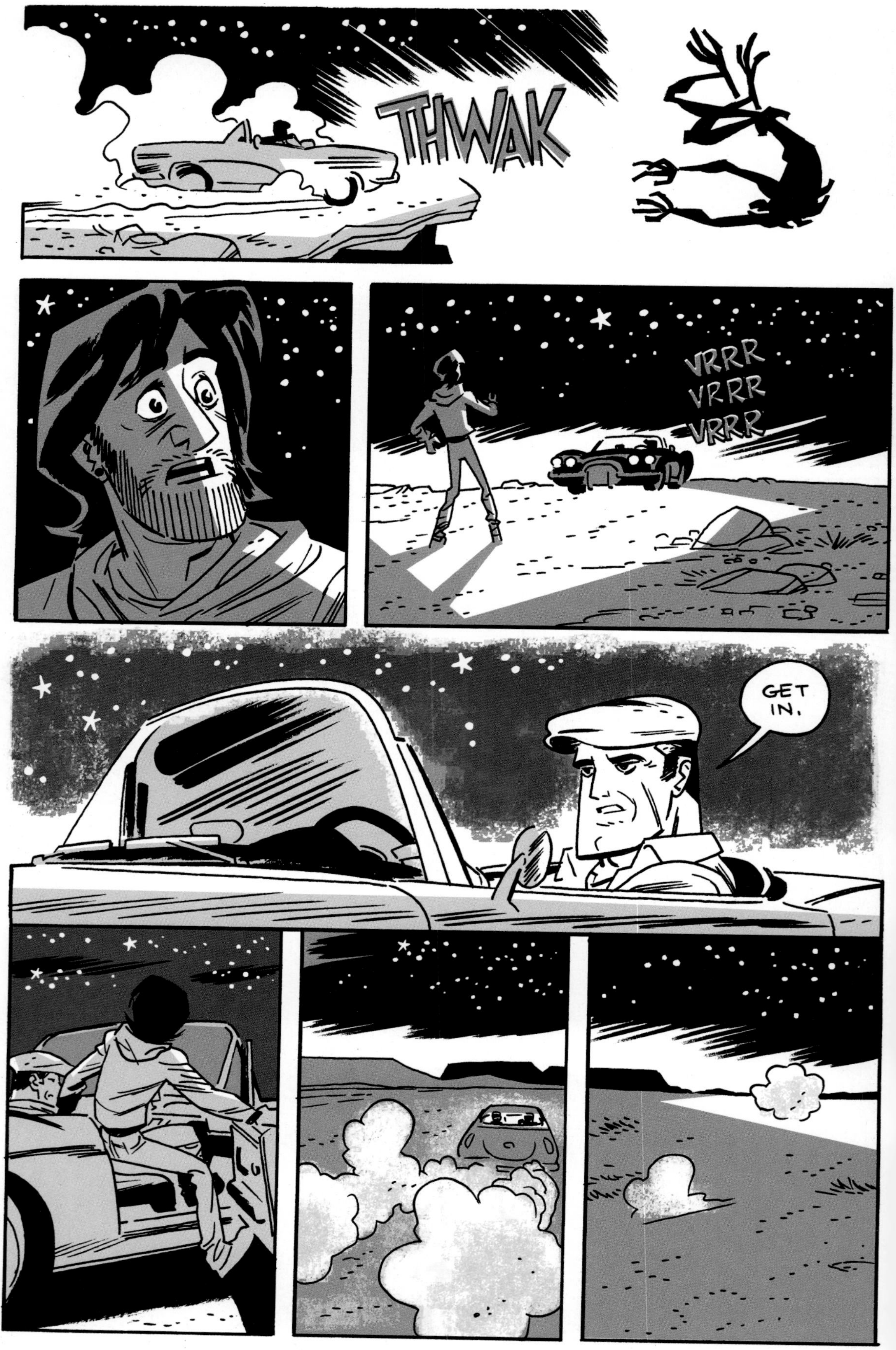
THWAK
VRRR
VRRR
VRRR
GET IN.

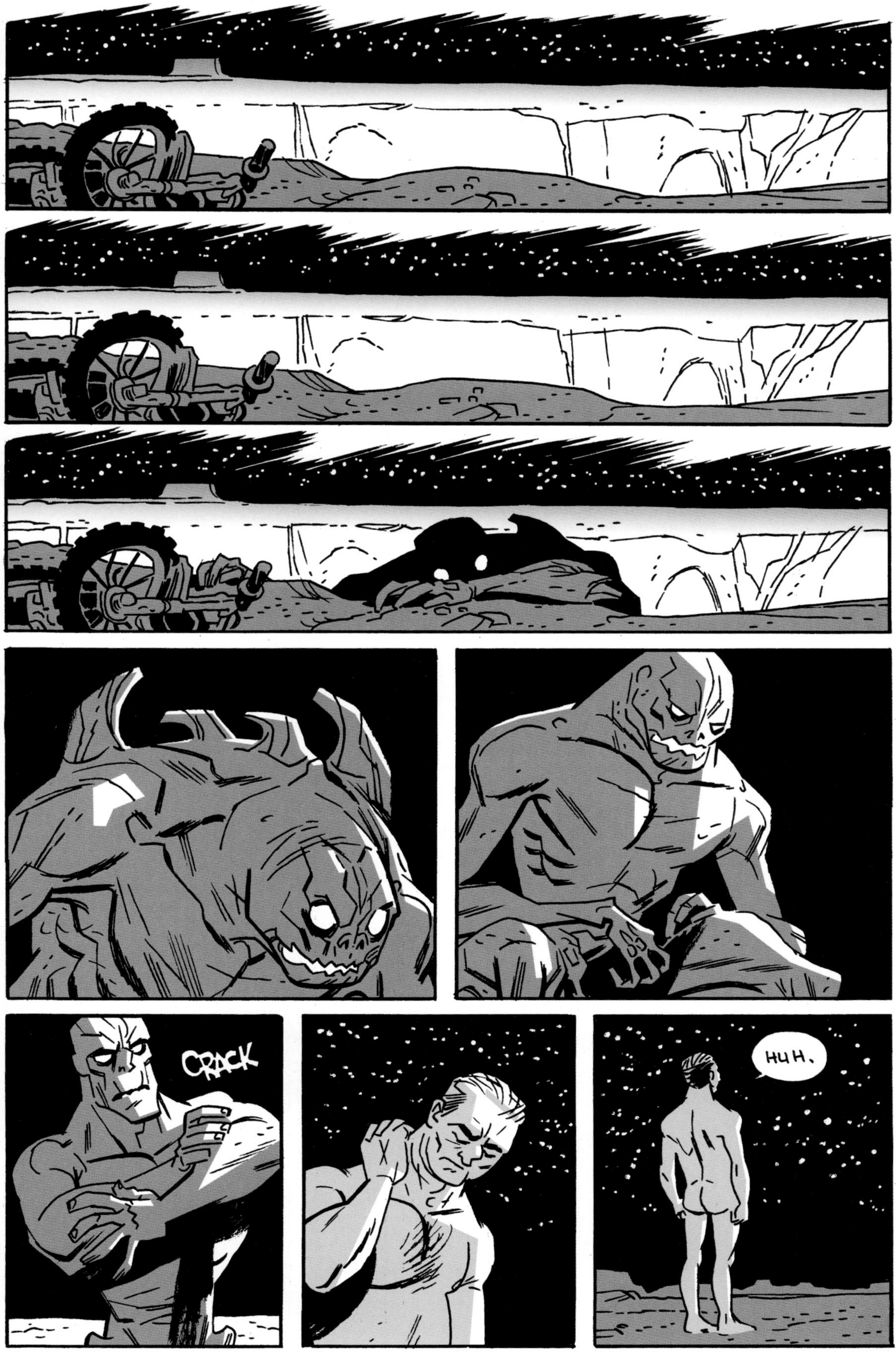
CRACK
HUH.

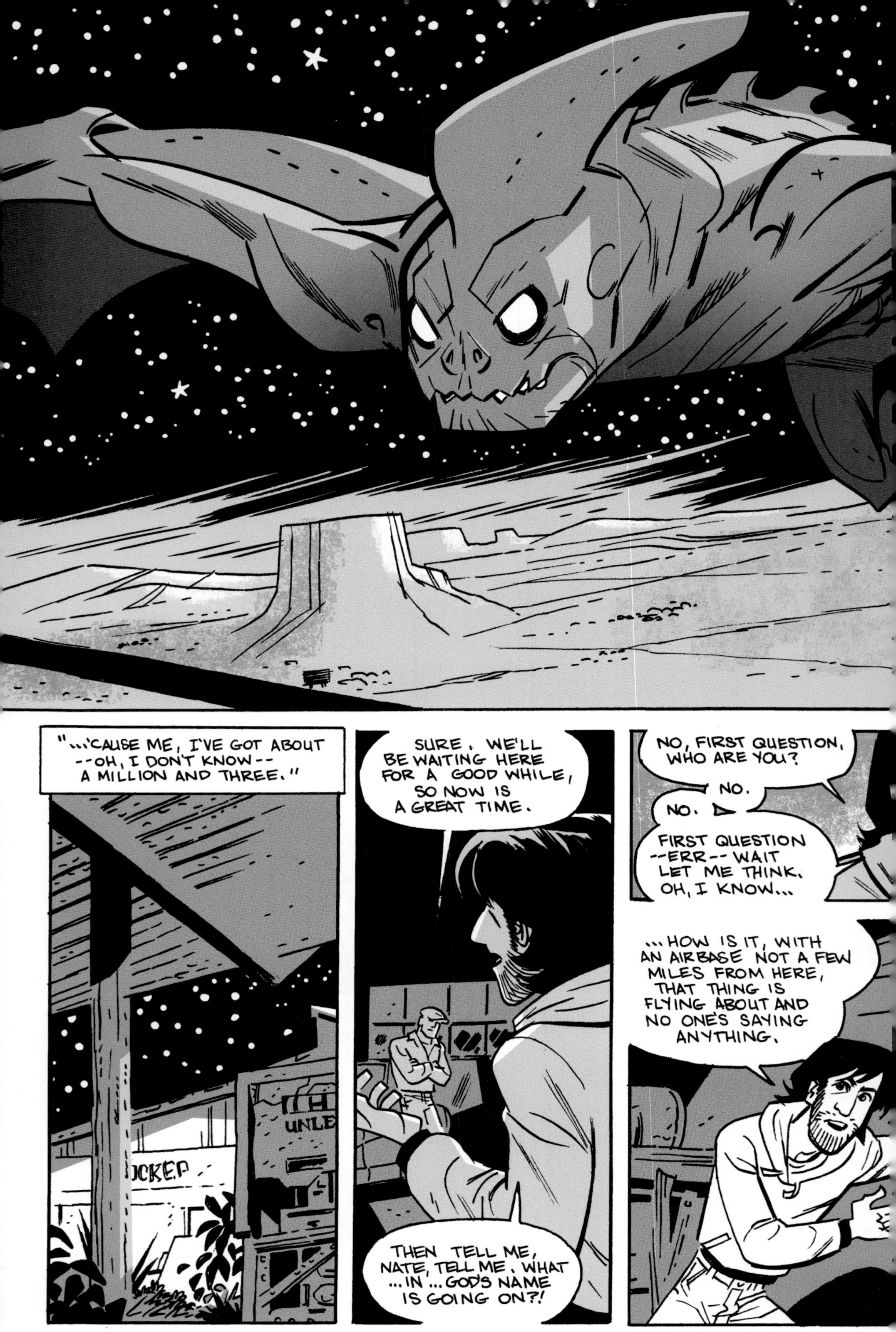
"...'CAUSE ME, I'VE GOT ABOUT --OH, I DON'T KNOW-- A MILLION AND THREE."
SURE. WE'LL BE WAITING HERE FOR A GOOD WHILE, SO NOW IS A GREAT TIME.
THEN TELL ME, NATE, TELL ME. WHAT ...IN ...GOD'S NAME IS GOING ON?!
NO, FIRST QUESTION, WHO ARE YOU?
NO.
NO.
FIRST QUESTION --ERR-- WAIT LET ME THINK. OH, I KNOW...
...HOW IS IT, WITH AN AIRBASE NOT A FEW MILES FROM HERE, THAT THING IS FLYING ABOUT AND NO ONE'S SAYING ANYTHING.

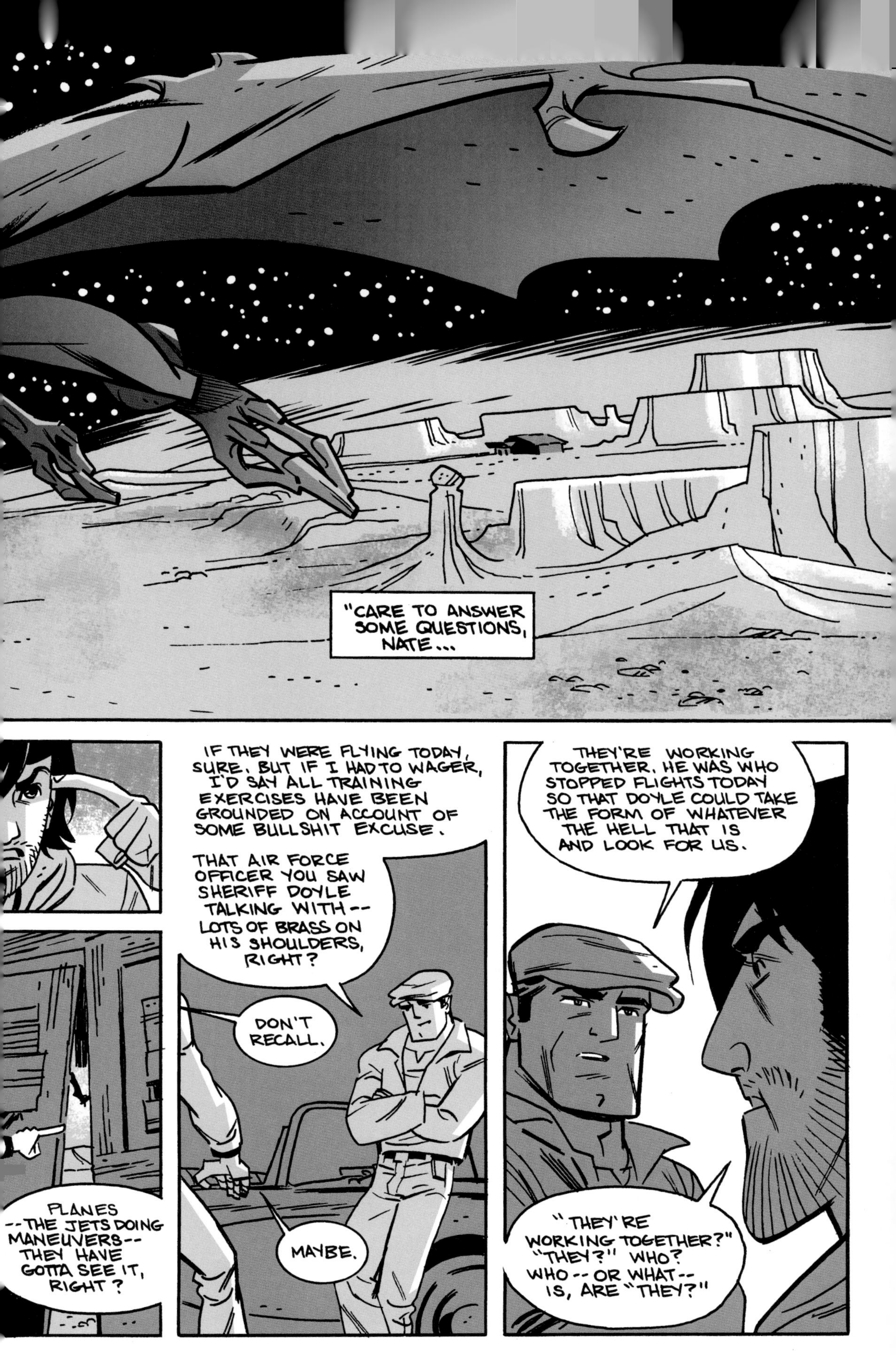
"CARE TO ANSWER SOME QUESTIONS, NATE...
PLANES --THE JETS DOING MANEUVERS-- THEY HAVE GOTTA SEE IT, RIGHT?
IF THEY WERE FLYING TODAY, SURE. BUT IF I HAD TO WAGER, I'D SAY ALL TRAINING EXERCISES HAVE BEEN GROUNDED ON ACCOUNT OF SOME BULLSHIT EXCUSE.
THAT AIR FORCE OFFICER YOU SAW SHERIFF DOYLE TALKING WITH -- LOTS OF BRASS ON HIS SHOULDERS, RIGHT?
DON'T RECALL.
MAYBE.
THEY'RE WORKING TOGETHER. HE WAS WHO STOPPED FLIGHTS TODAY SO THAT DOYLE COULD TAKE THE FORM OF WHATEVER THE HELL THAT IS AND LOOK FOR US.
"THEY'RE WORKING TOGETHER?" "THEY?" WHO? WHO -- OR WHAT -- IS, ARE "THEY?"

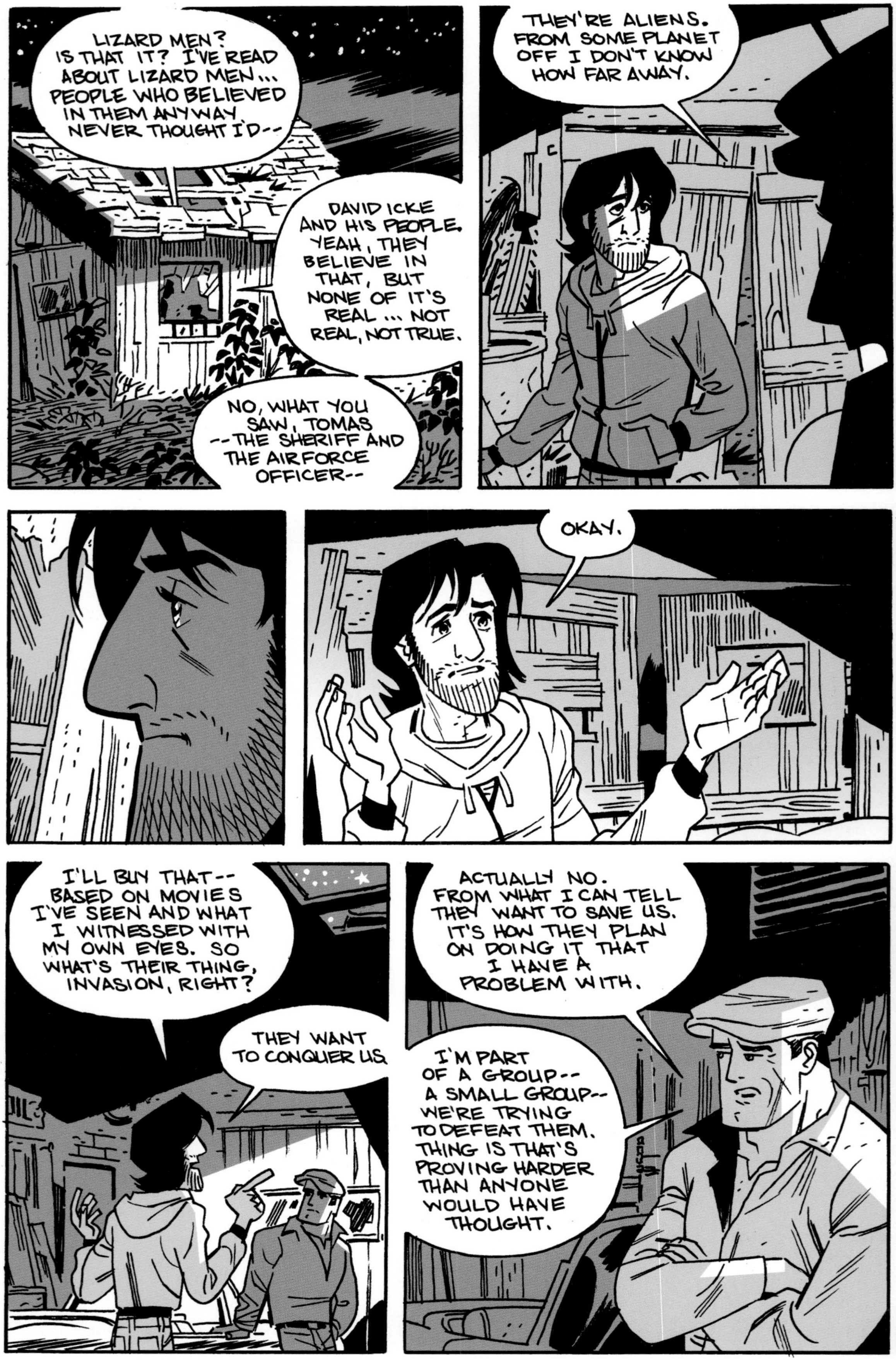
LIZARD MEN? IS THAT IT? I'VE READ ABOUT LIZARD MEN... PEOPLE WHO BELIEVED IN THEM ANYWAY. NEVER THOUGHT I'D--
DAVID ICKE AND HIS PEOPLE. YEAH, THEY BELIEVE IN THAT, BUT NONE OF IT'S REAL... NOT REAL, NOT TRUE.
NO, WHAT YOU SAW, TOMAS --THE SHERIFF AND THE AIRFORCE OFFICER--
THEY'RE ALIENS. FROM SOME PLANET OFF I DON'T KNOW HOW FAR AWAY.
OKAY.
I'LL BUY THAT-- BASED ON MOVIES I'VE SEEN AND WHAT I WITNESSED WITH MY OWN EYES. SO WHAT'S THEIR THING, INVASION, RIGHT?
THEY WANT TO CONQUER US.
ACTUALLY NO. FROM WHAT I CAN TELL THEY WANT TO SAVE US. IT'S HOW THEY PLAN ON DOING IT THAT I HAVE A PROBLEM WITH.
I'M PART OF A GROUP-- A SMALL GROUP-- WE'RE TRYING TO DEFEAT THEM. THING IS THAT'S PROVING HARDER THAN ANYONE WOULD HAVE THOUGHT.

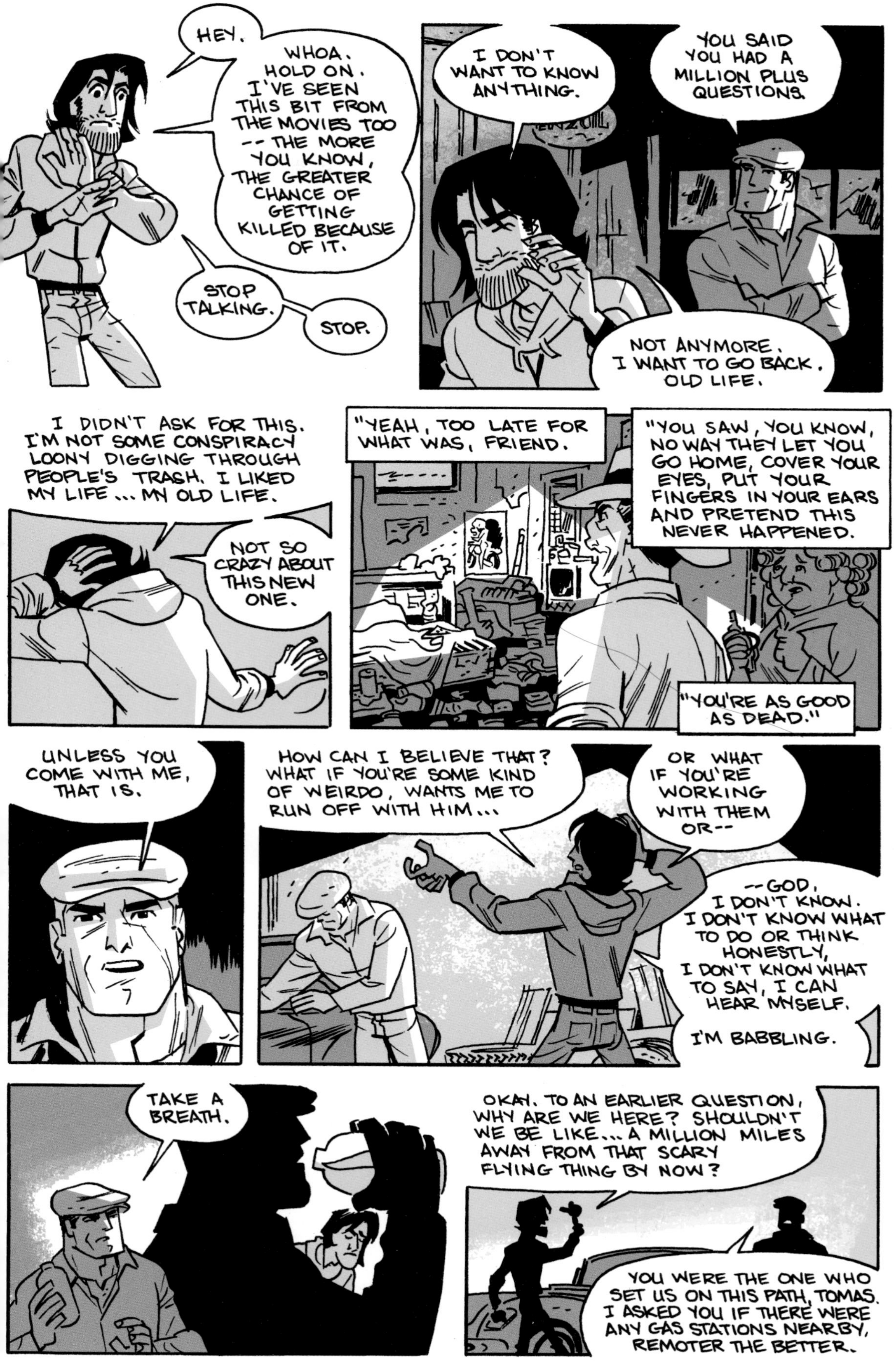
HEY.
WHOA. HOLD ON. I'VE SEEN THIS BIT FROM THE MOVIES TOO -- THE MORE YOU KNOW, THE GREATER CHANCE OF GETTING KILLED BECAUSE OF IT.
STOP TALKING.
STOP.
I DON'T WANT TO KNOW ANYTHING.
YOU SAID YOU HAD A MILLION PLUS QUESTIONS.
NOT ANYMORE. I WANT TO GO BACK. OLD LIFE.
I DIDN'T ASK FOR THIS. I'M NOT SOME CONSPIRACY LOONY DIGGING THROUGH PEOPLE'S TRASH. I LIKED MY LIFE ... MY OLD LIFE.
NOT SO CRAZY ABOUT THIS NEW ONE.
"YEAH, TOO LATE FOR WHAT WAS, FRIEND.
"YOU SAW, YOU KNOW, NO WAY THEY LET YOU GO HOME, COVER YOUR EYES, PUT YOUR FINGERS IN YOUR EARS AND PRETEND THIS NEVER HAPPENED.
"YOU'RE AS GOOD AS DEAD."
UNLESS YOU COME WITH ME, THAT IS.
HOW CAN I BELIEVE THAT? WHAT IF YOU'RE SOME KIND OF WEIRDO, WANTS ME TO RUN OFF WITH HIM...
OR WHAT IF YOU'RE WORKING WITH THEM OR--
--GOD, I DON'T KNOW. I DON'T KNOW WHAT TO DO OR THINK HONESTLY, I DON'T KNOW WHAT TO SAY, I CAN HEAR MYSELF.
I'M BABBLING.
TAKE A BREATH.
OKAY. TO AN EARLIER QUESTION, WHY ARE WE HERE? SHOULDN'T WE BE LIKE... A MILLION MILES AWAY FROM THAT SCARY FLYING THING BY NOW?
YOU WERE THE ONE WHO SET US ON THIS PATH, TOMAS. I ASKED YOU IF THERE WERE ANY GAS STATIONS NEARBY, REMOTER THE BETTER.

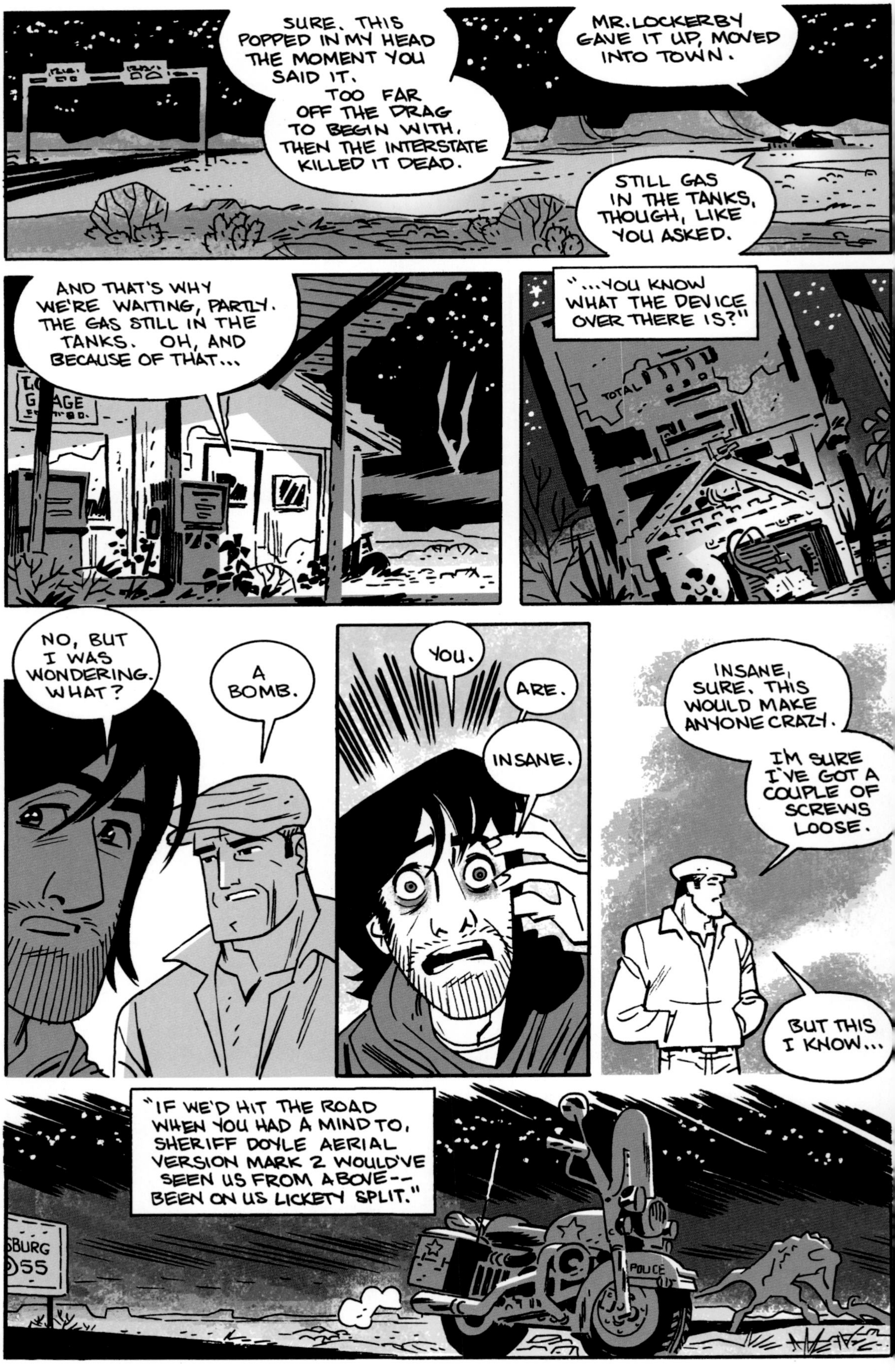

SURE. THIS POPPED IN MY HEAD THE MOMENT YOU SAID IT.
TOO FAR OFF THE DRAG TO BEGIN WITH, THEN THE INTERSTATE KILLED IT DEAD.
MR. LOCKERBY GAVE IT UP, MOVED INTO TOWN.
STILL GAS IN THE TANKS, THOUGH, LIKE YOU ASKED.
AND THAT'S WHY WE'RE WAITING, PARTLY. THE GAS STILL IN THE TANKS. OH, AND BECAUSE OF THAT...
"...YOU KNOW WHAT THE DEVICE OVER THERE IS?"
TOTAL
NO, BUT I WAS WONDERING. WHAT?
A BOMB.
YOU.
ARE.
INSANE.
INSANE, SURE. THIS WOULD MAKE ANYONE CRAZY.
I'M SURE I'VE GOT A COUPLE OF SCREWS LOOSE.
BUT THIS I KNOW...
"IF WE'D HIT THE ROAD WHEN YOU HAD A MIND TO, SHERIFF DOYLE AERIAL VERSION MARK 2 WOULD'VE SEEN US FROM ABOVE-- BEEN ON US LICKETY SPLIT."
SBURG
55
POLICE

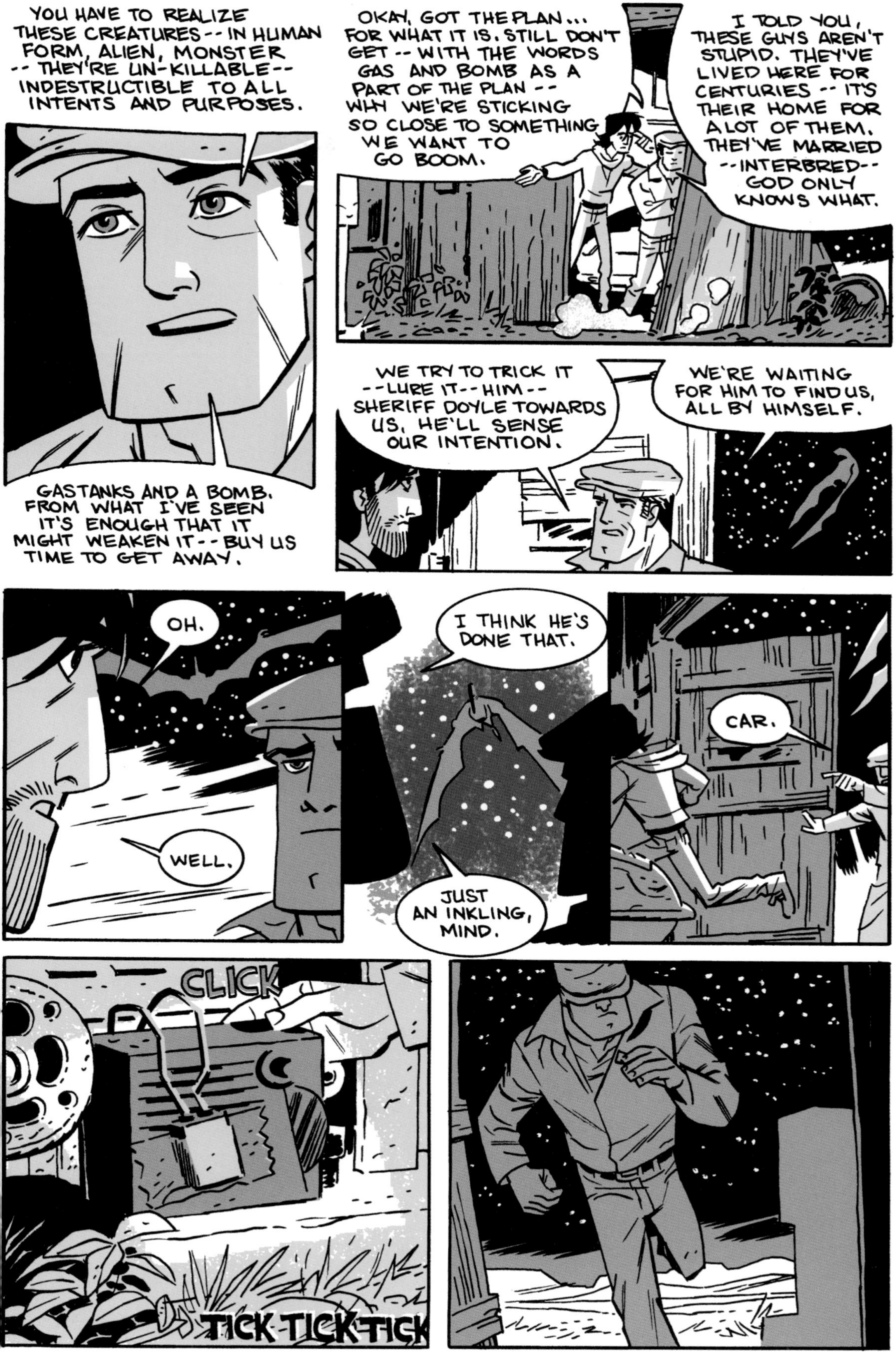
YOU HAVE TO REALIZE THESE CREATURES -- IN HUMAN FORM, ALIEN, MONSTER -- THEY'RE UN-KILLABLE -- INDESTRUCTIBLE TO ALL INTENTS AND PURPOSES.
GASTANKS AND A BOMB. FROM WHAT I'VE SEEN IT'S ENOUGH THAT IT MIGHT WEAKEN IT -- BUY US TIME TO GET AWAY.
OKAY, GOT THE PLAN... FOR WHAT IT IS. STILL DON'T GET -- WITH THE WORDS GAS AND BOMB AS A PART OF THE PLAN -- WHY WE'RE STICKING SO CLOSE TO SOMETHING WE WANT TO GO BOOM.
I TOLD YOU, THESE GUYS AREN'T STUPID. THEY'VE LIVED HERE FOR CENTURIES -- IT'S THEIR HOME FOR A LOT OF THEM. THEY'VE MARRIED -- INTERBRED -- GOD ONLY KNOWS WHAT.
WE TRY TO TRICK IT -- LURE IT -- HIM -- SHERIFF DOYLE TOWARDS US, HE'LL SENSE OUR INTENTION.
WE'RE WAITING FOR HIM TO FIND US, ALL BY HIMSELF.
OH.
WELL.
I THINK HE'S DONE THAT.
JUST AN INKLING, MIND.
CAR.
CLICK
TICK-TICK-TICK

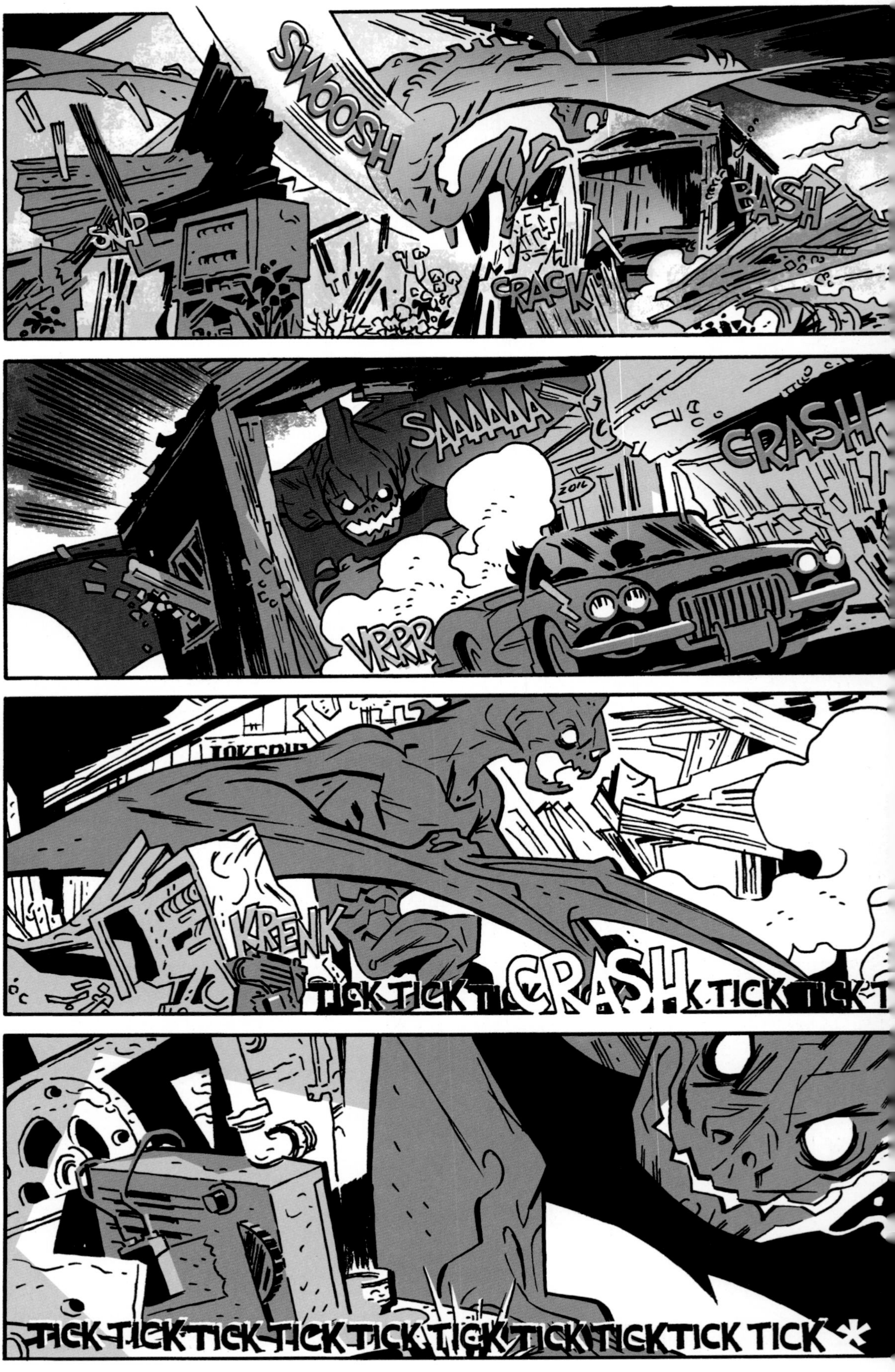
SWOOSH
SNAP
CRACK
BASH
SAAAAAA
CRASH
VRRR
KRRENK
TICK TICK
CRASH
TICK
TICK TICK TICK TICK TICK TICK TICK TICK TICK TICK

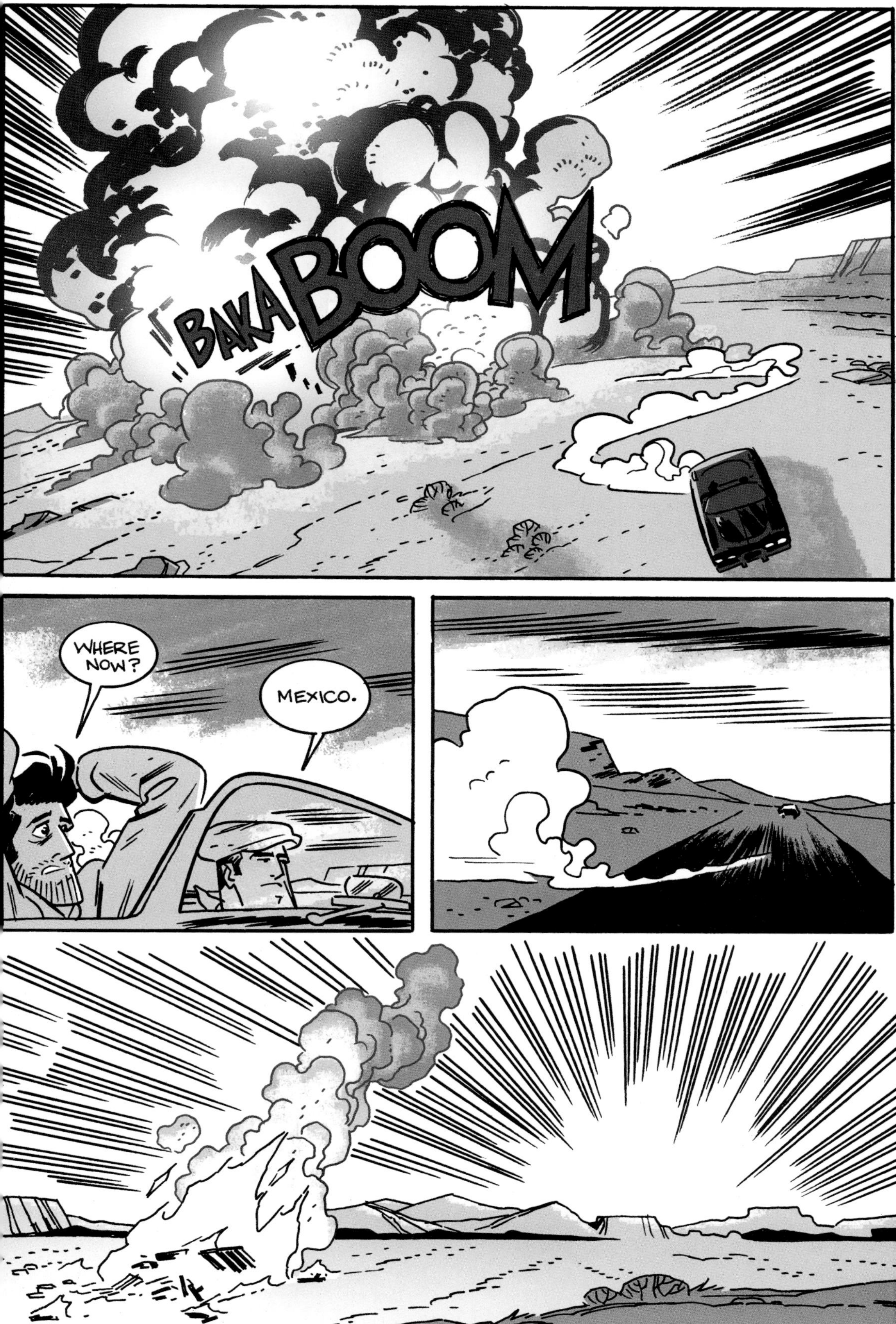
BAKA BOOM
WHERE NOW?
MEXICO.

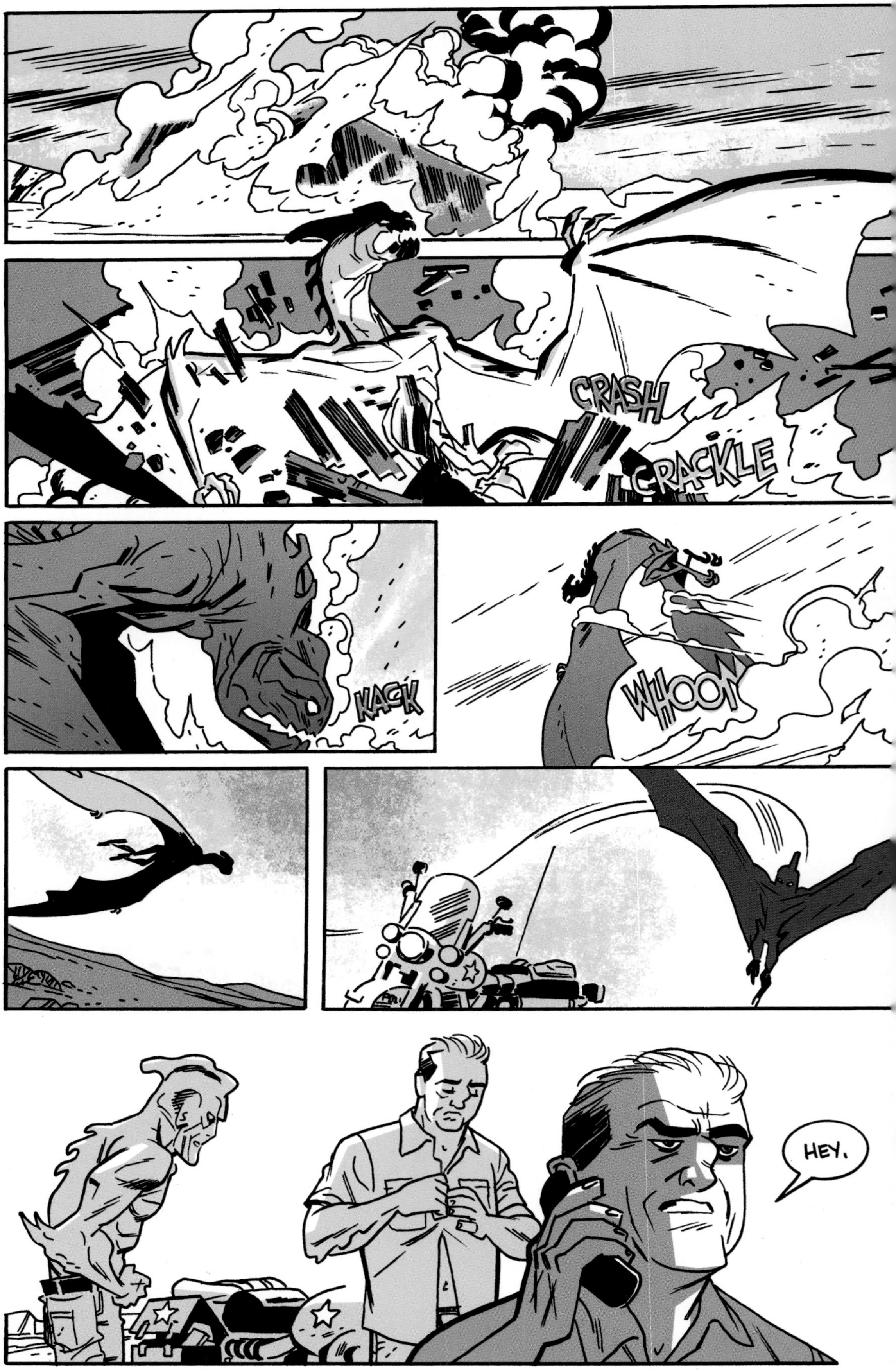
CRASH
CRACKLE
KACK
WHOOM
HEY.

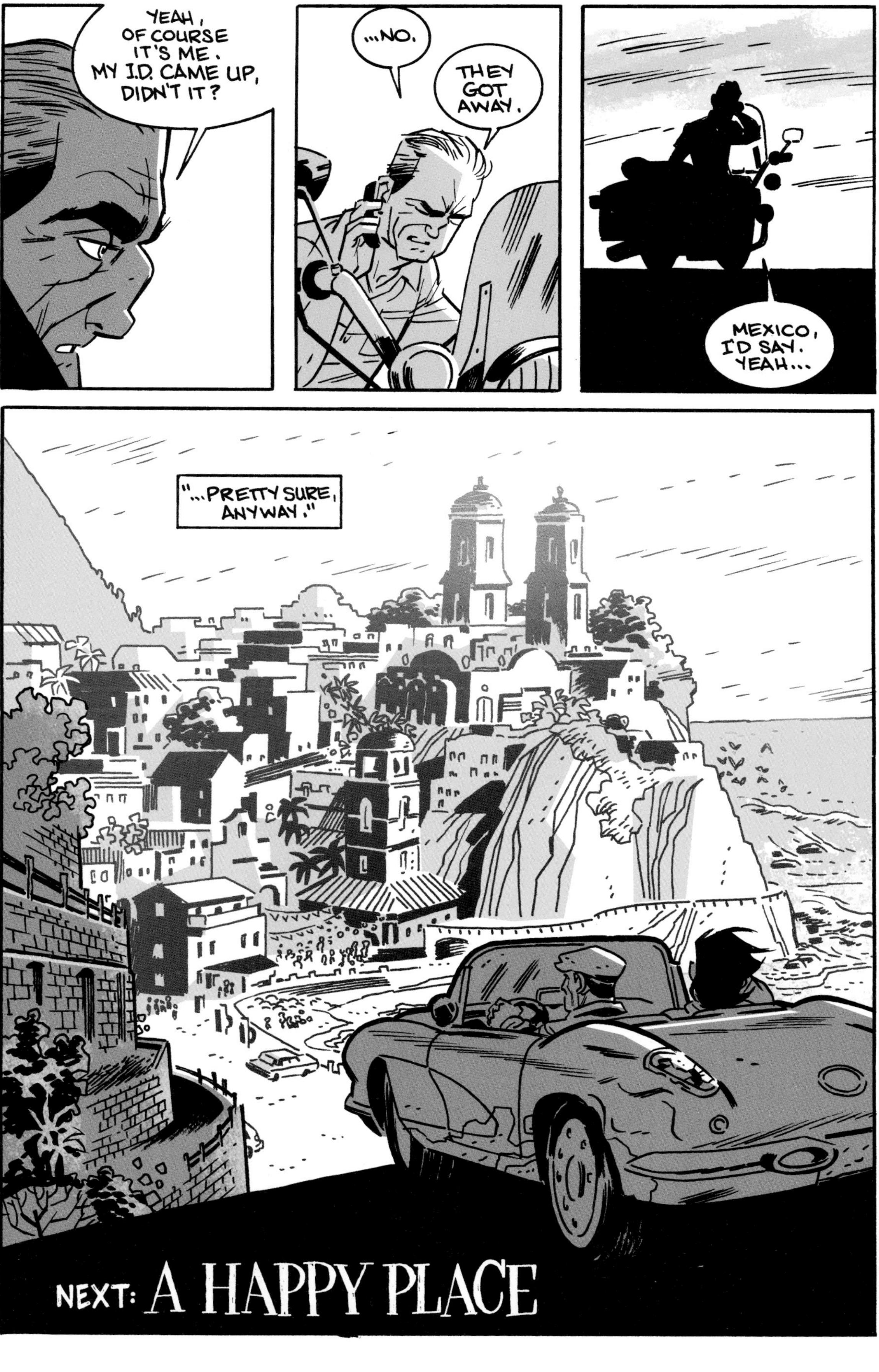
YEAH, OF COURSE IT'S ME. MY I.D. CAME UP, DIDN'T IT?
...NO.
THEY GOT AWAY.
MEXICO, I'D SAY. YEAH...
"...PRETTY SURE, ANYWAY."
NEXT: A HAPPY PLACE

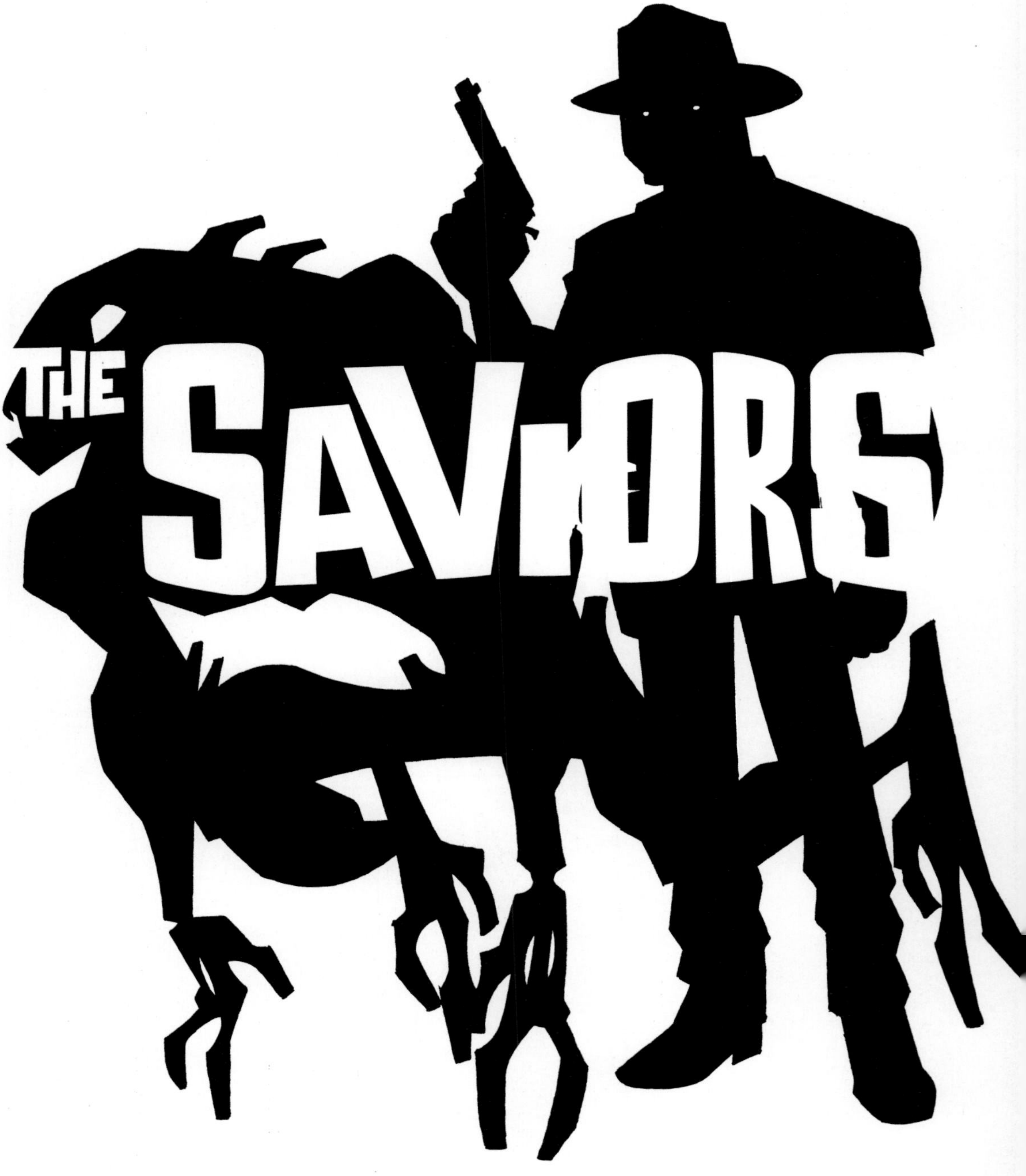
THE SAVIORS

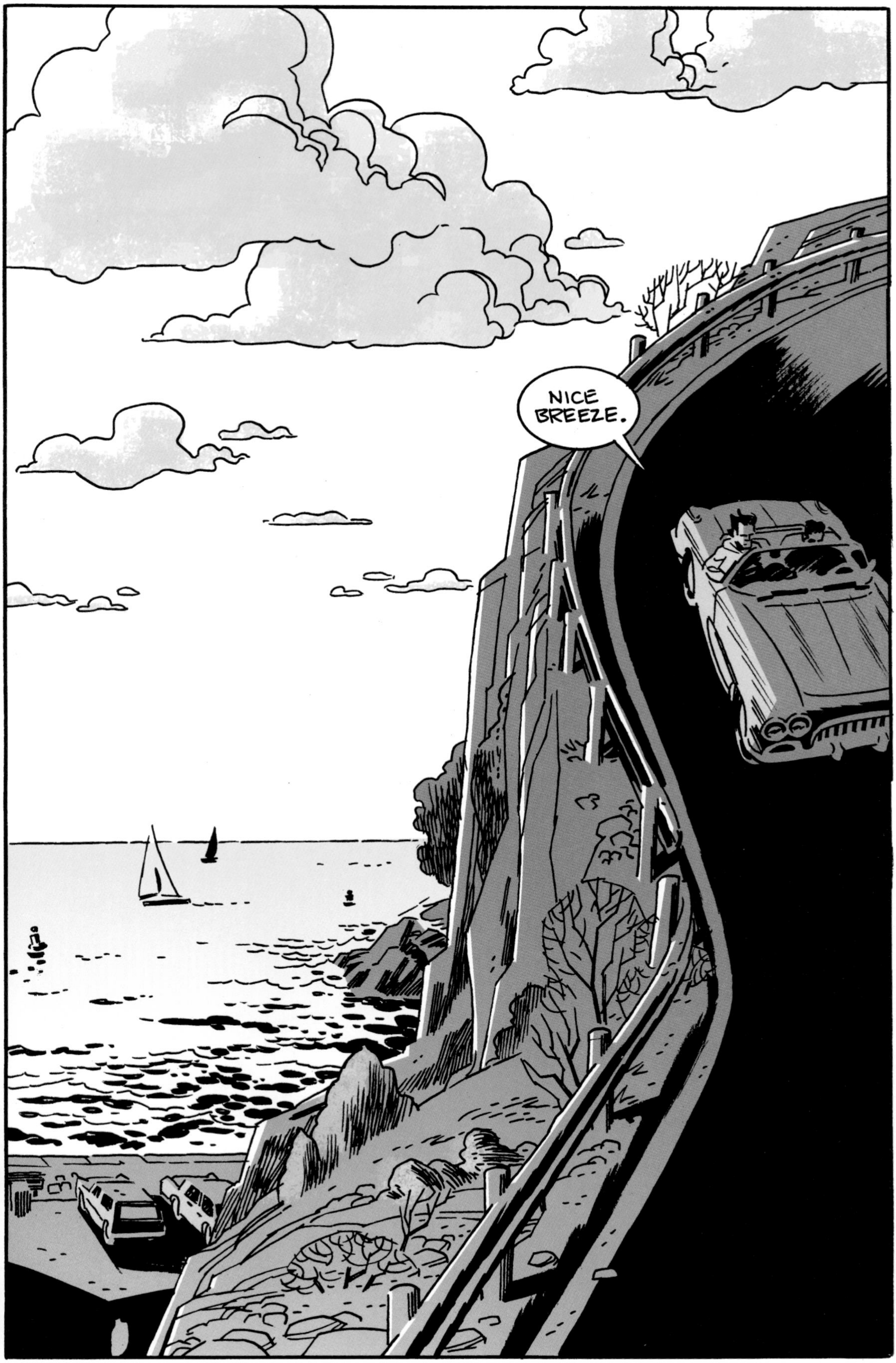
NICE BREEZE.

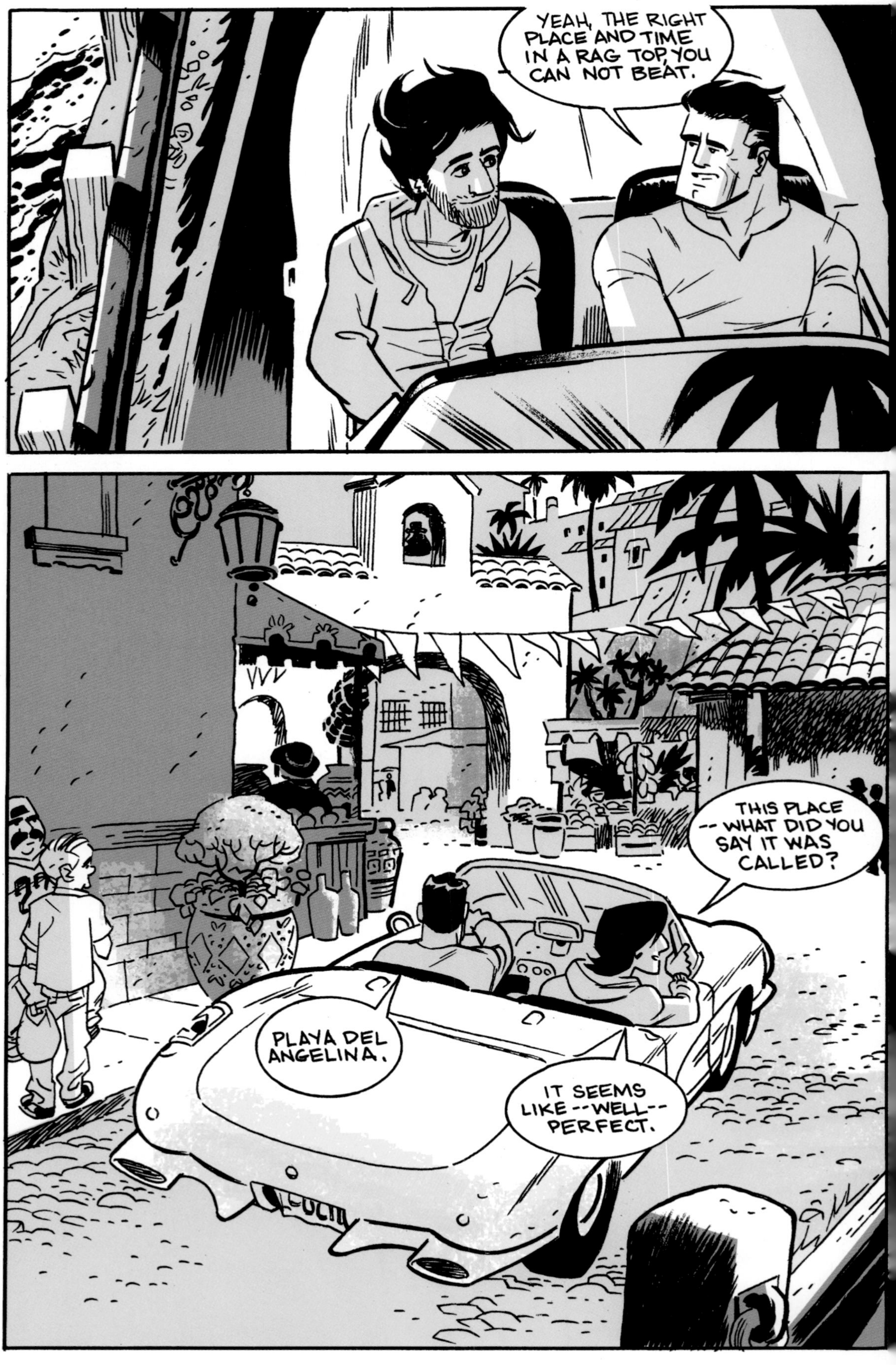
YEAH, THE RIGHT PLACE AND TIME IN A RAG TOP, YOU CAN NOT BEAT.
THIS PLACE -- WHAT DID YOU SAY IT WAS CALLED?
PLAYA DEL ANGELINA.
IT SEEMS LIKE -- WELL -- PERFECT.

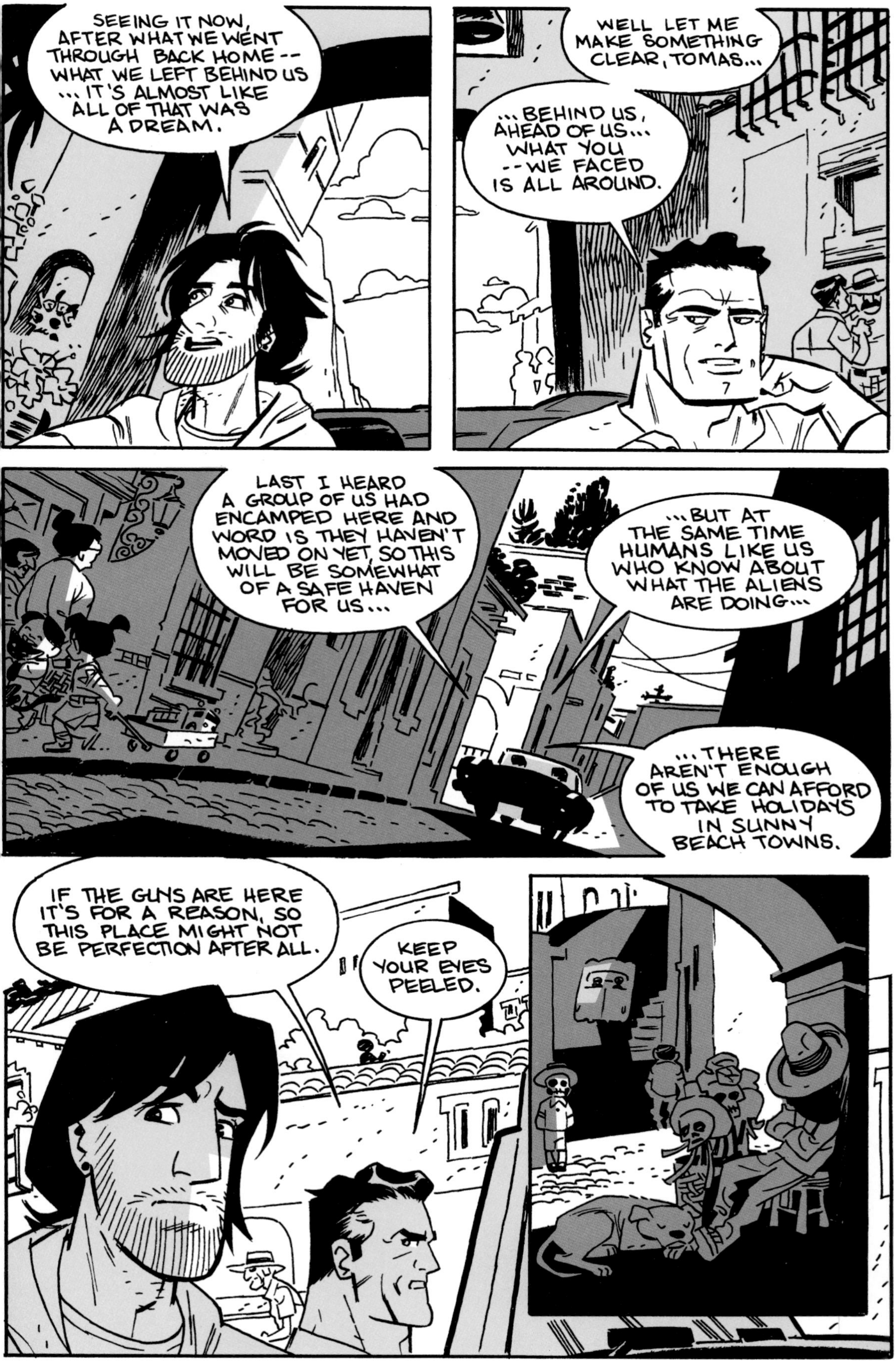
SEEING IT NOW, AFTER WHAT WE WENT THROUGH BACK HOME -- WHAT WE LEFT BEHIND US ... IT'S ALMOST LIKE ALL OF THAT WAS A DREAM.
WELL LET ME MAKE SOMETHING CLEAR, TOMAS...
...BEHIND US, AHEAD OF US... WHAT YOU --WE FACED IS ALL AROUND.
LAST I HEARD A GROUP OF US HAD ENCAMPED HERE AND WORD IS THEY HAVEN'T MOVED ON YET, SO THIS WILL BE SOMEWHAT OF A SAFE HAVEN FOR US...
...BUT AT THE SAME TIME HUMANS LIKE US WHO KNOW ABOUT WHAT THE ALIENS ARE DOING...
...THERE AREN'T ENOUGH OF US WE CAN AFFORD TO TAKE HOLIDAYS IN SUNNY BEACH TOWNS.
IF THE GUNS ARE HERE IT'S FOR A REASON, SO THIS PLACE MIGHT NOT BE PERFECTION AFTER ALL.
KEEP YOUR EYES PEELED.

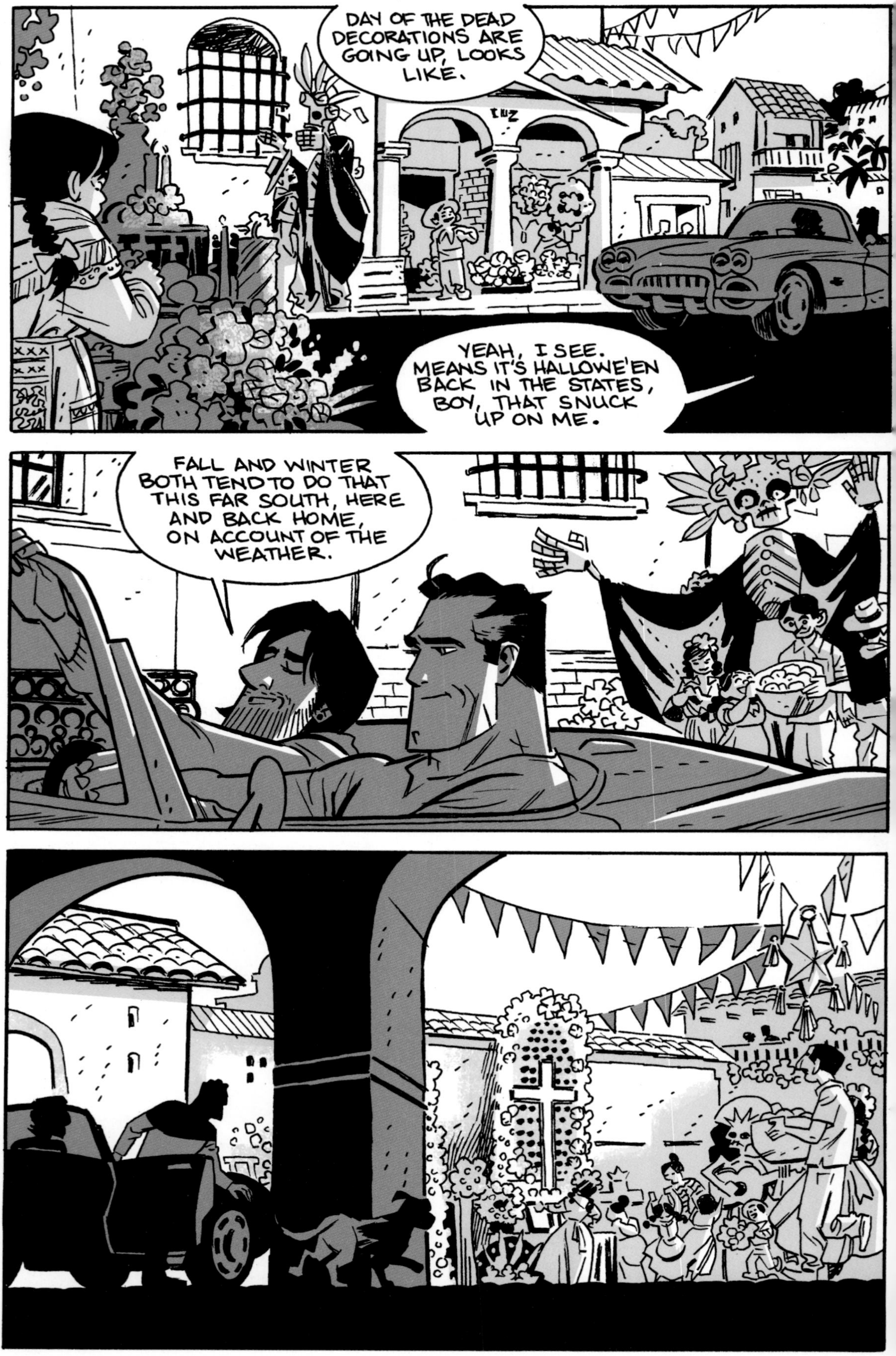

DAY OF THE DEAD DECORATIONS ARE GOING UP, LOOKS LIKE.
YEAH, I SEE. MEANS IT'S HALLOWE'EN BACK IN THE STATES, BOY, THAT SNUCK UP ON ME.
FALL AND WINTER BOTH TEND TO DO THAT THIS FAR SOUTH, HERE AND BACK HOME, ON ACCOUNT OF THE WEATHER.

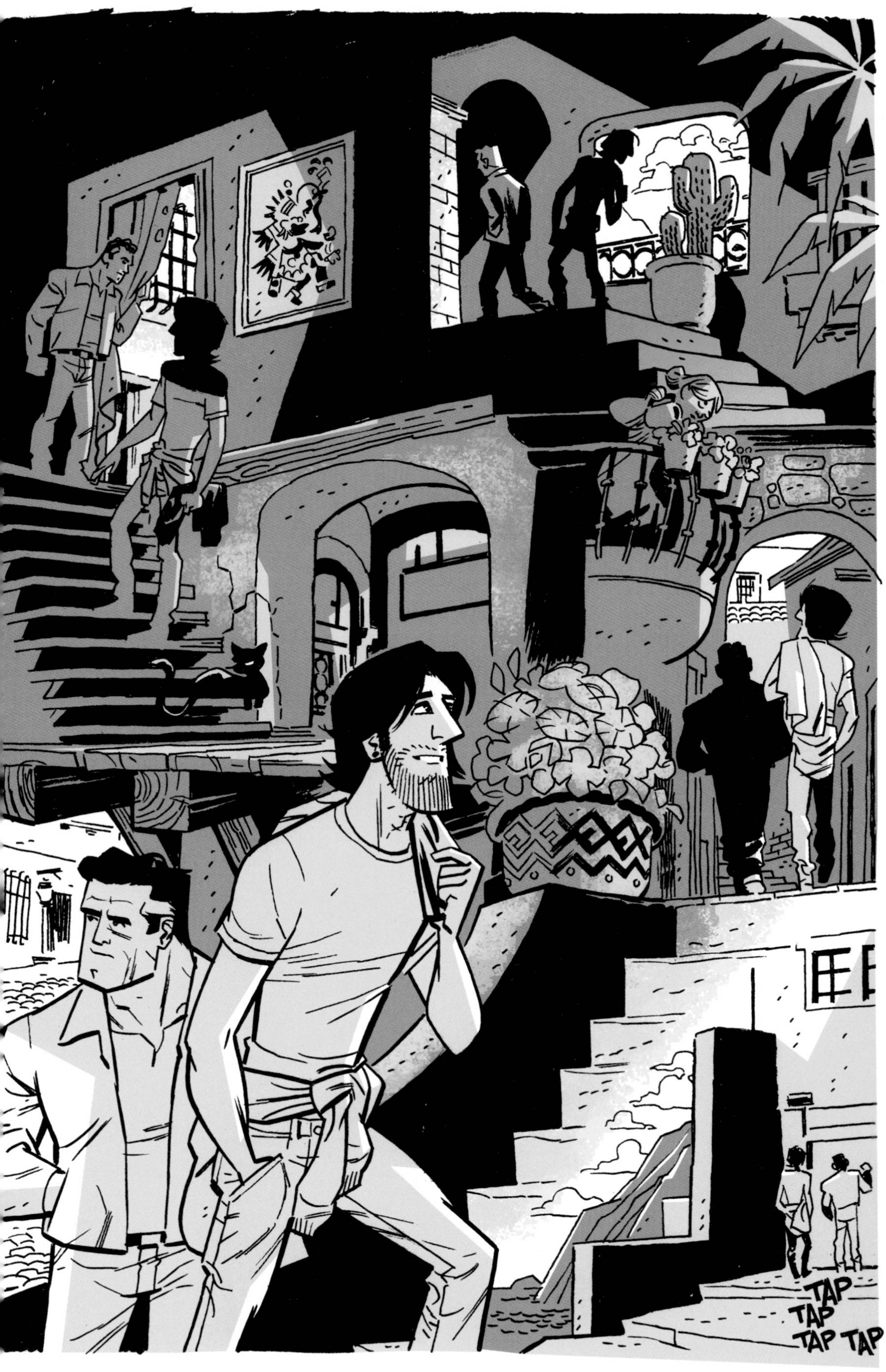
TAP
TAP
TAP TAP

NATE.

CARL.

IT'S BEEN A WHILE.

SO THIS IS TOMAS, A NEW RECRUIT. THROWN IN AT THE DEEP END, BUT HE SWAM TO THE EDGE, JUST ABOUT.

WAIT, NO, GUYS, I'M NOT A RECRUIT --I'M NOT-- THIS ISN'T SOMETHING I WANT TO BE A PART OF.

BOTH SIDES OF THE LAW.

ALL OVER EVERYWHERE TO INFLUENCE THE ACTIONS OF THE WORLD.

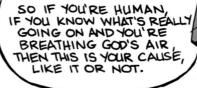

SO IF YOU'RE HUMAN, IF YOU KNOW WHAT'S REALLY GOING ON AND YOU'RE BREATHING GOD'S AIR, THEN THIS IS YOUR CAUSE, LIKE IT OR NOT.

AND YOU ARE?

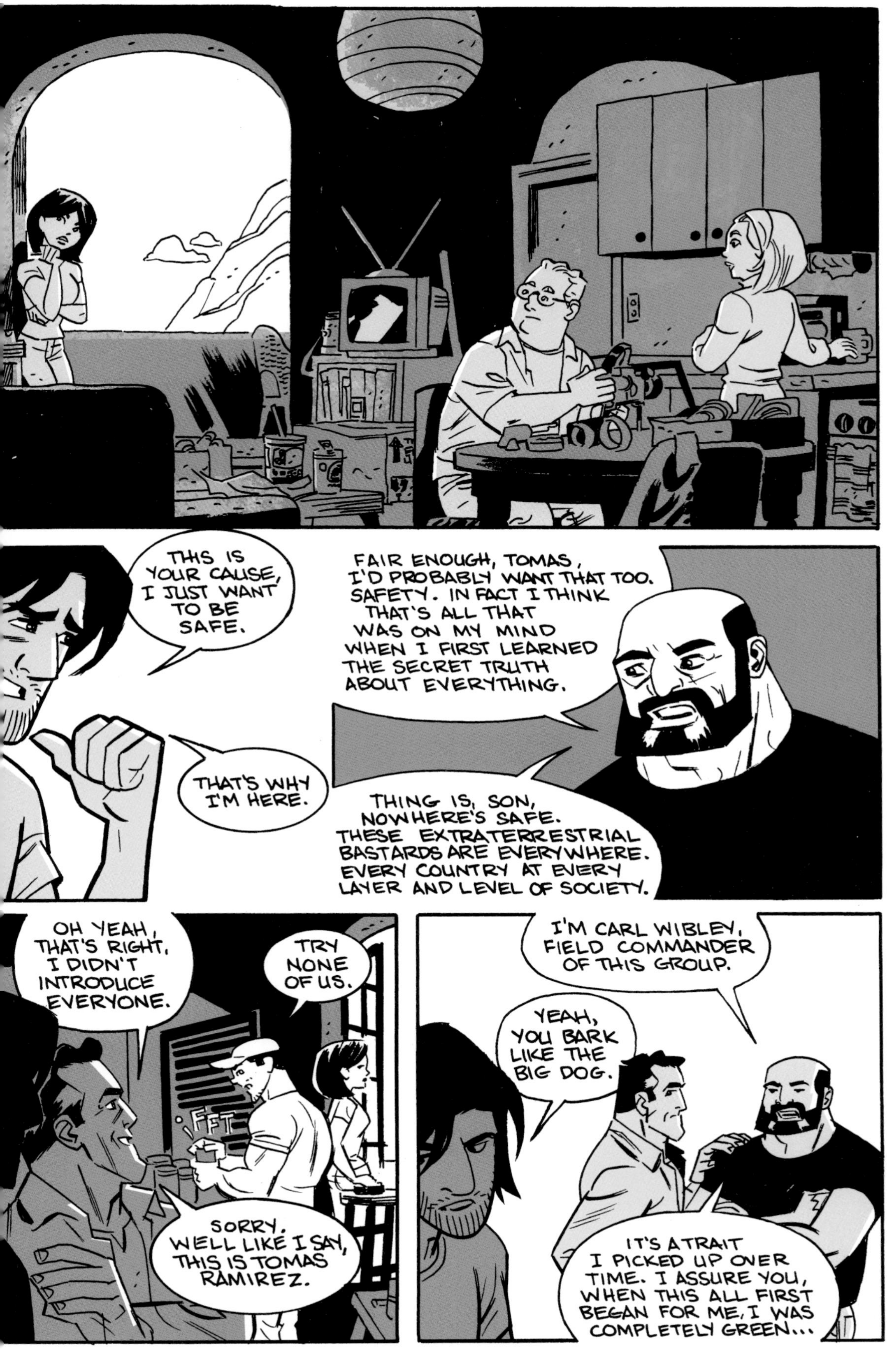
THIS IS YOUR CAUSE, I JUST WANT TO BE SAFE.
FAIR ENOUGH, TOMAS, I'D PROBABLY WANT THAT TOO. SAFETY. IN FACT I THINK THAT'S ALL THAT WAS ON MY MIND WHEN I FIRST LEARNED THE SECRET TRUTH ABOUT EVERYTHING.
THAT'S WHY I'M HERE.
THING IS, SON, NOWHERE'S SAFE. THESE EXTRATERRESTRIAL BASTARDS ARE EVERYWHERE. EVERY COUNTRY AT EVERY LAYER AND LEVEL OF SOCIETY.
OH YEAH, THAT'S RIGHT, I DIDN'T INTRODUCE EVERYONE.
TRY NONE OF US.
FFT
SORRY. WELL LIKE I SAY, THIS IS TOMAS RAMIREZ.
I'M CARL WIBLEY, FIELD COMMANDER OF THIS GROUP.
YEAH, YOU BARK LIKE THE BIG DOG.
IT'S A TRAIT I PICKED UP OVER TIME. I ASSURE YOU, WHEN THIS ALL FIRST BEGAN FOR ME, I WAS COMPLETELY GREEN...

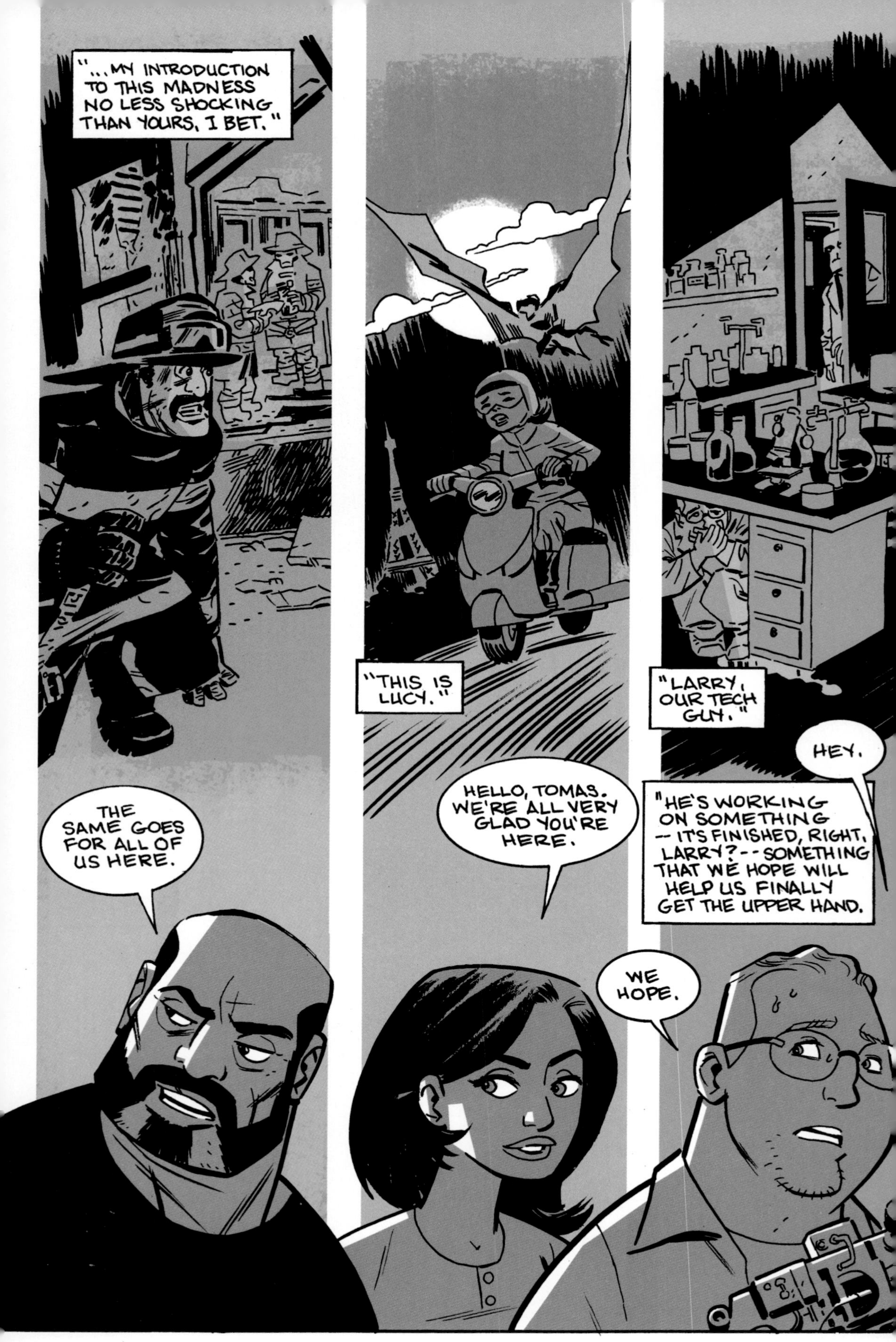
"...MY INTRODUCTION TO THIS MADNESS NO LESS SHOCKING THAN YOURS, I BET."
THE SAME GOES FOR ALL OF US HERE.
"THIS IS LUCY."
HELLO, TOMAS. WE'RE ALL VERY GLAD YOU'RE HERE.
"LARRY, OUR TECH GUY."
HEY.
"HE'S WORKING ON SOMETHING -- IT'S FINISHED, RIGHT, LARRY?-- SOMETHING THAT WE HOPE WILL HELP US FINALLY GET THE UPPER HAND.
WE HOPE.

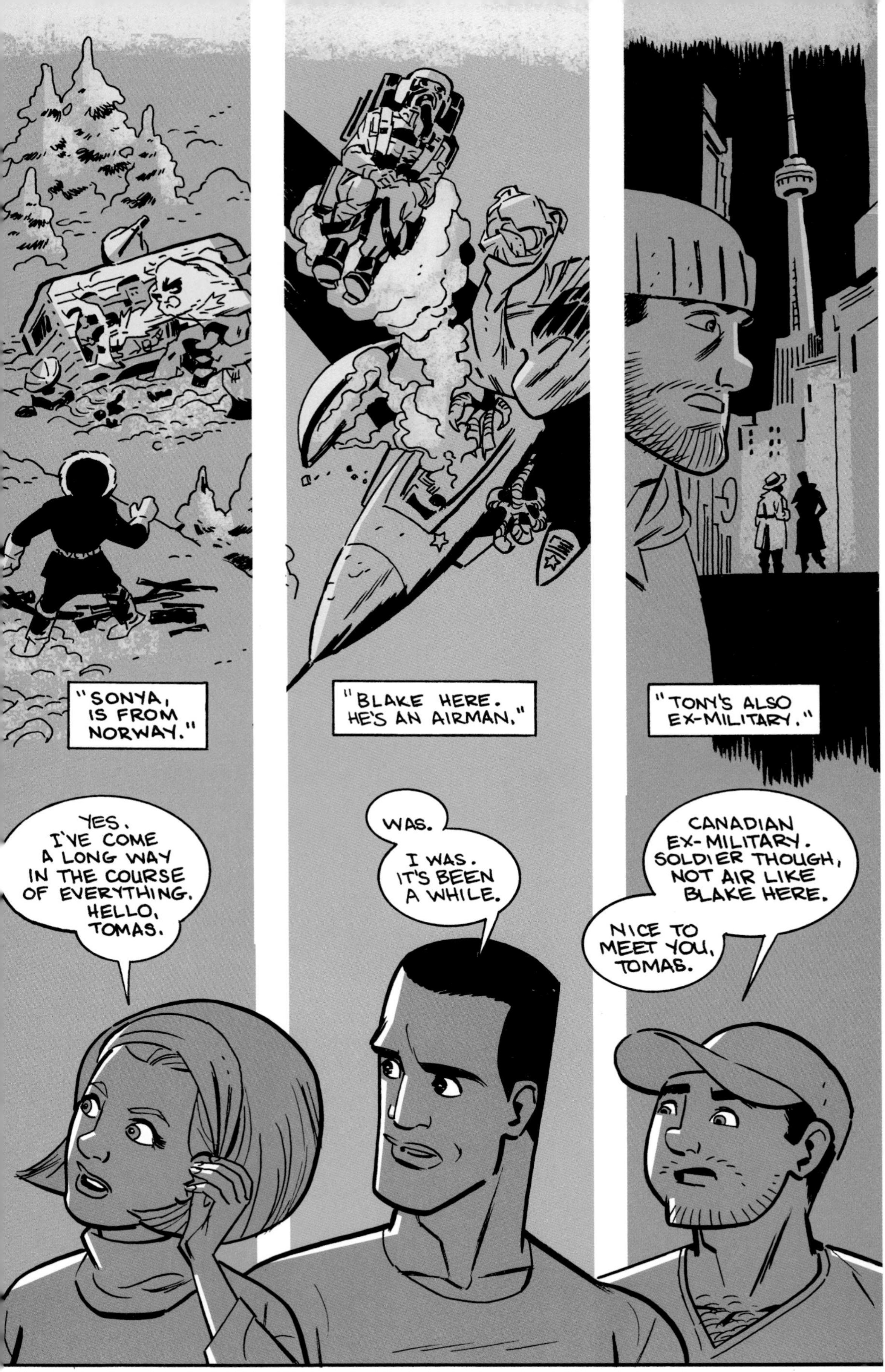
"SONYA, IS FROM NORWAY."
"BLAKE HERE. HE'S AN AIRMAN."
"TONY'S ALSO EX-MILITARY."
YES. I'VE COME A LONG WAY IN THE COURSE OF EVERYTHING. HELLO, TOMAS.
WAS.
I WAS. IT'S BEEN A WHILE.
CANADIAN EX-MILITARY. SOLDIER THOUGH, NOT AIR LIKE BLAKE HERE.
NICE TO MEET YOU, TOMAS.

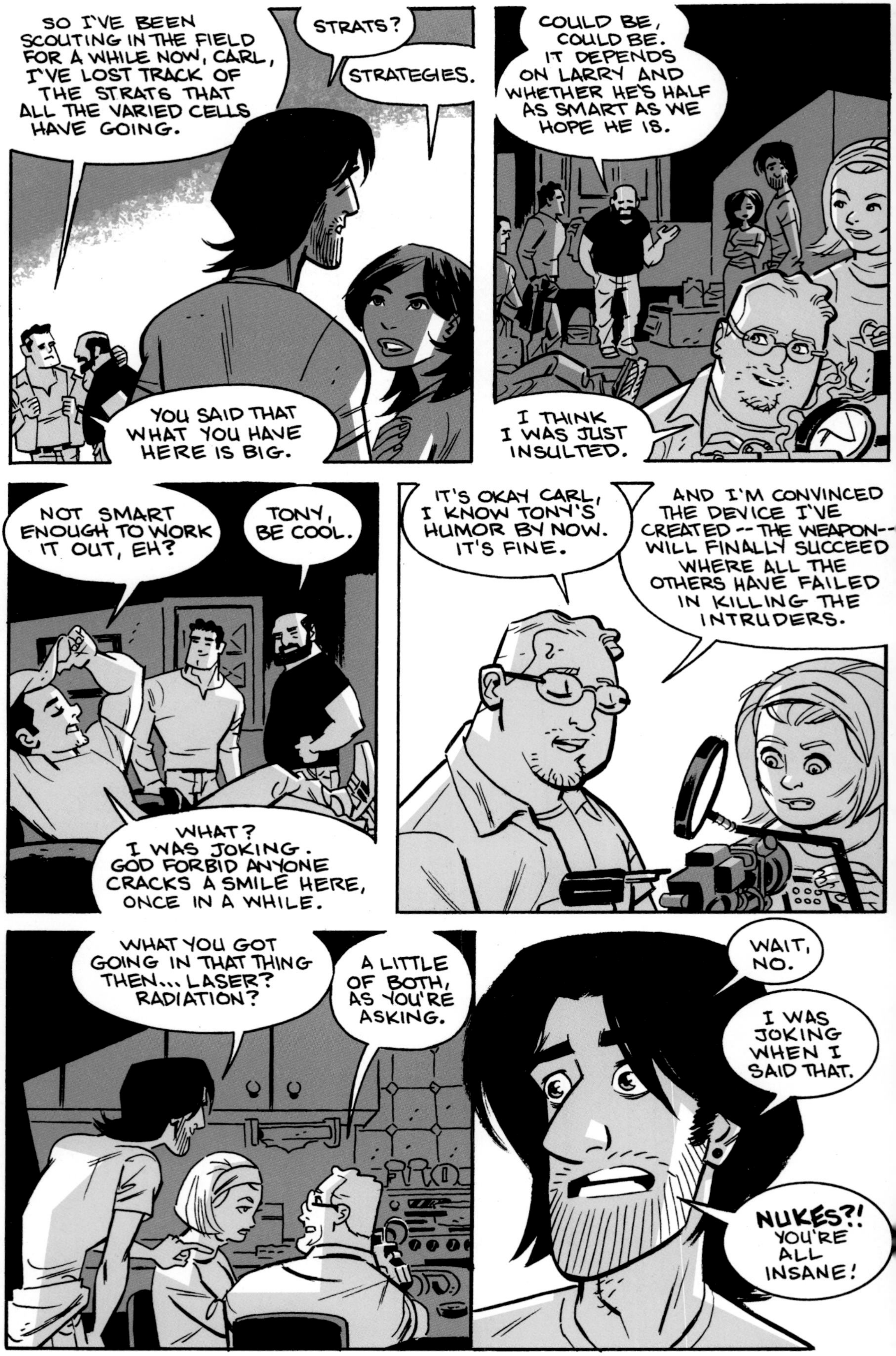
SO I'VE BEEN SCOUTING IN THE FIELD FOR A WHILE NOW, CARL, I'VE LOST TRACK OF THE STRATS THAT ALL THE VARIED CELLS HAVE GOING.
STRATS?
STRATEGIES.
YOU SAID THAT WHAT YOU HAVE HERE IS BIG.
COULD BE, COULD BE. IT DEPENDS ON LARRY AND WHETHER HE'S HALF AS SMART AS WE HOPE HE IS.
I THINK I WAS JUST INSULTED.
NOT SMART ENOUGH TO WORK IT OUT, EH?
TONY, BE COOL.
WHAT? I WAS JOKING. GOD FORBID ANYONE CRACKS A SMILE HERE, ONCE IN A WHILE.
IT'S OKAY CARL, I KNOW TONY'S HUMOR BY NOW. IT'S FINE.
AND I'M CONVINCED THE DEVICE I'VE CREATED -- THE WEAPON-- WILL FINALLY SUCCEED WHERE ALL THE OTHERS HAVE FAILED IN KILLING THE INTRUDERS.
WHAT YOU GOT GOING IN THAT THING THEN... LASER? RADIATION?
A LITTLE OF BOTH, AS YOU'RE ASKING.
WAIT, NO.
I WAS JOKING WHEN I SAID THAT.
NUKES?! YOU'RE ALL INSANE!

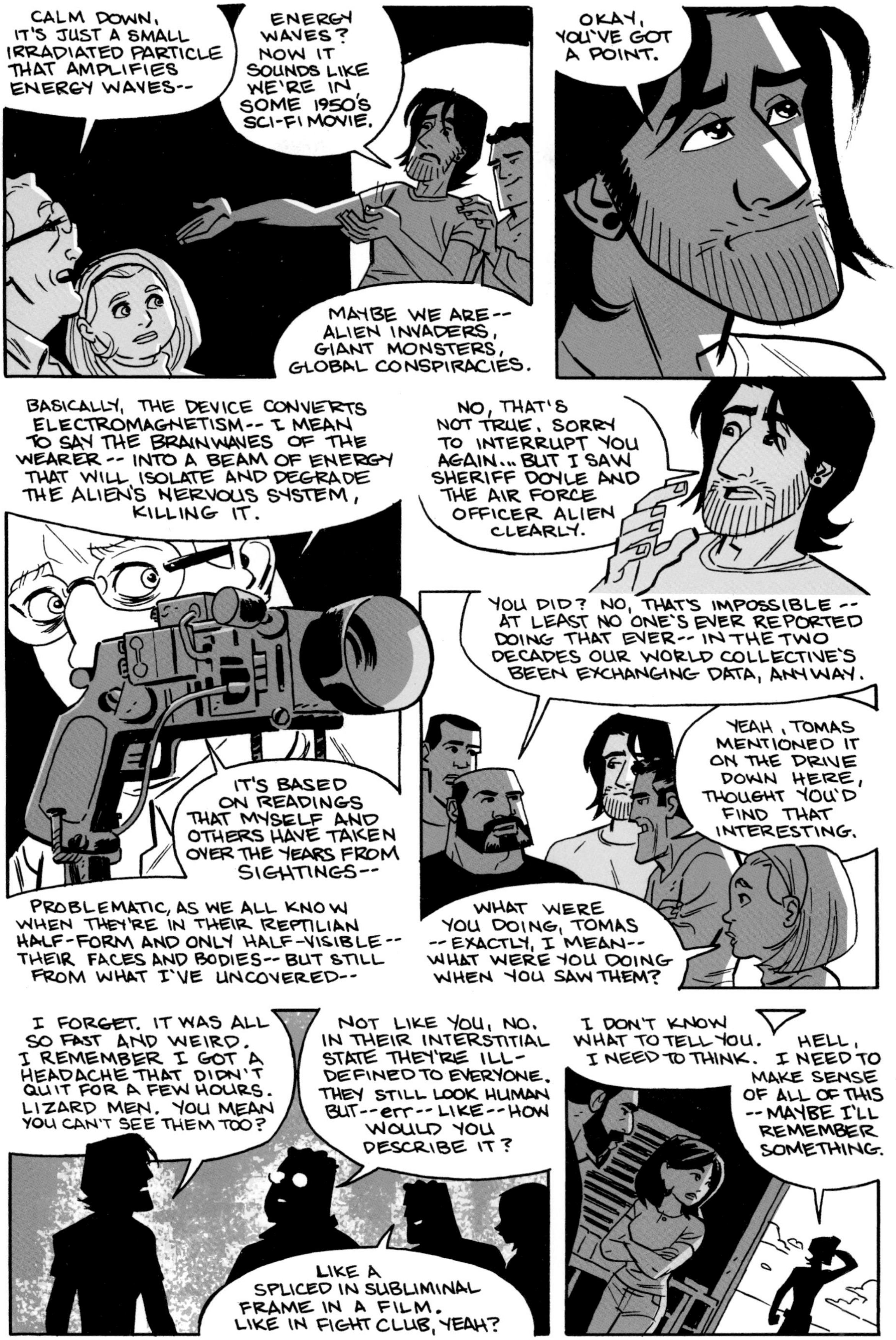
CALM DOWN, IT'S JUST A SMALL IRRADIATED PARTICLE THAT AMPLIFIES ENERGY WAVES--
ENERGY WAVES? NOW IT SOUNDS LIKE WE'RE IN SOME 1950'S SCI-FI MOVIE.
MAYBE WE ARE-- ALIEN INVADERS, GIANT MONSTERS, GLOBAL CONSPIRACIES.
OKAY, YOU'VE GOT A POINT.
BASICALLY, THE DEVICE CONVERTS ELECTROMAGNETISM-- I MEAN TO SAY THE BRAINWAVES OF THE WEARER-- INTO A BEAM OF ENERGY THAT WILL ISOLATE AND DEGRADE THE ALIEN'S NERVOUS SYSTEM, KILLING IT.
IT'S BASED ON READINGS THAT MYSELF AND OTHERS HAVE TAKEN OVER THE YEARS FROM SIGHTINGS--
PROBLEMATIC, AS WE ALL KNOW WHEN THEY'RE IN THEIR REPTILIAN HALF-FORM AND ONLY HALF-VISIBLE-- THEIR FACES AND BODIES-- BUT STILL FROM WHAT I'VE UNCOVERED--
NO, THAT'S NOT TRUE. SORRY TO INTERRUPT YOU AGAIN... BUT I SAW SHERIFF DOYLE AND THE AIR FORCE OFFICER ALIEN CLEARLY.
YOU DID? NO, THAT'S IMPOSSIBLE-- AT LEAST NO ONE'S EVER REPORTED DOING THAT EVER-- IN THE TWO DECADES OUR WORLD COLLECTIVE'S BEEN EXCHANGING DATA, ANYWAY.
YEAH, TOMAS MENTIONED IT ON THE DRIVE DOWN HERE, THOUGHT YOU'D FIND THAT INTERESTING.
WHAT WERE YOU DOING, TOMAS --EXACTLY, I MEAN-- WHAT WERE YOU DOING WHEN YOU SAW THEM?
I FORGET. IT WAS ALL SO FAST AND WEIRD. I REMEMBER I GOT A HEADACHE THAT DIDN'T QUIT FOR A FEW HOURS. LIZARD MEN. YOU MEAN YOU CAN'T SEE THEM TOO?
NOT LIKE YOU, NO. IN THEIR INTERSTITIAL STATE THEY'RE ILL-DEFINED TO EVERYONE. THEY STILL LOOK HUMAN BUT--err--LIKE--HOW WOULD YOU DESCRIBE IT?
LIKE A SPLICED IN SUBLIMINAL FRAME IN A FILM. LIKE IN FIGHT CLUB, YEAH?
I DON'T KNOW WHAT TO TELL YOU. I NEED TO THINK.
HELL, I NEED TO MAKE SENSE OF ALL OF THIS --MAYBE I'LL REMEMBER SOMETHING.

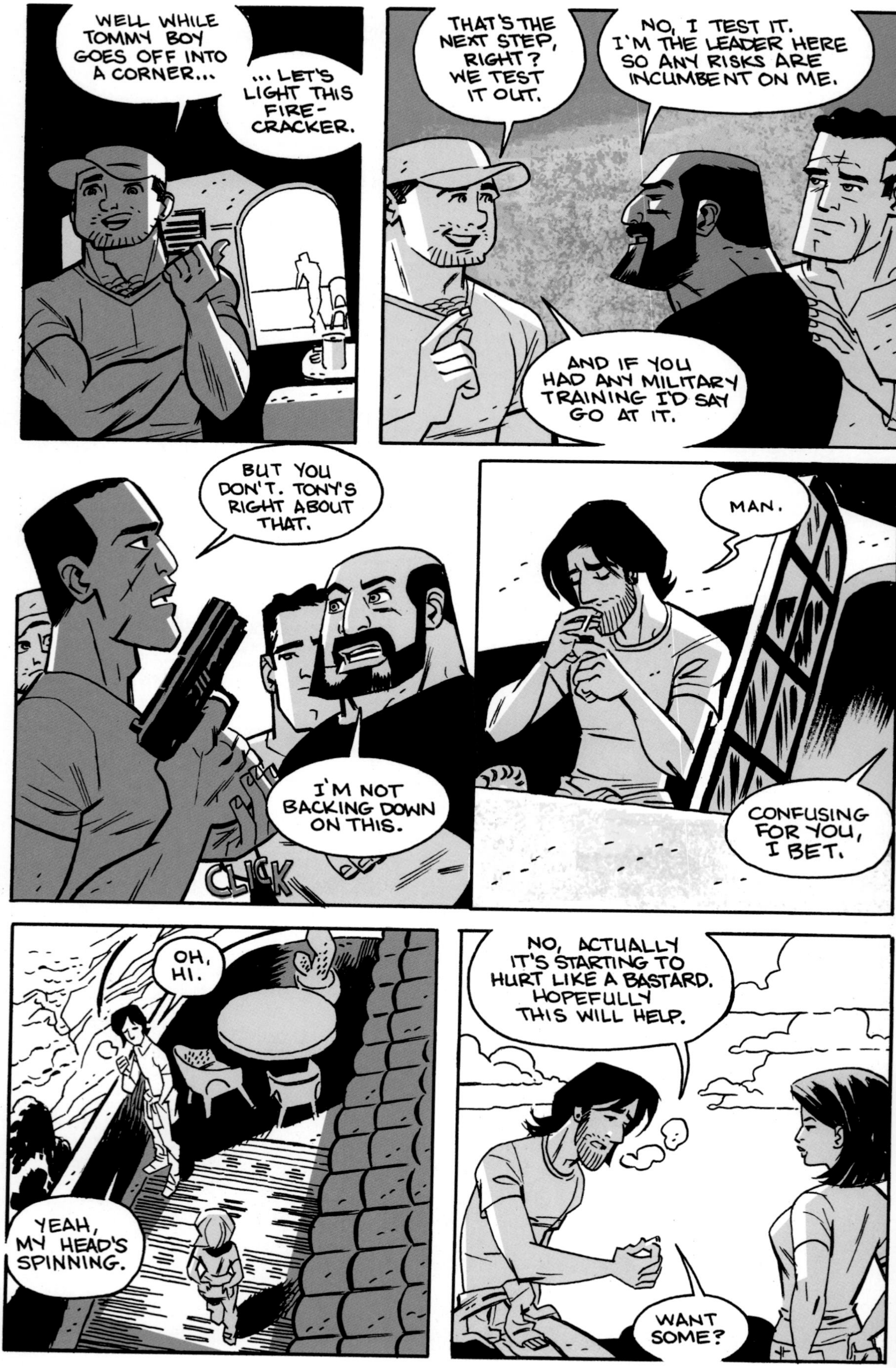
WELL WHILE TOMMY BOY GOES OFF INTO A CORNER...
...LET'S LIGHT THIS FIRE-CRACKER.
THAT'S THE NEXT STEP, RIGHT? WE TEST IT OUT.
NO, I TEST IT. I'M THE LEADER HERE SO ANY RISKS ARE INCUMBENT ON ME.
AND IF YOU HAD ANY MILITARY TRAINING I'D SAY GO AT IT.
BUT YOU DON'T. TONY'S RIGHT ABOUT THAT.
I'M NOT BACKING DOWN ON THIS.
CLICK
MAN.
CONFUSING FOR YOU, I BET.
OH, HI.
YEAH, MY HEAD'S SPINNING.
NO, ACTUALLY IT'S STARTING TO HURT LIKE A BASTARD. HOPEFULLY THIS WILL HELP.
WANT SOME?

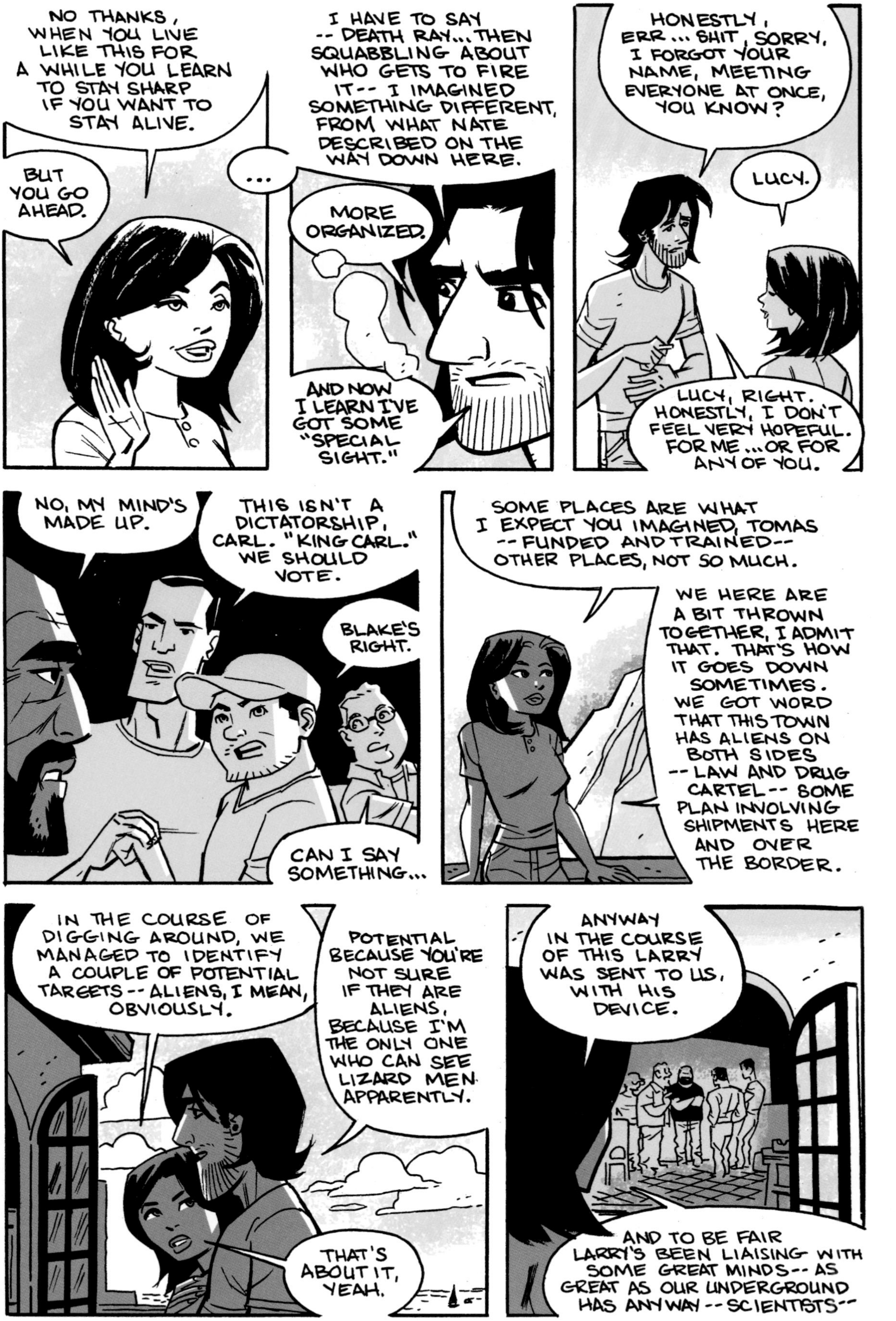
NO THANKS, WHEN YOU LIVE LIKE THIS FOR A WHILE YOU LEARN TO STAY SHARP IF YOU WANT TO STAY ALIVE.
BUT YOU GO AHEAD.
...
I HAVE TO SAY -- DEATH RAY... THEN SQUABBLING ABOUT WHO GETS TO FIRE IT-- I IMAGINED SOMETHING DIFFERENT, FROM WHAT NATE DESCRIBED ON THE WAY DOWN HERE.
MORE ORGANIZED.
AND NOW I LEARN I'VE GOT SOME "SPECIAL SIGHT."
HONESTLY, ERR... SHIT, SORRY, I FORGOT YOUR NAME, MEETING EVERYONE AT ONCE, YOU KNOW?
LUCY.
LUCY, RIGHT. HONESTLY, I DON'T FEEL VERY HOPEFUL. FOR ME... OR FOR ANY OF YOU.
NO, MY MIND'S MADE UP.
THIS ISN'T A DICTATORSHIP, CARL. "KING CARL." WE SHOULD VOTE.
BLAKE'S RIGHT.
CAN I SAY SOMETHING...
SOME PLACES ARE WHAT I EXPECT YOU IMAGINED, TOMAS -- FUNDED AND TRAINED-- OTHER PLACES, NOT SO MUCH.
WE HERE ARE A BIT THROWN TOGETHER, I ADMIT THAT. THAT'S HOW IT GOES DOWN SOMETIMES. WE GOT WORD THAT THIS TOWN HAS ALIENS ON BOTH SIDES -- LAW AND DRUG CARTEL -- SOME PLAN INVOLVING SHIPMENTS HERE AND OVER THE BORDER.
IN THE COURSE OF DIGGING AROUND, WE MANAGED TO IDENTIFY A COUPLE OF POTENTIAL TARGETS -- ALIENS, I MEAN, OBVIOUSLY.
POTENTIAL BECAUSE YOU'RE NOT SURE IF THEY ARE ALIENS, BECAUSE I'M THE ONLY ONE WHO CAN SEE LIZARD MEN. APPARENTLY.
THAT'S ABOUT IT, YEAH.
ANYWAY IN THE COURSE OF THIS LARRY WAS SENT TO US, WITH HIS DEVICE.
AND TO BE FAIR LARRY'S BEEN LIAISING WITH SOME GREAT MINDS-- AS GREAT AS OUR UNDERGROUND HAS ANYWAY -- SCIENTISTS--

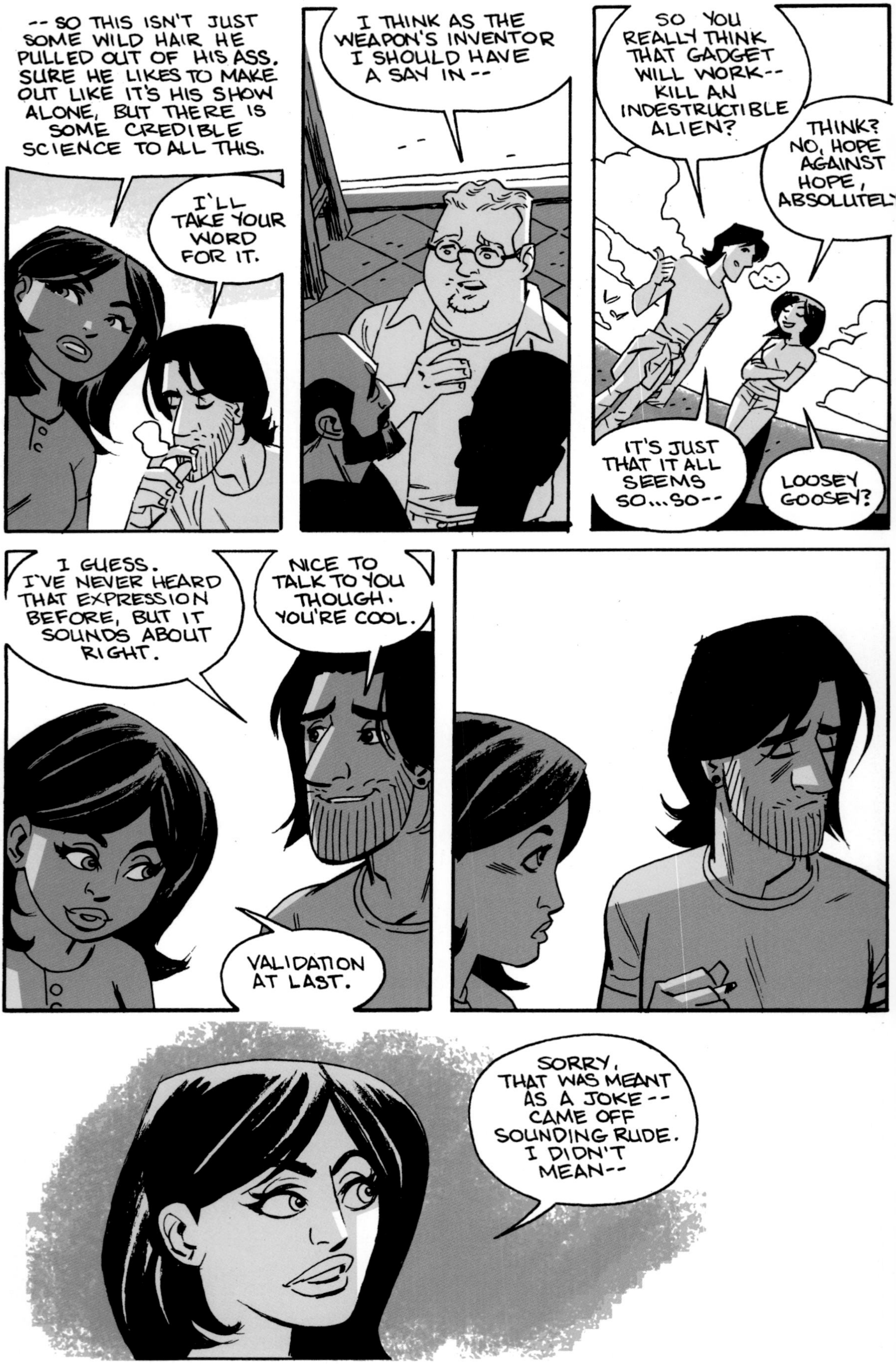
-- SO THIS ISN'T JUST SOME WILD HAIR HE PULLED OUT OF HIS ASS. SURE HE LIKES TO MAKE OUT LIKE IT'S HIS SHOW ALONE, BUT THERE IS SOME CREDIBLE SCIENCE TO ALL THIS.
I'LL TAKE YOUR WORD FOR IT.
I THINK AS THE WEAPON'S INVENTOR I SHOULD HAVE A SAY IN --
SO YOU REALLY THINK THAT GADGET WILL WORK-- KILL AN INDESTRUCTIBLE ALIEN?
THINK? NO, HOPE AGAINST HOPE, ABSOLUTEL
IT'S JUST THAT IT ALL SEEMS SO...SO--
LOOSEY GOOSEY?
I GUESS. I'VE NEVER HEARD THAT EXPRESSION BEFORE, BUT IT SOUNDS ABOUT RIGHT.
NICE TO TALK TO YOU THOUGH. YOU'RE COOL.
VALIDATION AT LAST.
SORRY, THAT WAS MEANT AS A JOKE-- CAME OFF SOUNDING RUDE. I DIDN'T MEAN--

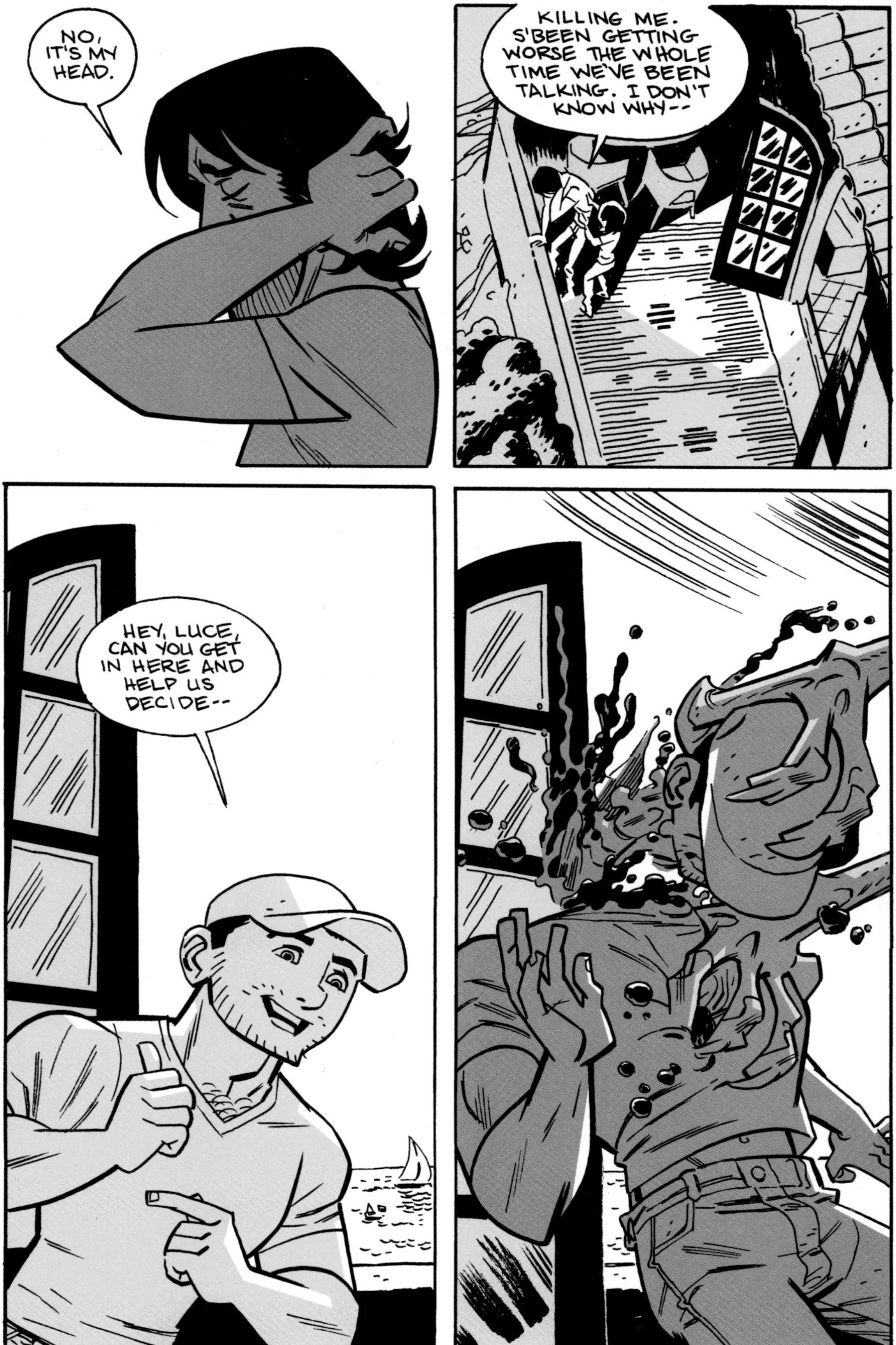
NO, IT'S MY HEAD.
KILLING ME. S'BEEN GETTING WORSE THE WHOLE TIME WE'VE BEEN TALKING. I DON'T KNOW WHY--
HEY, LUCE, CAN YOU GET IN HERE AND HELP US DECIDE--

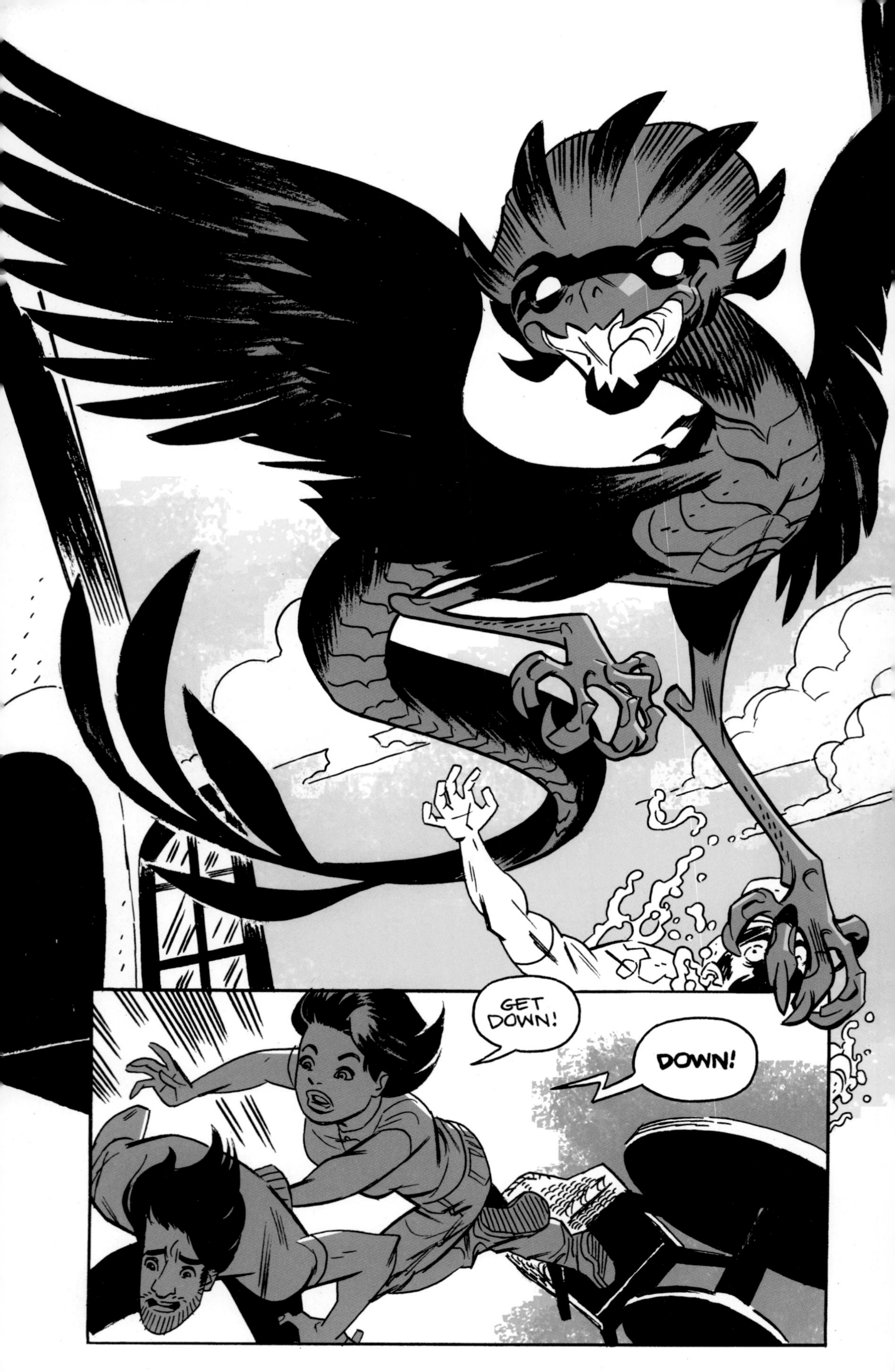
GET DOWN!
DOWN!

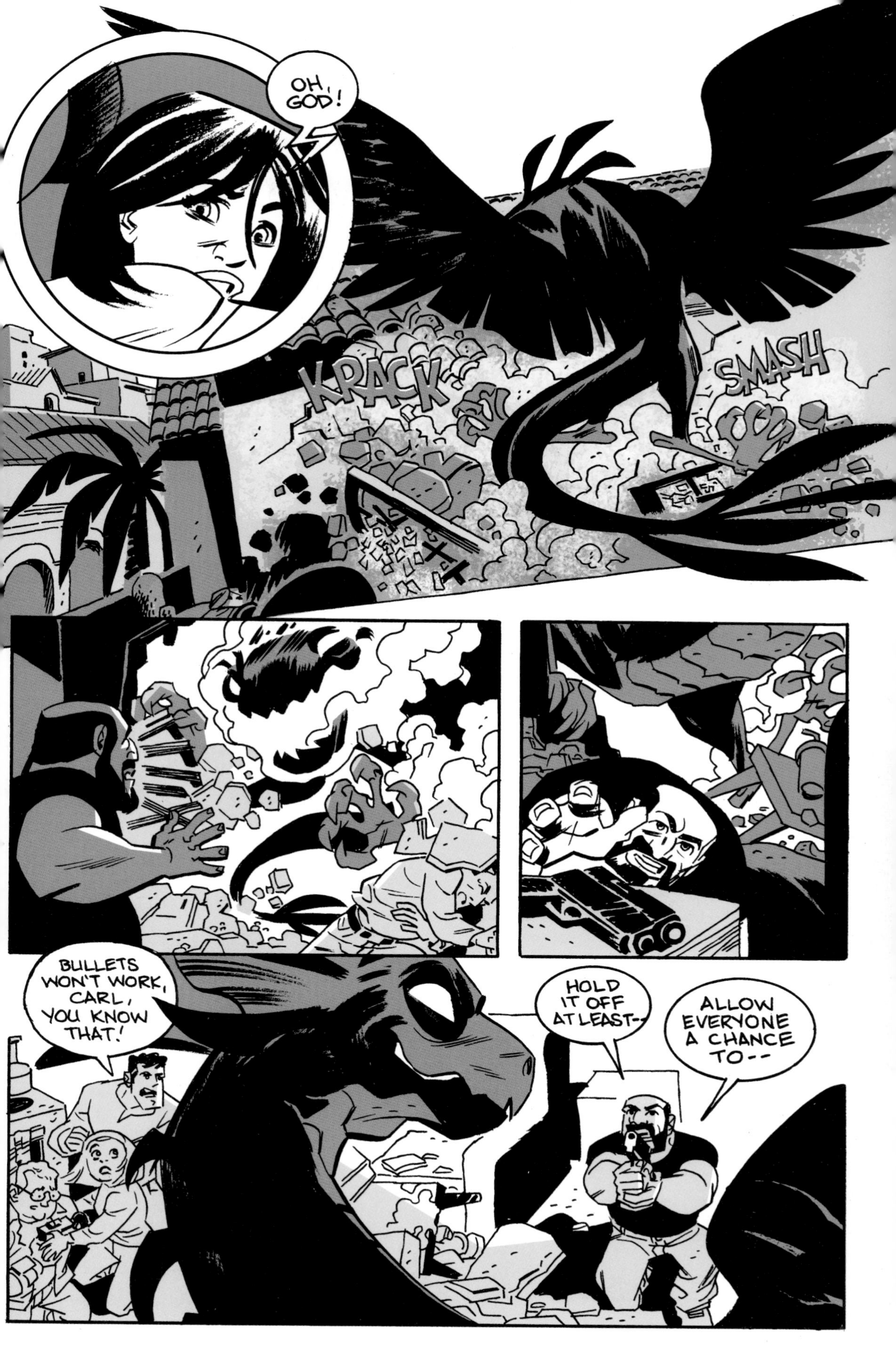
OH, GOD!
KRACK
SMASH
BULLETS WON'T WORK, CARL, YOU KNOW THAT!
HOLD IT OFF AT LEAST--
ALLOW EVERYONE A CHANCE TO--

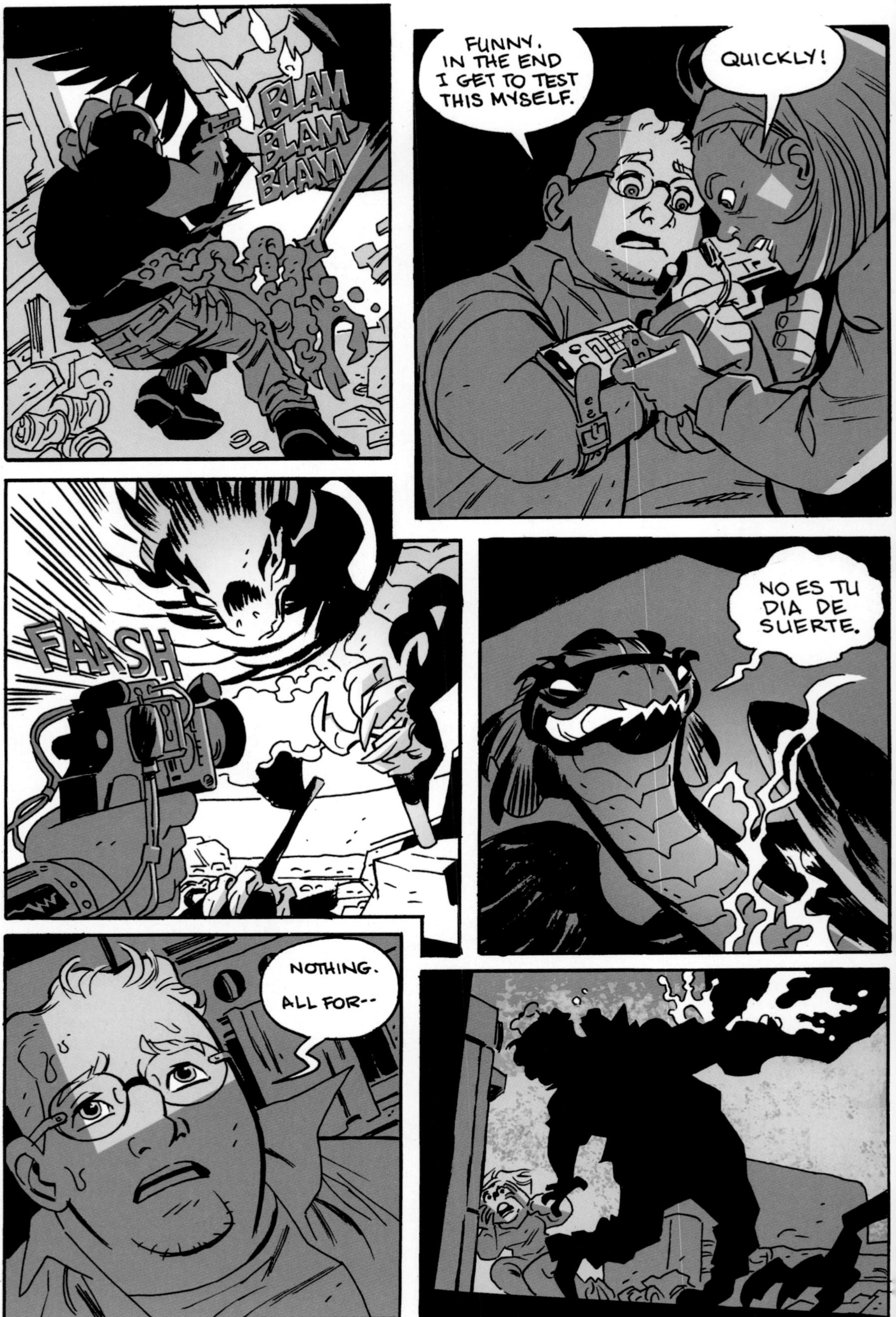
BLAM
BLAM
BLAM
FUNNY. IN THE END I GET TO TEST THIS MYSELF.
QUICKLY!
FAASH
NO ES TU DIA DE SUERTE.
NOTHING.
ALL FOR--

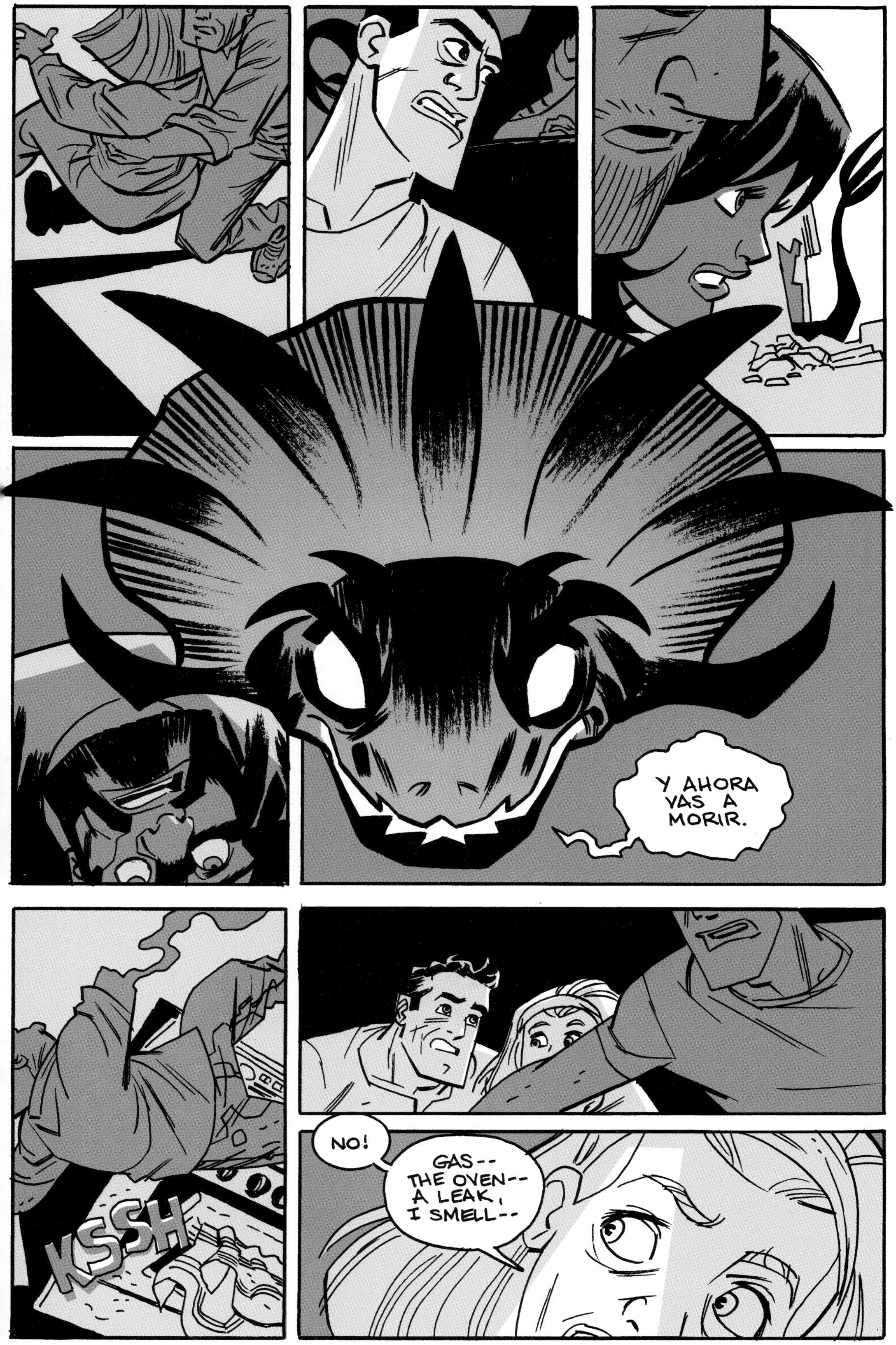
Y AHORA VAS A MORIR.
KSSH
NO!
GAS-- THE OVEN-- A LEAK, I SMELL--

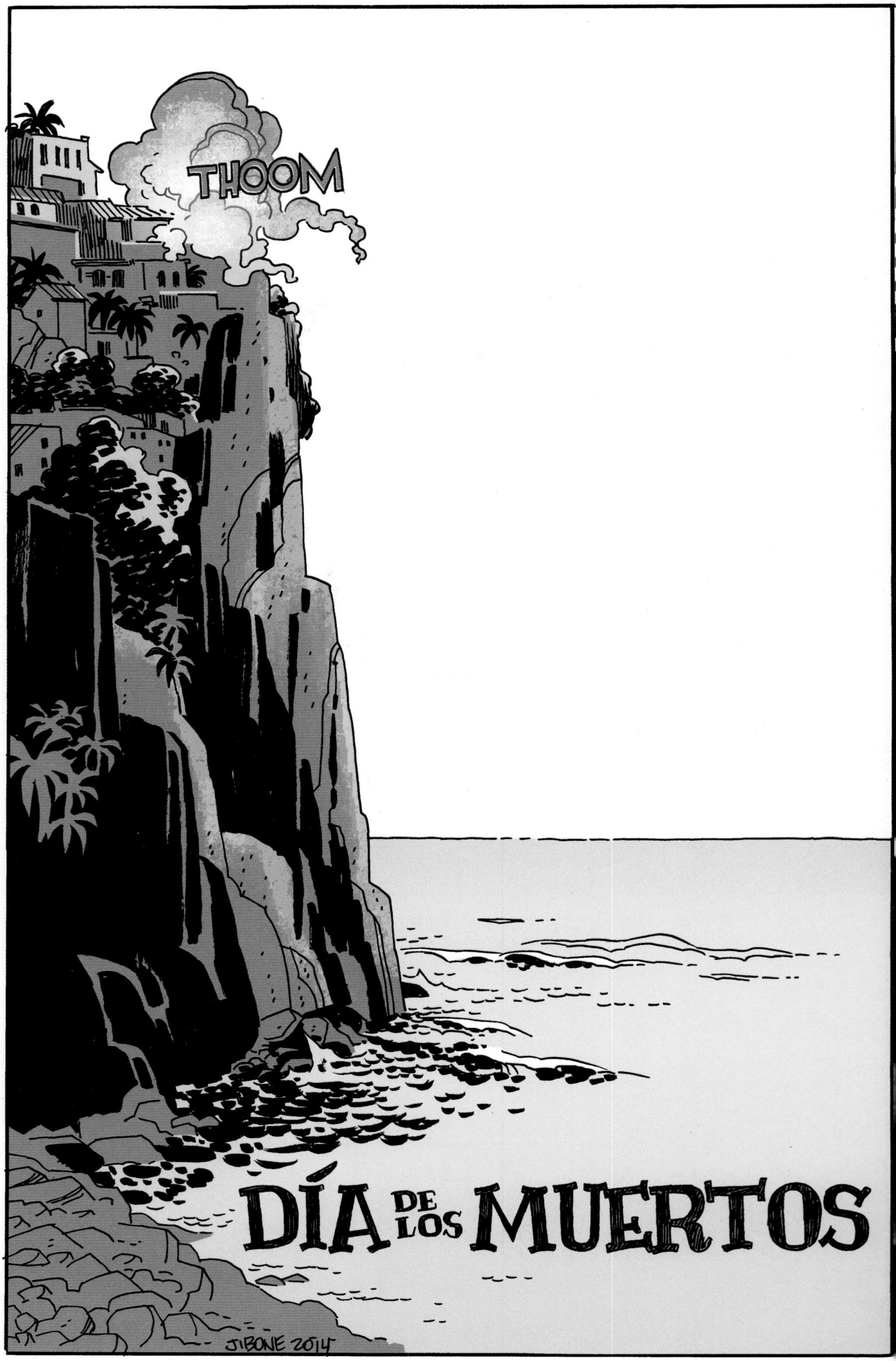
THOOM
DÍA DE LOS MUERTOS
JIBONE 2014

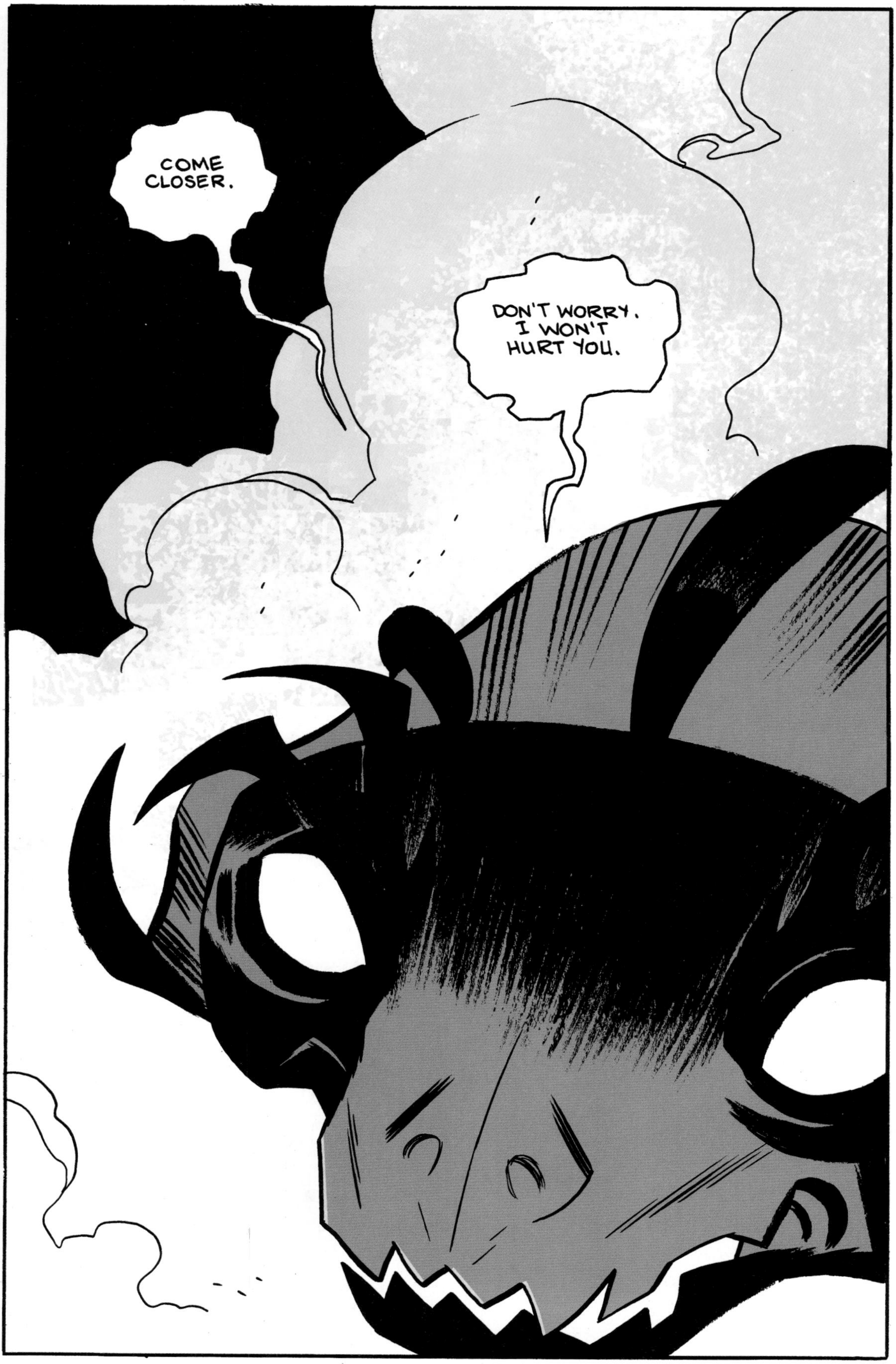
COME CLOSER.
DON'T WORRY. I WON'T HURT YOU.

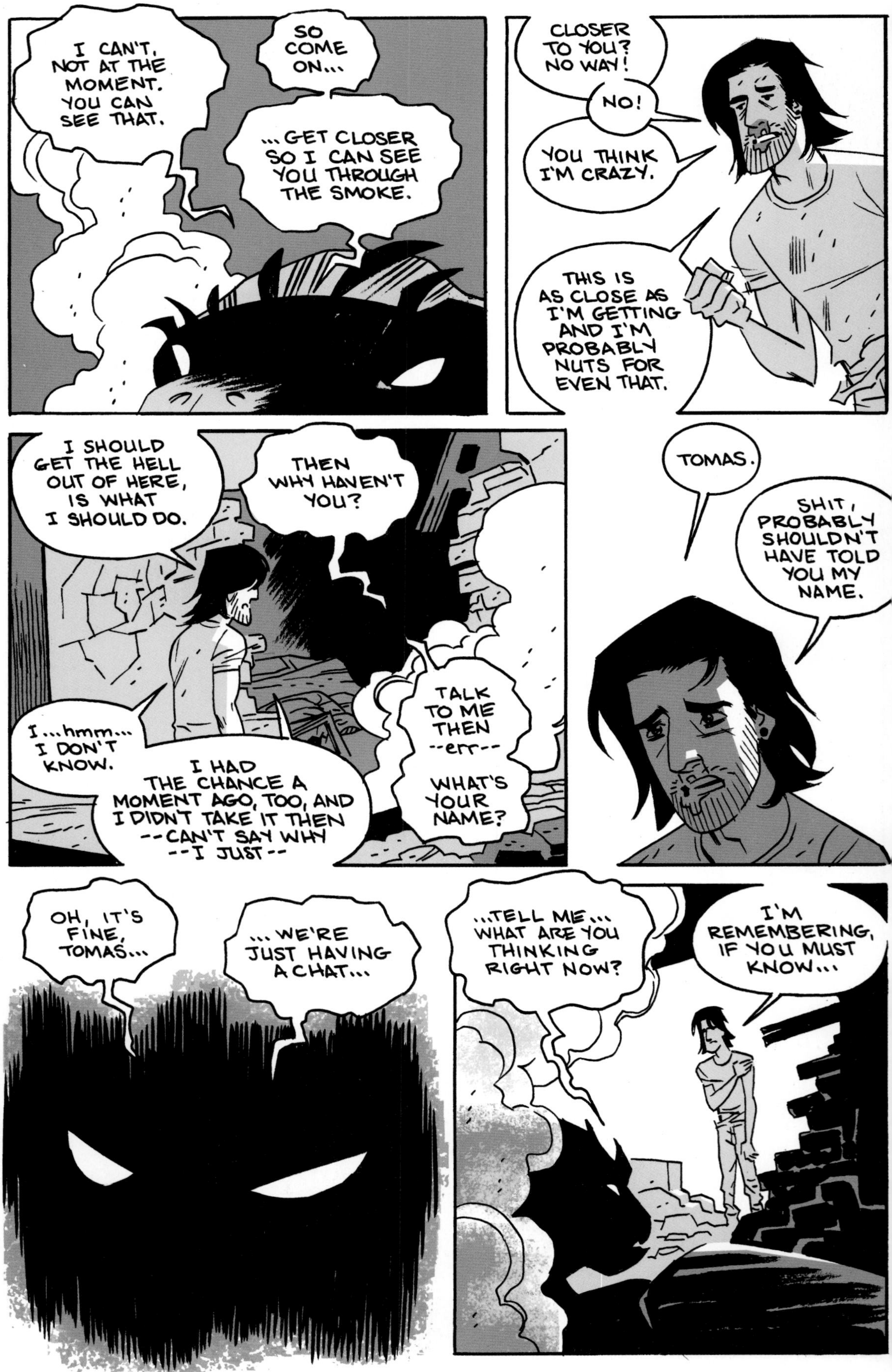
I CAN'T. NOT AT THE MOMENT. YOU CAN SEE THAT.
SO COME ON...
...GET CLOSER SO I CAN SEE YOU THROUGH THE SMOKE.
CLOSER TO YOU? NO WAY!
NO!
YOU THINK I'M CRAZY.
THIS IS AS CLOSE AS I'M GETTING AND I'M PROBABLY NUTS FOR EVEN THAT.
I SHOULD GET THE HELL OUT OF HERE, IS WHAT I SHOULD DO.
THEN WHY HAVEN'T YOU?
I...hmm... I DON'T KNOW.
I HAD THE CHANCE A MOMENT AGO, TOO, AND I DIDN'T TAKE IT THEN --CAN'T SAY WHY --I JUST--
TALK TO ME THEN --err--
WHAT'S YOUR NAME?
TOMAS.
SHIT, PROBABLY SHOULDN'T HAVE TOLD YOU MY NAME.
OH, IT'S FINE, TOMAS...
...WE'RE JUST HAVING A CHAT...
...TELL ME... WHAT ARE YOU THINKING RIGHT NOW?
I'M REMEMBERING, IF YOU MUST KNOW...

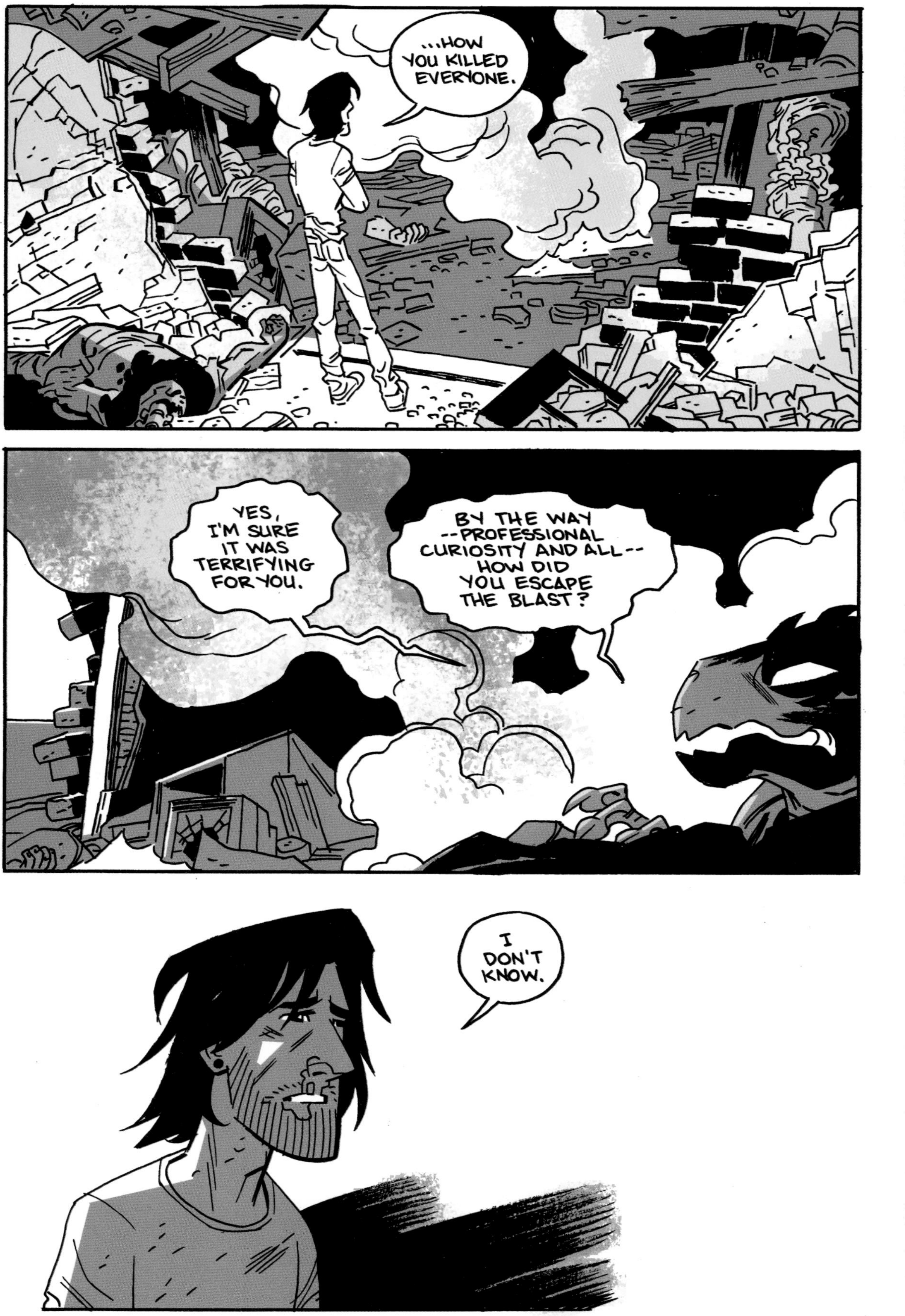
...HOW YOU KILLED EVERYONE.
YES, I'M SURE IT WAS TERRIFYING FOR YOU.
BY THE WAY --PROFESSIONAL CURIOSITY AND ALL-- HOW DID YOU ESCAPE THE BLAST?
I DON'T KNOW.

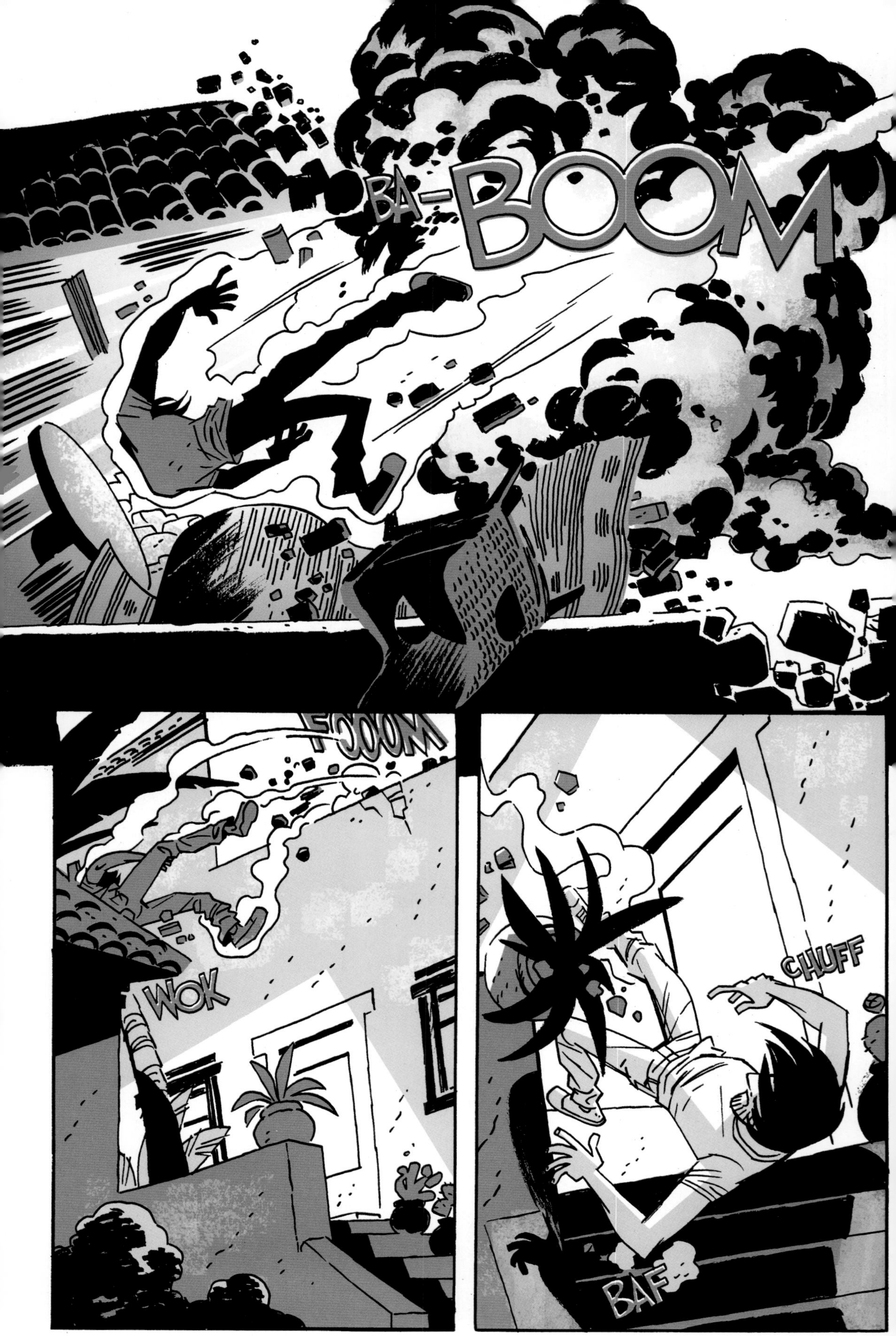
BA-BOOM
FOOOM
WOK
CHUFF
BAF

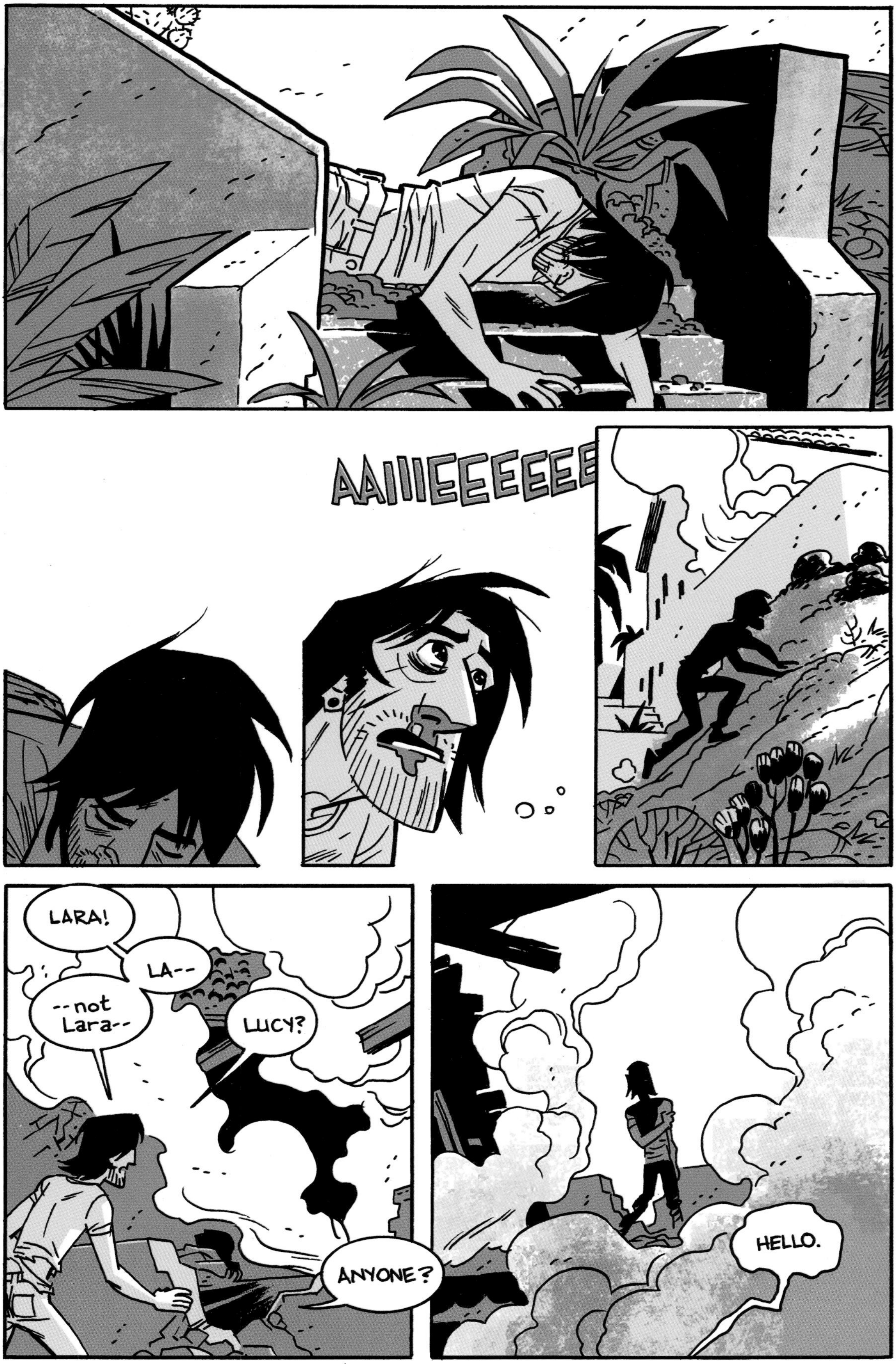
AAIIIEEEEEE
LARA!
LA--
--not Lara--
LUCY?
ANYONE?
HELLO.

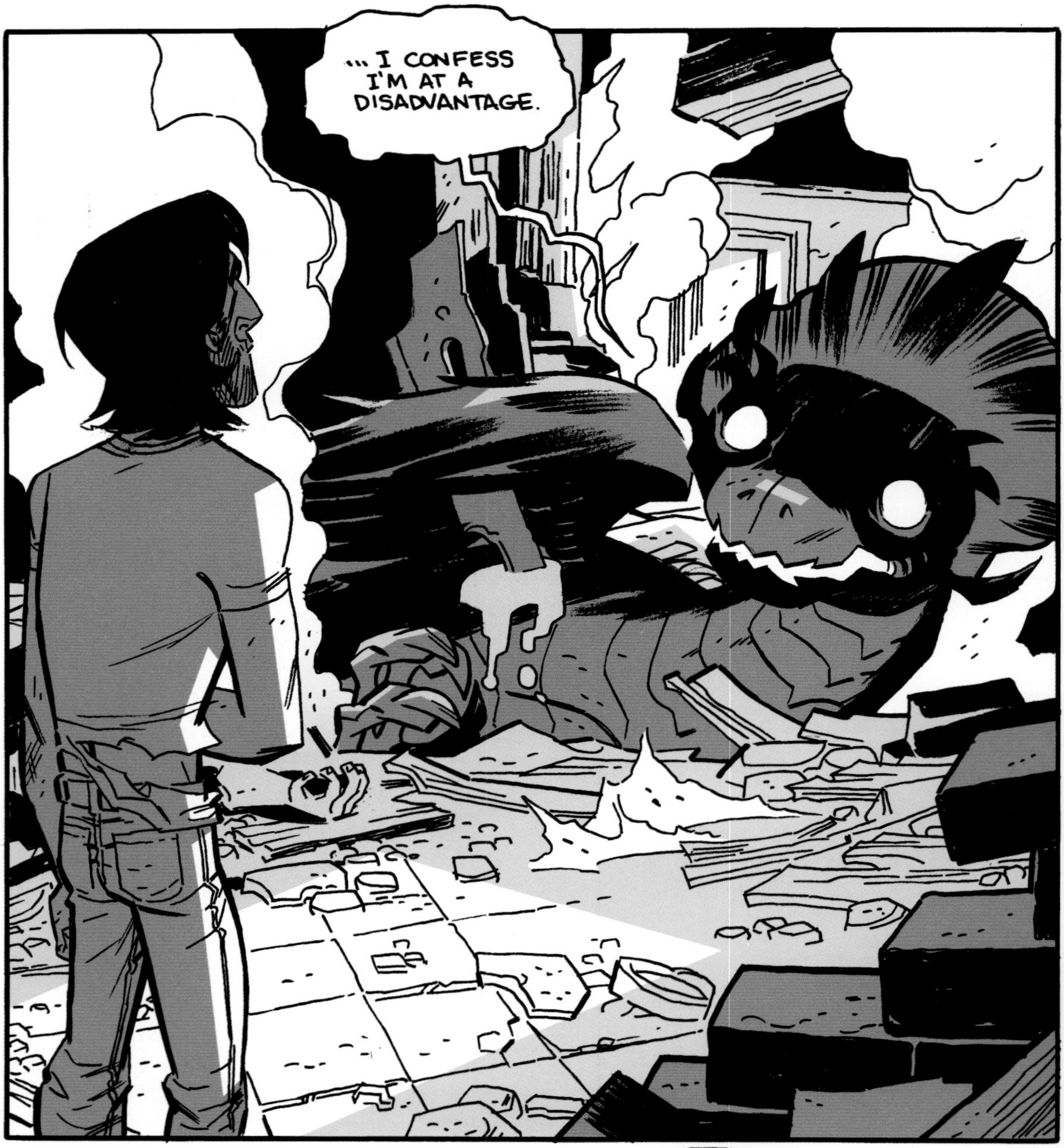
...I CONFESS I'M AT A DISADVANTAGE.

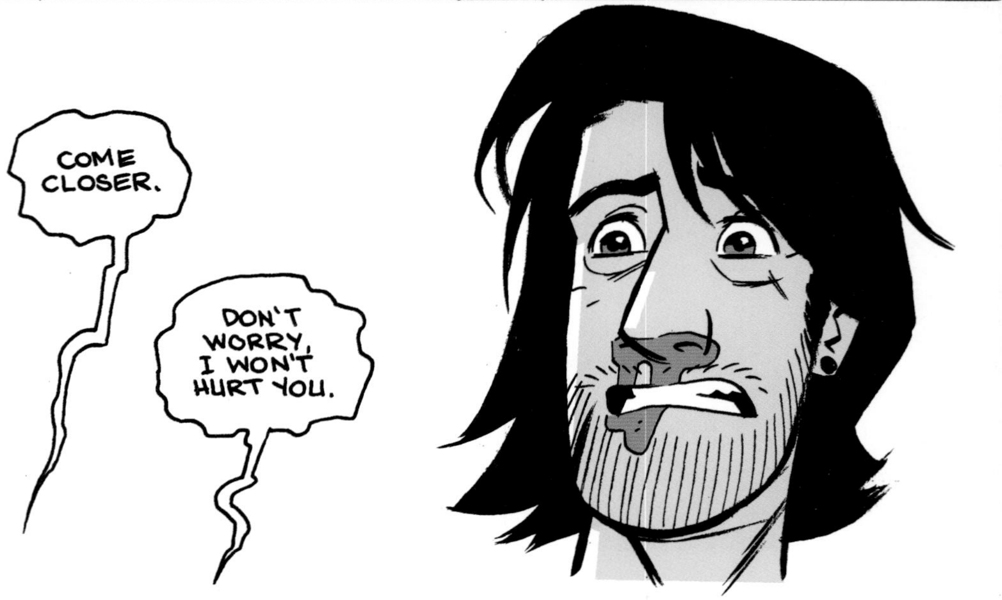
COME CLOSER.
DON'T WORRY, I WON'T HURT YOU.

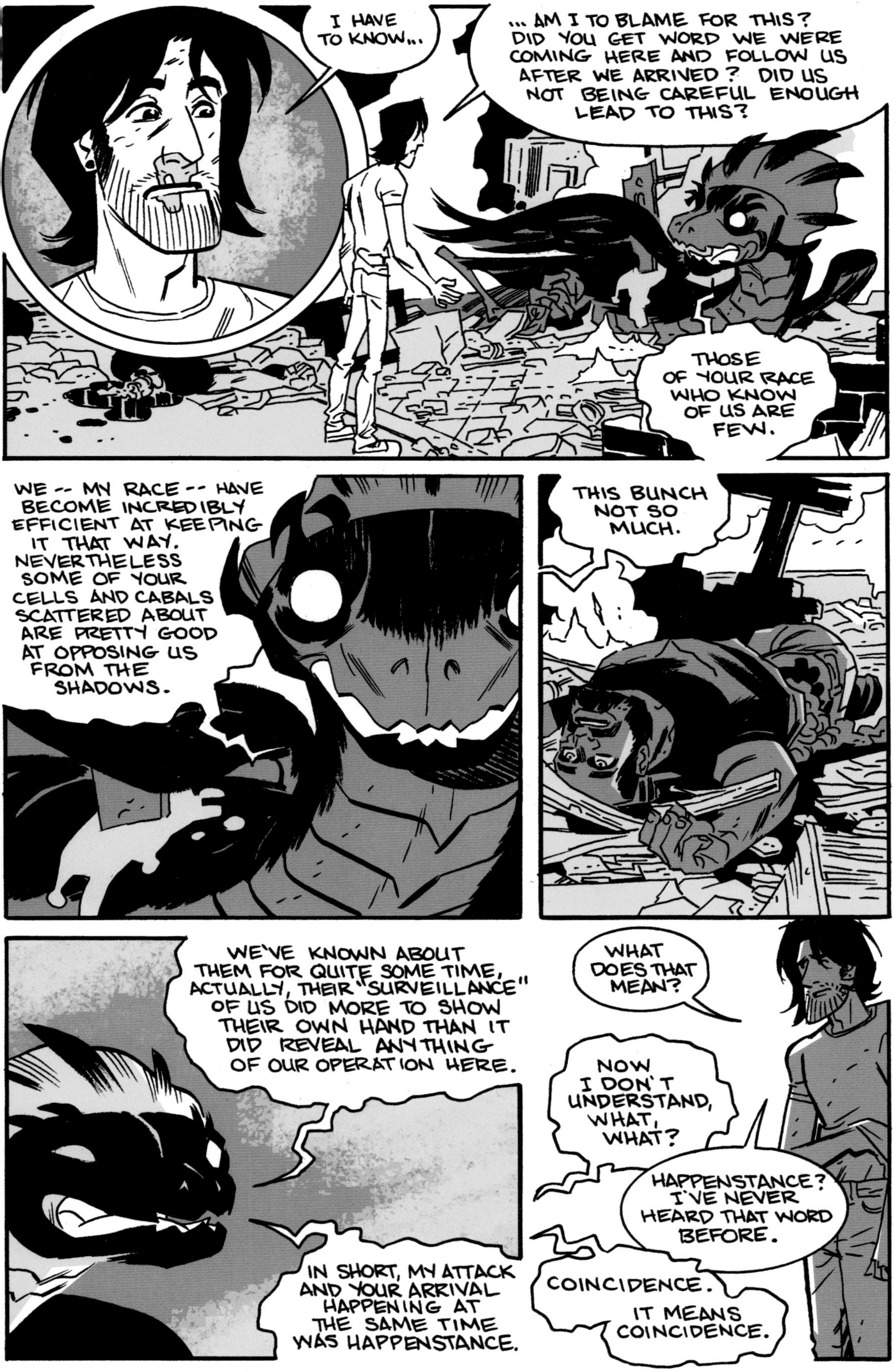
I HAVE TO KNOW...
...AM I TO BLAME FOR THIS? DID YOU GET WORD WE WERE COMING HERE AND FOLLOW US AFTER WE ARRIVED? DID US NOT BEING CAREFUL ENOUGH LEAD TO THIS?
THOSE OF YOUR RACE WHO KNOW OF US ARE FEW.
WE -- MY RACE -- HAVE BECOME INCREDIBLY EFFICIENT AT KEEPING IT THAT WAY. NEVERTHELESS SOME OF YOUR CELLS AND CABALS SCATTERED ABOUT ARE PRETTY GOOD AT OPPOSING US FROM THE SHADOWS.
THIS BUNCH NOT SO MUCH.
WE'VE KNOWN ABOUT THEM FOR QUITE SOME TIME, ACTUALLY, THEIR "SURVEILLANCE" OF US DID MORE TO SHOW THEIR OWN HAND THAN IT DID REVEAL ANYTHING OF OUR OPERATION HERE.
IN SHORT, MY ATTACK AND YOUR ARRIVAL HAPPENING AT THE SAME TIME WAS HAPPENSTANCE.
WHAT DOES THAT MEAN?
NOW I DON'T UNDERSTAND, WHAT, WHAT?
HAPPENSTANCE? I'VE NEVER HEARD THAT WORD BEFORE.
COINCIDENCE.
IT MEANS COINCIDENCE.

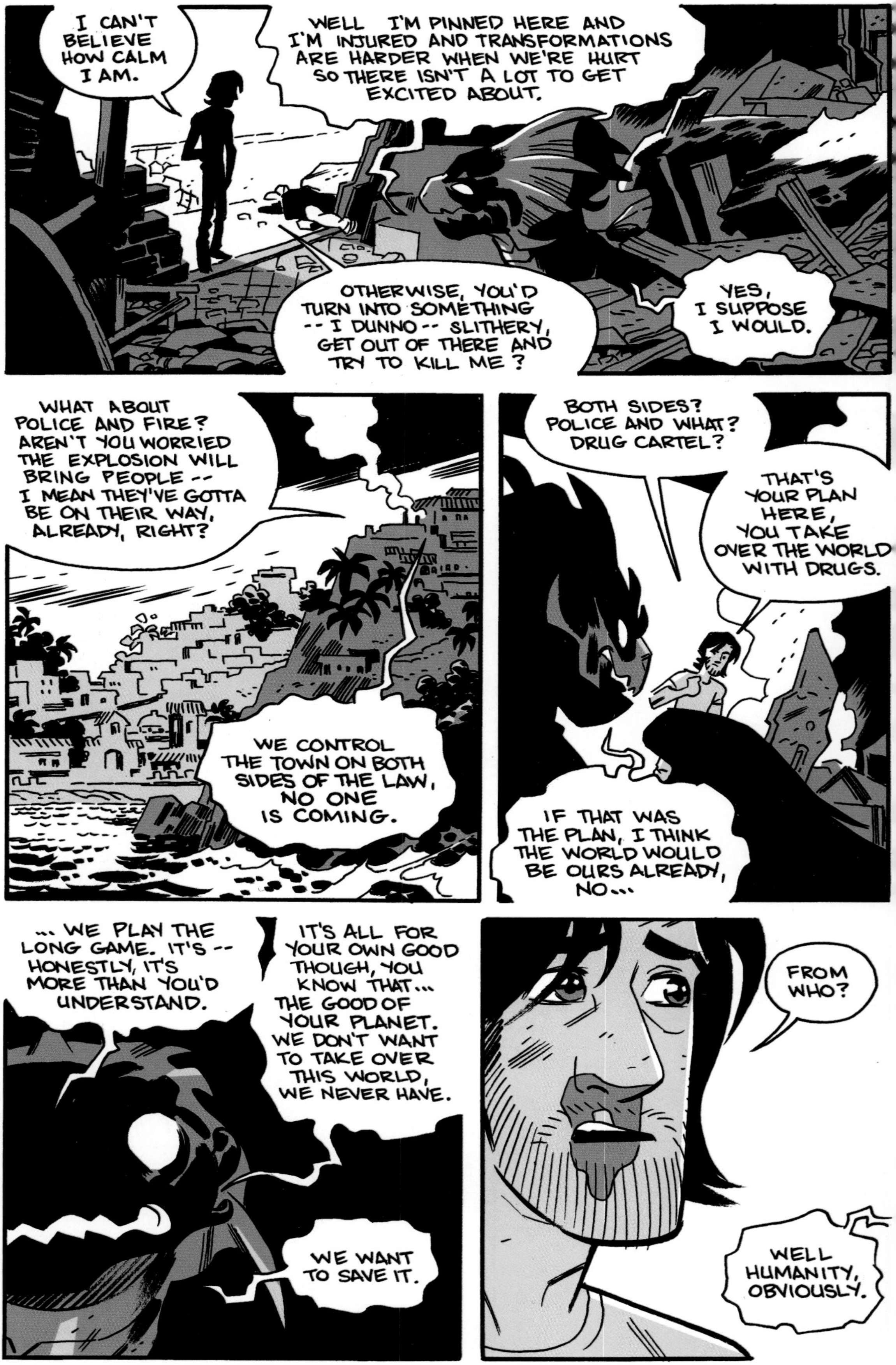
I CAN'T BELIEVE HOW CALM I AM.
WELL I'M PINNED HERE AND I'M INJURED AND TRANSFORMATIONS ARE HARDER WHEN WE'RE HURT SO THERE ISN'T A LOT TO GET EXCITED ABOUT.
OTHERWISE, YOU'D TURN INTO SOMETHING -- I DUNNO -- SLITHERY, GET OUT OF THERE AND TRY TO KILL ME ?
YES, I SUPPOSE I WOULD.
WHAT ABOUT POLICE AND FIRE? AREN'T YOU WORRIED THE EXPLOSION WILL BRING PEOPLE -- I MEAN THEY'VE GOTTA BE ON THEIR WAY, ALREADY, RIGHT?
WE CONTROL THE TOWN ON BOTH SIDES OF THE LAW, NO ONE IS COMING.
BOTH SIDES? POLICE AND WHAT? DRUG CARTEL?
THAT'S YOUR PLAN HERE, YOU TAKE OVER THE WORLD WITH DRUGS.
IF THAT WAS THE PLAN, I THINK THE WORLD WOULD BE OURS ALREADY, NO...
... WE PLAY THE LONG GAME. IT'S -- HONESTLY, IT'S MORE THAN YOU'D UNDERSTAND.
IT'S ALL FOR YOUR OWN GOOD THOUGH, YOU KNOW THAT... THE GOOD OF YOUR PLANET. WE DON'T WANT TO TAKE OVER THIS WORLD, WE NEVER HAVE.
WE WANT TO SAVE IT.
FROM WHO?
WELL HUMANITY, OBVIOUSLY.

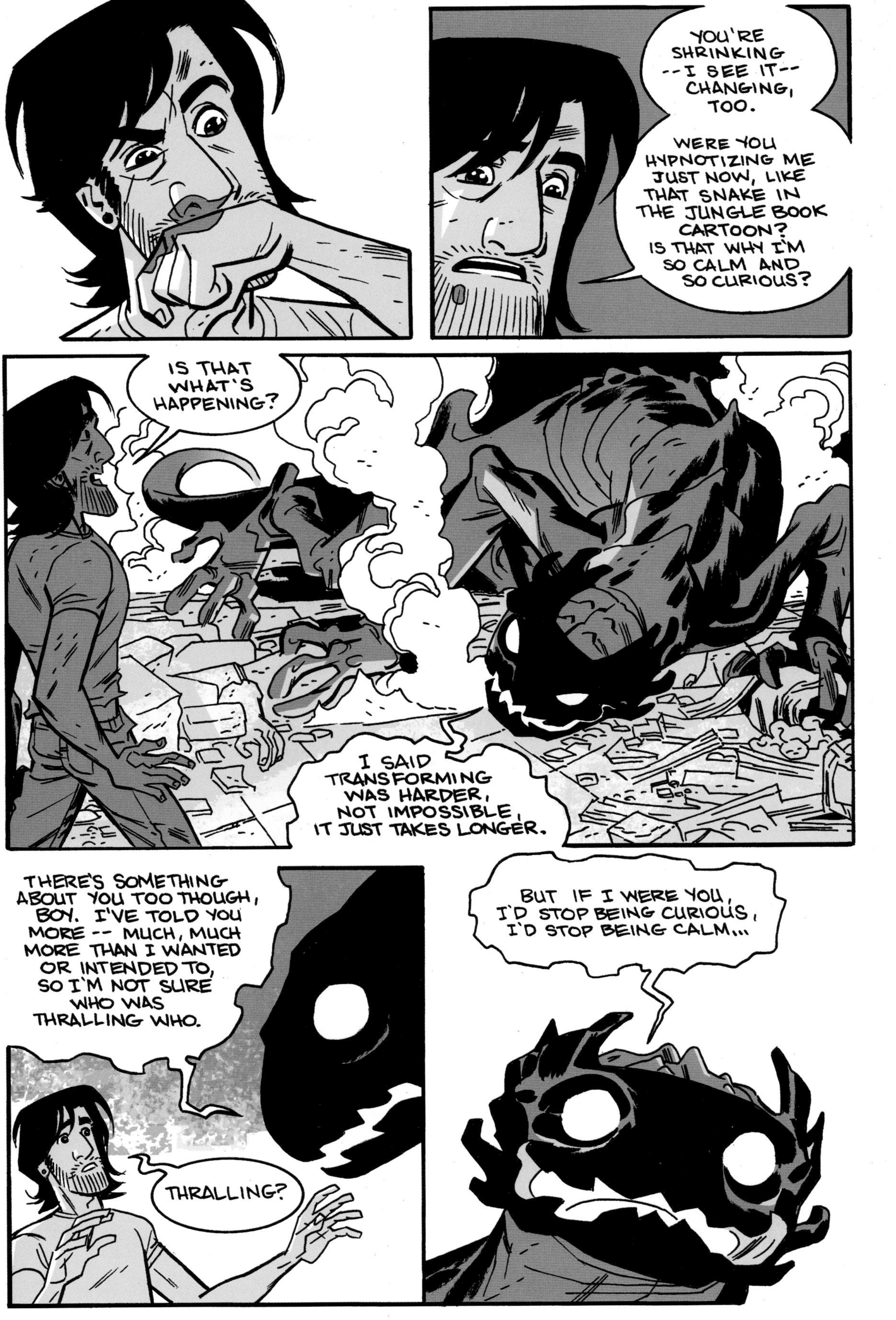
YOU'RE SHRINKING --I SEE IT-- CHANGING, TOO.
WERE YOU HYPNOTIZING ME JUST NOW, LIKE THAT SNAKE IN THE JUNGLE BOOK CARTOON? IS THAT WHY I'M SO CALM AND SO CURIOUS?
IS THAT WHAT'S HAPPENING?
I SAID TRANSFORMING WAS HARDER, NOT IMPOSSIBLE, IT JUST TAKES LONGER.
THERE'S SOMETHING ABOUT YOU TOO THOUGH, BOY. I'VE TOLD YOU MORE -- MUCH, MUCH MORE THAN I WANTED OR INTENDED TO, SO I'M NOT SURE WHO WAS THRALLING WHO.
THRALLING?
BUT IF I WERE YOU, I'D STOP BEING CURIOUS, I'D STOP BEING CALM...

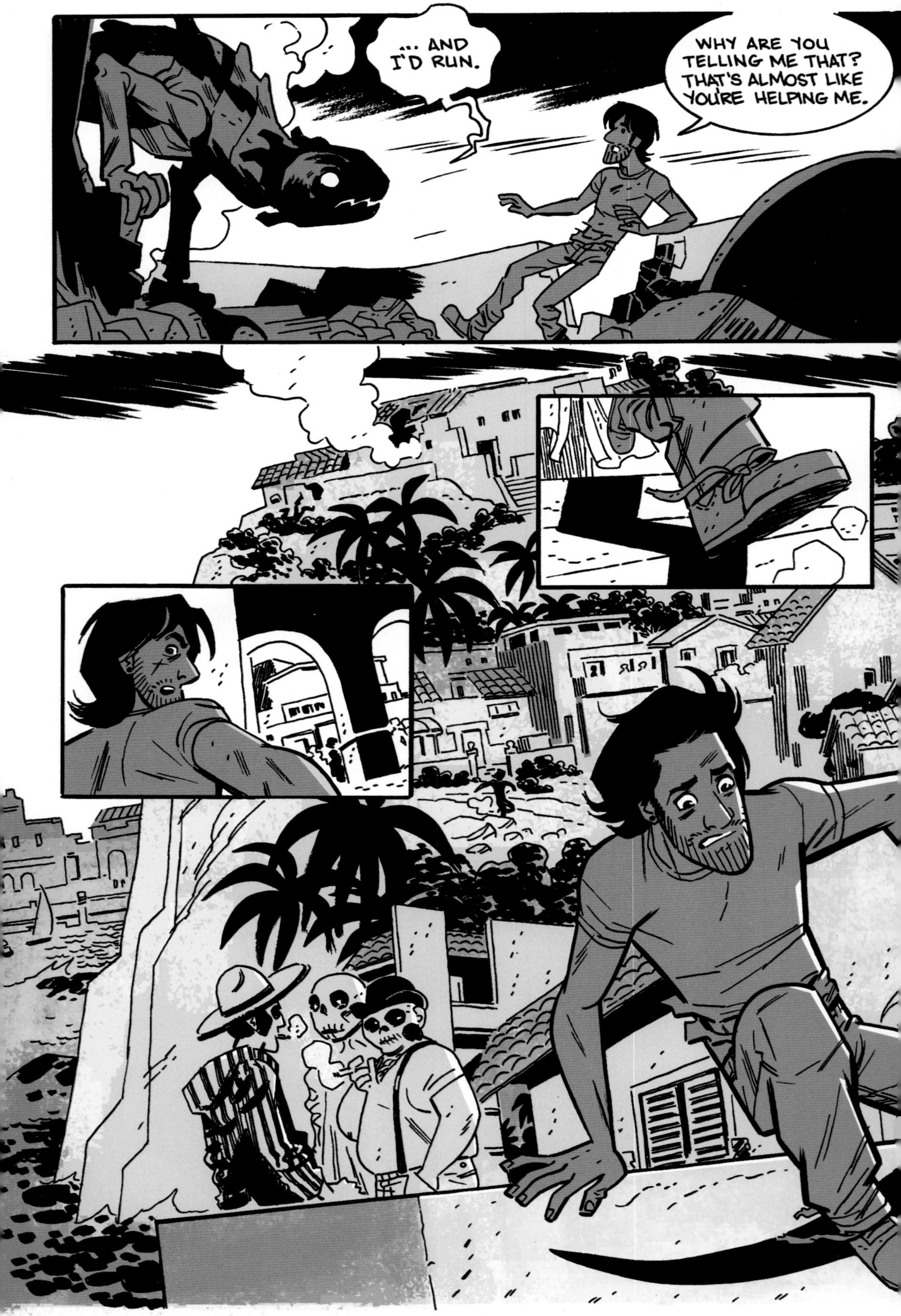
... AND I'D RUN.
WHY ARE YOU TELLING ME THAT? THAT'S ALMOST LIKE YOU'RE HELPING ME.

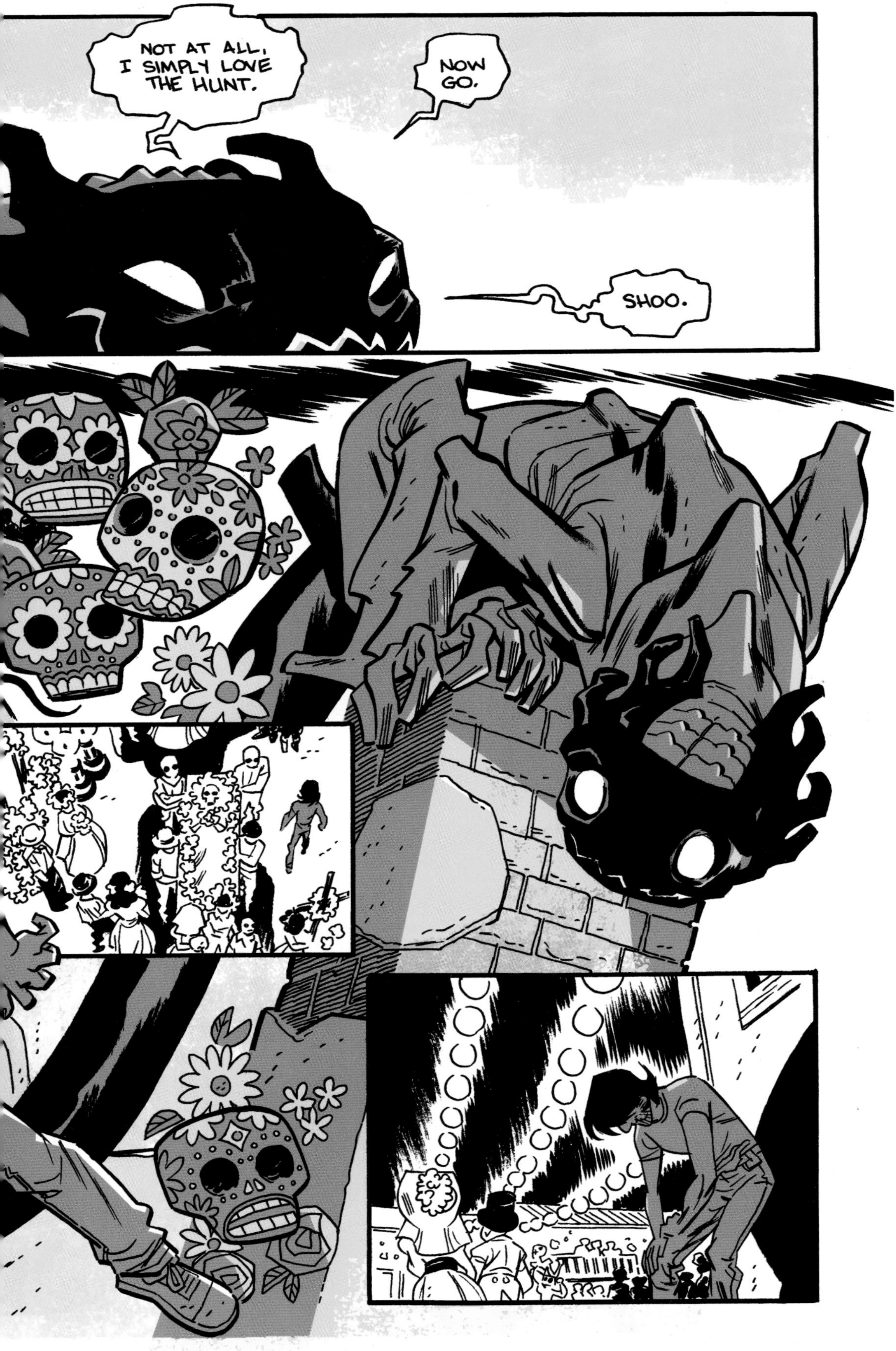
NOT AT ALL, I SIMPLY LOVE THE HUNT.
NOW GO.
SHOO.

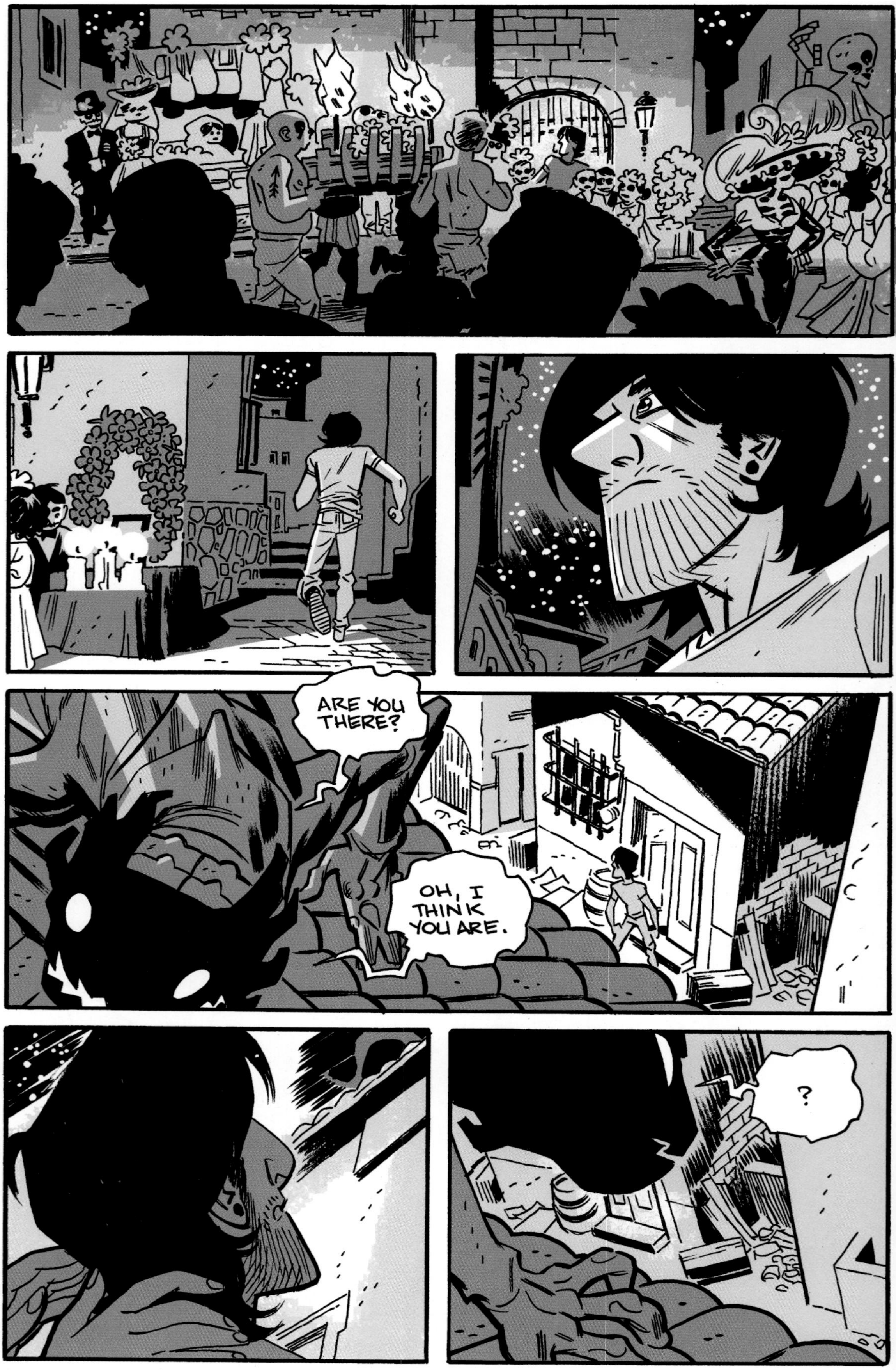
ARE YOU THERE?
OH, I THINK YOU ARE.
?

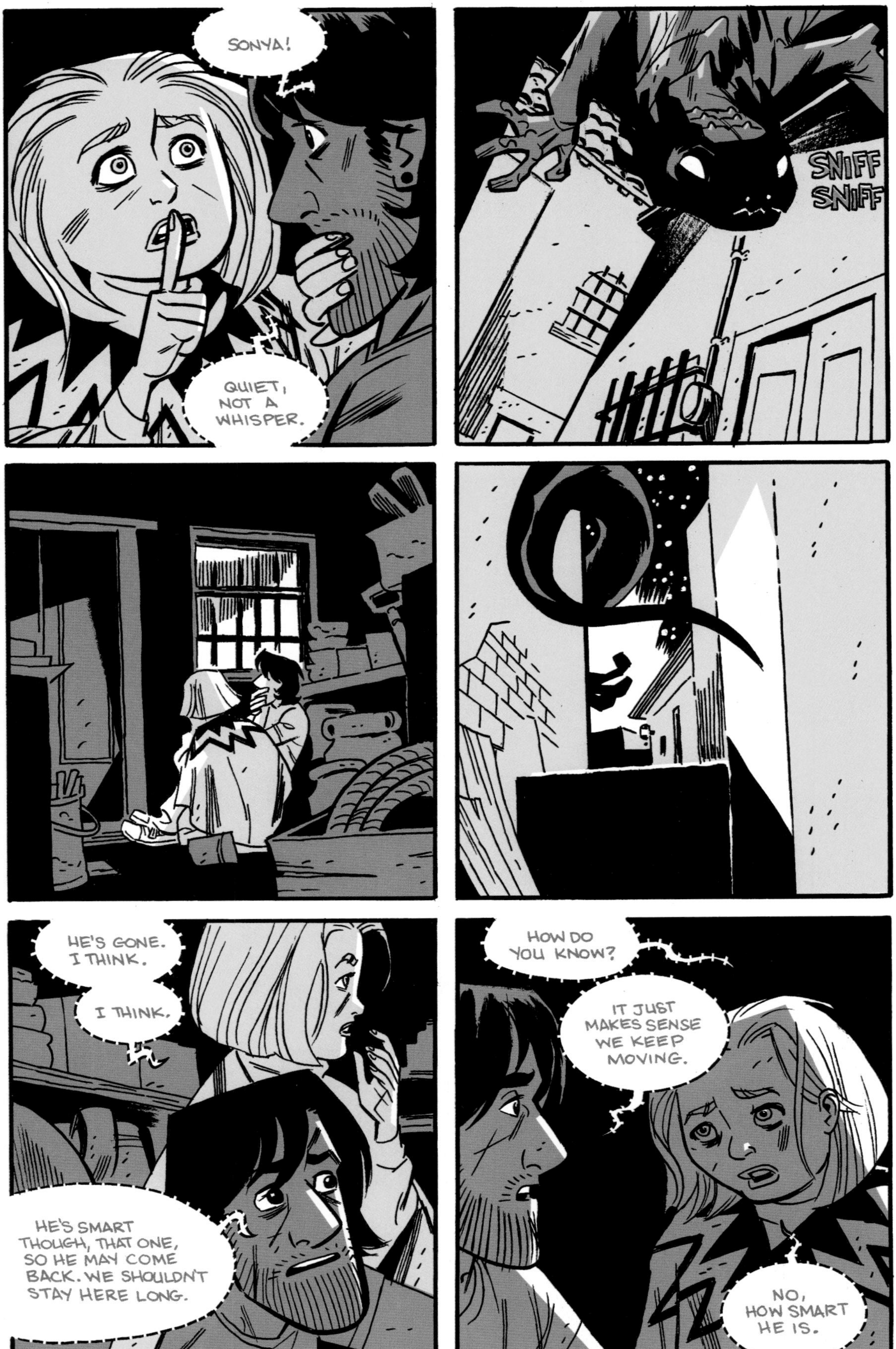
SONYA!
QUIET, NOT A WHISPER.
SNIFF SNIFF
HE'S GONE. I THINK.
I THINK.
HE'S SMART THOUGH, THAT ONE, SO HE MAY COME BACK. WE SHOULDN'T STAY HERE LONG.
HOW DO YOU KNOW?
IT JUST MAKES SENSE WE KEEP MOVING.
NO, HOW SMART HE IS.

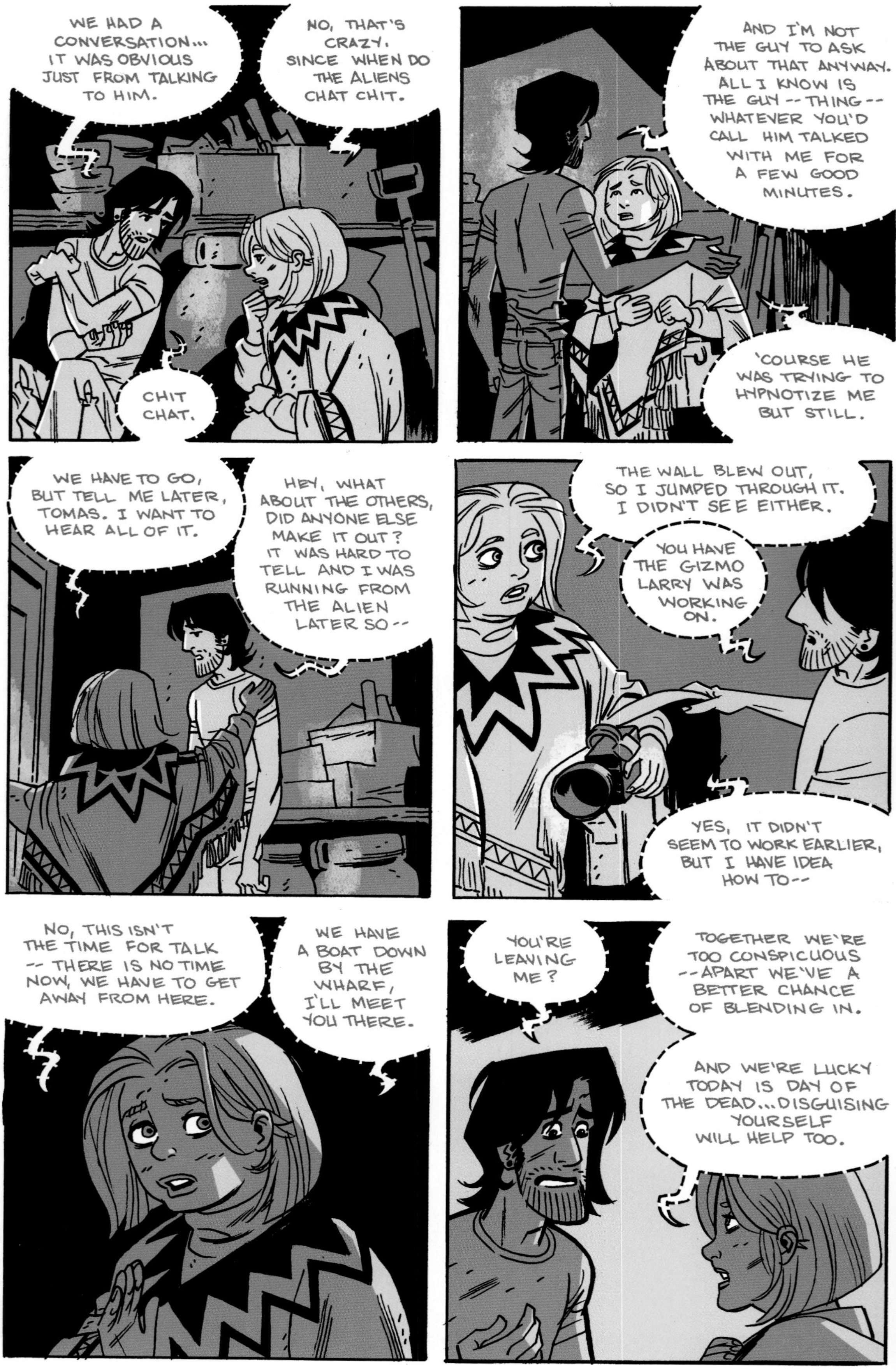
WE HAD A CONVERSATION... IT WAS OBVIOUS JUST FROM TALKING TO HIM.
NO, THAT'S CRAZY. SINCE WHEN DO THE ALIENS CHAT CHIT.
CHIT CHAT.
AND I'M NOT THE GUY TO ASK ABOUT THAT ANYWAY. ALL I KNOW IS THE GUY -- THING -- WHATEVER YOU'D CALL HIM TALKED WITH ME FOR A FEW GOOD MINUTES.
'COURSE HE WAS TRYING TO HYPNOTIZE ME BUT STILL.
WE HAVE TO GO, BUT TELL ME LATER, TOMAS. I WANT TO HEAR ALL OF IT.
HEY, WHAT ABOUT THE OTHERS, DID ANYONE ELSE MAKE IT OUT? IT WAS HARD TO TELL AND I WAS RUNNING FROM THE ALIEN LATER SO--
THE WALL BLEW OUT, SO I JUMPED THROUGH IT. I DIDN'T SEE EITHER.
YOU HAVE THE GIZMO LARRY WAS WORKING ON.
YES, IT DIDN'T SEEM TO WORK EARLIER, BUT I HAVE IDEA HOW TO--
NO, THIS ISN'T THE TIME FOR TALK -- THERE IS NO TIME NOW, WE HAVE TO GET AWAY FROM HERE.
WE HAVE A BOAT DOWN BY THE WHARF, I'LL MEET YOU THERE.
YOU'RE LEAVING ME?
TOGETHER WE'RE TOO CONSPICUOUS --APART WE'VE A BETTER CHANCE OF BLENDING IN.
AND WE'RE LUCKY TODAY IS DAY OF THE DEAD...DISGUISING YOURSELF WILL HELP TOO.

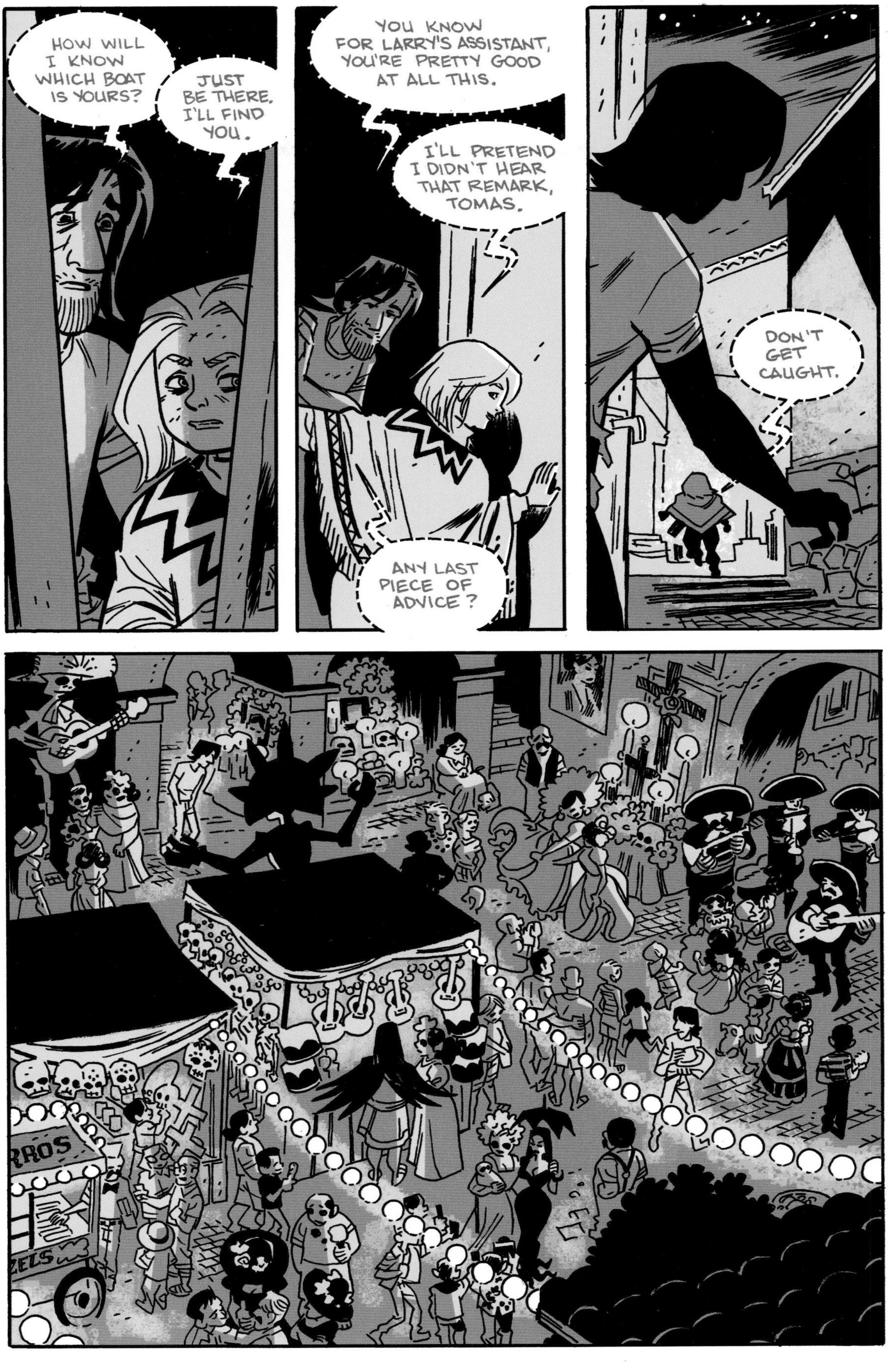
HOW WILL I KNOW WHICH BOAT IS YOURS?
JUST BE THERE. I'LL FIND YOU.
YOU KNOW FOR LARRY'S ASSISTANT, YOU'RE PRETTY GOOD AT ALL THIS.
I'LL PRETEND I DIDN'T HEAR THAT REMARK, TOMAS.
ANY LAST PIECE OF ADVICE?
DON'T GET CAUGHT.

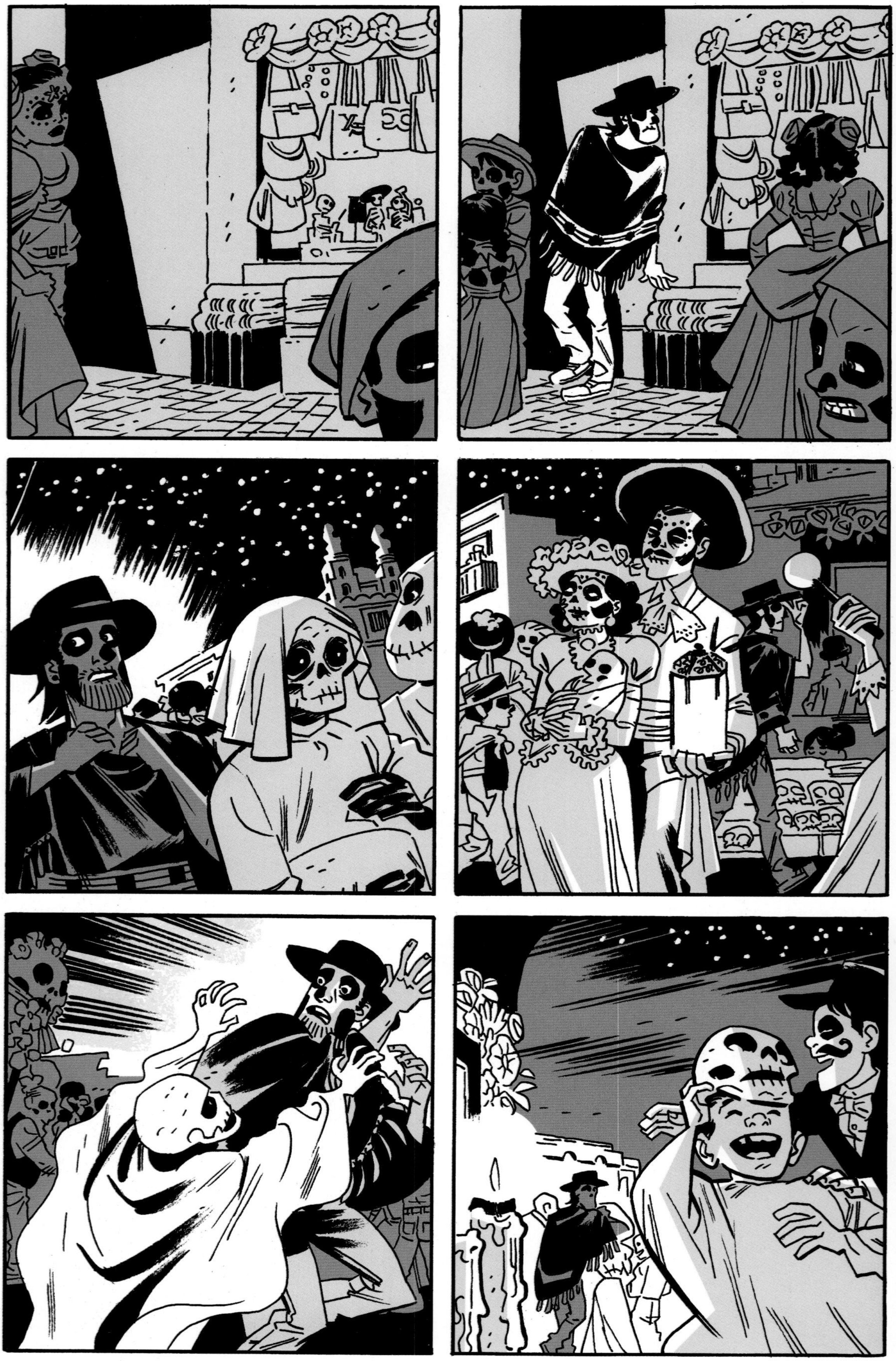

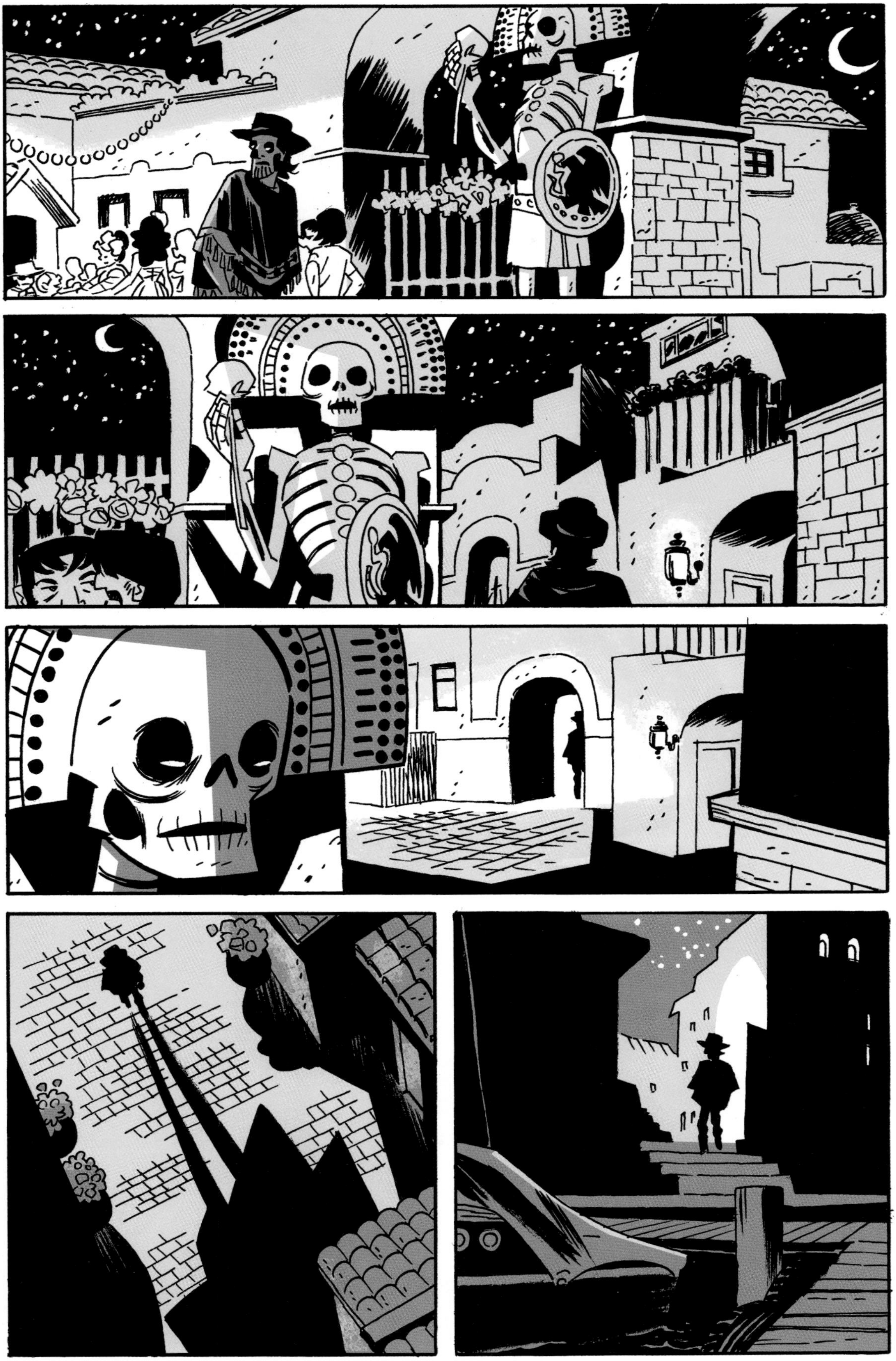

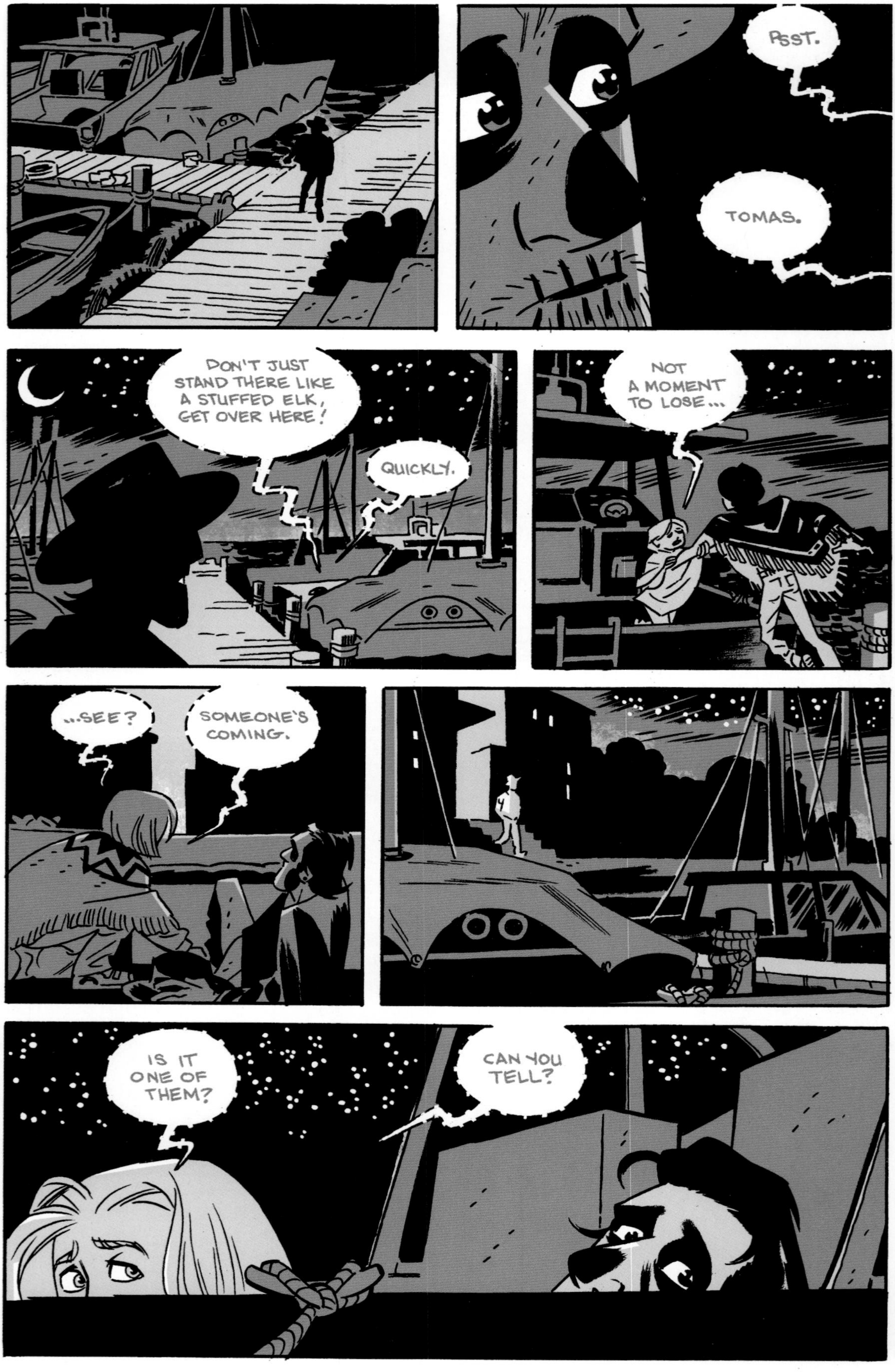
PSST.
TOMAS.
DON'T JUST STAND THERE LIKE A STUFFED ELK, GET OVER HERE!
QUICKLY.
NOT A MOMENT TO LOSE...
..SEE?
SOMEONE'S COMING.
IS IT ONE OF THEM?
CAN YOU TELL?

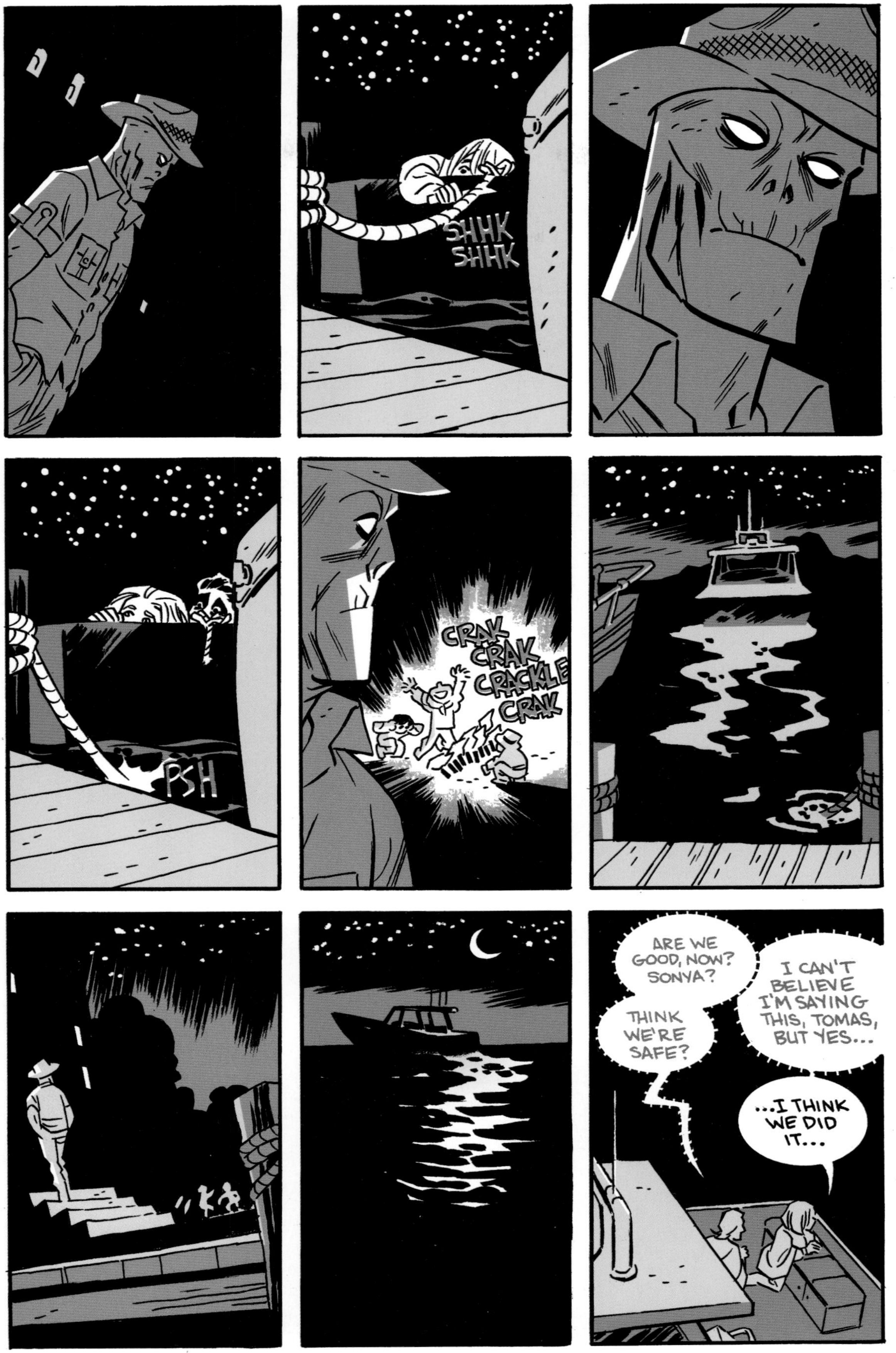
SHHK
SHHK
PSH
CRAK
CRAK
CRACKLE
CRAK
ARE WE GOOD, NOW? SONYA?
THINK WE'RE SAFE?
I CAN'T BELIEVE I'M SAYING THIS, TOMAS, BUT YES...
...I THINK WE DID IT...

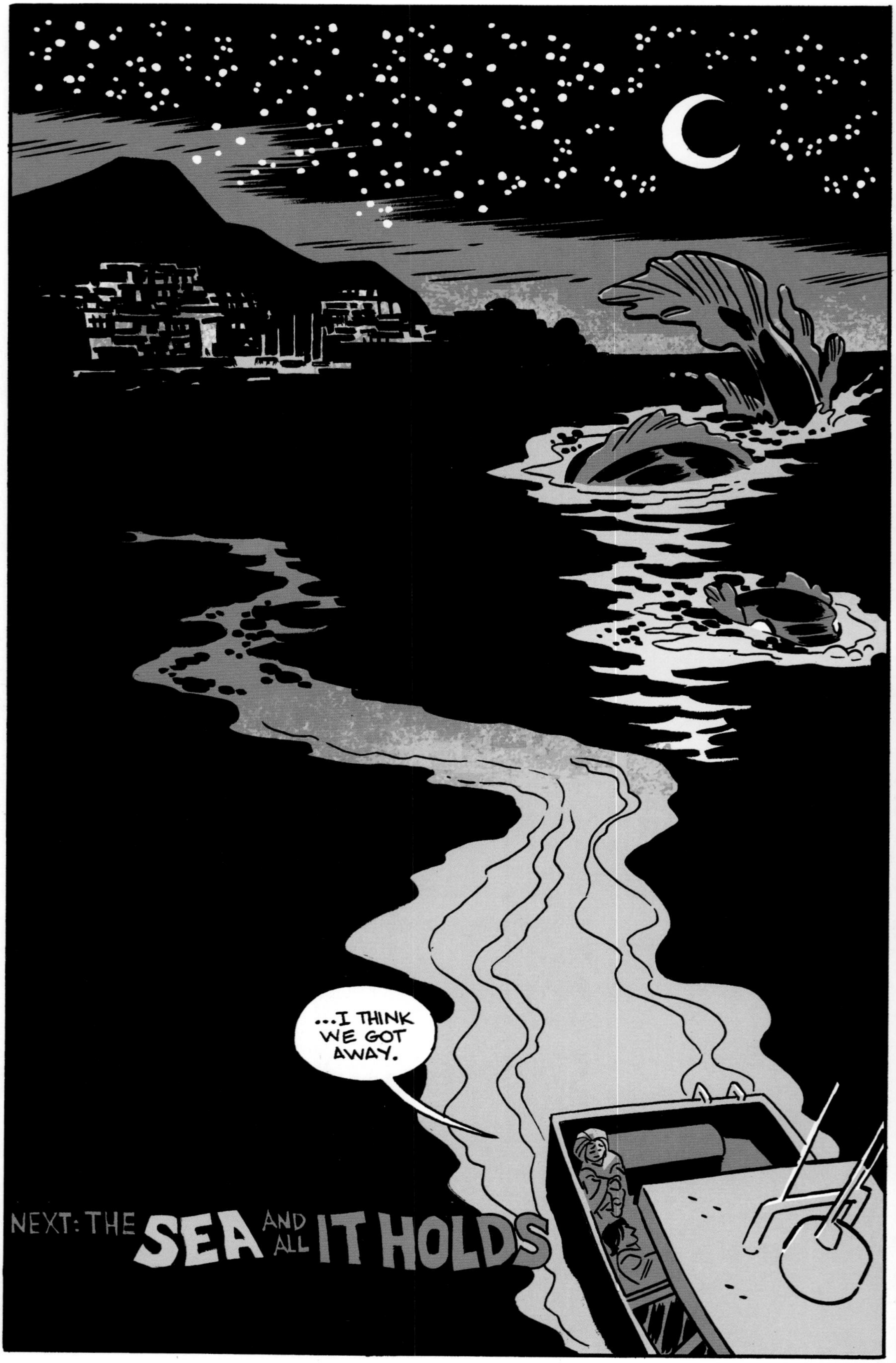
...I THINK WE GOT AWAY.
NEXT: THE SEA AND ALL IT HOLDS

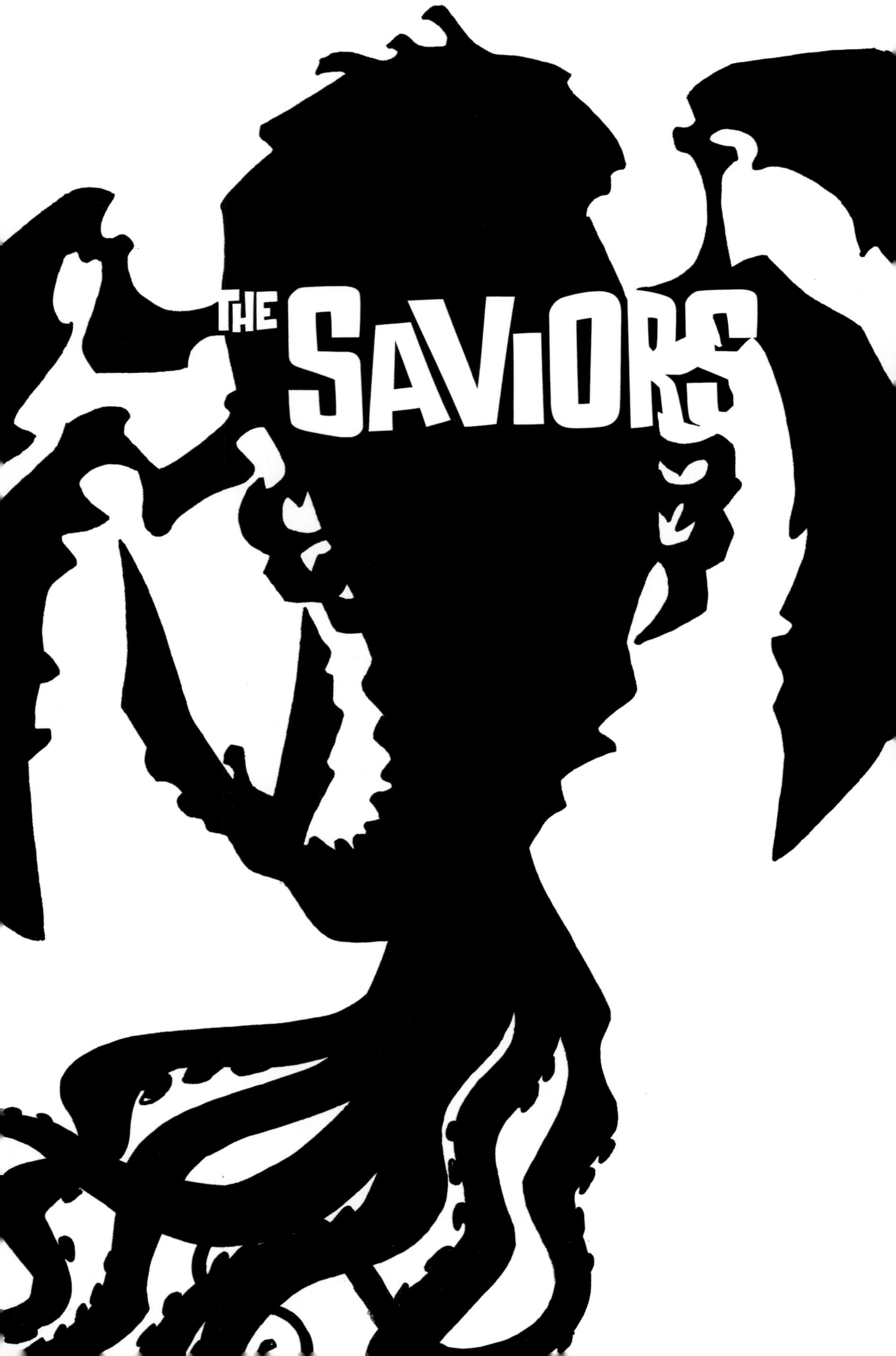
THE SAVIORS

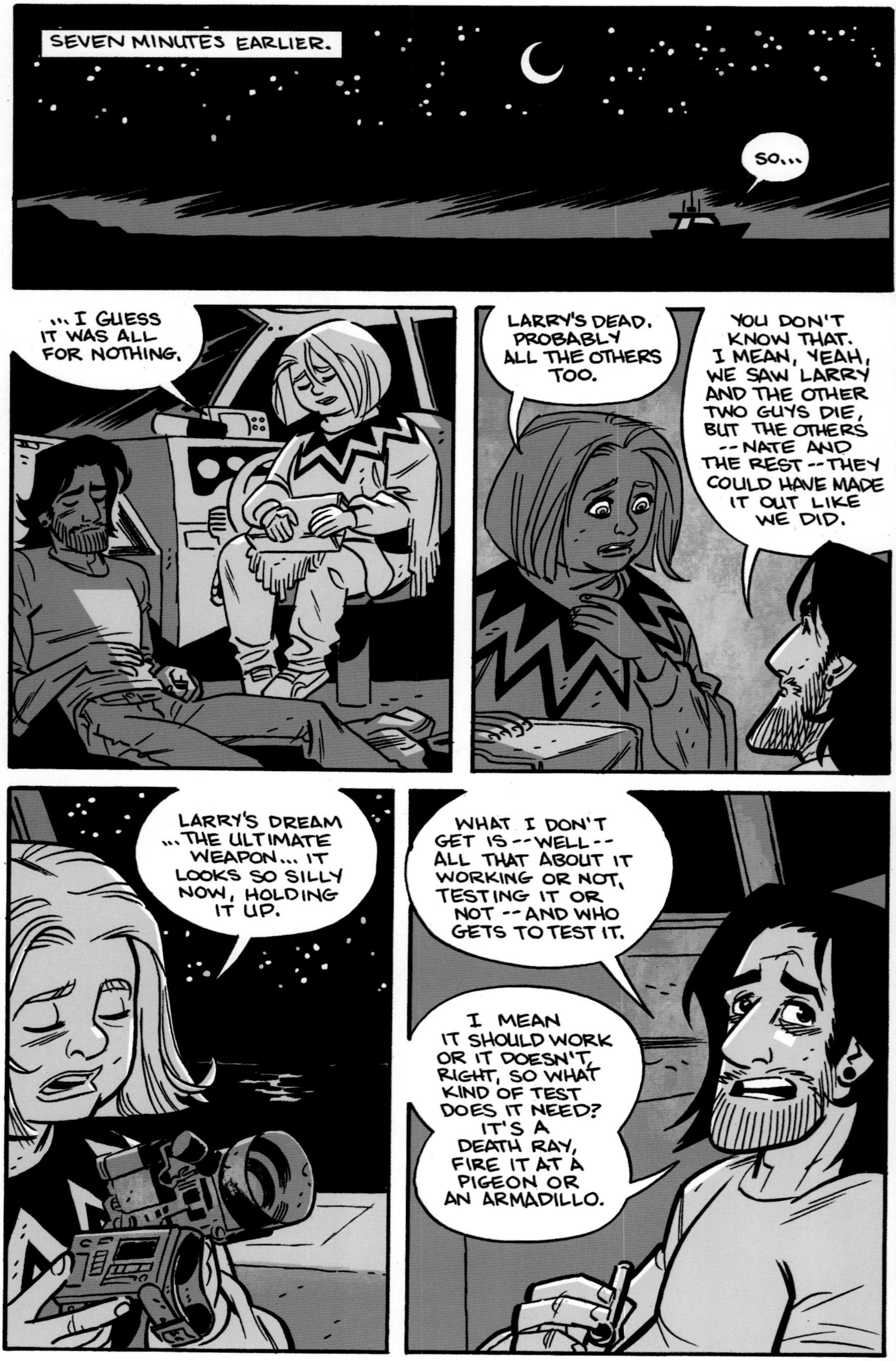
SEVEN MINUTES EARLIER.
SO...
...I GUESS IT WAS ALL FOR NOTHING.
LARRY'S DEAD. PROBABLY ALL THE OTHERS TOO.
YOU DON'T KNOW THAT. I MEAN, YEAH, WE SAW LARRY AND THE OTHER TWO GUYS DIE, BUT THE OTHERS --NATE AND THE REST--THEY COULD HAVE MADE IT OUT LIKE WE DID.
LARRY'S DREAM ...THE ULTIMATE WEAPON... IT LOOKS SO SILLY NOW, HOLDING IT UP.
WHAT I DON'T GET IS--WELL-- ALL THAT ABOUT IT WORKING OR NOT, TESTING IT OR NOT--AND WHO GETS TO TEST IT.
I MEAN IT SHOULD WORK OR IT DOESN'T, RIGHT, SO WHAT KIND OF TEST DOES IT NEED? IT'S A DEATH RAY, FIRE IT AT A PIGEON OR AN ARMADILLO.

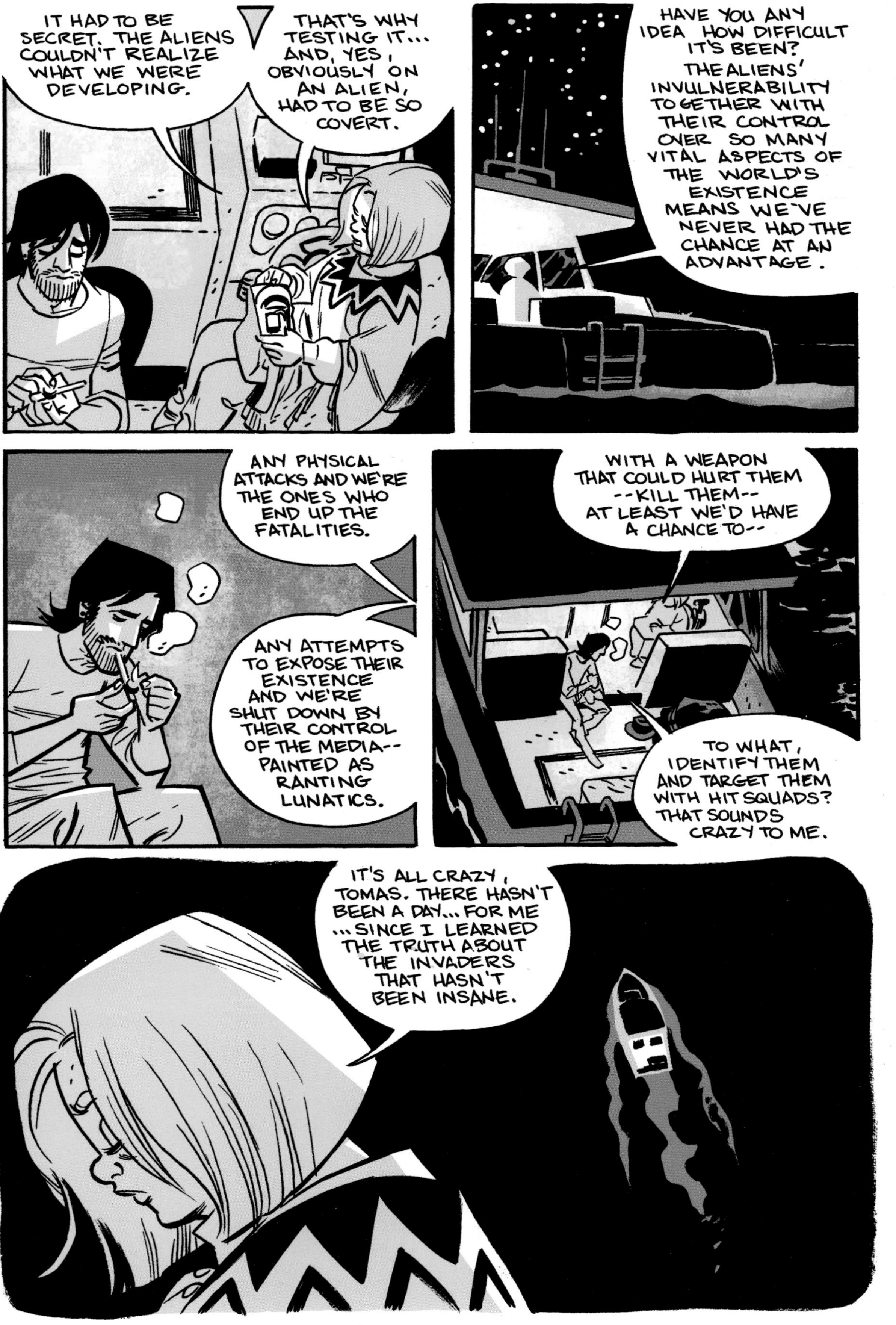
IT HAD TO BE SECRET. THE ALIENS COULDN'T REALIZE WHAT WE WERE DEVELOPING.
THAT'S WHY TESTING IT... AND, YES, OBVIOUSLY ON AN ALIEN, HAD TO BE SO COVERT.
HAVE YOU ANY IDEA HOW DIFFICULT IT'S BEEN?
THE ALIENS' INVULNERABILITY TOGETHER WITH THEIR CONTROL OVER SO MANY VITAL ASPECTS OF THE WORLD'S EXISTENCE MEANS WE'VE NEVER HAD THE CHANCE AT AN ADVANTAGE.
ANY PHYSICAL ATTACKS AND WE'RE THE ONES WHO END UP THE FATALITIES.
ANY ATTEMPTS TO EXPOSE THEIR EXISTENCE AND WE'RE SHUT DOWN BY THEIR CONTROL OF THE MEDIA-- PAINTED AS RANTING LUNATICS.
WITH A WEAPON THAT COULD HURT THEM --KILL THEM-- AT LEAST WE'D HAVE A CHANCE TO--
TO WHAT, IDENTIFY THEM AND TARGET THEM WITH HIT SQUADS? THAT SOUNDS CRAZY TO ME.
IT'S ALL CRAZY, TOMAS. THERE HASN'T BEEN A DAY... FOR ME ...SINCE I LEARNED THE TRUTH ABOUT THE INVADERS THAT HASN'T BEEN INSANE.

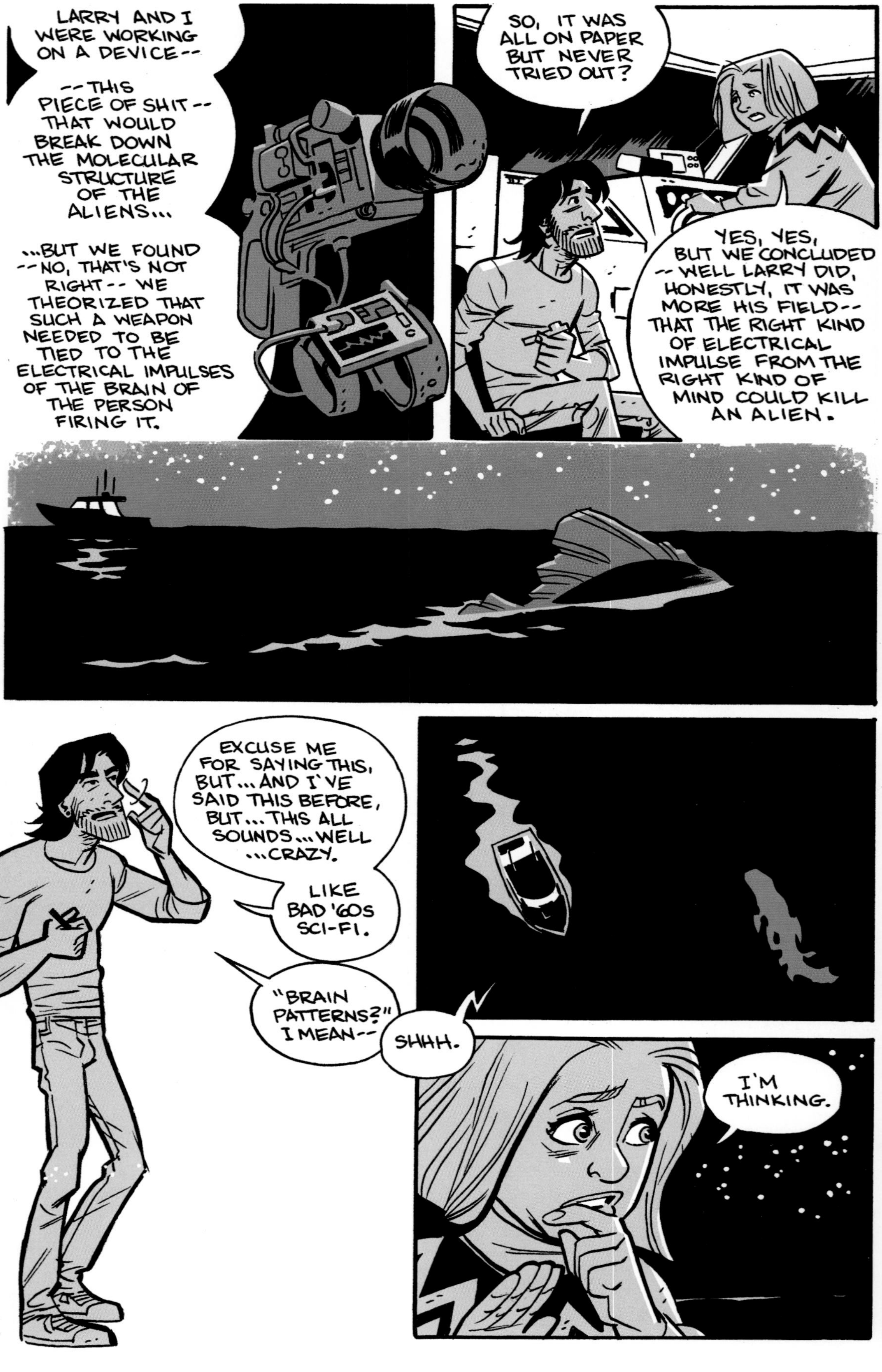
LARRY AND I WERE WORKING ON A DEVICE--
--THIS PIECE OF SHIT-- THAT WOULD BREAK DOWN THE MOLECULAR STRUCTURE OF THE ALIENS...
...BUT WE FOUND --NO, THAT'S NOT RIGHT-- WE THEORIZED THAT SUCH A WEAPON NEEDED TO BE TIED TO THE ELECTRICAL IMPULSES OF THE BRAIN OF THE PERSON FIRING IT.
SO, IT WAS ALL ON PAPER BUT NEVER TRIED OUT?
YES, YES, BUT WE CONCLUDED --WELL LARRY DID, HONESTLY, IT WAS MORE HIS FIELD-- THAT THE RIGHT KIND OF ELECTRICAL IMPULSE FROM THE RIGHT KIND OF MIND COULD KILL AN ALIEN.
EXCUSE ME FOR SAYING THIS, BUT...AND I'VE SAID THIS BEFORE, BUT...THIS ALL SOUNDS...WELL ...CRAZY.
LIKE BAD '60S SCI-FI.
"BRAIN PATTERNS?" I MEAN--
SHHH.
I'M THINKING.

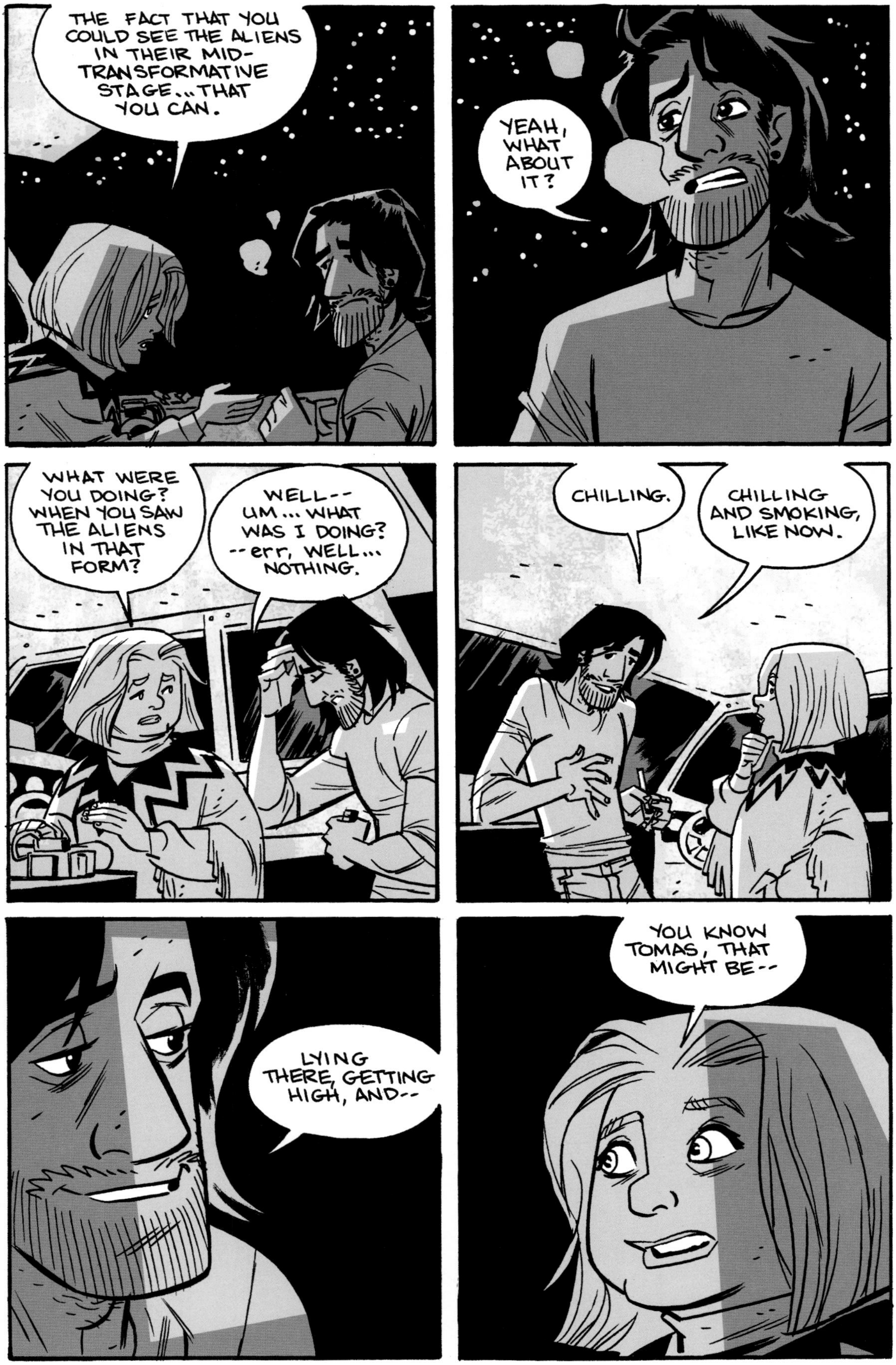
THE FACT THAT YOU COULD SEE THE ALIENS IN THEIR MID-TRANSFORMATIVE STAGE... THAT YOU CAN.
YEAH, WHAT ABOUT IT?
WHAT WERE YOU DOING? WHEN YOU SAW THE ALIENS IN THAT FORM?
WELL-- UM... WHAT WAS I DOING? --err, WELL... NOTHING.
CHILLING.
CHILLING AND SMOKING, LIKE NOW.
LYING THERE, GETTING HIGH, AND--
YOU KNOW TOMAS, THAT MIGHT BE--

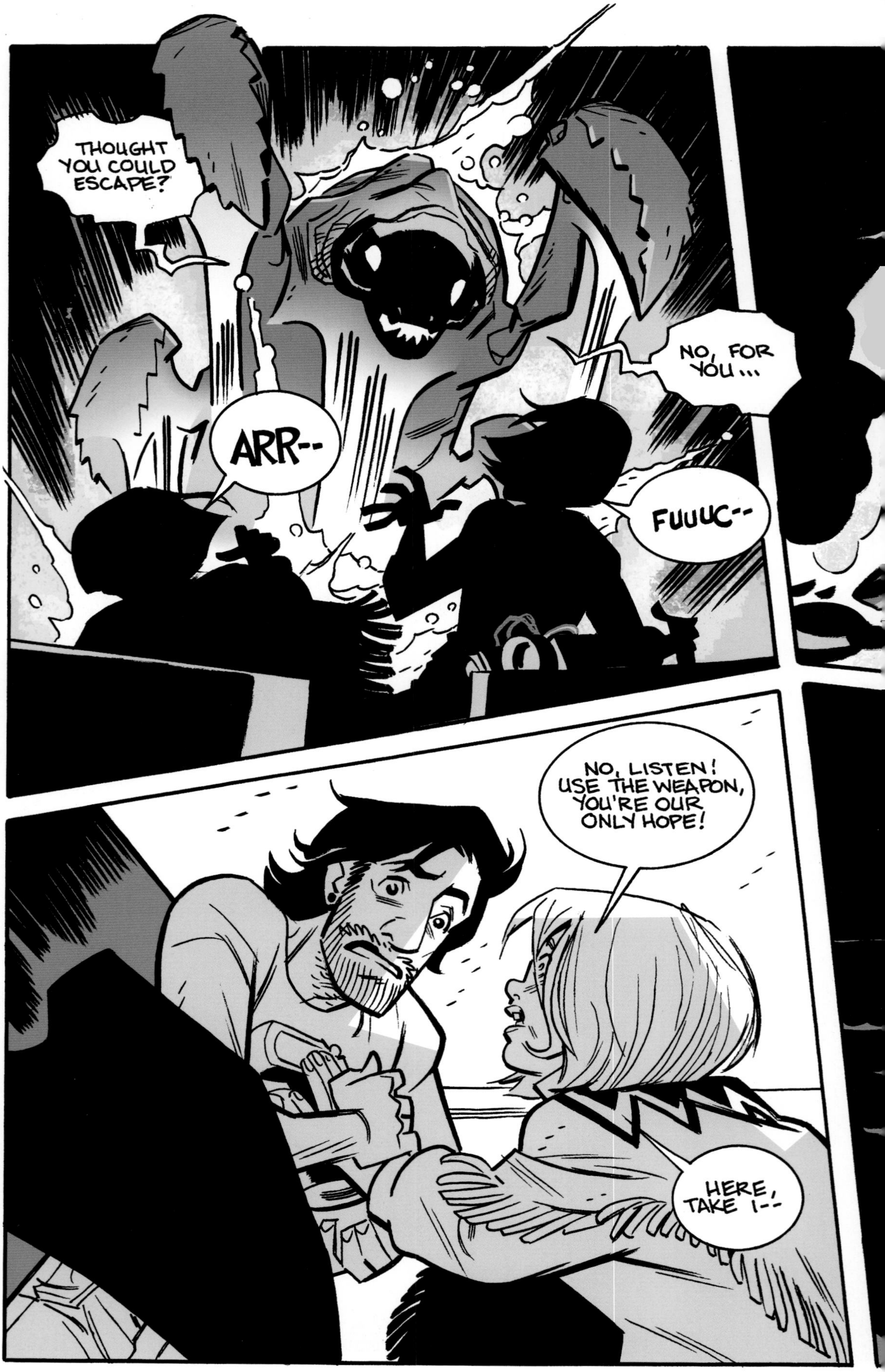
THOUGHT YOU COULD ESCAPE?
ARR--
NO, FOR YOU...
FUUUC--
NO, LISTEN! USE THE WEAPON, YOU'RE OUR ONLY HOPE!
HERE, TAKE I--

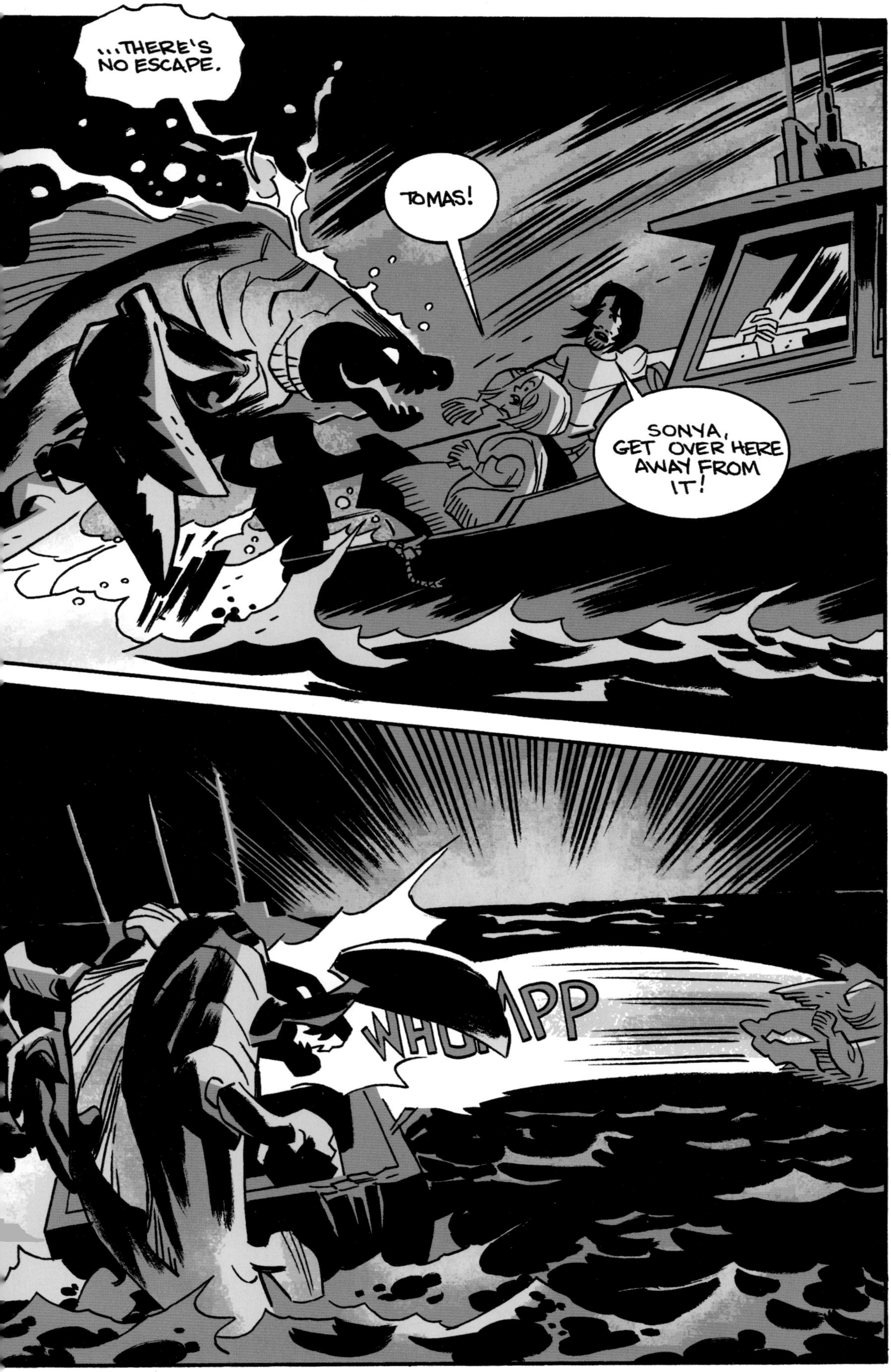
...THERE'S NO ESCAPE.
TOMAS!
SONYA, GET OVER HERE AWAY FROM IT!
WHUMPP

YOUR BRAIN...
YOUR BRAIN...
...I THINK THE DRUGS HAVE CHANGED IT...
USE THE WEAPON!
TRY TO--
TEST--
GLUB--
TRY TO--
--
--
PLIP

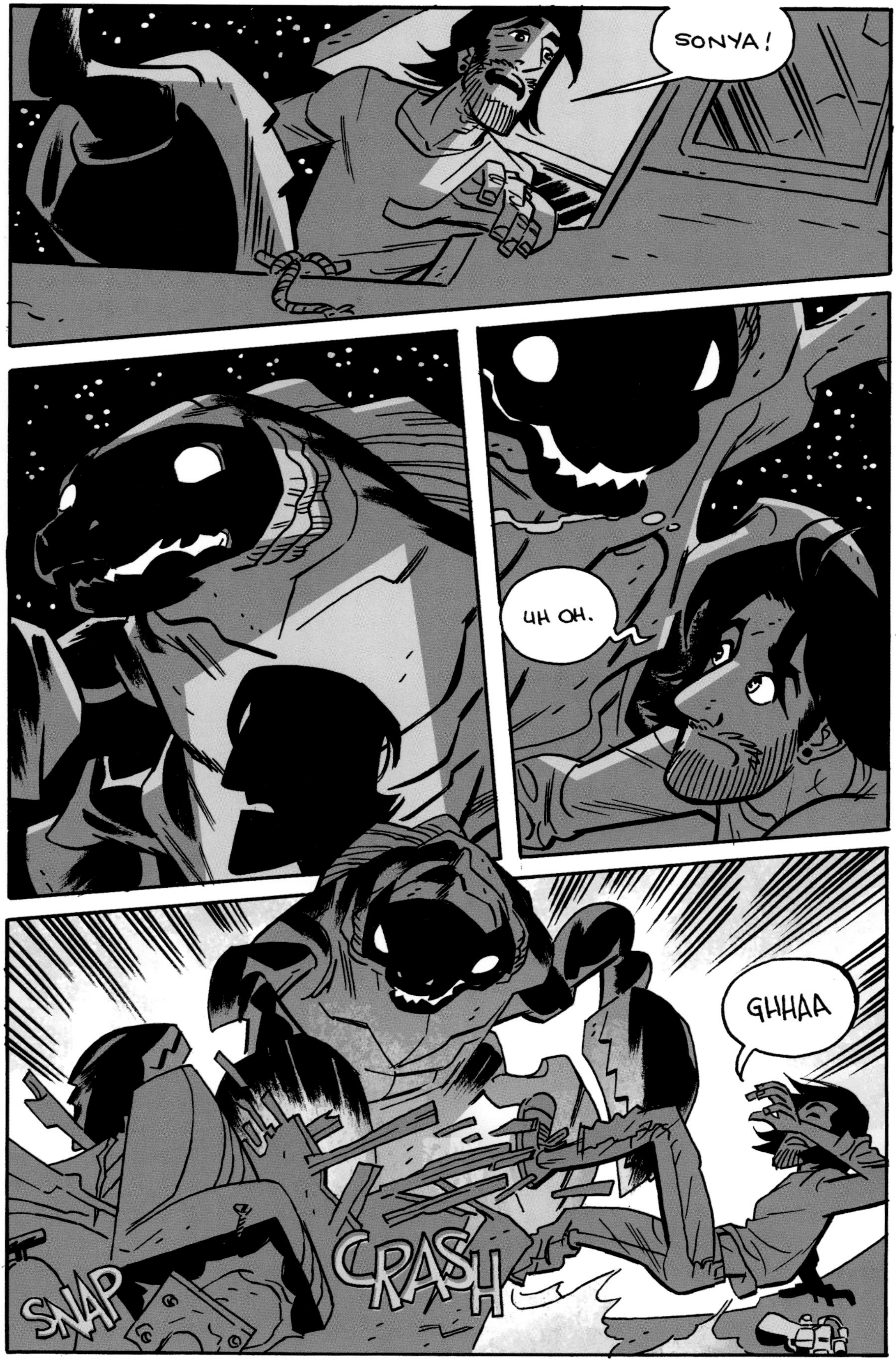
SONYA!
UH OH.
GHHAA
SNAP
CRASH

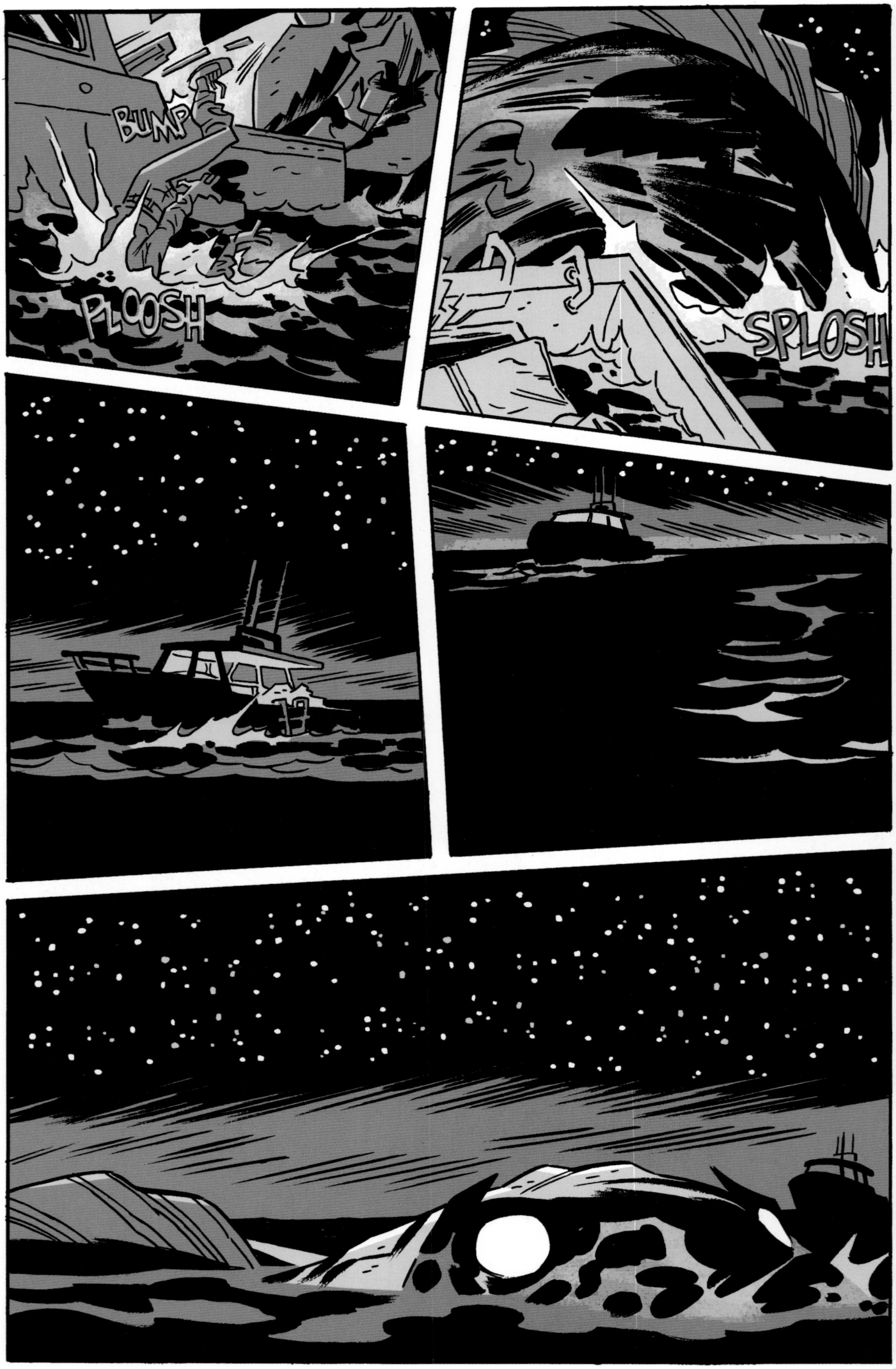
BUMP
PLOOSH
SPLOSH

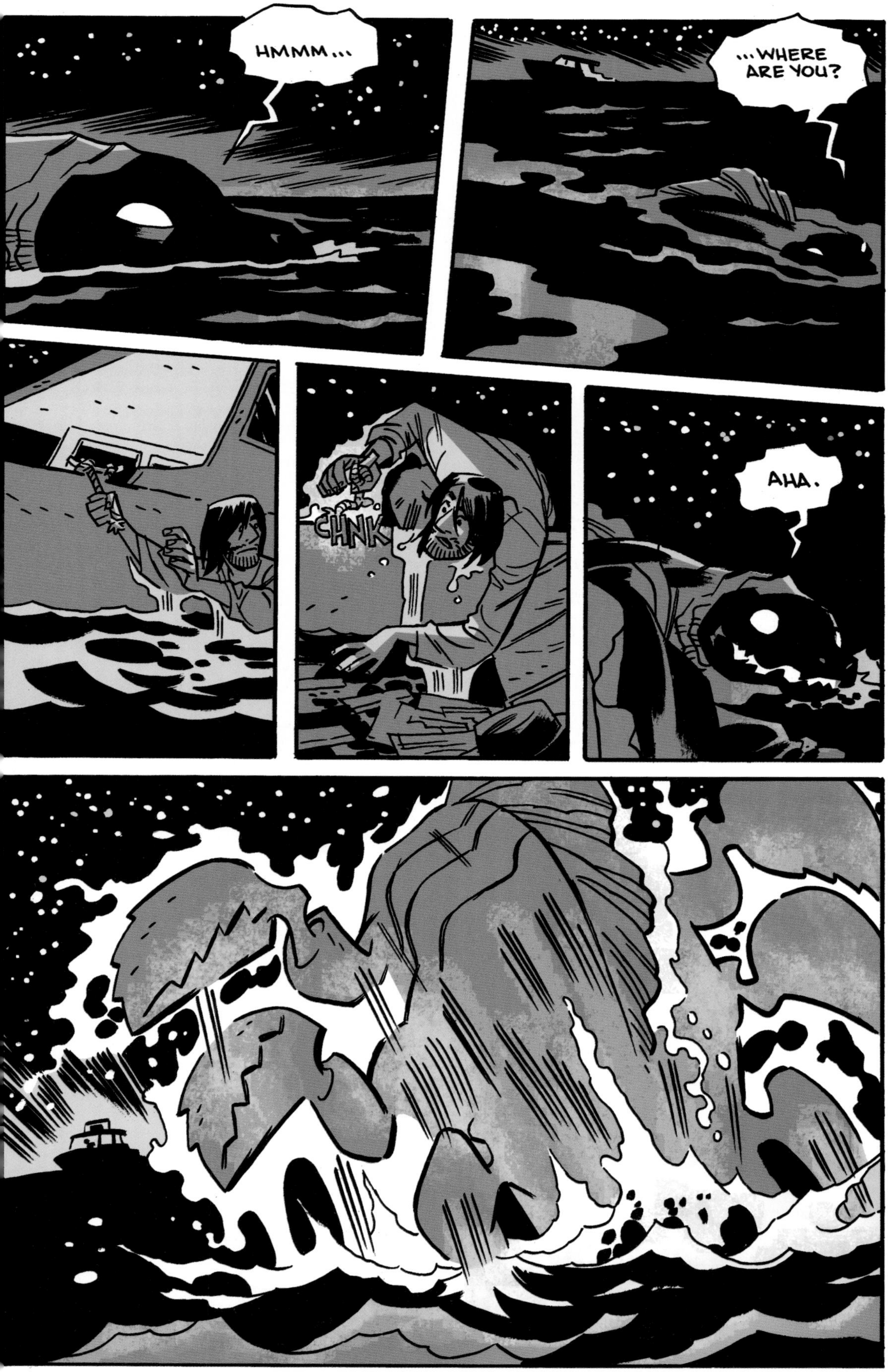
HMMM...
...WHERE ARE YOU?
CHNK
AHA.

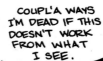COUPL'A WAYS I'M DEAD IF THIS DOESN'T WORK FROM WHAT I SEE.

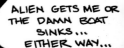ALIEN GETS ME OR THE DAMN BOAT SINKS... EITHER WAY...

HOPE THIS WORKS.

YOU WERE NEVER GOING TO ESCAPE ME, YOU DO KNOW THAT?

I'M A HUNTER. LOVE TO. IN HUMAN FORM IT'S DUCKS AND SUCH. IN MY TRUE FORM... WELL...

YOU'RE MORE FUN THAN A DUCK.

CRUNCH

KSH

HOPE I'M STONED ENOUGH.

FUCK.

I WISH I'D SMOKED MORE POT.

FAASH

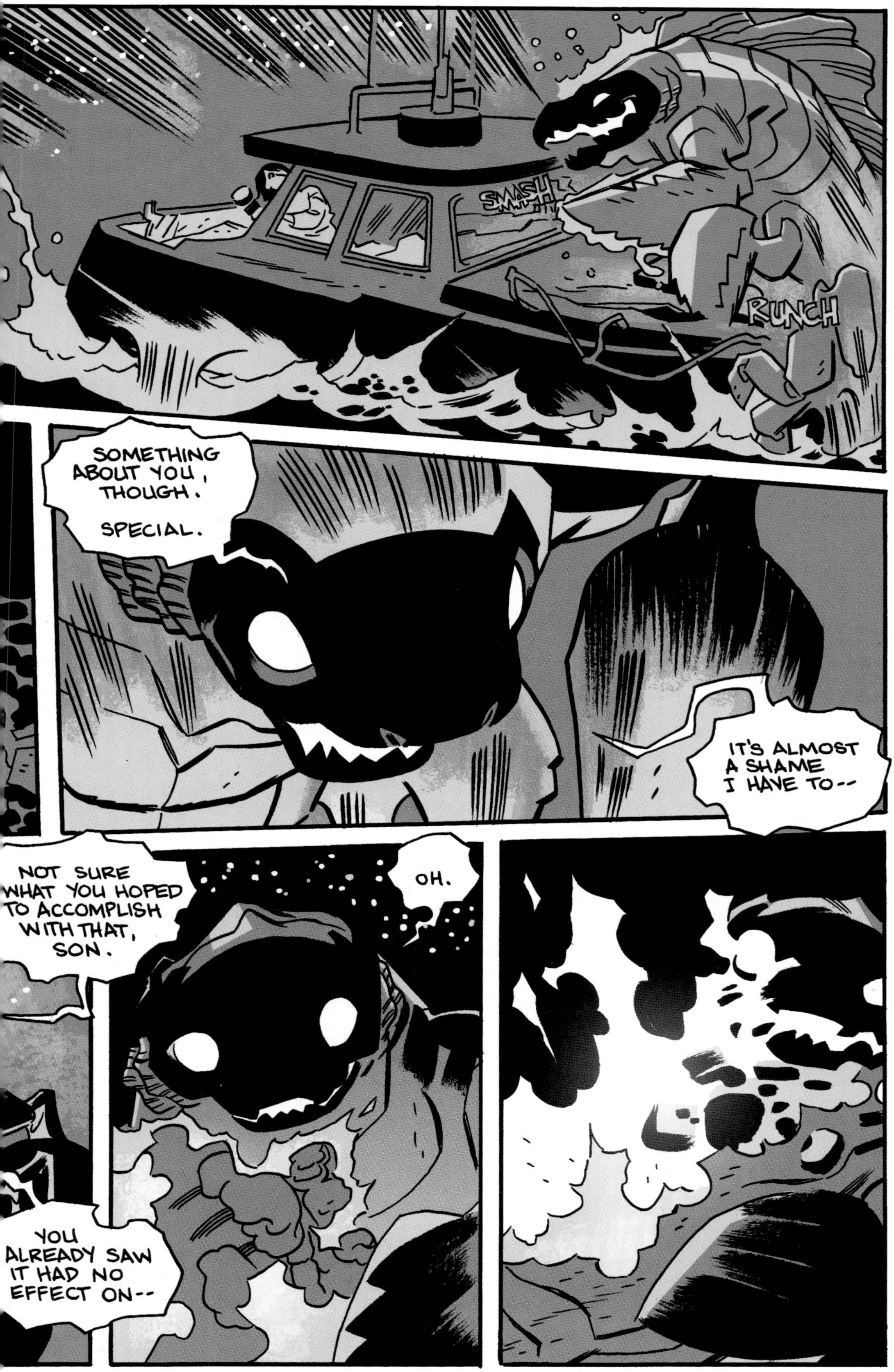
SMASH
RUNCH
SOMETHING ABOUT YOU, THOUGH.
SPECIAL.
IT'S ALMOST A SHAME I HAVE TO--
NOT SURE WHAT YOU HOPED TO ACCOMPLISH WITH THAT, SON.
OH.
YOU ALREADY SAW IT HAD NO EFFECT ON--

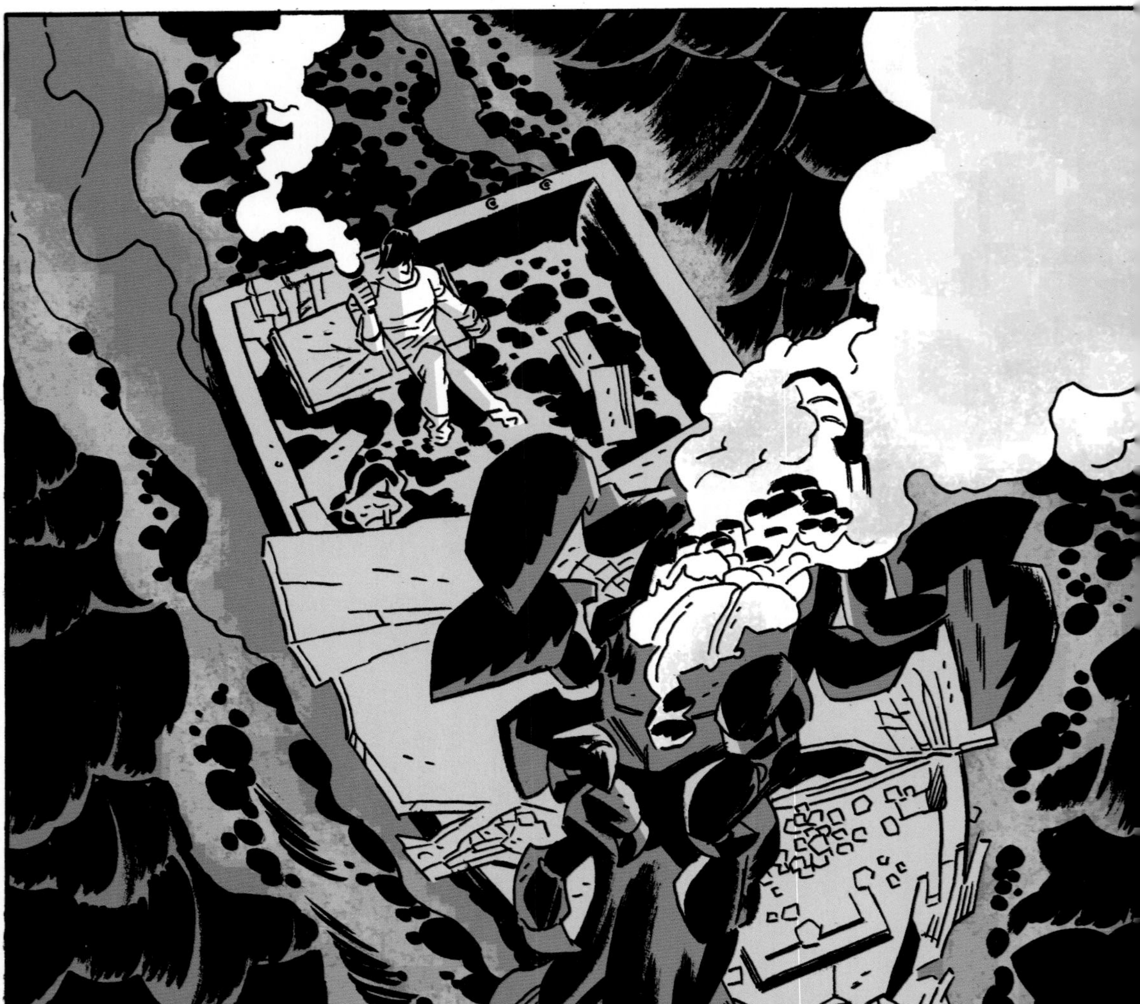
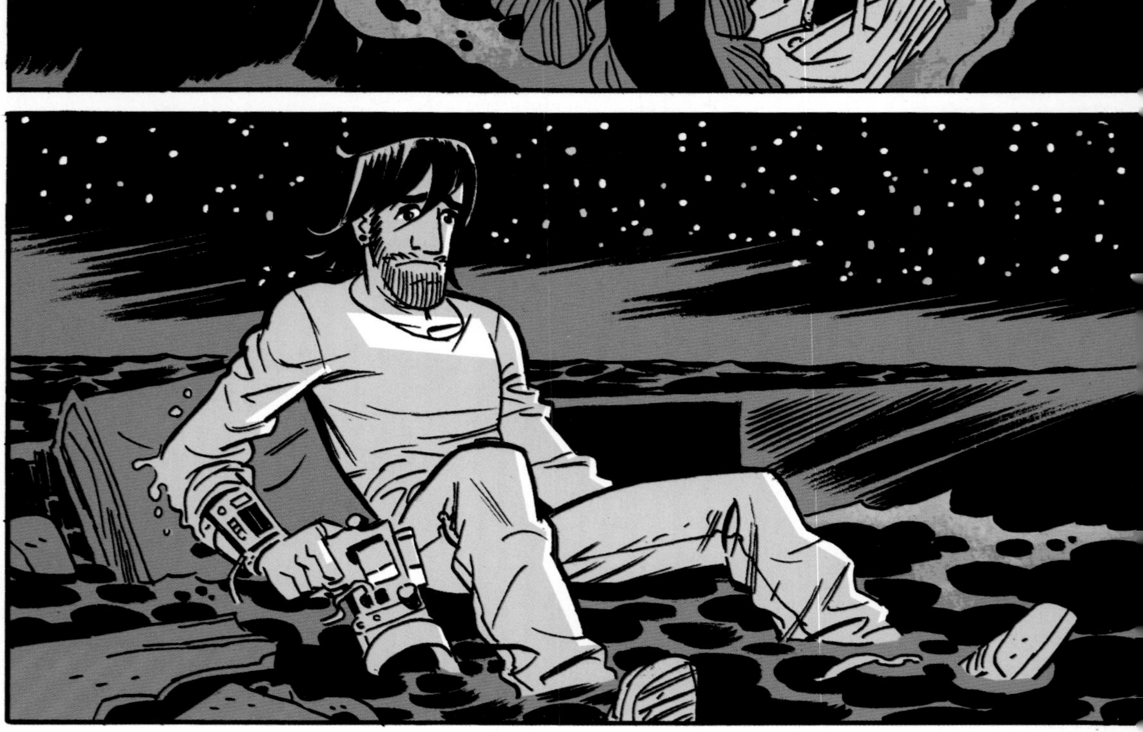

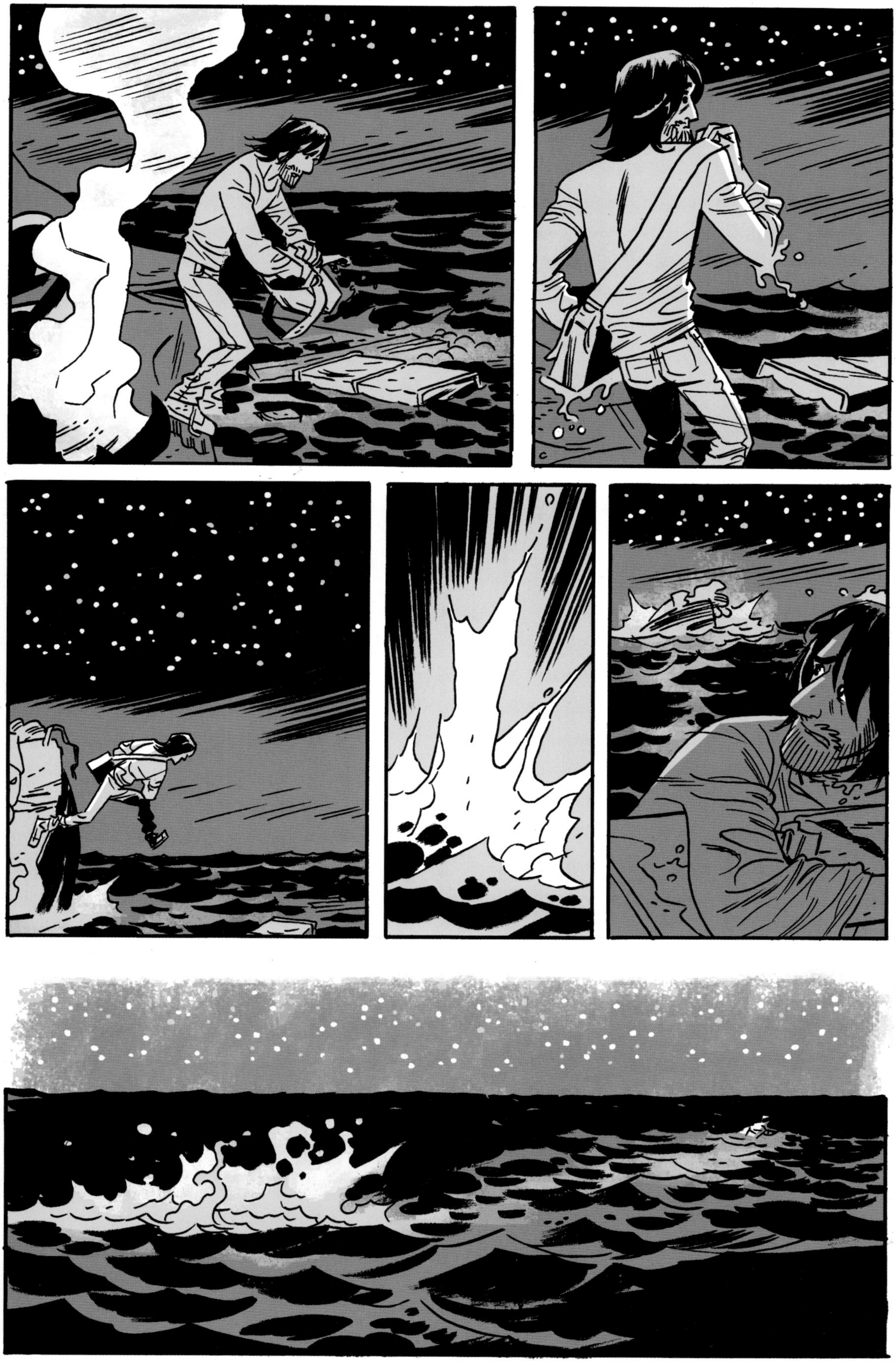

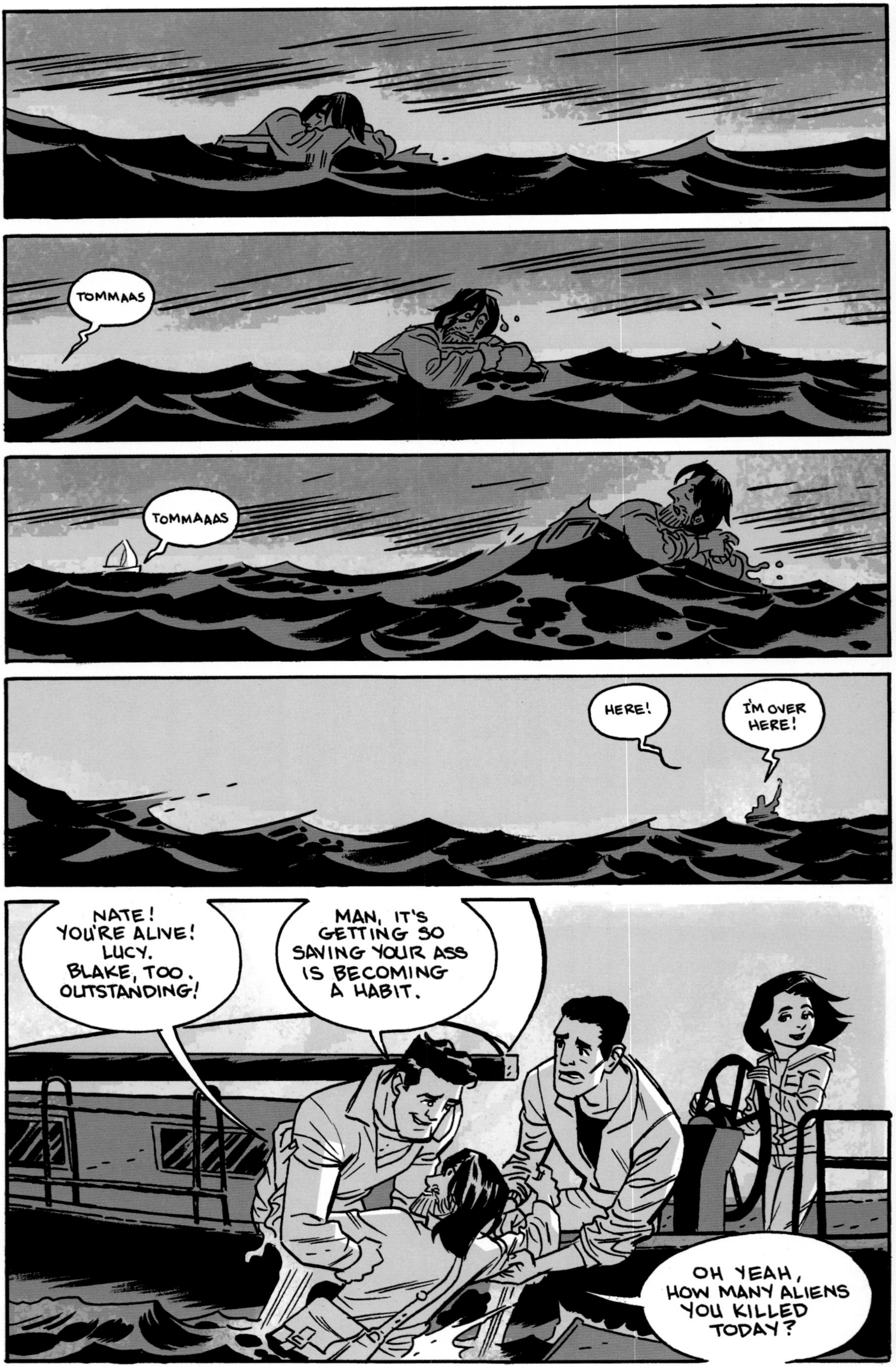
TOMMAAS
TOMMAAAS
HERE!
I'M OVER HERE!
NATE! YOU'RE ALIVE! LUCY. BLAKE, TOO. OUTSTANDING!
MAN, IT'S GETTING SO SAVING YOUR ASS IS BECOMING A HABIT.
OH YEAH, HOW MANY ALIENS YOU KILLED TODAY?

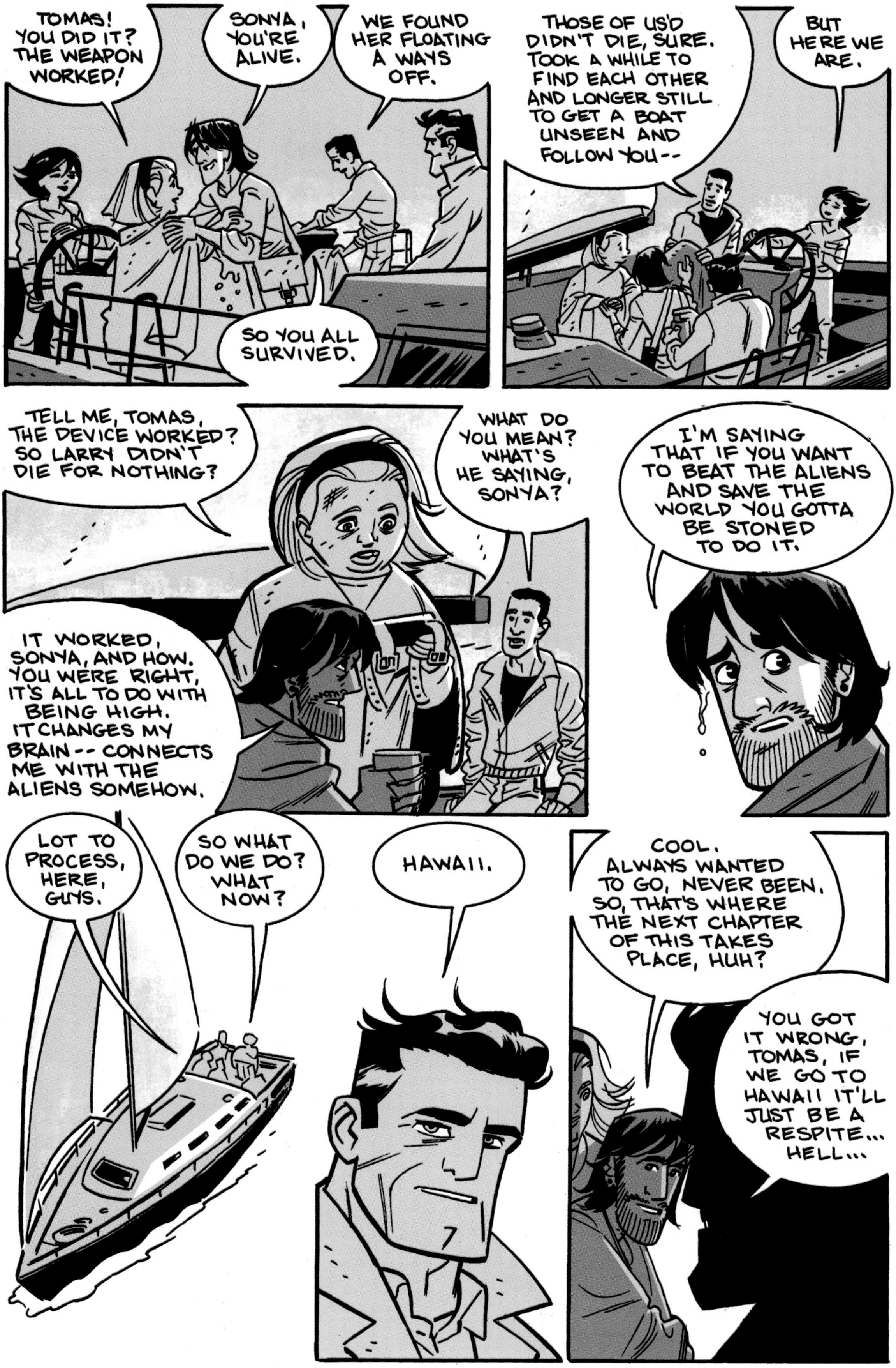
TOMAS! YOU DID IT? THE WEAPON WORKED!
SONYA, YOU'RE ALIVE.
WE FOUND HER FLOATING A WAYS OFF.
SO YOU ALL SURVIVED.
THOSE OF US'D DIDN'T DIE, SURE. TOOK A WHILE TO FIND EACH OTHER AND LONGER STILL TO GET A BOAT UNSEEN AND FOLLOW YOU--
BUT HERE WE ARE.
TELL ME, TOMAS, THE DEVICE WORKED? SO LARRY DIDN'T DIE FOR NOTHING?
WHAT DO YOU MEAN? WHAT'S HE SAYING, SONYA?
IT WORKED, SONYA, AND HOW. YOU WERE RIGHT, IT'S ALL TO DO WITH BEING HIGH. IT CHANGES MY BRAIN-- CONNECTS ME WITH THE ALIENS SOMEHOW.
I'M SAYING THAT IF YOU WANT TO BEAT THE ALIENS AND SAVE THE WORLD YOU GOTTA BE STONED TO DO IT.
LOT TO PROCESS, HERE, GUYS.
SO WHAT DO WE DO? WHAT NOW?
HAWAII.
COOL. ALWAYS WANTED TO GO, NEVER BEEN. SO, THAT'S WHERE THE NEXT CHAPTER OF THIS TAKES PLACE, HUH?
YOU GOT IT WRONG, TOMAS, IF WE GO TO HAWAII IT'LL JUST BE A RESPITE... HELL...

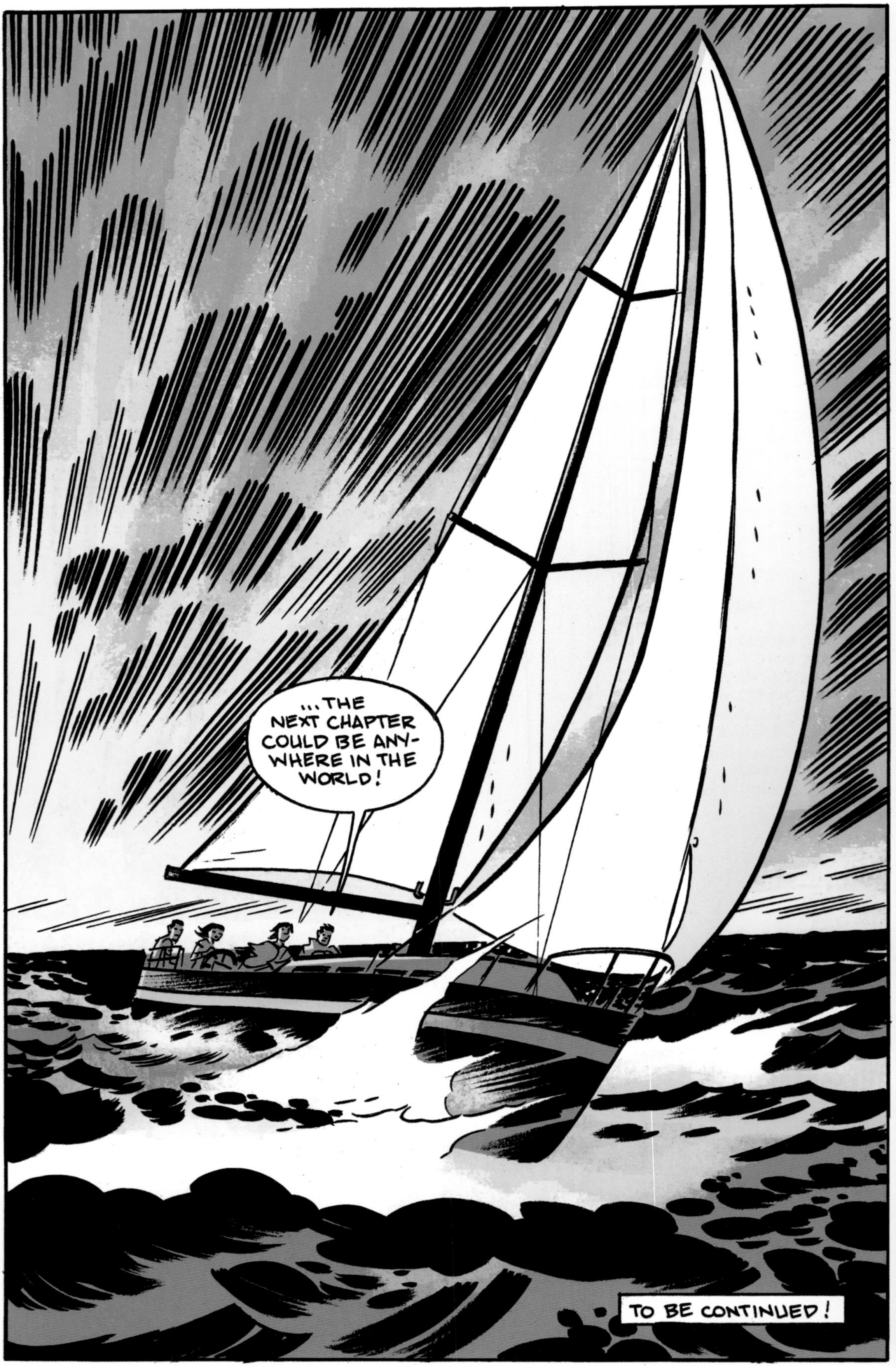
...THE NEXT CHAPTER COULD BE ANY-WHERE IN THE WORLD!
TO BE CONTINUED!

THE SAVIORS

CREATED BY
JAMES ROBINSON
& J.BONE

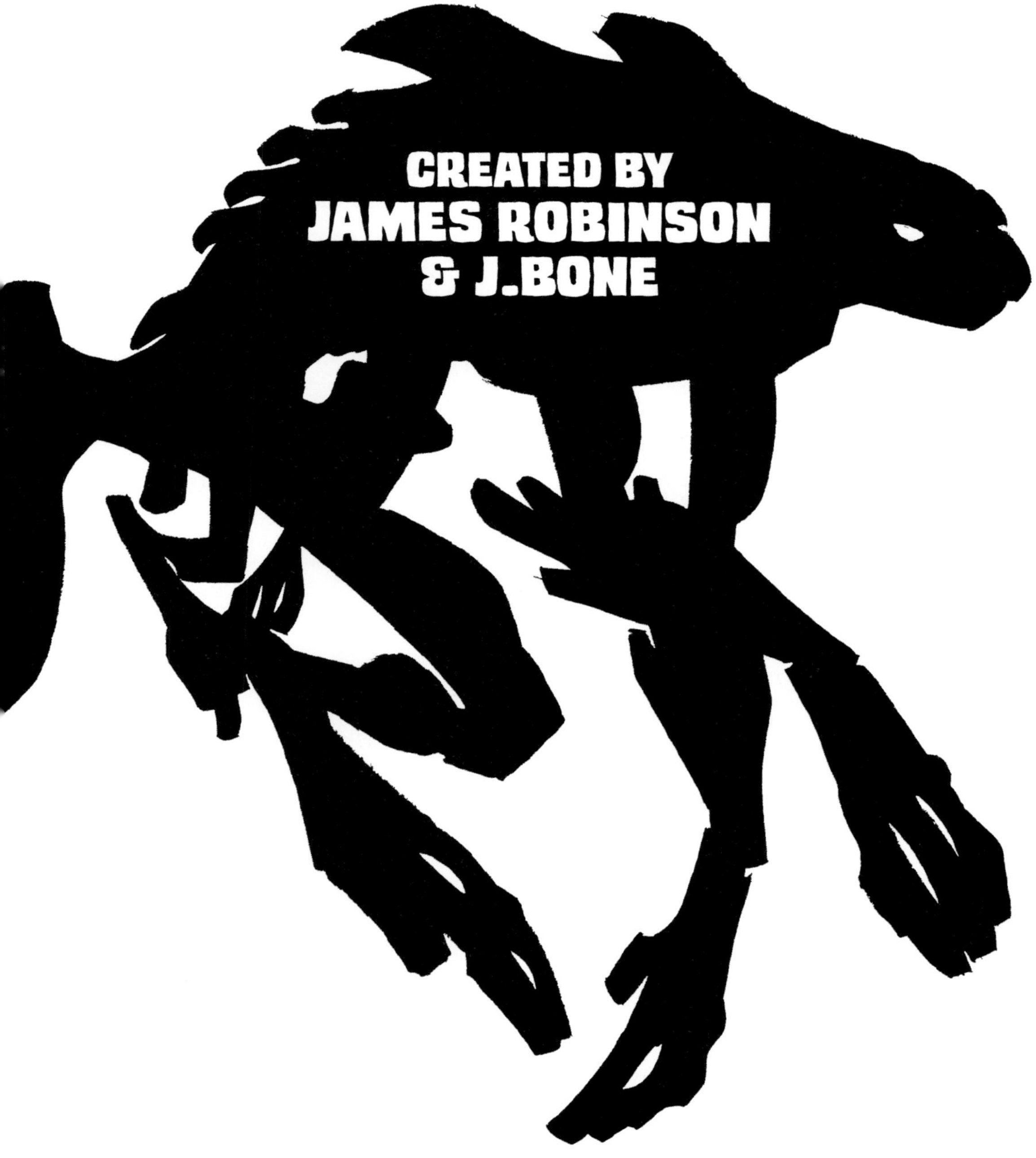

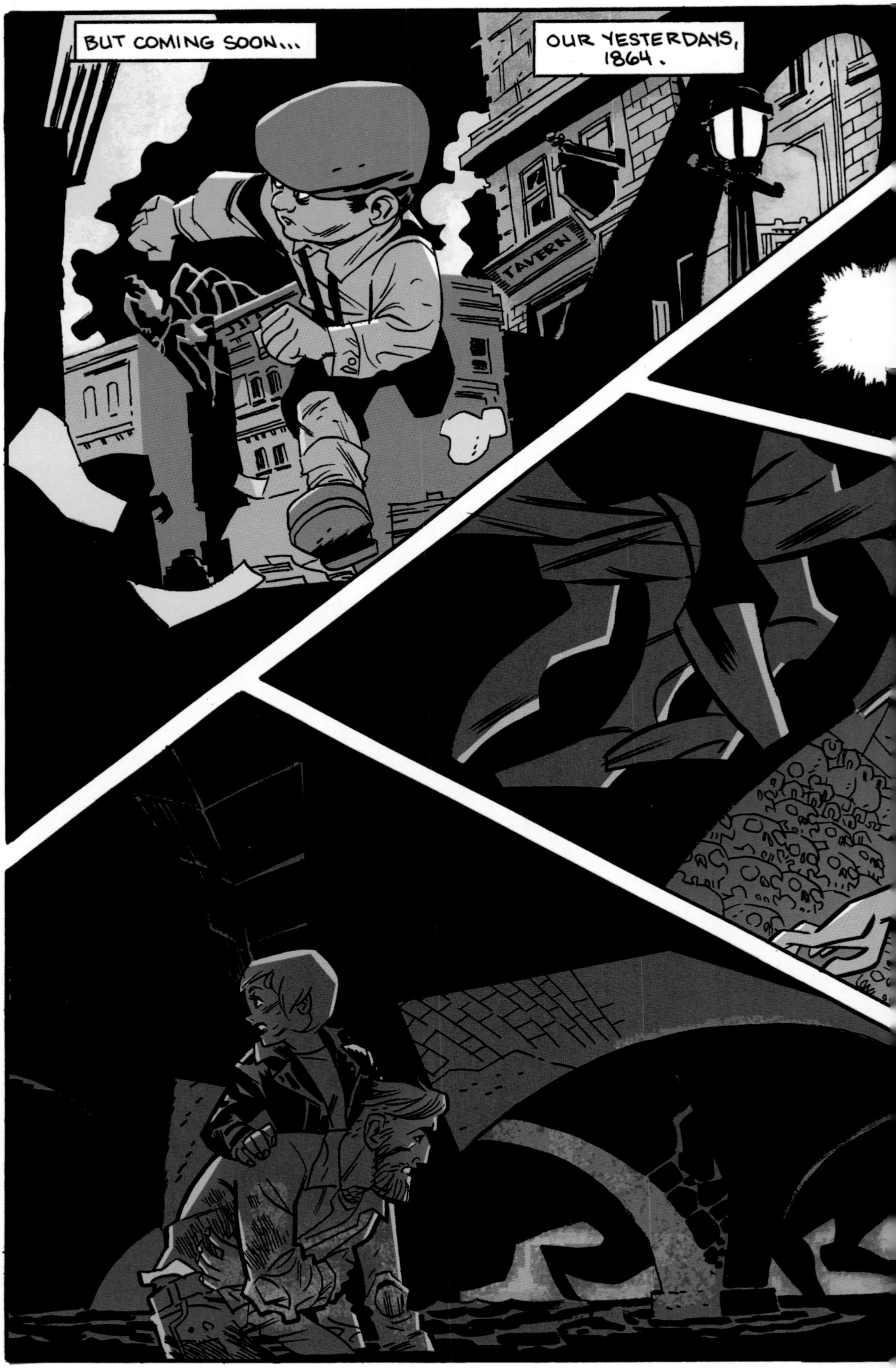
BUT COMING SOON...
OUR YESTERDAYS, 1864.
TAVERN

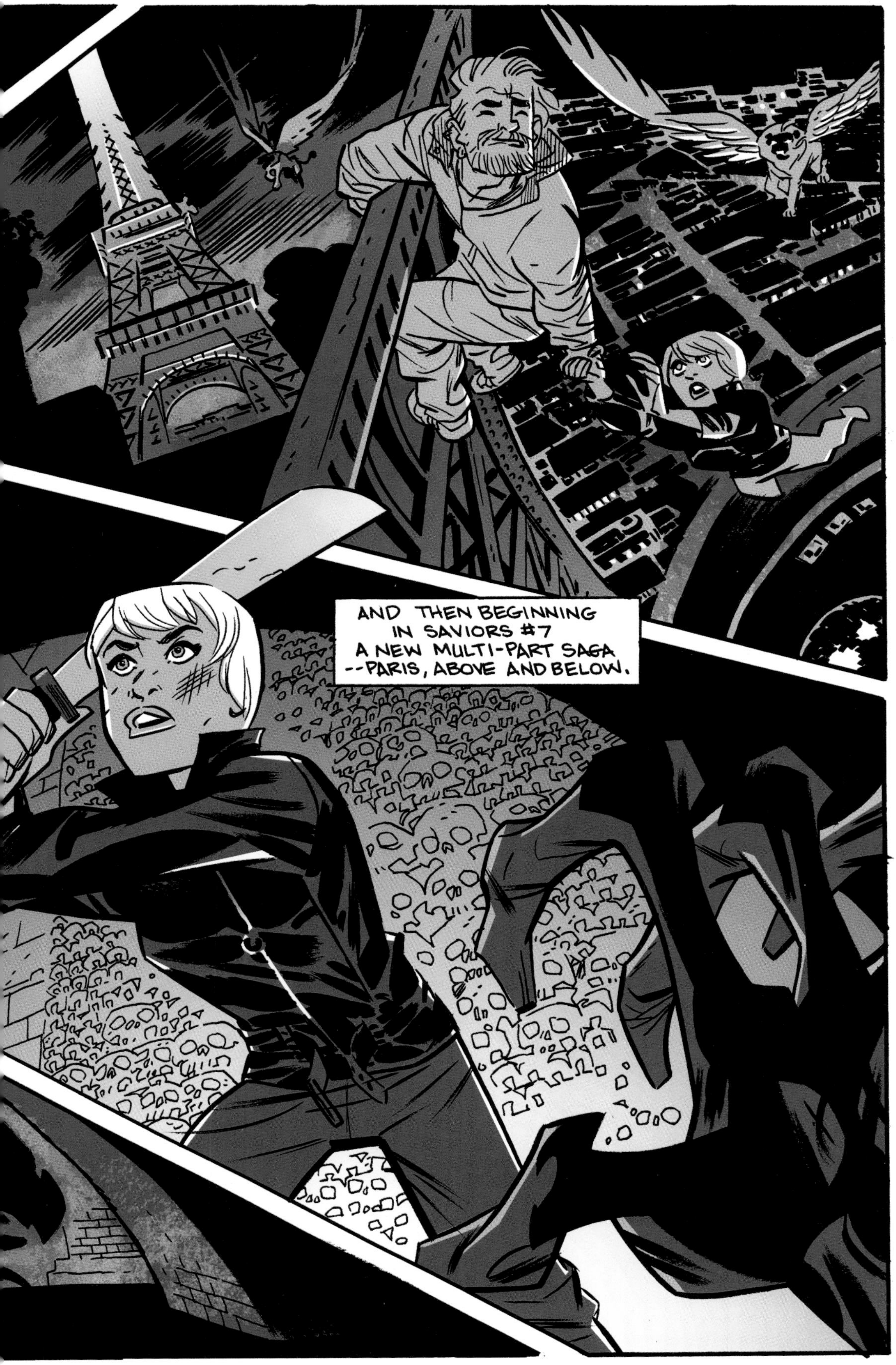
AND THEN BEGINNING
IN SAVIORS #7
A NEW MULTI-PART SAGA
--PARIS, ABOVE AND BELOW.

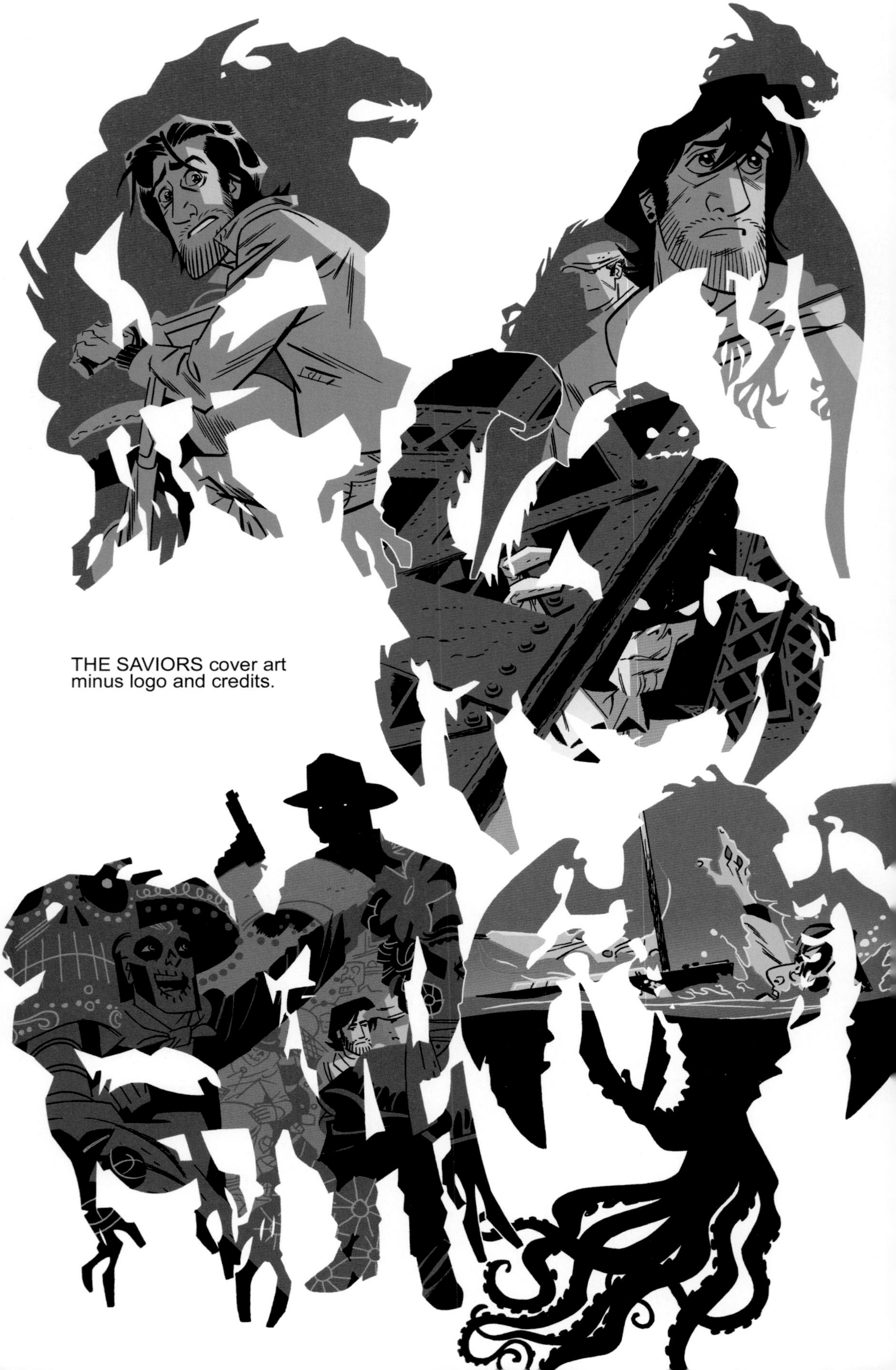

THE SAVIORS cover art
minus logo and credits.

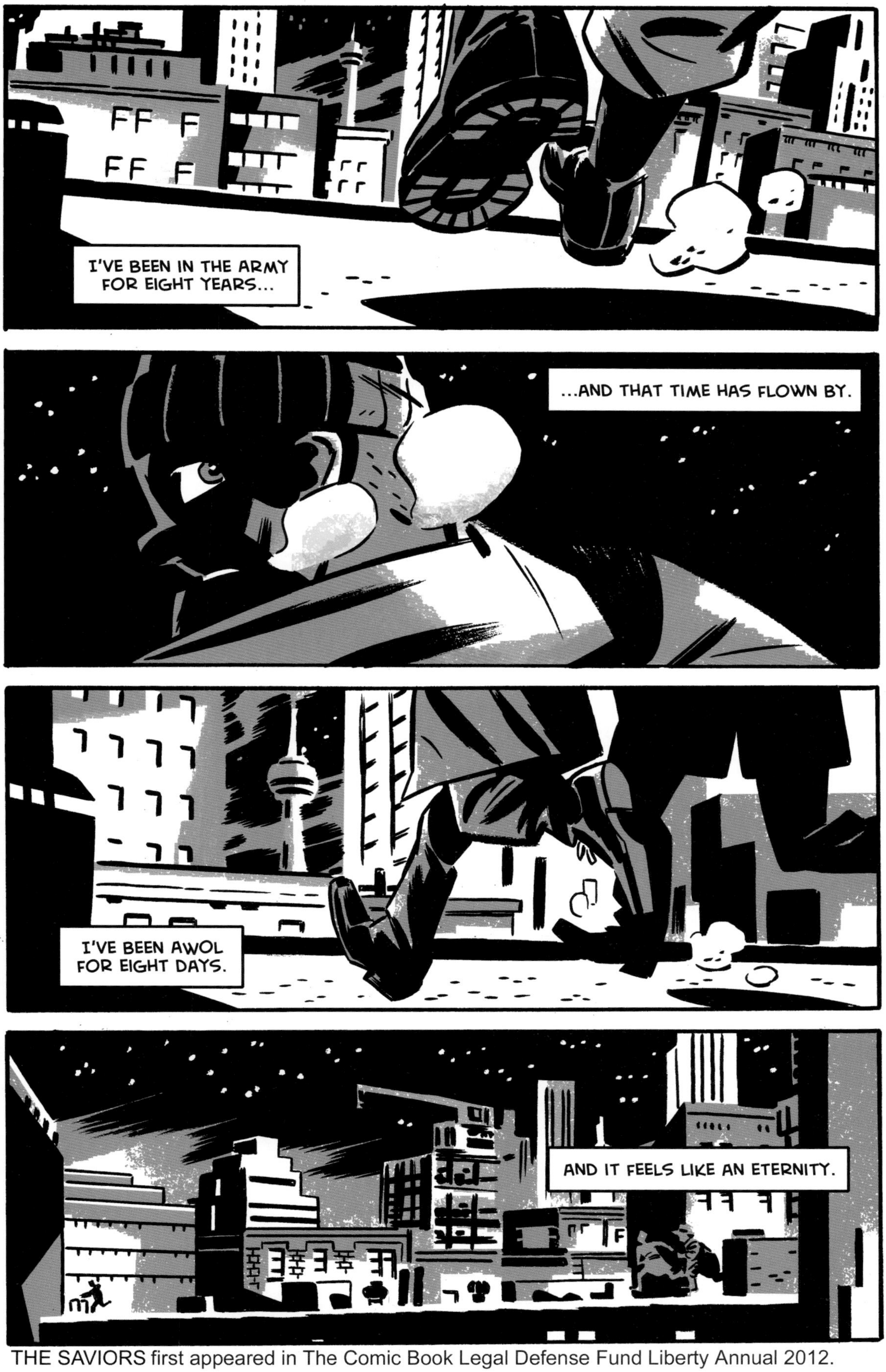
I'VE BEEN IN THE ARMY FOR EIGHT YEARS...
...AND THAT TIME HAS FLOWN BY.
I'VE BEEN AWOL FOR EIGHT DAYS.
AND IT FEELS LIKE AN ETERNITY.

THE SAVIORS first appeared in The Comic Book Legal Defense Fund Liberty Annual 2012.

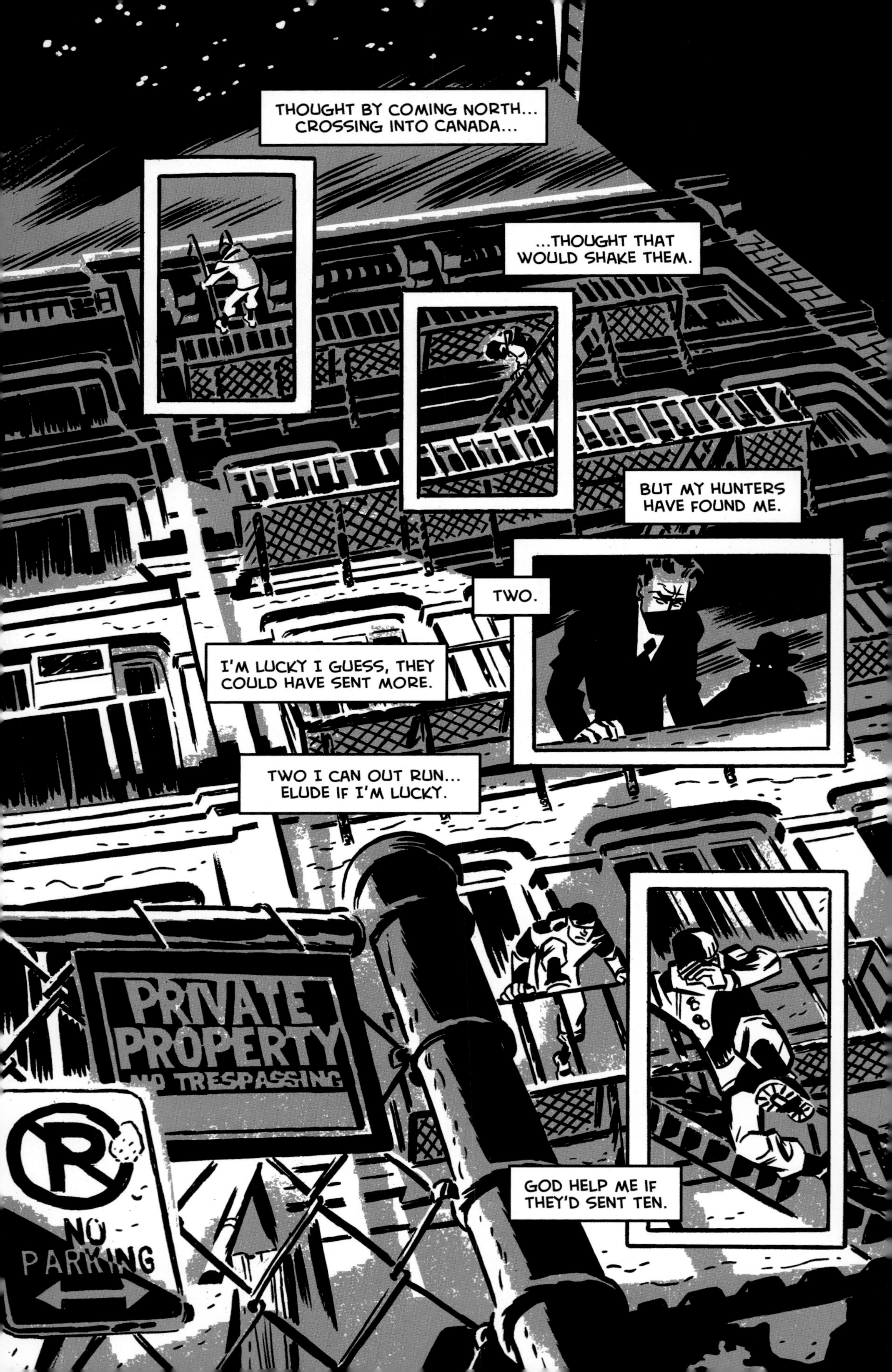
THOUGHT BY COMING NORTH... CROSSING INTO CANADA...
...THOUGHT THAT WOULD SHAKE THEM.
BUT MY HUNTERS HAVE FOUND ME.
TWO.
I'M LUCKY I GUESS, THEY COULD HAVE SENT MORE.
TWO I CAN OUT RUN... ELUDE IF I'M LUCKY.
PRIVATE PROPERTY
NO TRESPASSING
NO PARKING
GOD HELP ME IF THEY'D SENT TEN.

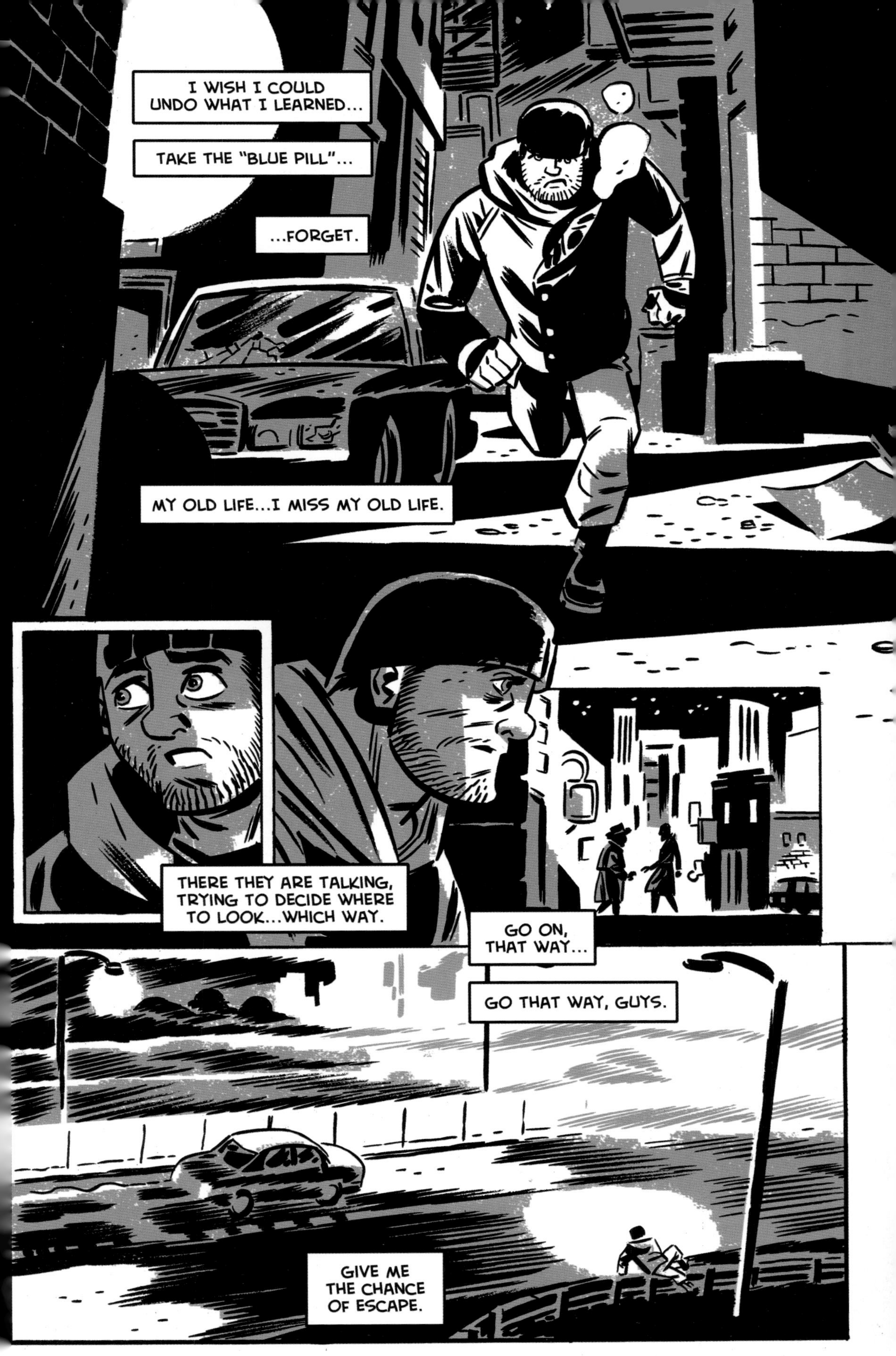
I WISH I COULD UNDO WHAT I LEARNED...
TAKE THE "BLUE PILL"...
...FORGET.
MY OLD LIFE...I MISS MY OLD LIFE.
THERE THEY ARE TALKING, TRYING TO DECIDE WHERE TO LOOK...WHICH WAY.
GO ON, THAT WAY...
GO THAT WAY, GUYS.
GIVE ME THE CHANCE OF ESCAPE.

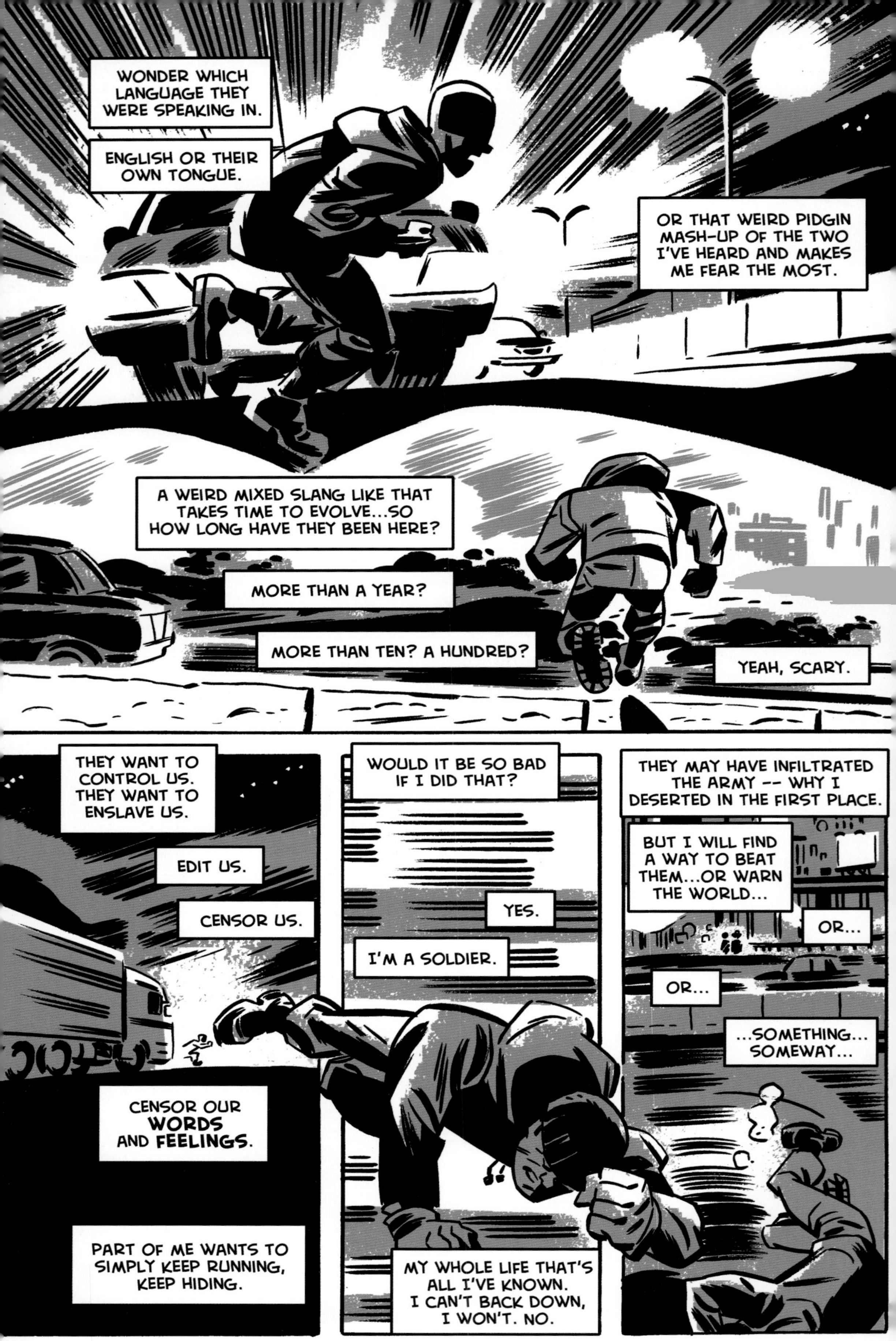
WONDER WHICH LANGUAGE THEY WERE SPEAKING IN.
ENGLISH OR THEIR OWN TONGUE.
OR THAT WEIRD PIDGIN MASH-UP OF THE TWO I'VE HEARD AND MAKES ME FEAR THE MOST.
A WEIRD MIXED SLANG LIKE THAT TAKES TIME TO EVOLVE...SO HOW LONG HAVE THEY BEEN HERE?
MORE THAN A YEAR?
MORE THAN TEN? A HUNDRED?
YEAH, SCARY.
THEY WANT TO CONTROL US. THEY WANT TO ENSLAVE US.
EDIT US.
CENSOR US.
CENSOR OUR **WORDS** AND **FEELINGS**.
PART OF ME WANTS TO SIMPLY KEEP RUNNING, KEEP HIDING.
WOULD IT BE SO BAD IF I DID THAT?
YES.
I'M A SOLDIER.
MY WHOLE LIFE THAT'S ALL I'VE KNOWN. I CAN'T BACK DOWN, I WON'T. NO.
THEY MAY HAVE INFILTRATED THE ARMY -- WHY I DESERTED IN THE FIRST PLACE.
BUT I WILL FIND A WAY TO BEAT THEM...OR WARN THE WORLD...
OR...
OR...
...SOMETHING... SOMEWAY...

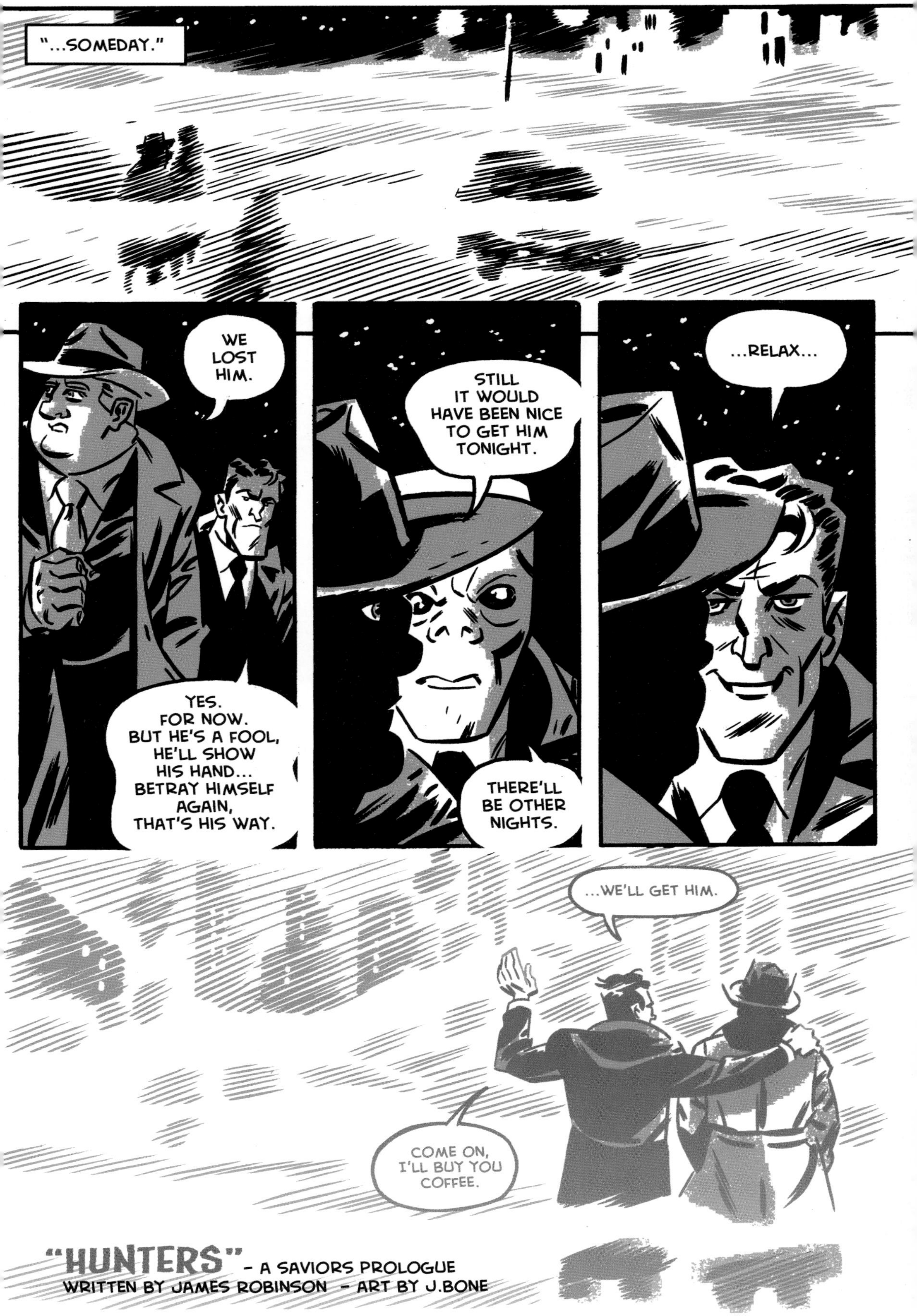
"...SOMEDAY."
WE LOST HIM.
YES. FOR NOW. BUT HE'S A FOOL, HE'LL SHOW HIS HAND... BETRAY HIMSELF AGAIN, THAT'S HIS WAY.
STILL IT WOULD HAVE BEEN NICE TO GET HIM TONIGHT.
THERE'LL BE OTHER NIGHTS.
...RELAX...
...WE'LL GET HIM.
COME ON, I'LL BUY YOU COFFEE.

"HUNTERS" - A SAVIORS PROLOGUE
WRITTEN BY JAMES ROBINSON - ART BY J.BONE

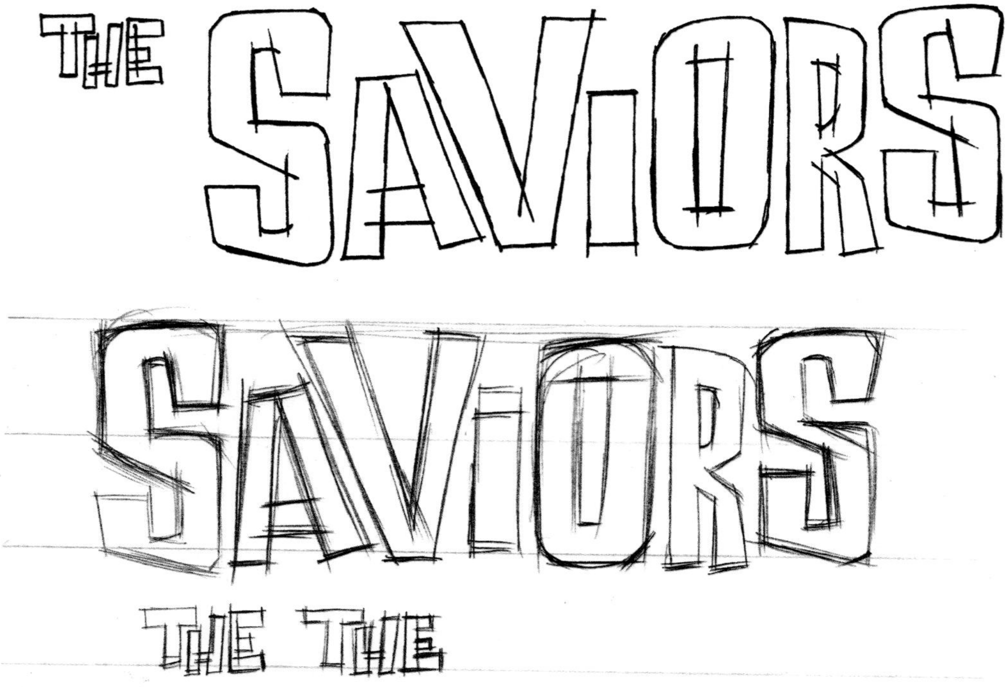
THE SAVIORS
SAVIORS
THE THE

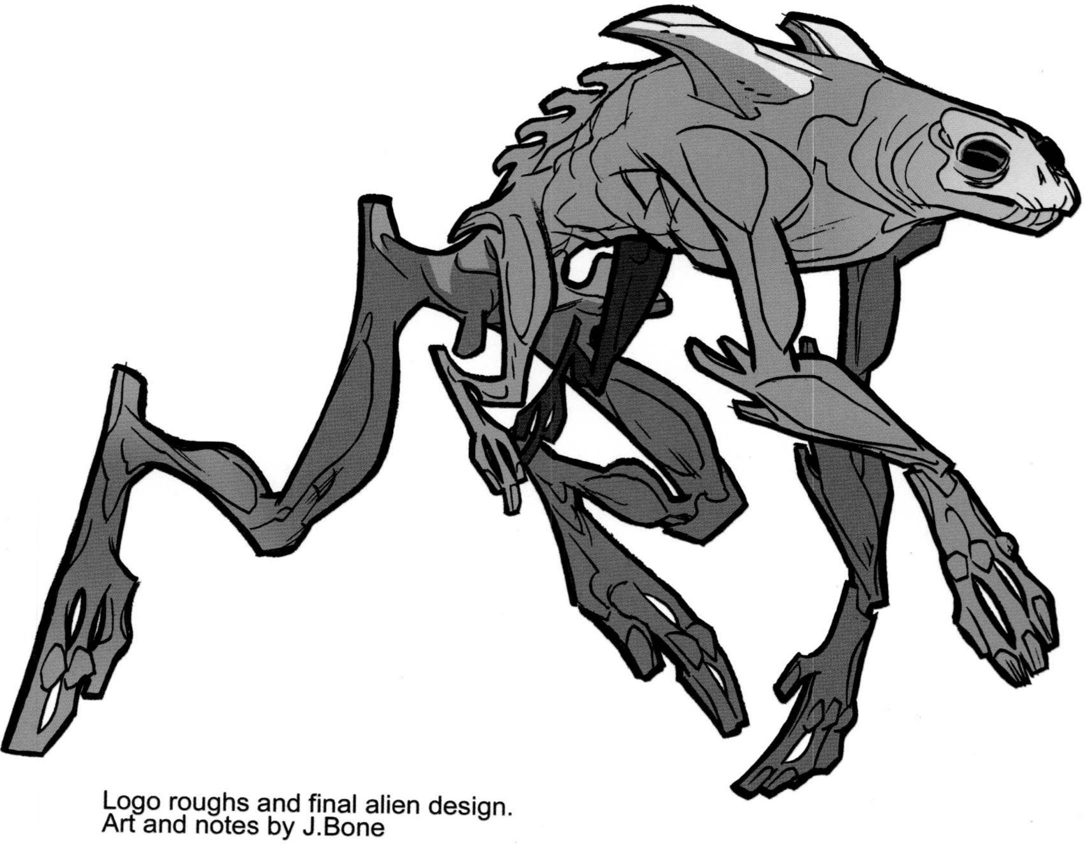

Logo roughs and final alien design.
Art and notes by J.Bone

Tomas Ramirez -- the look for Tomas started working for me when I decided to base him on my friend Alex. He's 6'5" (or 6'7"...tall. Very tall. And handsome). Height would make Tomas feel like an outsider and be a disadvantage when trying to hide in a crowd.

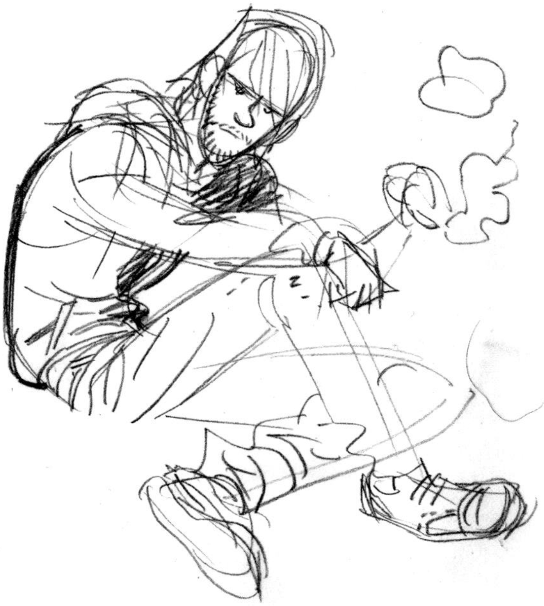

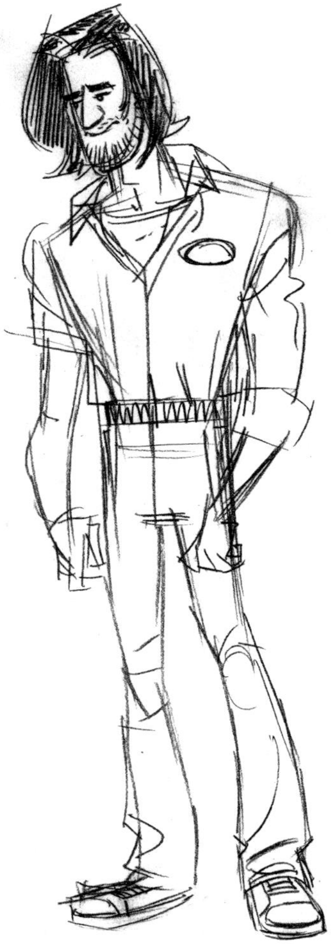

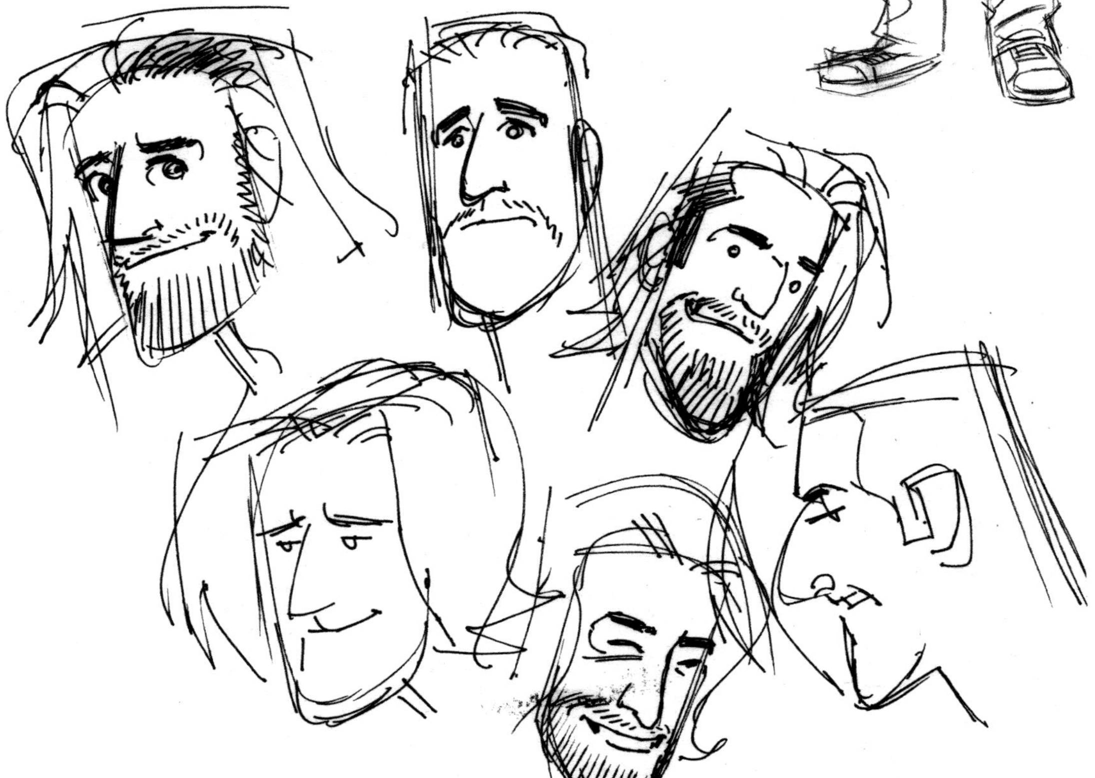

Fun Fact -- Alex is also the model for Jon from the Eisner Award-winning Image comics series SEX CRIMINALS.

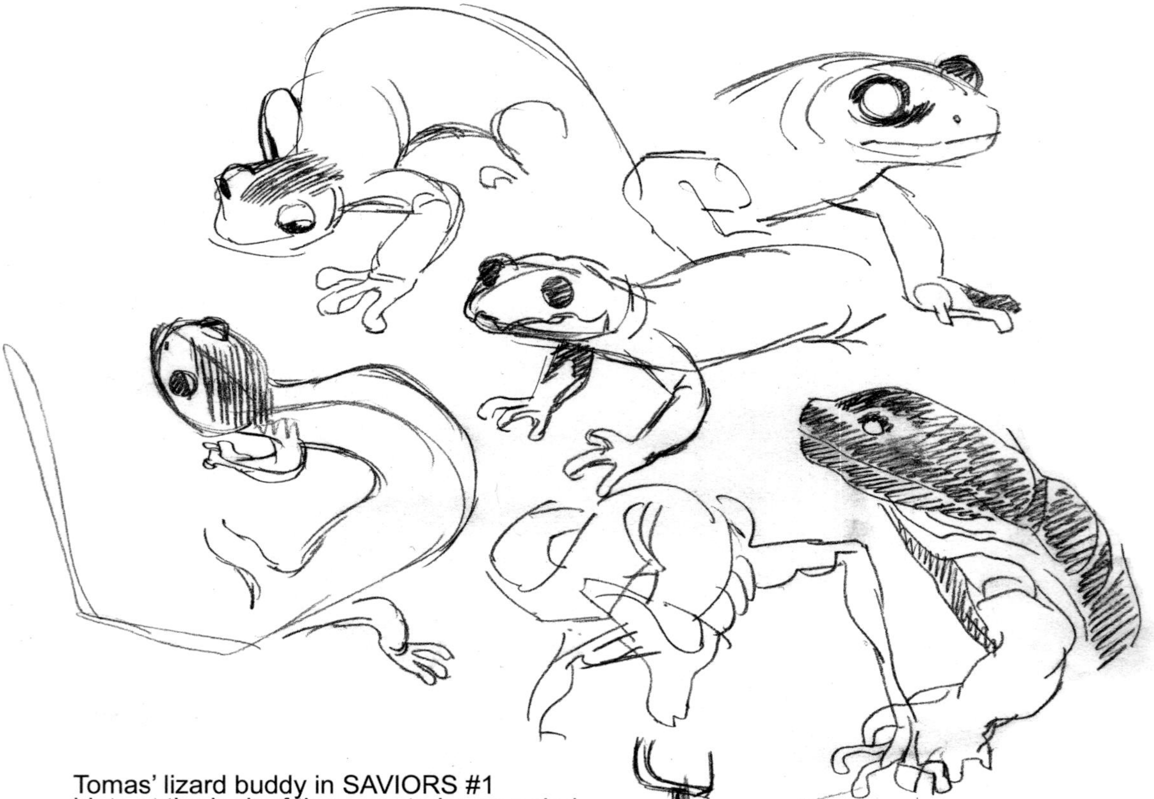

Tomas' lizard buddy in SAVIORS #1
hints at the look of the soon-to-be-revealed
monstrous alien transformation.

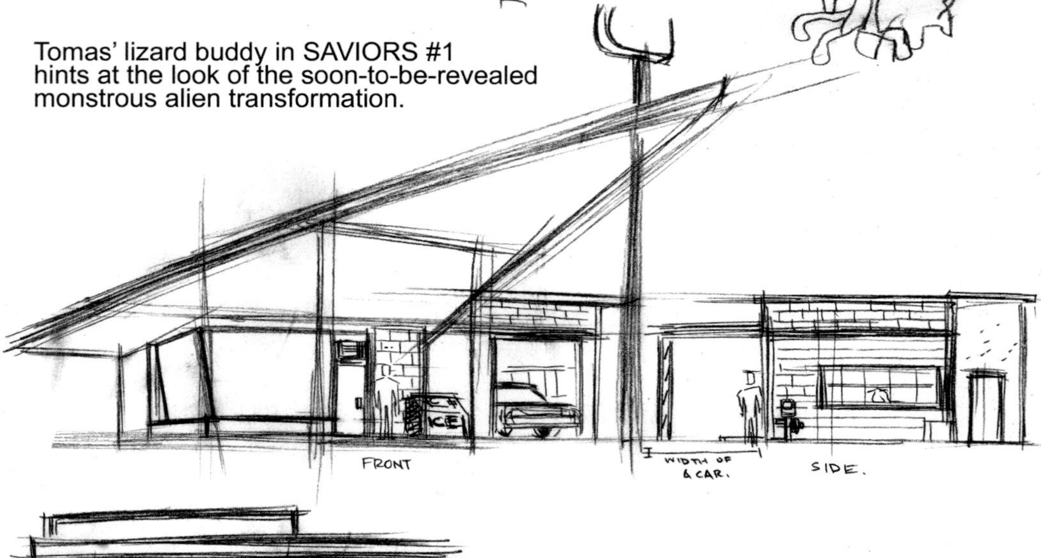
ICE
FRONT
WIDTH OF A CAR.
SIDE.

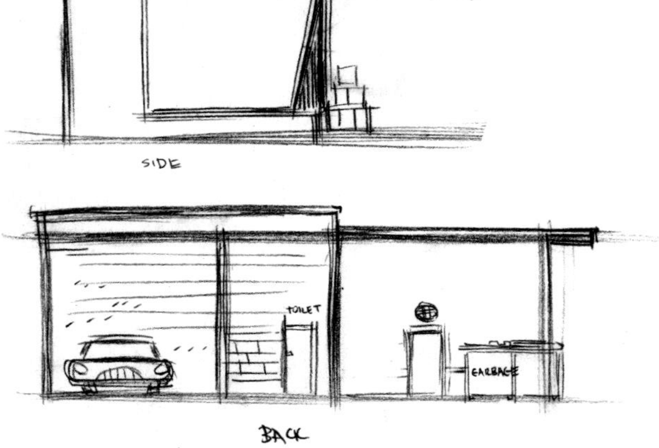
SIDE
TOILET
GARBAGE
BACK

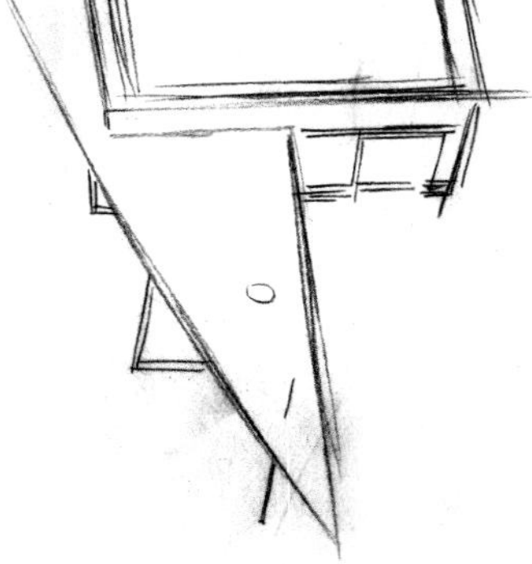

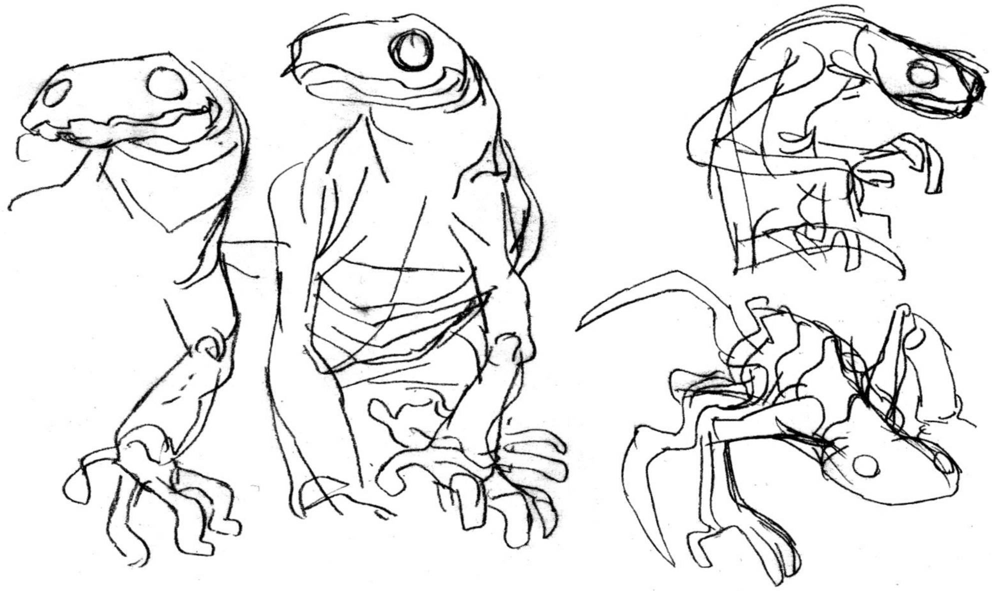

The transformed alien in issue four is based on salamanders but with scorpion-like joints and exo-skeleton/armor.

The '50s style gas station is not only fun to draw but pays homage to small-town alien invasion movies from that era.

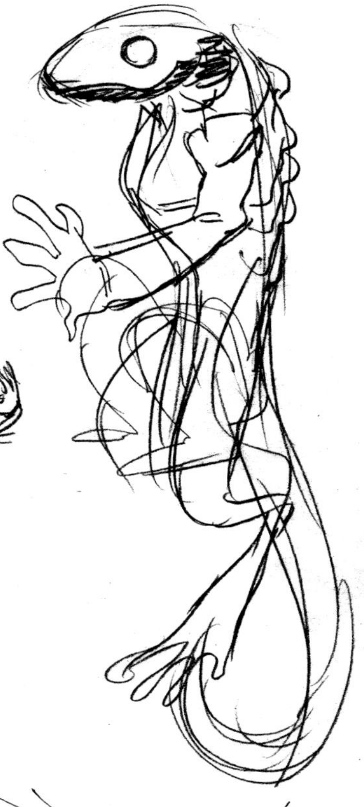

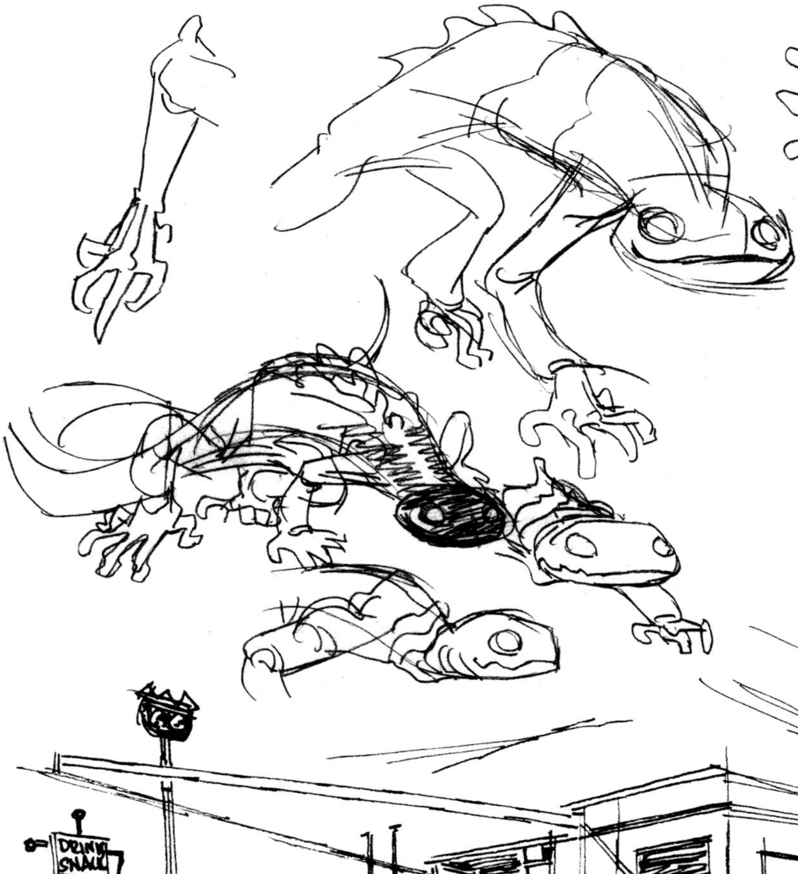

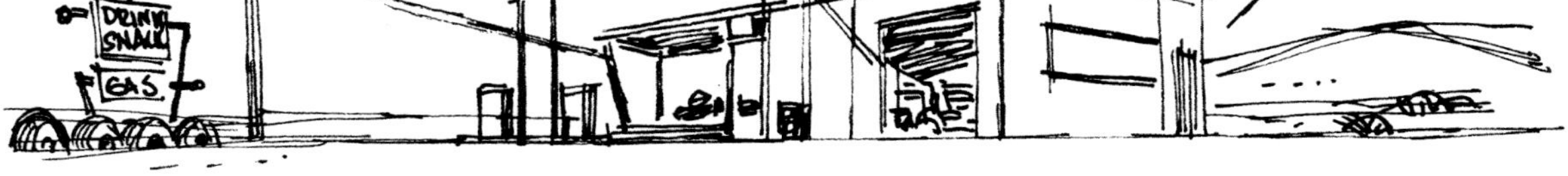
GAS.

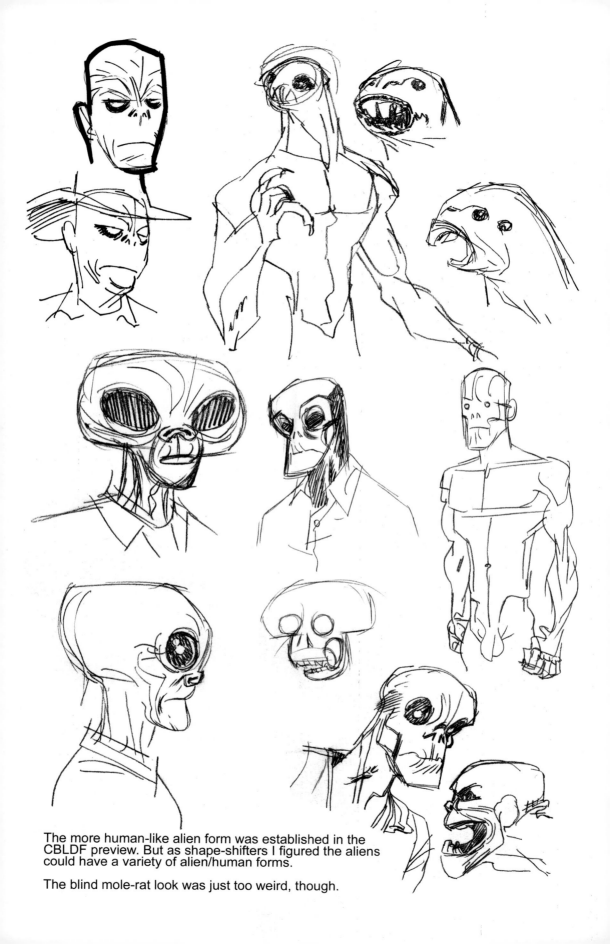

The more human-like alien form was established in the CBLDF preview. But as shape-shifters I figured the aliens could have a variety of alien/human forms.

The blind mole-rat look was just too weird, though.

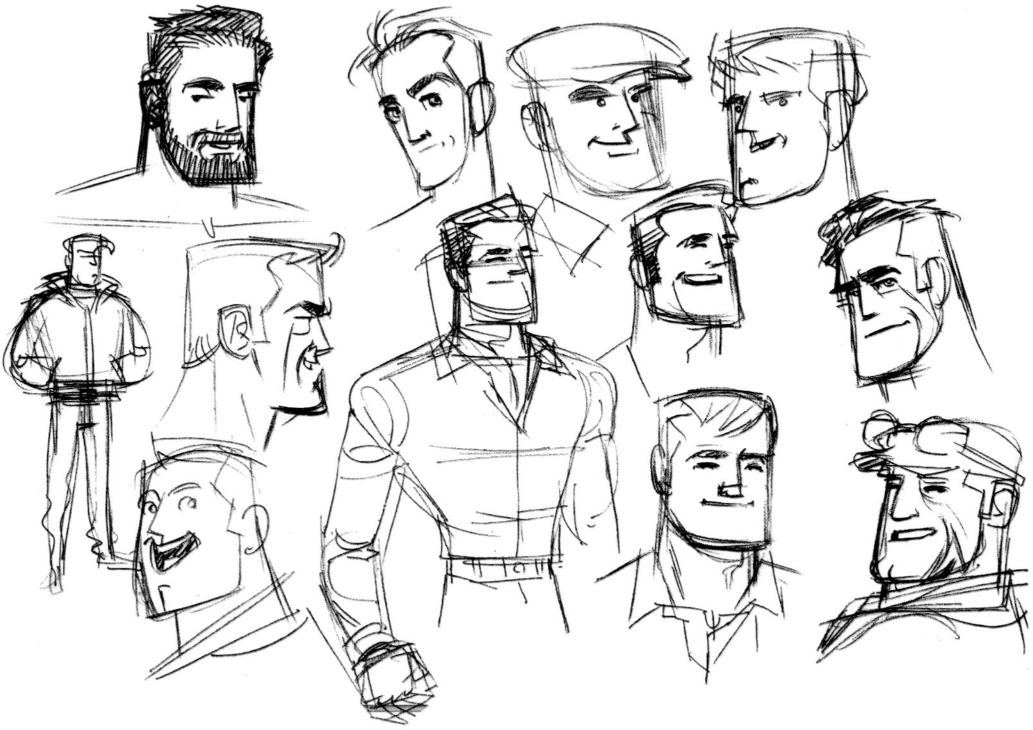

In James' script Nate is described as a "George Clooney type". Having a real-world person in mind when drawing helps bring personality to a character. I really got to work my "acting" chops in Nate's scenes with Tomas.

Also shown -- rough drawing of monstrous Doyle.

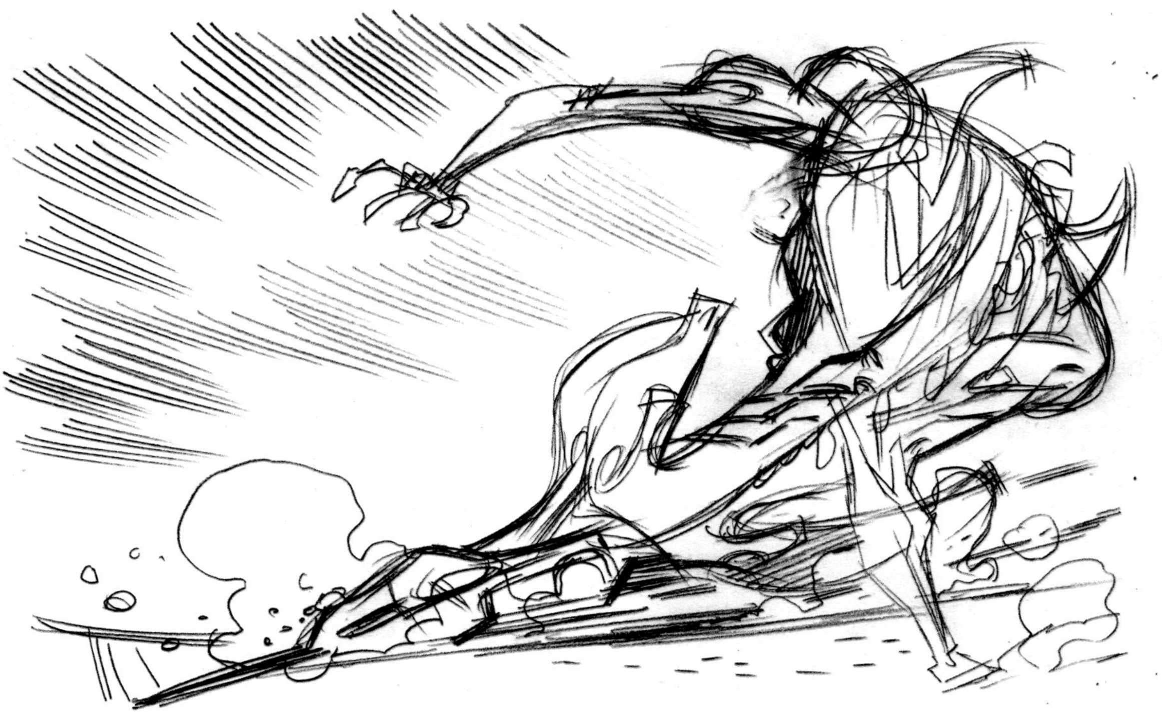

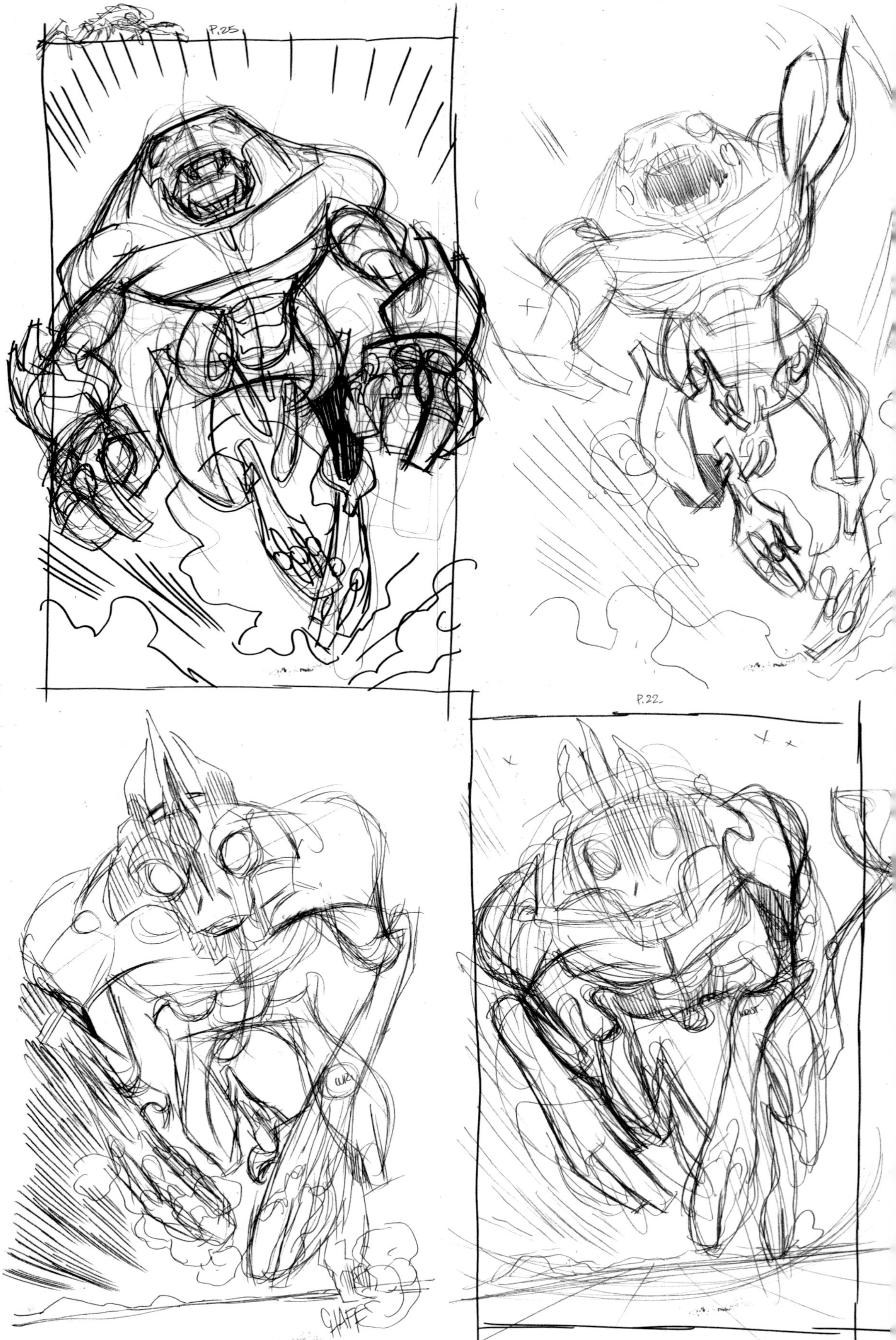
P.25
P.22

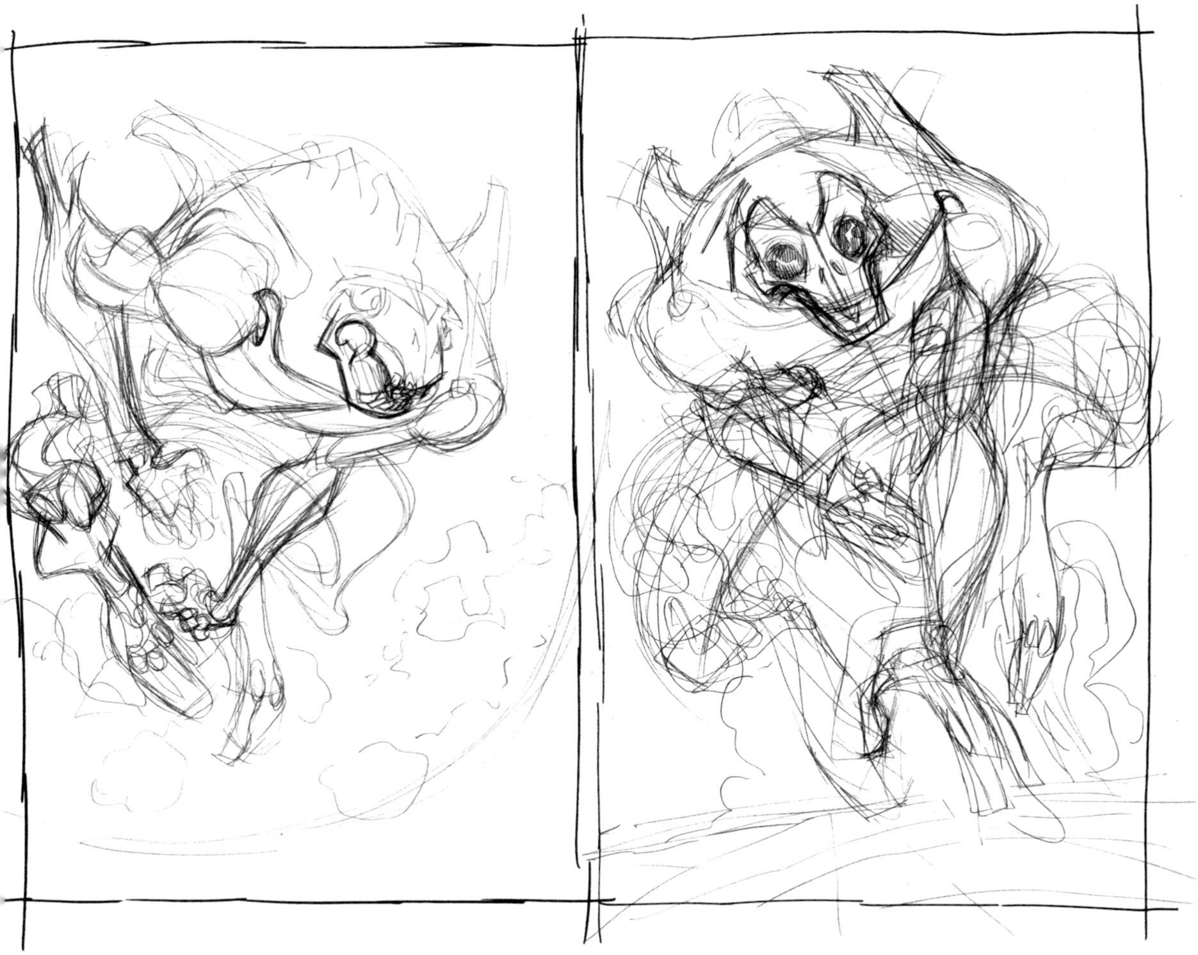

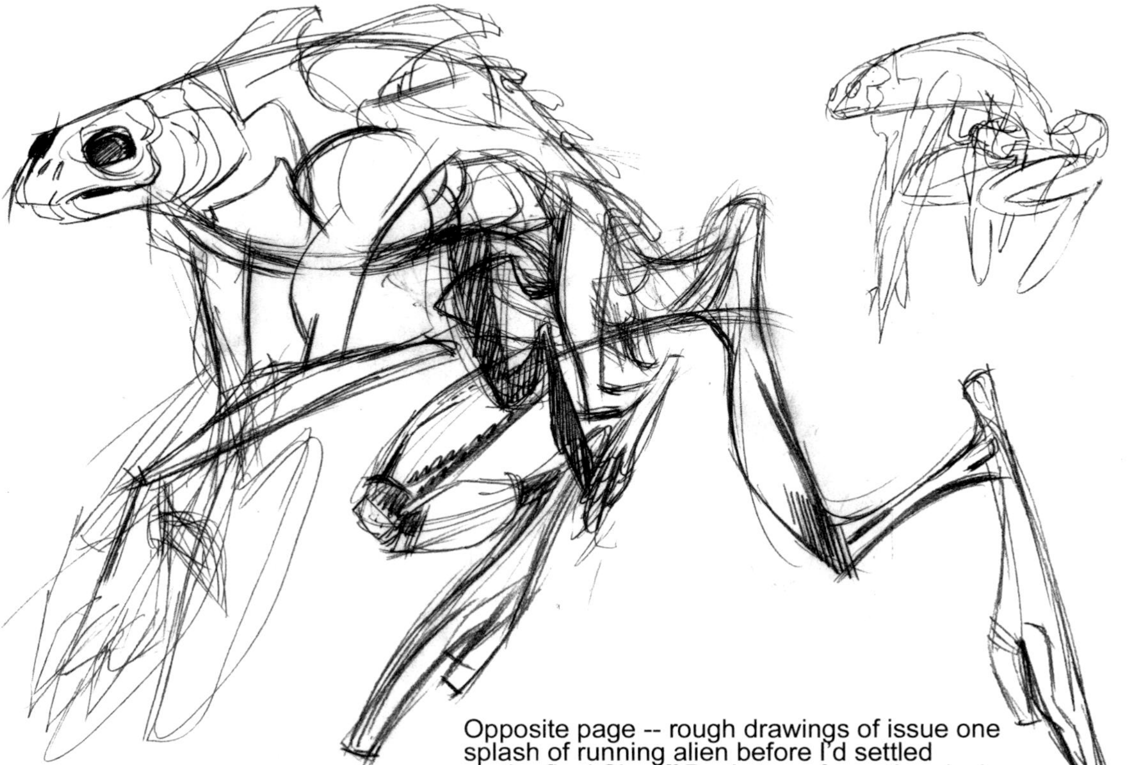

Opposite page -- rough drawings of issue one splash of running alien before I'd settled on the final Sheriff Doyle transformation design.

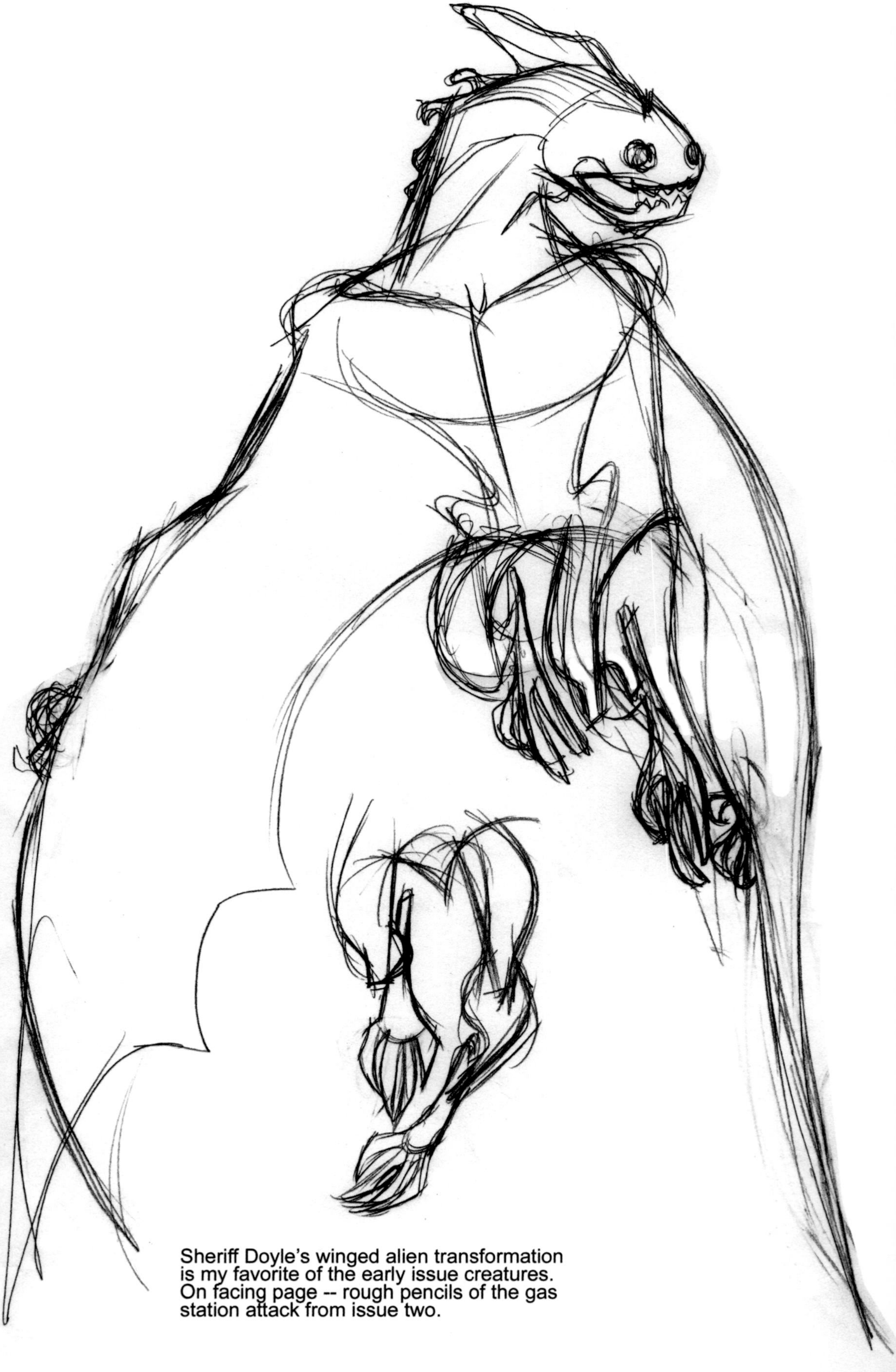

Sheriff Doyle's winged alien transformation is my favorite of the early issue creatures. On facing page -- rough pencils of the gas station attack from issue two.

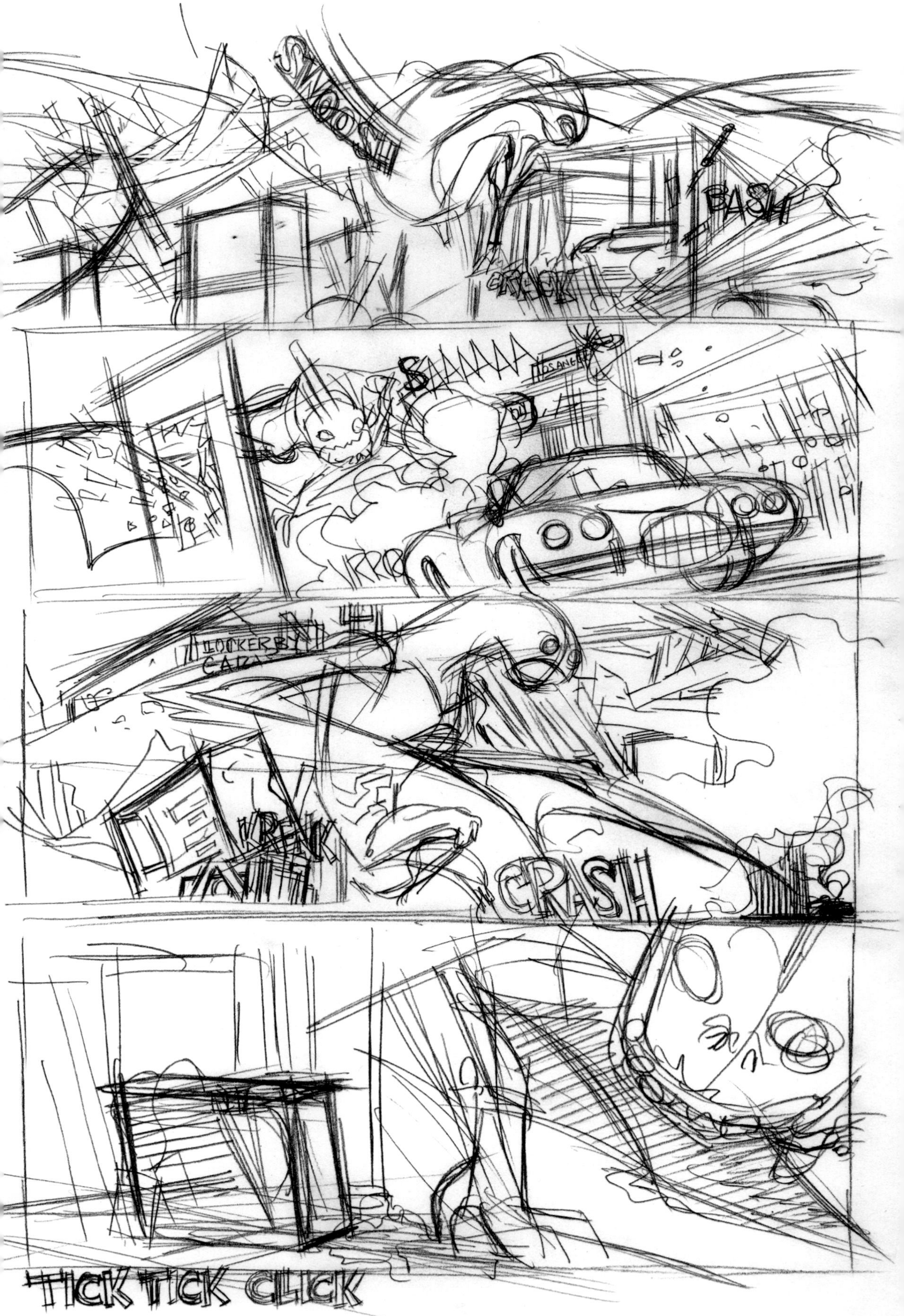
BASH
CREAK
CRASH
TICK TICK CLICK

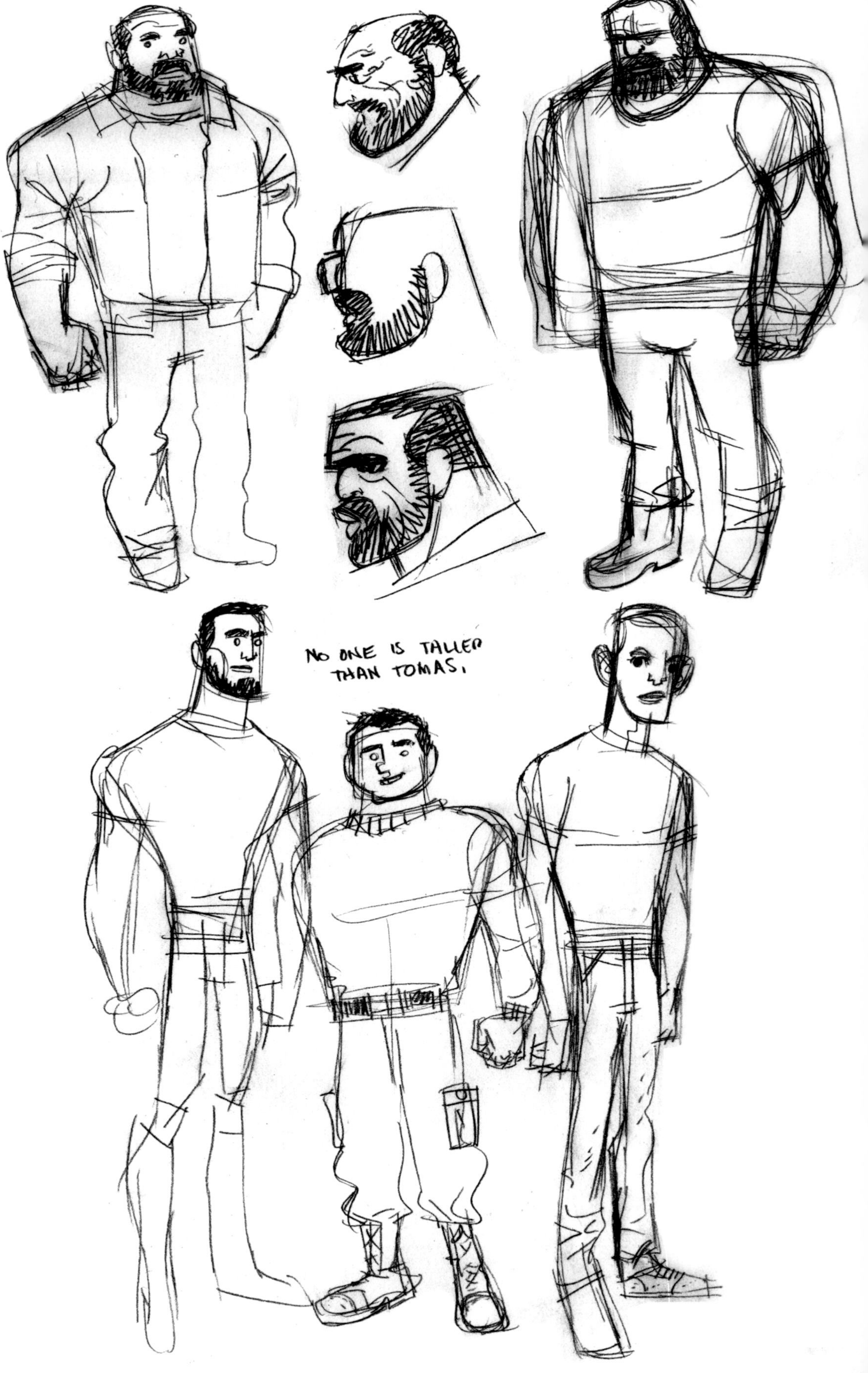
NO ONE IS TALLER THAN TOMAS.

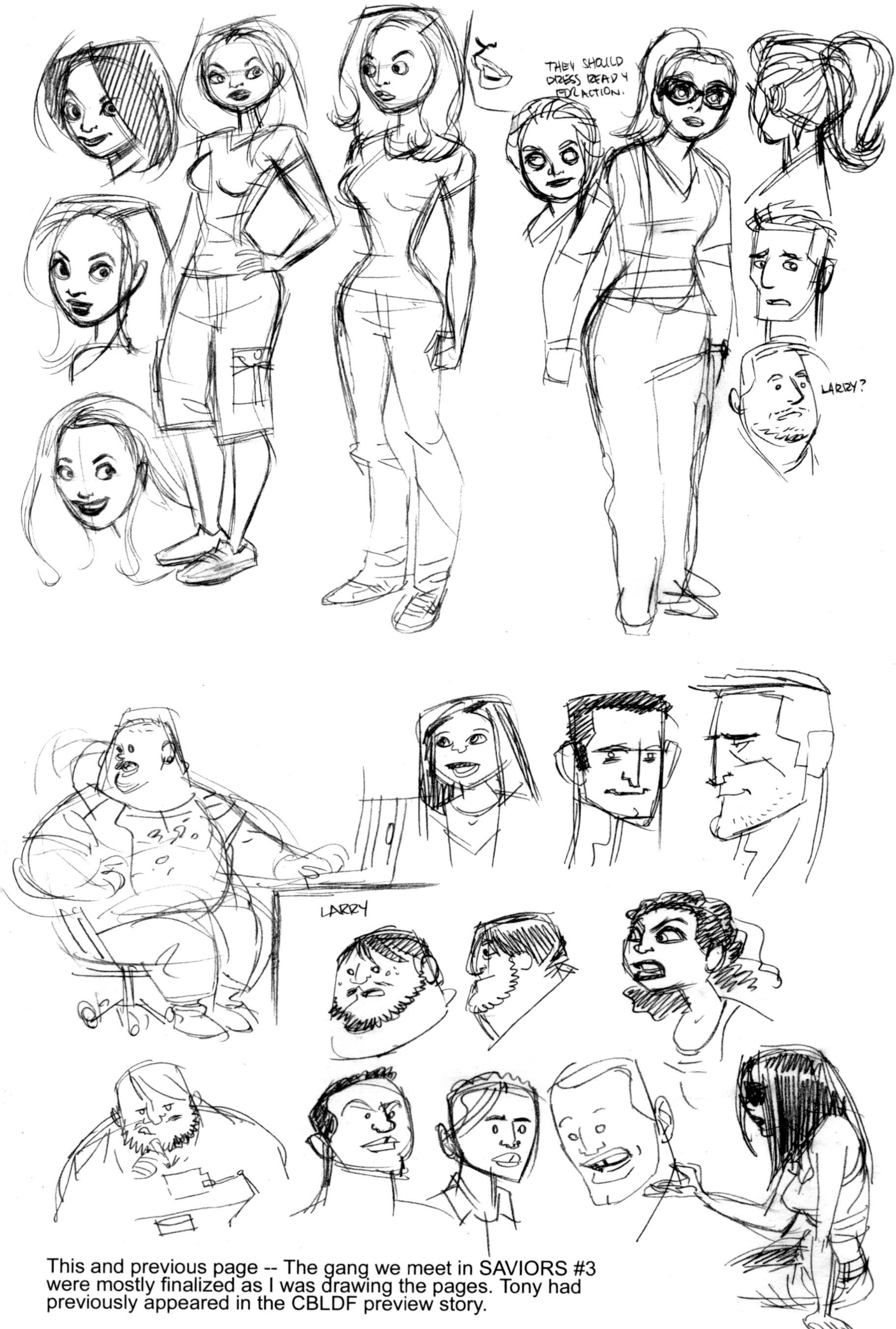
THEY SHOULD
DRESS READY
FOR ACTION.
LARRY?
LARRY

This and previous page -- The gang we meet in SAVIORS #3 were mostly finalized as I was drawing the pages. Tony had previously appeared in the CBLDF preview story.

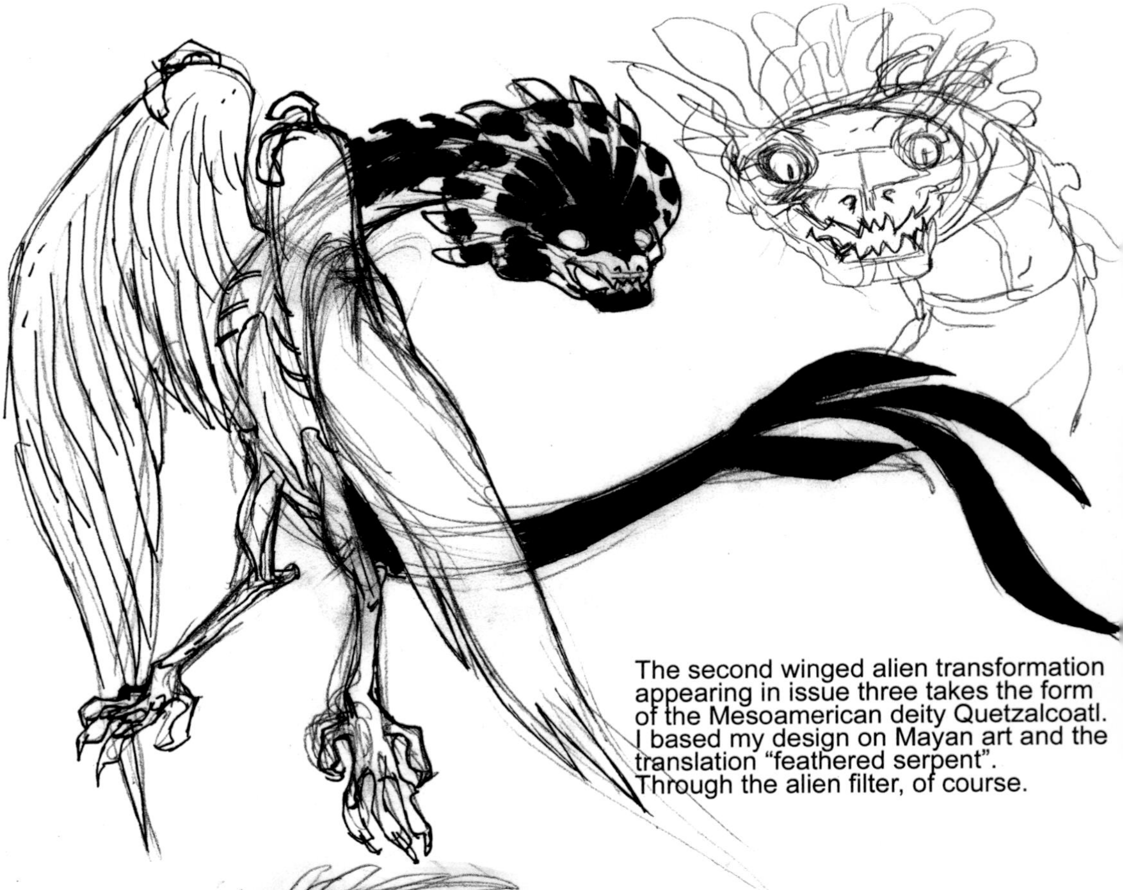

The second winged alien transformation appearing in issue three takes the form of the Mesoamerican deity Quetzalcoatl. I based my design on Mayan art and the translation "feathered serpent". Through the alien filter, of course.

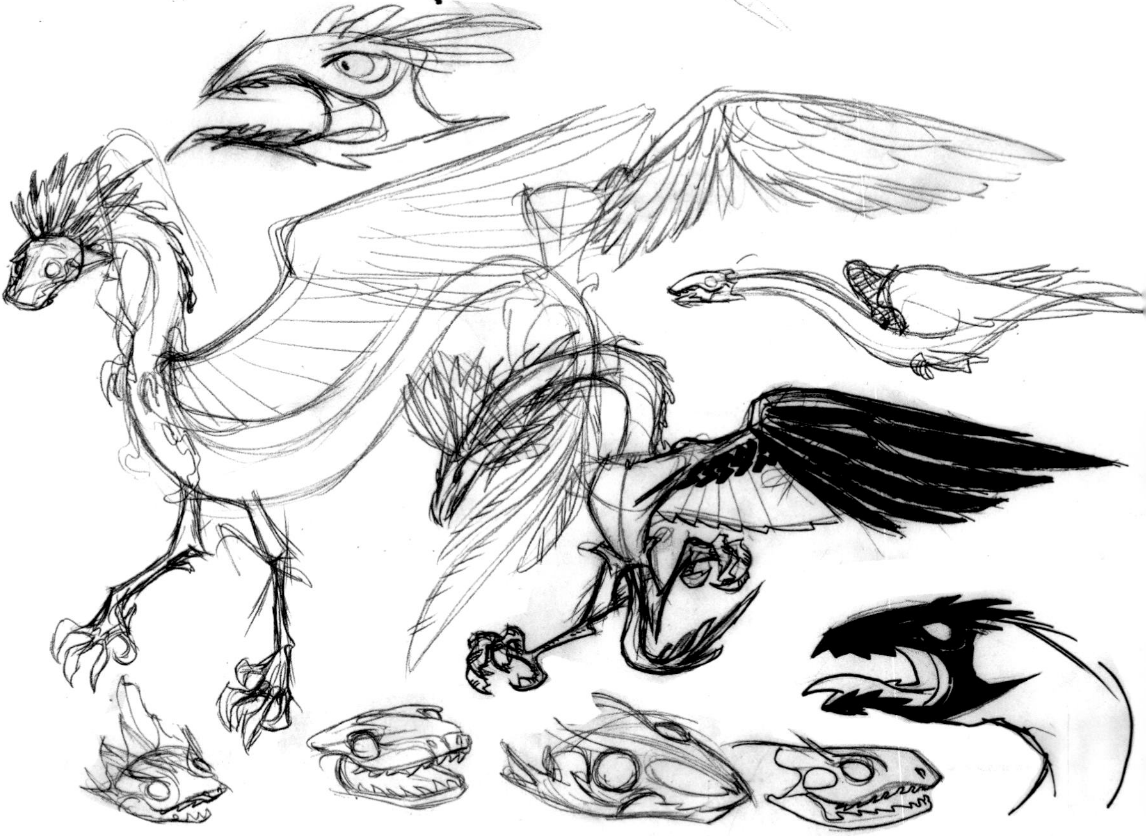

Another favorite monster is this guy, the water creature from issue five.

The ocean holds many terrifying wonders and I looked at them all before settling on a nightmarish moray eel/isopod/crocodile hybrid.

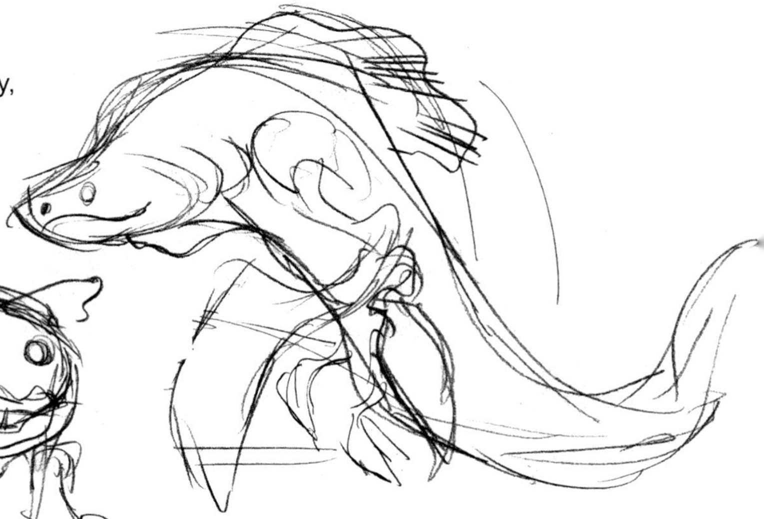

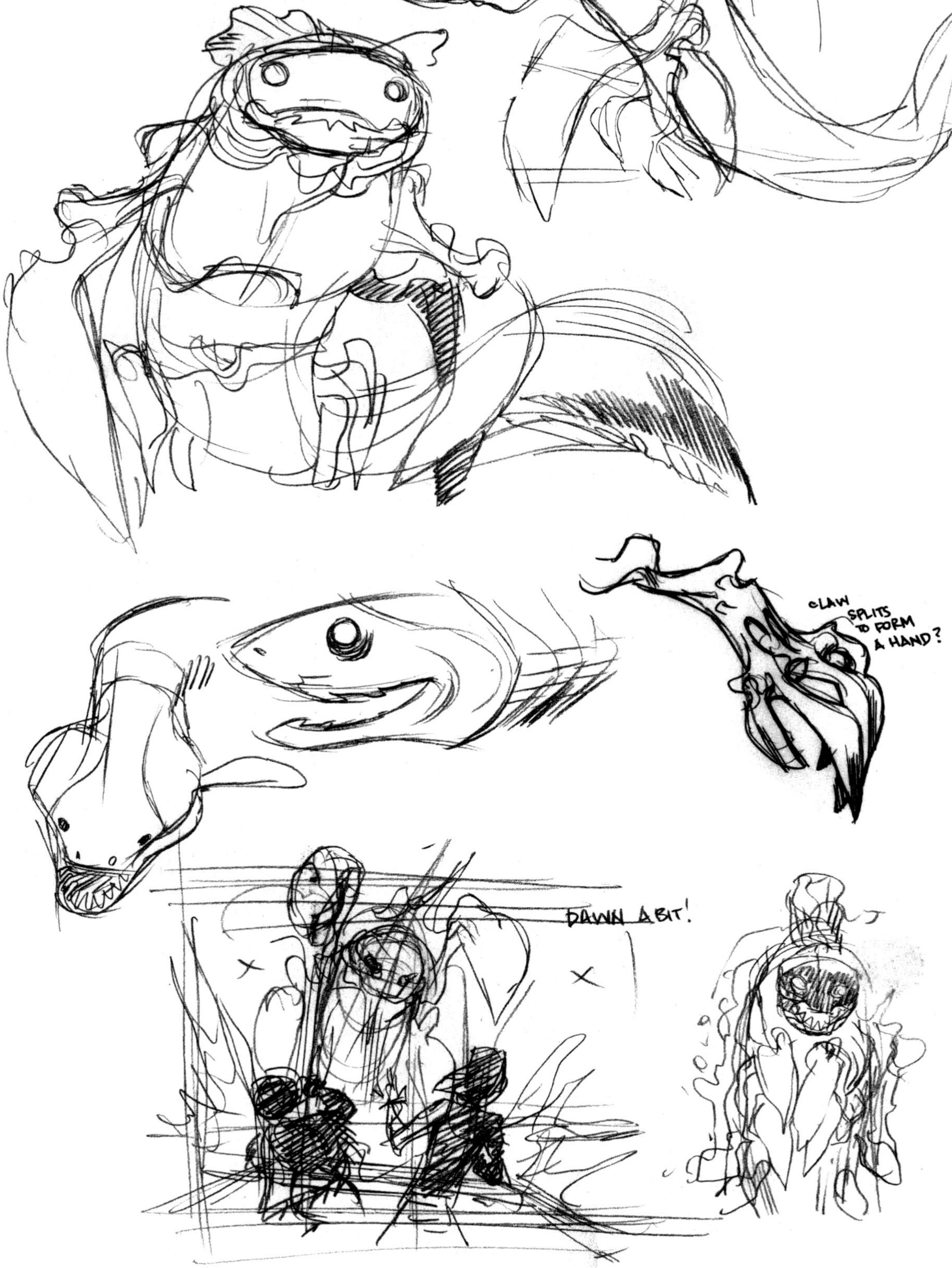
CLAW SPLITS TO FORM A HAND?
DAWN A BIT!

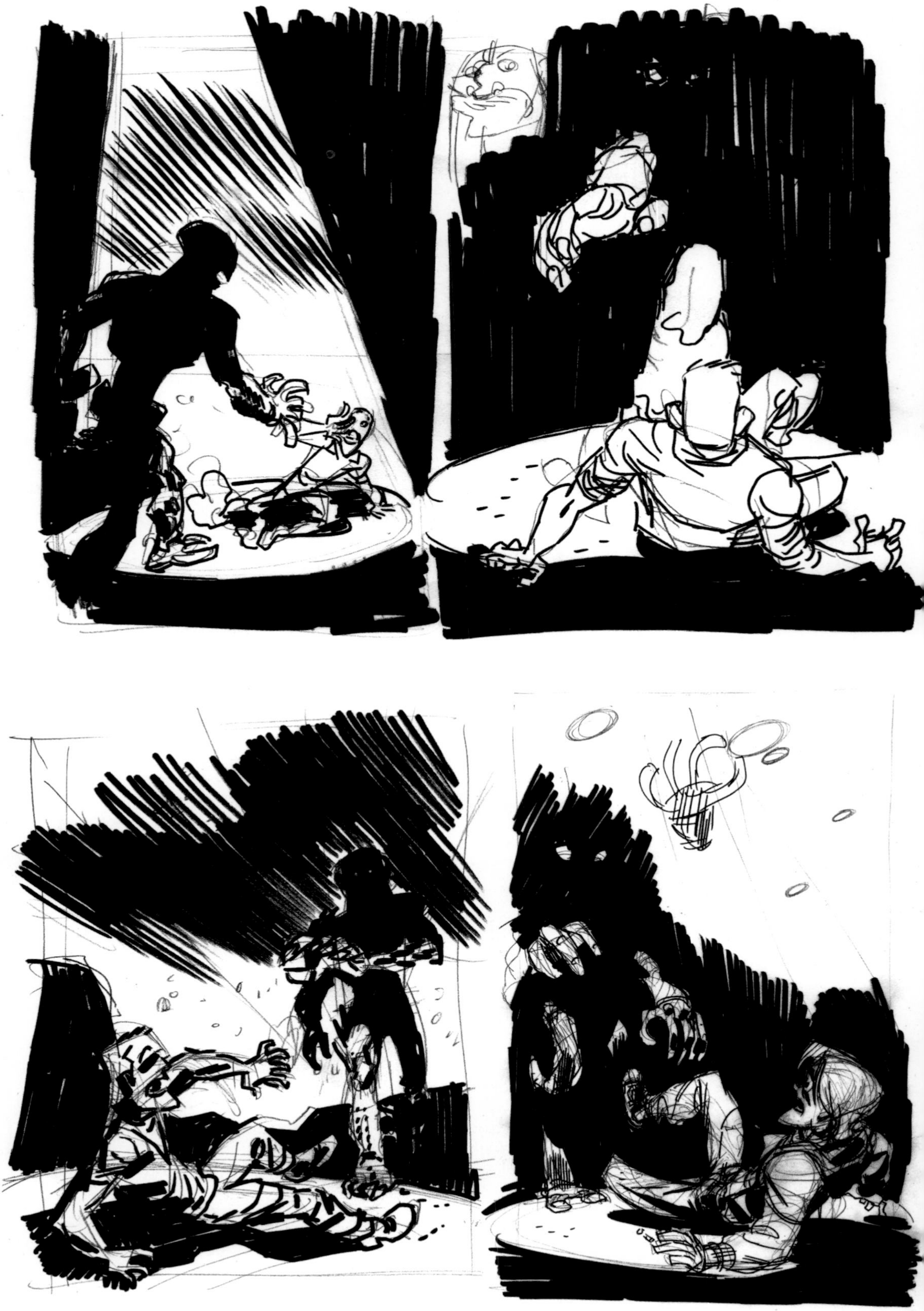

This, and facing page -- rough sketches for the IMAGE Expo announcement.

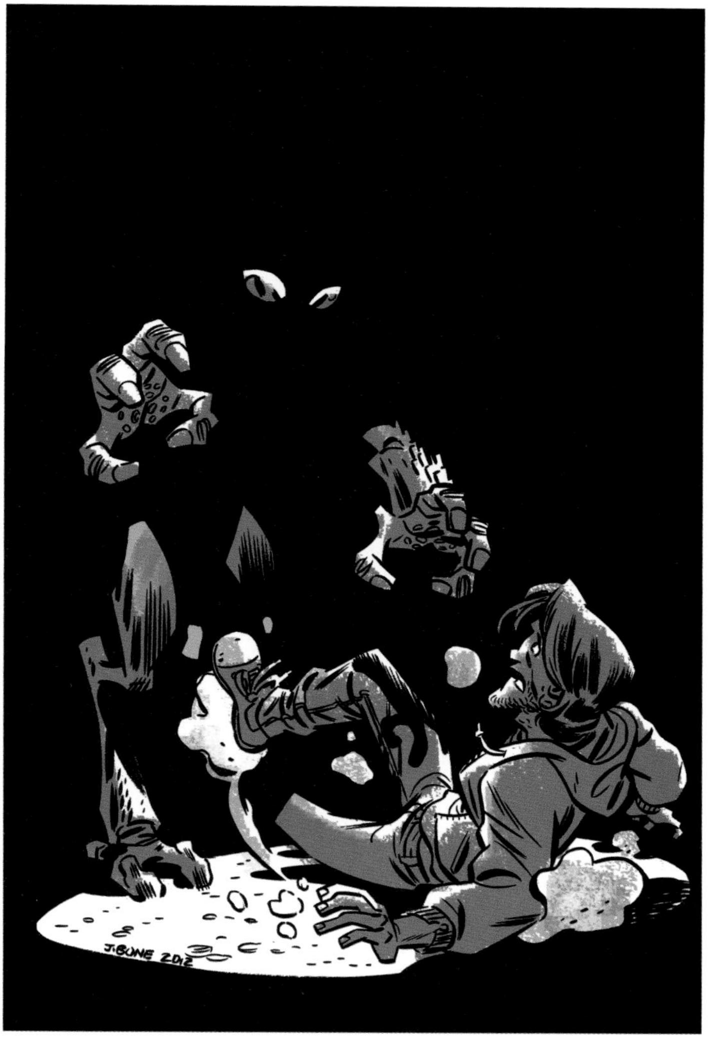
J.BONE 2012

This is the very first image created to announce THE SAVIORS at Image Expo.

Obviously I hadn't figured out Tomas or the look of the aliens in natural form at this time. James and I had the beginnings of an alien invasion plot with the idea that the invaders think they're doing good in the world.

We talked for hours about the tone and story we wanted to tell. I had never drawn a horror/monster comic and really wanted to work with James. This was also my chance to work in a less cartoony style just to expand my portfolio a bit.

Like any good '50s monster movie, our story would start in a small desert town with only a few characters before expanding to reveal a global threat.

The shape-shifting abilities allowed me to draw different types of monsters, which I had a lot of fun doing. James suggested the aliens use elements of Earth animals native to whatever area they inhabit, filtered through the grotesque alien physique.

I'm pleased to finally share my sketches and some of the thinking that goes into drawing a comic book.

J BONE
2016

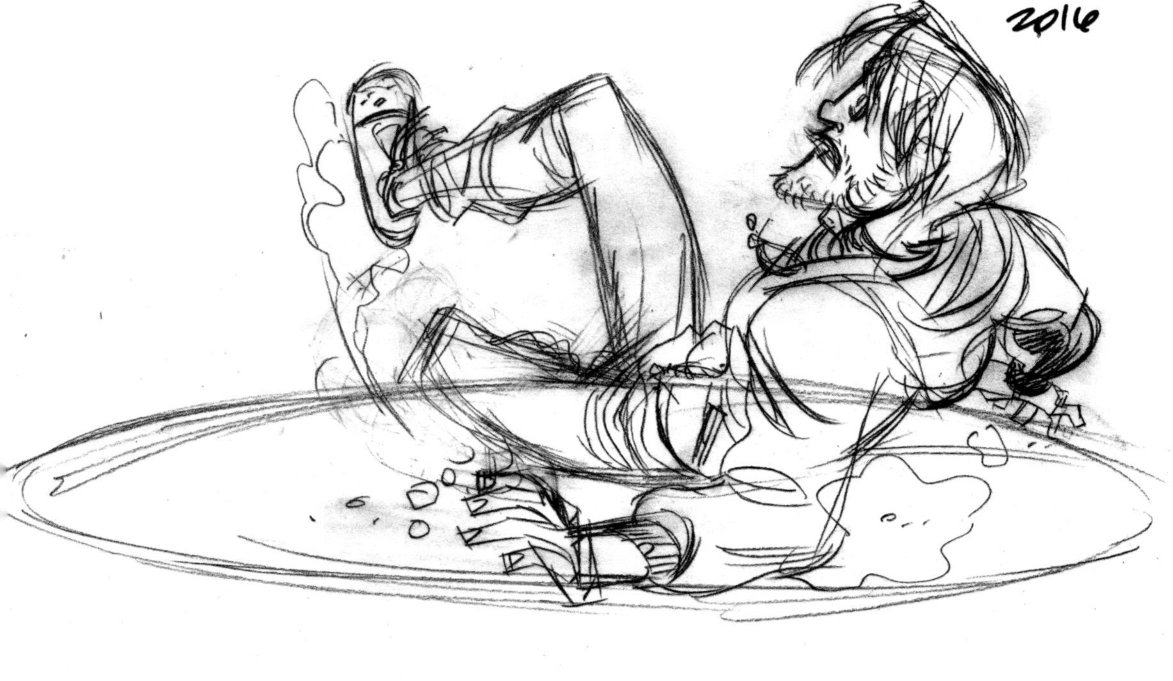

BIOS

JAMES ROBINSON

James Robinson was born in Great Britain, but has lived in the U.S. since 1989 where he began working in comics initially for DC and Dark Horse Comics. Among his more known and regarded works are *Grendel Tales: Four Devils, One Hell*, sundry *Legends of the Dark Knight* arcs, *Superman, Justice League of America* and *Earth 2*. He is perhaps most well known for his award-winning runs on both *Starman* and *Leave It To Chance*.

After a long working relationship with DC Comics, James made the switch to Marvel Comics where he's written runs of *All-New Invaders, Fantastic Four, Squadron Supreme* and *Scarlet Witch*. Currently he is also writing *Grand Passion* for Dynamite Comics.

As an Image creator James has written both THE SAVIORS and AIRBOY.

James resides in Las Vegas with his wife Alyson and his dog Rex.

J. BONE

J. Bone is an Eisner Award-nominated Canadian comic book artist and writer. His credits include DC Comics' *Batman: The Brave and the Bold* and *Super Friends, Rocketeer: Hollywood Horror* and *Rocketeer at War* for IDW, and THE SAVIORS for Image Comics. He was the inker on the Eisner Award-winning one-shot *Batman/The Spirit* as well as *The Spirit* ongoing with artist Darwyn Cooke.

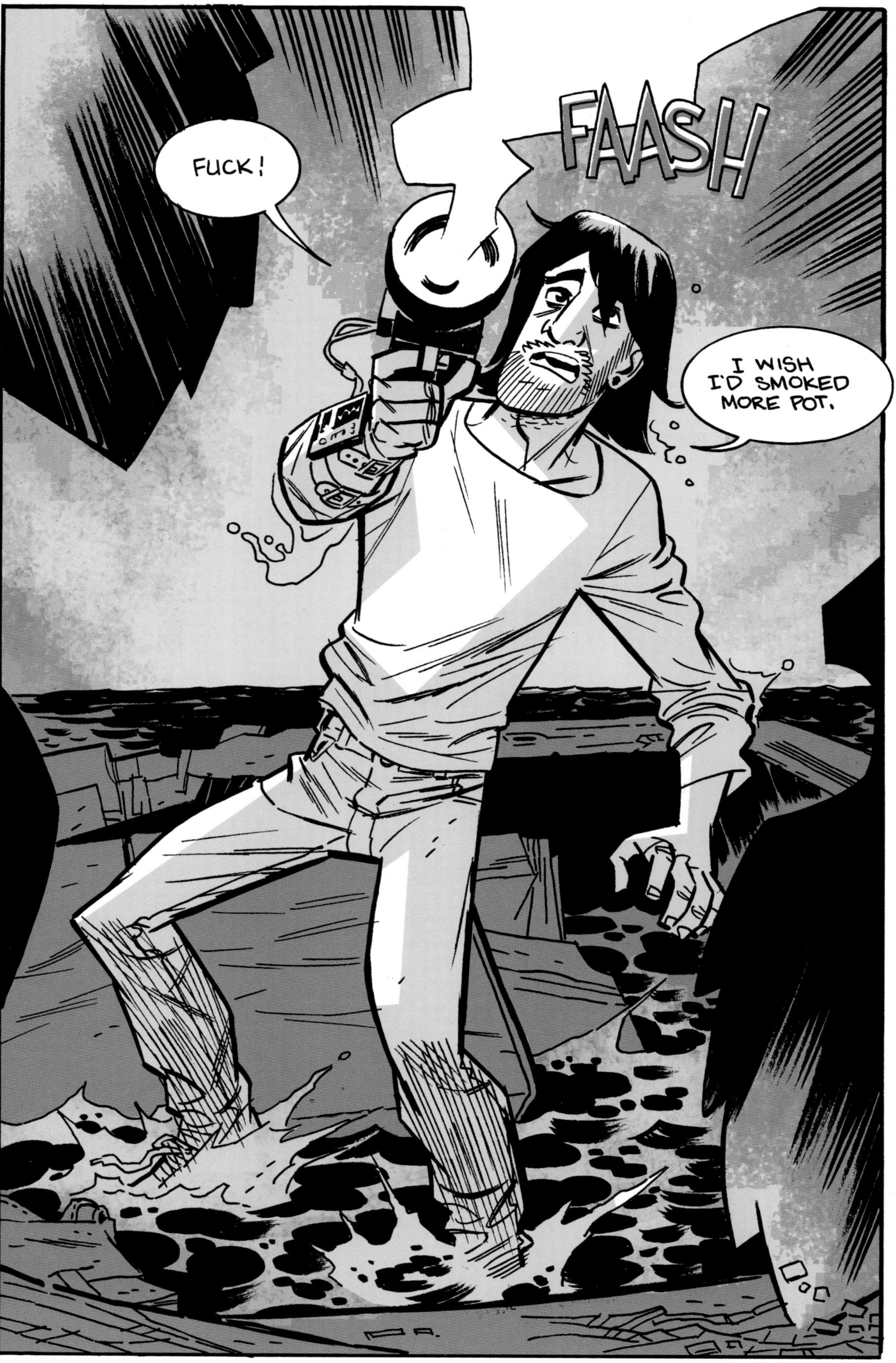
FUCK!
FAASH
I WISH I'D SMOKED MORE POT.

THE SAVIORS